A PASSION
IN THE BLOOD

A
PASSION
IN THE
BLOOD

Arabella Seymour

G. P. PUTNAM'S SONS
NEW YORK

G. P. Putnam's Sons
Publishers Since 1838
200 Madison Avenue
New York, NY 10016

Library of Congress Cataloging in Publication Data

Seymour, Arabella, date.
 A passion in the blood.

 I. Title.
PR6069.E73P3   1985   823'.914   85-9348
ISBN 0-399-13095-0

Printed in the United States of America
1 2 3 4 5 6 7 8 9 10

For my daughter

✳ Contents ✳

Part IX
May 1834

Part X
February 1837

Part XI
March 1837

Part XII
October 1837

Part XIII
April 1838

Part XIV
May 1838

PART I
March 1830

❋ 1 ❋

Afterward, Sam Loam could never remember what woke him, long before dawn. Outside, somewhere, he could hear his dogs barking in the yard. Beyond the window a leafless branch tapped; softly, rhythmically, like a ghostly hand questing entrance to a room. Then it stopped, and the barking of his dogs ceased, and there was silence once more.

He lay there for a while, restless without knowing why. He could not fall back into sleep. He turned this way and then that. Then the sudden cantering of a horse made him sit bolt upright in bed. That was the moment he knew something had happened.

It was too early for any of his men to be coming into the yard. None of the horses were fed or watered until five o'clock, and it was still half-dark outside the window. He could see the murky gray-blackness, through a chink in the curtains where they had not been drawn all the way across. Rubbing his eyes he pushed back the bedclothes and groped his way across the floor. When he pulled back the curtains and looked beyond his fence onto the Downs, he let out an oath of surprise. Behind him, his wife stirred, trying to raise herself on one elbow.

"Sam, in God's name, what is it?"

He went on staring, like a dumb thing, scarcely able to believe his own eyes. "That girl. It's her. Her who was here yesterday, asking for work." His voice rose to a sudden shout. "Bloody Jesus, look at her, woman! She's put a spell on that nag of Russell's!"

From where he stood he could see them, the girl and the half-wild creature, not two separate living things but one; she stood at his head, her hands outstretched toward him; caressing his muzzle, his neck, entwining her fingers in his mane. Then she walked slowly all around him, touching him gently, her lips moving continuously, until she reached his left side and swung herself into the saddle. The animal started, lurched forward, tossing its head; but instead of kicking and plunging as any unridden colt would be expected to do, it obediently walked, then trotted, then cantered. Sam rushed over to the bed and pulled his wife from it like a madman. "That savage took a lump out of my arm and not three of us could fasten its saddle on! Look at it, will you, as gentle as a sheep!" He pulled on his breeches, grabbed a shirt, jerkin, and his working boots, and ran down-stairs as if he was a crazed man.

The girl smiled impudently at him when he flung open the door to the yard, stark blue eyes staring at him through her dark, windswept hair.

"Are you going to change your mind about giving me work now, Mr. Loam?"

He knew that he ought to be angry with her. Give her the rough side of his tongue; maybe threaten her with the constable, even, for trespassing on his land. She deserved it, the cocksure little bitch. She'd climbed over his fence, picked the lock on his stable door, and helped herself to an animal worth a small fortune, an animal not even his; a colt that belonged to a man who was not only a prominent member of the local aristocracy but also happened to be one of his most important clients. Nor had she so much as said she was sorry. She was calmly sitting astride the beast now, the same horse that yesterday had taken a bite out of his arm, kicked two of his men, and refused to let any of them so much as fasten on its saddle.

"You little bitch, you. Where in hell did you learn to handle horses like that?"

She still didn't look sorry for stealing it.

"I didn't learn. I just have a way with them, that's all."

She stood in the kitchen by the fire Kate Loam was busy kindling, looking at him solemnly.

"I need work, Mr. Loam. Don't send me away like you did yesterday." There was a trace of a pleading note in her voice that had not been there, then.

"It's a thrashing, not work, that you're wanting. For two pence I ought to put you across that stool and tan your arse." He caught his wife's eye and fought down a smile. "Don't you know what happens to horse thieves in these parts? They hang 'em. Not content with climbing over into my property and breaking into my stables you stole the horse as well."

"I didn't steal it. Stealing's when you take something and don't mean to bring it back."

"Don't answer me back. You helped yourself to it without asking and when you take something without asking that's thieving, you hear? That nag belongs to Lord Russell and Lord Russell's a big man in these parts. If anything happens to it while it's been trusted to my care 'is Lordship'd have my guts for garters and yours as well."

"If you'd given me the chance yesterday to show you what I could do, I wouldn't have needed to take it."

There was a short silence, broken only by the sound of Kate Loam clattering about with the dishes.

"All right. So you've shown me what you can do; you can handle horses. But like I told you yesterday rough riding's grown men's work. If you want to risk breaking your neck every day, that's all right by me. What isn't is that if you did I'd have your father down here, threatening to break mine."

"I haven't got a father."

"Your mother, then. You're under age for a start."

"I'm nearly sixteen!"

Sam turned away and began to pace the bare floor, stroking his chin. Yes, she was something special. But he couldn't tell her that to her face.

"Where does your mother think you are now, then?"

"Asleep, in bed. By the time she wakes up I'll be long back."

She stood there, the begging look still in her eyes, in the same old, tattered clothes she'd worn yesterday. She was tall for her age. Too thin, shabby. But she had a curious, refined look about her, like a greyhound, and his quick eyes that never missed much saw that the bonnet and cloak she wore had once been fine, quality stuff, clothes that gentry might wear. Her dark hair was thick and matted from the wind, and had blown carelessly about her face, and Sam stared at her in the same knowing way he might stare at a new filly—over-lean, gone in her coat—and think, *With the right feeding and a good grooming she'll be a real beauty next year,* and saw something striking under the poverty and neglect. Her voice, too, had struck him, when she'd walked into his yard yesterday and asked him for work, for it was no rough common girl's voice, but the voice of somebody brought up among gentry.

All at once, he stopped pacing and turned back to her.

"All right. If you want work, I reckon I can give you plenty." Her blue, catlike eyes lit up. "I pay ten shillings a week with meals thrown in, and a new pair of boots every quarter." He glanced down at hers, worn and shabby. "But understand this, Anna Brodie." He remembered the name from yesterday, and for some reason it had become imprinted in his memory. "Don't expect any favors because you're a female; you won't get any. No shirking. No privileges. I pay you the same as I pay the men and you do the same work they do . . . understand?"

"Yes, I understand you. And I never expected any privileges."

"Well, now you're here and you've woken us up, you might as well stay and eat breakfast with us." He pointed in the direction of the long trestle table and benches. "After that you'd best saddle yourself one of my hunters and ride back home before your folks have half the county out, looking for you." They both sat down, opposite each other on the wooden benches. "You can start tomorrow, six o'clock. No later. No earlier. And if you cause any trouble with the men you'll be out." She nodded, and her lips turned up slightly at the corners in the beginnings of a smile; almost, he thought, as if she was unused to any act of kindness and had no idea how she should respond to it. She tucked into the meal his wife put in front of her as if she hadn't eaten for days; and he watched her, thinking how his father and grandfather would have turned in their graves at even the thought of a slip of a girl being offered rough-riding work in the yard they'd built up between them.

There'd been Loams breaking in young blood horses for the lords and gentry up on the Downs for as long as anyone about Epsom could remember. Sam's grandfather had started it, two generations ago, with no more than a good pair of hands, his savings from half a lifetime's laboring in racing stables, and a lot of know-how about what unpredictable, high-mettled animals liked and what they didn't. He'd got himself a reputation second to none and a small fortune put by when he'd handed the business over to his son, Young Tom, who'd carried on and expanded the stables to cope with the ever-increasing inflow of horses, and was still known as Young Tom even when he was in his sixties. By the time Sam was ready to take over reins it was a thriving yard, three times bigger than it had been in his grandfather's day and still growing, the well-to-do owners of running horses sending their unbroken young stock to Epsom from as far away as Doncaster and York.

At fifty he could number more than two dozen Derby or Guineas winners who'd passed through his yard on their way to glory, was on nodding terms with most of the local lords and gentry, and knew every tout, blackleg, and turf villain for miles around. What Sam Loam didn't know about racing and running horses wasn't worth knowing. Few things ever surprised him. Except for this morning, when he'd dragged himself, half-asleep still, to the bedroom window and looked down on the most amazing sight he'd ever set eyes on in all of his fifty years.

She still puzzled him, this thin, pale girl who'd walked into his yard out of nowhere and cast a spell over a savage, half-wild horse he'd been in two minds to tell milord Russell was untrainable, yet told him almost nothing of herself that he wanted to know. Where she came from. Why she was here. There was no one bearing her family name that had ever lived within thirty miles of Epsom, of that much he was sure.

Anna Brodie. Anna Brodie. There was something, if only he could remember, that was curiously familiar about that name.

It was the bitterest March in living memory. Across the hard, frost-covered ground Anna and Clara Brodie walked, heads down, not speaking, battling against the icy wind. Now and again they staggered when their frozen feet slipped in an unseen pothole, or caught against a clod of turf. Both wore tattered, patched capes that were small defense against the pitiless cold, and battered secondhand bonnets that had both seen better days, long since.

This high ground, halfway between Epsom and Walton Parish, was the coldest place on all of Epsom Downs. On a clear day, you could look down across the dip below to the racecourse and Durdans, one of the great houses that belonged to the local gentry, and beyond it to the woods. There were many such houses in the district, great sprawling mansions that belonged to the rich, most of them with stables behind them that housed not only their hacks and hunters and carriage horses but also their blood-stock, which were trained on the Downs by their training grooms and raced on the course at Epsom. Another, now, suddenly loomed into their sight, its tall red-bricked chimneys rising from the line of trees, a high wall encircling its rambling, shrub-filled grounds, austere, forbidding entry, like a castle under siege. Anna paused and caught at her sister's hand, pointing toward it.

When they reached its high iron wrought gates they stopped, and pressed their cold faces against the narrow bars.

Only part of the great house could be glimpsed from the spot at which they stood. A solitary corner, a portion of a large window with the glass glinting, starlike, in the early morning light. They could see the sweep of the drive, lined by leafless trees, and the flowerless bushes that lay sleeping until the summer sun would draw forth from them a riot of scent and color. It was so like that other house, their father's house, the house that had always been barred to them, nestling like a jewel in the hollow of a hand, that Anna looked at it sullenly, almost savagely, in stark, resentful silence. A rich man's house. A house built from the labor and misery and hunger of others. What did they know, those privileged, protected inside, of real suffering, real pain, real fear, real hunger? She thought, bitterly, of the half-bare attic room that she and her sister shared in the miserable little cottage up there, on the loneliest part of the Downs. The cracks in the walls. The green, rancid damp that crept, insidiously, from ceiling to floor. The scurrying sound of the rats overhead as they lay there, shivering beneath their threadbare blankets on the straw pallets that served as their beds. The beds in the grand bedrooms beyond the tall iron gates would be warm from the fires lit by the servants in the hearths. They would be carved from the finest woods, their curtains fashioned from the finest velvets and brocades to keep out the cold winter drafts. There would be fine carpets on the polished floors, and a gold clock on the marble mantlepiece. There might be paintings adorning the walls, themselves covered by fine silk, and on the beds there would be the finest white linen sheets, and real feather mattresses.

Gripping the iron railings, Anna glanced up. One each side of the great gates, mounted on massive pillars, were two heraldic beasts with chains about their necks, the owner's coat of arms emblazoned on the shields they held between their feet.

Like his gates. Like his coat of arms. Like the house at Mildenhall, where they could never enter. Their father's house.

Her mind and her bitterness ran on and on, like a stone rolling downhill, unable to stop until it had reached its natural halting place.

The empty larder. The empty wood basket at the cold hearth of the kitchen grate. The gray, lifeless ashes that no longer held warmth. The pitiful sound of their mother's coughing, and weeping, on the other side of the thin bedroom wall in the early hours.

There would be a great kitchen in the house beyond the locked gates. There would be huge gray flagstones on the floor and a massive fireplace, stoked in winter with the whole trunks of trees. There would be a long table in the center of the kitchen, and a larder that was hung with legs of mutton and sides of beef, and game. And on the oak sideboard would stand bowls of vegetables and fruit, in readiness to take up to the dining room above, where the fruit would adorn bowls of crystal and silver set upon a tablecloth of snow-white linen.

She could see the dining room set for dinner. There would be huge candelabra at either end of the long table, and in the center a lavish arrangement of exotic flowers, picked an hour before from the hothouse. The silver cutlery would gleam in the soft candlelight, and the laughter and idle chatter of the guests would fill the air as they consumed course after course from fine, gold-edged, porcelain plates, Wedgwood or Spode, with the family crest embossed on the delicate china. She could imagine them, in their silks and satins, discussing the price of fat cattle and sheep and trivial society gossip, talking of their horses as if they were merely things of no feeling, to be worked and exploited and bartered and sold, and not creatures of sensitivity and beauty.

She did not know anyone inside that great house at the end of the sweeping drive, but she hated and despised them for what they were, for what they represented.

"Who lives here?" Clara's voice, breaking into her half dream.

"I don't know. Only some rich man would live here."

Clara shrugged, and moved away from the gate. It was getting lighter. It was getting late. They should be on their way. But Anna did not move.

"I can see the roof of a stable from here. There, beyond those trees near the house." Her blue eyes were fixed upon some point that Clara could not see, and was not interested in. "I've a mind to climb over and see."

Into Clara's eyes, less blue, less brilliant, came a look of fear. "No. No, Anna. You can't. It's trespassing. If they catch you they might think that you were trying to get into the house, to steal . . ."

Anna's strong, striking face held only scorn. "Then they'd be wrong, wouldn't they? I only want to have a look at their horses. Now give me a leg up against this wall!" Reluctantly, without enthusiasm, Clara did as she was told.

"Anna, please don't."

"I'll be ten minutes, no more."

"Hurry, Anna, before someone comes!"

In a swift, graceful movement, Anna had scaled the high wall and slipped over it, landing almost noiselessly on the ground at the other side. She had already forgotten Clara. She stood up, brushing dead leaves and twigs from her skirt, and made her way stealthily through the dense screen of bushes and trees.

She came upon the house suddenly, unexpectedly, a great gray stone edifice far larger than she had imagined it from the glimpse through the tall locked gate. Boldly, she pushed away a branch that hung in her path, and began to walk across the expanse of lawn that led to the house, stretching before her with its carpet of fallen leaves, her booted feet leaving strange, glistening white footprints in the dew. She kept her eyes on the house, that massive, forbidding gray thing with so many windows, slumbering in the early dawn like some gigantic dog, awaiting its master's call. In a moment the house was behind her and she found herself at a tall white gate, through which she could see the coach house and the stables. Smiling, she climbed it with ease and dropped softly onto the grass at the other side.

Both stable blocks were locked and bolted. Curiously, the door to the big coach house was not only unlocked, but half open.

It was dark inside. She stood there, until her eyes had become accustomed to the dim light. Then in a kind of wonderment, she walked among the coaches and carriages, pausing to examine every one. This would be like the inside of his coach house. Her father's coach house. As in this one, there would be the great carriage, emblazoned with the family coat of arms, used for grand occasions. She reached inside and touched the soft velvet of the upholstered seats. On the box where the coachman sat there was a cushion of scarlet velvet, edged with rich gold fringe. Its body shone, and the servants had removed every vestige of dirt from the wheels. Anna could picture them, on their knees, sweating, bending down in the dirt to do their work. Cleaning. Polishing. Going over every part again and again to make certain it was right. She moved away, pitying them and despising them for their servitude.

There was a curricle, with enormous wheels. A trap. A second carriage, less grand than the first. Three post chaises, black and yellow, gleaming like ebony, as painstakingly polished as the carriage. Then she turned away and began to walk back toward the half-open door. Her curiosity had been satisfied. It was getting late now. She had already stayed too long. She could picture Clara, waiting still, crouching in the long grass on the other side of the brick wall, wringing her hands, shivering, wondering when she was coming back. Anna quickened her step. The coach house door creaked as she pushed it open, letting in a thin ray of gray daylight from outside. Then she stopped, abruptly, taken by surprise.

He stood there looking at her, as startled as she was, a shotgun in one hand. Then the dismay in his face turned to anger.

"What in hell's name do you think you're doing on my land, you bloody gypsy?"

"I'm not a gypsy." Her voice startled him. No, nobody with that voice could be a gypsy. It was a refined voice, the voice of someone brought up among gentry. He looked at her tattered clothes and stared harder, intrigued. Anna stared back without flinching.

"You're trespassing, whoever you are. This is private property." The same words Sam Loam had used to her, yesterday morning, when she had broken into his yard.

"All right. I climbed over your wall and thought I'd have a look around before anyone was up. Now I've looked I'm going again. Let's leave it at that, shall we?" Her insolence for the moment made him speechless. He ran his keen, light eyes over her too-slender figure, the long, dark, tangled hair that blew about her face. A striking face. A face impossible to forget. He'd slept little. Long before dawn he'd been up, pacing, restless, unable to find peace within himself, unable to stop the wild thoughts that stampeded around and around inside his head. He was not drunk now, only slightly tipsy.

"You little bitch. You need somebody to teach you manners." He reached out, took a handful of her loose hair, and pulled her toward him; then he kissed her, roughly, on the lips. She slapped him so savagely across the mouth that he reeled backward and almost lost his footing, stunned by the strength in her hand.

"Who's going to teach them to me? You, rich man?"

At his shout of pain and surprise his two gun dogs appeared, growling and snapping at her, but she stood her ground and showed no fear of them. To his astonishment they stopped barking, suddenly, and lay down at her feet. One of them began to lick her hand. A feeling of outrage blazed in him, without warning.

"Get out of here, at once. Now, before I set my guard dogs on you!"

She gave him one parting look of scorn. Then she went. Unhurriedly, arrogantly. As if the land she was walking on was hers, not his.

He strode back across the deserted courtyard and entered the house by a back door. The servants were up and about now; from the kitchens below he could hear the familiar sounds. A voice snapping orders, the clanking of pots and pans. The smell of food sickened him, though he had eaten nothing since the day before. In the hallway his butler, coming from another room, stopped at the unexpected sight of him, about so early.

"Good morning, Lord Russell."

He spoke a few casual words in return. He had no appetite for conversation, he wanted to be alone again. The abrupt meeting with the girl outside his coach house had somehow upset and disquieted him, without his understanding why. Mounting the stairs in twos he went up to the second floor and hesitated outside the door of one of the many rooms. Then he unlocked it and went inside.

He stood there, on the threshold of her bedroom, staring at the drapes still drawn across the windows. At the heavy, curtained bed of gold satin where a weak trickle of light picked out the exquisite embroidery of the ornate canopy. Then he went over to the windows and pulled back the drapes, savagely, flooding the neglected room with sudden sunlight. Then he turned away, opened the doors of the wardrobe, and began to pull out the row of gowns inside it.

They were all beautiful, costly, scarcely worn; all hung with tiny, scented sachets of lavender and rose petals; but despite them he could still smell the unpleasant, unmistakable odor of neglect. It nauseated him. When he had emptied the wardrobe he went over to the tallboy, then the chest of drawers; everything was exactly as she had left it. The white, delicate lawn petticoats and chemises; gloves, stockings, stays. He knelt there, staring at them, unable to touch them, even. He went over to the window and opened it to breathe in the fresh, cold air as an antidote to his revulsion. Finally, he rang the bell cord that would sound in the servants' hall below. It was dust-coated, a faded powder blue. Last pulled by her hand to summon her maid. He let it go, swiftly, as if the touch of it might contaminate him.

After several minutes a housemaid appeared in the doorway.

"Yes, milord?" He could see her barely concealed surprise. Over the floor, the counterpane of the bed, the whole contents of the wardrobe had been scattered. The drawers of the tallboy were still open.

"Get someone to take all these things away. Empty the drawers. Take everything."

"Everything, milord?"

"That is what I said. Have it all taken down into the gardens and burned." He turned away, expecting her to go, but she stood for a moment, her eyes roaming over the sea of velvets, silks, satins, and tarlatans, mesmerized, without understanding. Most of them never worn, worth a small fortune, all to be taken away and burned on a fire. She would have given her right arm for one of those beautiful gowns, and he wanted to destroy them.

"Burned, milord? What, all of them?"

He swung round on her.

"Yes, all of them. Lady Russell has been dead for more than two years. She will hardly have need of them now." He could not control the bitterness in his voice. He hated this room, loathed it; each time he passed the door to his own bedroom at the end of the same corridor his flesh would creep, thinking of her clothes, her possessions, still there, exactly as she had left them. By destroying everything that had been hers perhaps he could exorcise his feelings of pain and guilt.

He caught sight of his reflection in her mirror. The face was drawn, his eyes stared back at him, dull and hollow from their tired sockets, wearied by the long journey of the past few days and the grinding strain of the hated secret he was obliged to keep. For a moment the face of the strange girl, the girl who had struck him in the courtyard, swam before him in the depths of the mirror, her blue eyes mocking, her dark hair a tangle, blowing about her face; then the image faded and his own reflection reappeared.

The servants returned, a few moments later, with his butler.

"When these things have been taken away, I wish the bed to be stripped." He glanced at it, suppressing a shudder. On that white, starched pillow he fancied he could still see that other face, the face of his wife, her hair spread out behind her like a pale cape. High above him, echoing into the canopy, he could hear her wild, taunting laugh. "Burn the sheets. Burn the pillows. Everything. Throw it on the fire with the rest." He ignored their expressions of surprise, and the unspoken questions. Why now, after so long? "When the room has been stripped bare I wish it closed up. Do you understand?"

"Yes, milord. You have a visitor, milord, waiting downstairs. I showed him into the morning room."

"A visitor, at this hour? But no one knew that I returned here last night. Who is it?"

"Mr. Hindley, sir."

"Very well." Troubled, angry, still tired from lack of sleep, he strode out of the room.

Hindley. Hindley. When would that cursed name cease to haunt him?

✳ 3 ✳

There was a little group of men clustered about Sam Loam's yard when Anna and Clara opened the gate and let themselves inside. They were idling before starting work, talking, laughing amongst themselves; when they caught sight of the two girls they stopped, abruptly. Someone at the back of the group began to whisper. Another laughed. Beside her, Anna felt her sister's steps falter, and she grasped her firmly by the hand.

"They're just his men. They're not important. Take no notice of them. Walk on by."

"Why are they staring at us like that, Anna?"

"Because they're ignorant. They don't know any better."

"You didn't tell Mama that you'd be working with all these men. Rough men, laboring men." Her cheeks coloring, Clara averted her eyes from them. "She'd never let you if she knew."

"She'll never know. Because neither you nor I will tell her." She stopped, and stared into her sister's eyes. "Mama's ill, Clara. She's not been well for almost a year, since she caught the cough. The bailiffs are after her again. They found out where we are and they followed her. She's too ill to take in any more sewing, and we can't starve. It's the work I want. If I can work with horses I don't give a damn who else is here. Do you understand?" Clara hung her head, without speaking, and they walked on. As they came up to the little group of rough riders Anna nodded to them; politely, coldly. Her mother had always taught her to be courteous, even to the very humble. She could read in their curious stares that Sam Loam had already told them she was coming; and she could understand their curiosity; it was the other staring, the staring that she knew came only from men's eyes, that angered and revolted her. But she remembered Sam's warning, from yesterday, about making trouble, and she walked on without speaking. Behind her, the men's silence became loud whispering, and her sharp ears caught remarks that drew deep color to her sister's cheeks. She stopped walking at once, her hand resting on the latch of Sam's front door. She looked at each of them in turn with her angry, vivid blue eyes. There was an instant hush.

"My sister has just asked me why you were staring at us." Beside her, she felt Clara cringe with embarrassment. "She asked me because we were brought up to believe that only ignorant people stare at a stranger. I told her you did it because you don't know any better." The barb went home. No one spoke. No one moved. One or two of the men who had been smirking and nudging each other hung their heads and looked away. Then, slowly, the little group broke up and went off to different parts of the yard to work. Anna waited until every one of them had gone. Then she knocked on the door and let herself in.

"Anna, you oughtn't to have spoken to them like that!"

"Why not? It was true."

"But it'll cause trouble, don't you understand?"

"Only of their making. They got what they deserved."

"But they'll resent you now. You could see it in their faces. They'll think you talked to them that way because you think you're better than they are."

"I am better than they are." Her voice was harsh, impatient. "I have better manners. And I tamed a colt that threw three of them on their arses."

"Anna!" Clara stopped, abruptly, having caught sight of Sam Loam on the stairs. In one hand he held a bridle; in the other his working boots.

"Well, what's this you've brought me, Anna Brodie? Another rough rider looking for work?"

"This is my sister, Clara."

"So I see by the likeness. Can you ride, too?"

"Not so well as Anna, sir."

Sam bit his lip to hide a smile. He'd been called many things in his long life, but this was the first time anyone had called him sir. He let his keen eyes rest on the younger girl for a moment, sizing her up. Dark, very pretty, with the same wide blue eyes as her sister, but they lacked the vividness and color of Anna's; she was nervous, unsure of herself, respectful; all the things the older girl was not, as if she had been fashioned from all the leftover pieces, a weaker, paler imitation of the original.

"Mr. Loam, could I speak to you outside?" He could see by the look on her face that whatever it was she wanted to say, she didn't want either her sister or his wife to hear. He shrugged. "I reckon so." He turned to Clara. "Sit yourself down by the fire, lass. You look chilled through. Kate? Give her something to eat." Outside he put his hands on his hips. "Well, let's be hearing it."

"It's about money."

"Oh?" He was watching her face shrewdly.

"I know when you took me on, you said I wouldn't get any favors. As far as the work is concerned, I don't expect any. What I wanted to ask was if you'd let me have my first week's wages today, instead of at the end of the week. I have my reasons for asking." She hesitated, fighting a losing battle with her pride. "That's why I brought Clara with me. If you can give me the ten shillings now, she can take it back to my mother."

"You mean your mother's got no money indoors, is that it?"

"Yes, that's it."

"If it's food you're wanting to buy with it, I'll get Kate to pack you a basket. Your sister can take it home with her."

"That's kind of you, Mr. Loam. But it's not just the food." She bit her lip, forcing out the words. "The bailiffs have come after my mother again. They followed us from Saffron Walden. She's frightened they'll have her up in front of the magistrate, and if she can't pay they can arrest her for debt." There were no tears in her eyes. But he could tell by the bitterness in her voice that she was telling him the truth. "They know she's sick, that she's got nothing left of any value they can take; but they won't leave her alone. They won't be satisfied until they've hounded her to death."

"How much does she owe, then?"

"Five guineas."

"Then ten shillings wouldn't satisfy them, would it?"

"It'd stave them off, till I earned more."

"And what would you live off if you gave them that?"

She hesitated, reluctant to tell him any more. She had already said far more than she'd meant to. "My mother's been taking in sewing, since things got bad for us. Jessie helps her, when she gets too tired; she's always lived with us, she used to be a servant when Mama was a girl." She had told him so much, she might as well tell him the rest. All but one thing. That was her secret, that must remain where it was, locked away. "We lived in a cottage on her uncle's estate, until he died. Then as soon as he was dead and buried his widow stopped the allowance that he paid us and threw us out." There was anger in her voice, but no self-pity. He admired that. "We had nowhere to go. With what money there was left we took the first stagecoach from the town and ended up here. We came to Epsom because that was where the stagecoach was going." Yes, he remembered now; one of his men had mentioned that a pale young woman, a widow by her garb, had got off the Epsom stage more than a week ago with two girls and an older woman, maybe a servant. He hadn't thought much of it at the time, but the descriptions fitted. And, he'd heard since, they'd been lodging up in the old dilapidated cottage that'd been empty for years, on the west side of Mickleham Downs.

"All right, I'll make a bargain with you. I won't give you an advance on your earnings . . . you'll get them at the end of the week, same as the men do. But for taming Lord Russell's colt I'm prepared to pay extra." Her eyes brightened. "Five guineas for the job . . . and you can pay your bailiffs off with it."

"I'm grateful, Mr. Loam."

She felt a sudden, unexpected moment of weakness, when she would have liked to have told him more; about what had happened to her inside the mansion grounds that morning, about the scene on his doorstep with his men, but she held back. She had kept her own counsel and kept her feelings hidden for so long that even his kindness could not break her of the habit of silence.

He said, mildly teasing, "Reckon when it gets out that I've gone and hired a girl rough rider, you and me'll be the talk of the Downs."

She looked up at him with that special way she had, mischief in her eyes and her head cocked on one side.

"I can stand it if you can."

Later that evening, sitting by the fire with his wife, Sam Loam leaned back in his chair and drew slowly on his pipe.

"The girl's a natural. I never saw such balance, and that Selim nag of Russell's had never even had a saddle on. And she's got the hands, too. Like magic. Pity she wasn't born a boy."

"A boy?"

"Yes. She's got flair, that one. She could do anything she liked with a horse. If she was a boy, she'd be a great jockey, better than the Chifneys or Hem Robinson. If you'd seen her with that nag, you'd know what I mean. It's something . . . just something she's got that you can't teach. It's a gift. And you got to be born with it. And that colt, he knew it, too. They know, horses do." The smoke from his pipe rose upward in a winding column to the ceiling. "If only Ralph Russell could have seen her, when she rode the colt into my yard . . . his face'd have been a sight for sore eyes! And to think I was about to send the nag back to him as a bad job. Ay, she's worth her weight in gold, young Anna Brodie."

Her name still lingered with him, elusively, for he was almost certain that, somewhere, he had heard it before. Brodie. Brodie. No. For the moment his memory failed him, and it would not come. But it would, later, he was sure of it.

PART II
April 1830

❋ 4 ❋

There was little heat left in the fire now. The single candle was half burned down, spluttering in its pool of melted wax, the flame swaying to and fro in the draft. Screwing up her eyes to see better, Anna bent closer to the garment she held in her hands, studying the fine, almost invisible stitching. Her mother was so skilled, so clever. Ill as she was, even with the warmer weather, she'd taken the old, forgotten roll of material down from the dusty attic trunk and turned it into a fashionable, exquisite gown any lady would be proud to wear. Turning it over in the murky light, then holding it up to examine with her sharp eyes, Anna could see no difference between what her mother had created with her needle and thread and the picture she had copied it from. A fashion plate, cut from a lady's magazine that Mercy Troggle, the corn chandler's daughter, had filched from milady's waste paper basket up at the big house.

"You're set on going, then?" Jessie's voice, with its soft Suffolk burr, reproachful from the other side of the room. Twenty years in her mother's service gave Jessie the privilege of speaking her mind. " 'Tisn't right, not a girl brought up proper like you've bin, going near racegrounds." She didn't wait for Anna's answer. "Never 'ave heard of such a monstrous, scandalous thing . . . a young lady of your sort, rubbing shoulders with a pack of thieves and villains!"

"I can take care of myself. And the thieves and villains."

"Your ma's too easy with you, my girl. And I told 'er so, and all! It's bad enough you working in that 'orse-breaker's yard, keeping company with a lot of rough, common men . . ." Anna sighed. Clara's words, too. "But you must get it into your 'ead that you'll make a spectacle of yourself being seen in public on a raceground!" On and on, a dog with a bone.

"Jessie, this is Derby Day. Special. Don't you understand that? On Derby Day there'll be a lot of women at Epsom. From all over. From York, Newmarket, London. Everywhere. It's the most important day in the year . . . even parliament closes for the Derby."

A snort of disgust. "Shame on 'em, then." Outraged, she heaved herself from the chair, grumbling beneath her breath as she always did when Anna had the better of her. "Well, I can see full well I'm wasting me breath on you, my girl . . . you'll just go right ahead, no matter what, and do what you've set your mind to, anyhow."

Anna hid the beginnings of a smile.

"Jessie, it's the sport of kings."

"Sport of kings my eye. Pastime of the devil, more like." She picked up a pile of soiled dishes from the table and shuffled off into the scullery, leaving Anna alone. From one of the little attic rooms upstairs, there came the muffled sound of a sharp, rasping cough.

"Go and see if your ma's all right; I'll tend to what needs seeing to down 'ere." Jessie turned back to the soiled dishes, rubbing her tired eyes on the back of her big, work-roughened hand. She'd spent more than twenty years serving her beloved mistress, a girl of fifteen and as pretty as a picture when she'd first set eyes on her, so long ago. A humble maid she'd been then, in good Doctor Flood's house, and the singing and laughter she'd smiled to hear from Anna Maria then had stood her in good stead for all the bad times that were to follow on, after. The first, ill-fated marriage to that rogue, Richard Rowe . . . no, no. She mustn't think back on that, not now. It was all done and over with. Then the worse-than-ill-fated liaison with Edward Brodie, father of Anna and Clara, and the tears and heartache when, to save him from scandal and ruin, she'd let him go. Jessie had been with her mistress for so long and through so much that long since she had ceased to be regarded as a servant. Anna Maria was still her life. As the disciples had followed Christ, Jessie had stuck by her through thick and thin, unquestioningly, without complaint. What hurt her most was to see her a pale ghost of the girl she'd once been; weak, ailing, struggling to survive ill health and cruel misfortune. Her Anna Maria, who once had everything of the best, reduced to living like a pauper.

There was no self-pity. Jessie was low-born and humble, a cobbler's eleventh daughter, and her whole life had been spent in the service of others, first her parents, then her first job, at thirteen, when she'd packed up her meager belongings in a bundle and gone to work at the big house, for Lord Eglinton, ten miles from Saffron Walden. Her life had been hard then, and she reckoned resignedly, it always would be. No doubt there were plenty of others worse off.

But she wasn't bitter, only angry. Bitterness was a canker, like jealousy. If you gave in to it, it ended by eating you alive. That was why she was so worried about young Anna. She blamed her father for all her mother's ills, and her hatred for him was so great that Jessie was afraid of something she couldn't define, or even quite understand, but that hovered, menacingly, like a gypsy's curse.

Anna was awake, long before dawn. The dark sky outside was heavy, with gathering clouds that lay low across the sweep of the Downs. Rain for the Derby. Leaving Clara still sleeping she crept from the attic and made her way downstairs, the gray velvet gown draped across one arm. The stone floor was cold to her bare feet. When she had lit the fire she washed and dressed herself, and sat at the tiny window brushing out her long, dark hair as she watched the weak sunlight rising above the green of the low hills.

They were still sleeping when she left, mounted on the borrowed horse from Sam Loam's yard, riding astride as she always did. She had spent the whole evening before brushing and grooming him, and as the early light fell upon his flanks and neck his bay coat gleamed like satin. At the stile in Patton's Field she joined forces with young Matthew Troggle, the corn chandler's lad, who was waiting for her as they had arranged. As she rode up, he sprang to his feet, brown eyes bolting from their sockets. In her new gown and with her hair brushed he scarcely recognized her.

"Morning, Anna. Why, you're a sight for sore eyes."

"We'd best get going, before the roads are full." Gently, she eased her horse to a standstill.

"No need to use the roads. We can ride straight through Walton Parish, bypass Woodcote Park, and come out on the course itself." He pulled himself into the saddle.

"But Woodcote Park's private land." Not that that worried her. But if they were seen by Sir Gilbert Heathcote's gamekeeper, he might stop them and turn them back, wasting precious time.

"There's no one about, not this early. I've done it before."

"All right. If we see anyone, we separate and ride straight past them at a gallop."

They started off, walking their horses. There was plenty of time.

"You'll be the first female what's ever set foot on the course. Come tonight, you'll 'ave set a fair few tongues wagging, I reckon."

She laughed, her breath rising in the chilly air and mingling with the horses'.

"They haven't seen anything yet."

The first thing that astonished her was the size of the crowd. A week ago, a few days, even, the Downs and the villages roundabout were well-nigh empty. Today, the masses swarmed in their thousands and there was no room to be had at any of the posting inns as far as Sutton and Cheam. Some had been sleeping out on the Downs for days, suffering the wretched weather; some had walked from as far off as London and beyond. Along every road and track every carriage, cart, or wagon that could hold human beings and go along was bursting at the seams.

"Where do they all come from, Mattie?"

"You name the place, and you'll find the folk that've traveled from it. London, Sussex, Kent. From Newmarket. And from as far off as Taunton in the south and Doncaster and York up north. That's what the Derby does to some folk. Casts a spell on 'em. There's no other race like it. Never will be. Why, even parliament closes for it."

She had never seen or been in anything like it, the vast Derby crowd. The noise deafened her, hurting her eardrums, more than when they'd driven through the packed streets of London, on the Epsom-bound stage. There were musicians, jugglers, acrobats. Men with performing monkeys and dancing bears. Gypsies with bright-colored booths bedecked with streamers where you could buy a pennyworth of ale and hot pies, and stalls where you could try to hit a row of skittles with a ball, for a halfpenny a turn. There were dancers in strange costumes and organ-grinders with performing dogs, and an old gypsy woman, withered as a baked apple, who read palms for sixpence, and for a shilling promised to foretell the winner of the Derby.

When it began to rain, Matthew pulled off his jacket and draped it over Anna's head. "Come on. This'll keep the worst off us. 'Old me 'and and we'll shove our way through this bloody—begging your pardon—blessed lot, and make our way to the edge of the course on this side." He took her hand, screwing up his eyes against the rain, which was getting heavier. "If anyone shoves you, give 'em a dig with your elbow or a kick in the shins. There's so many 'ere, they won't know where it come from."

"But this is the wrong side of the course. The saddling and the horses are on the other side, in front of the grandstand."

"We can't go there, Anna. It's not allowed. Even ladies from the gentry 'ave to stop inside the ladies' room what's bin built for 'em, in the new grandstand, unless they've come with someone who's got a private box. No female can go out on the course."

"Why not?"

He stared at her, exasperated, hampered by his inborn inability to express himself.

"'Cos it ain't done, that's why not. You've turned enough 'eads among this lot, coming down in the roughnecks and gypsies in that smart get-up. If you get seen on the other side, where the lords and gentlemen are, you'll be the talk of every mouth this side of the county."

She shrugged.

"Is that all?"

"But they'll stop you, don't you understand? Women just ain't allowed near the Warren, not unless they're on their way to the grandstand and they're being escorted."

"What are you doing, then?"

"But I ain't a gentleman."

For a few moments they were separated, while the crowd jostled around and in between them. Then Anna took his jacket from her head and lay it on his arm. She smiled, so that he wouldn't feel slighted.

"If you won't come with me I shall just have to go alone."

Edward Brodie stood alone in the crowded gallery, leaning against the balcony and staring out at the driving rain. Before him in the Warren some of the grooms were already saddling their horses for the Derby, trying to shield their eyes from the downpour, already drenched to the skin. The grass was now a sea of mud. He stared at the familiar scene without really seeing it, sick with disappointment and rage, tired of the press of people in the salon, tired of the false condolences of false friends, who he knew were only too delighted that his colt had been scratched from the race when it had gone lame. The forfeited entrance fee, the five thousand guineas, even, that he'd wagered on it among his aquaintances and friends, meant nothing beside the galling knowledge that with all his wealth and power and priceless breeding stock, he had never even come close to his ambition of breeding a Derby winner until now; and now it was unfit to run.

Perhaps he deserved his ill fortune. Perhaps after all his cynicism there really was a God and he was being punished for his sins. Maybe there really was a Supreme Being who looked down and saw all the cruel and callous acts he had committed in his life, and had found, for him, the ultimate punishment. Sipping his glass of brandy without tasting it, he stood there for a while longer. He was no longer even interested in the outcome of the race. He set the glass down, only half-finished, and walked slowly along the length of the gallery until he reached the end. It was then that he caught sight of her, walking through the driving rain as if it didn't exist, every head turning to stare after her as she passed.

His heart began to beat wildly. There was no mistake; she was so like her mother that that face could not belong to anyone else. He turned and ran back along the gallery into the crowded salon, pushing his way roughly through the press of people, ignoring their shouts of protest and surprise. When he had reached the bottom of the staircase and fought his way to the entrance, he could see her, making her way through the half-deserted paddock where she suddenly stopped, in front of a dark bay colt whose jockey he recognized as Sam Day. He caught up with her, fighting for his breath.

For a few moments he watched her as she stood there, staring at the colt with the same expression people used when they stared at the Holy Cross, on the altars of churches. Then she turned, suddenly, and caught sight of him. Across the horse's back they looked at each other. He smiled. She did not smile back. Sam Day was given a leg up by the groom and the dark bay colt moved off, leaving a void between them. Uncertainly he stepped into it, his hands outstretched toward her.

"*Anna?* . . . Is it really you?" He was oblivious to anything else around him. The rain. The turning heads. He did not even wonder what she was doing here, a solitary female among a sea of men. No place for a young girl to be. Rain dripped from the brim of his top hat and ran down his neck. Rain trickled into his eyes and down his cheeks, as if he had been weeping. "Anna?" he said again, when she continued to stand there, looking at him.

"The last time I saw you, you cut us dead, in the market square at Bury Saint Edmunds." The hate in her voice sent a chill through him. "You didn't want to know me that day. You turned your face the other way, so that your wife and sons would think I was a stranger. You disowned me.

Now, I disown you." Abruptly, she turned on her heel and walked away into the milling crowd of grooms and jockeys, rushing to get their mounts off to post. For a moment he hesitated, wondering if he should run after her before it was too late. But as he felt curious eyes staring his way he suddenly remembered who he was, and what would happen if any part of his past that concerned Anna Maria should become common knowledge. He turned back, shielding his eyes from the rain, and returned to the grandstand and his private box.

He sat there, his head in his hands, in a deep, unshakable depression. He could not remember afterward how long he sat there. Through the fourteen false starts in the race. Through the shouting and cheering and curses of the others in the adjoining boxes, whose bets had been lost. Behind him he could hear the noise of crowds quitting the building, but still he stayed where he was, the same half-drunk glass of brandy in his hand. Only when the grandstand was almost empty did he get to his feet and walk out, slowly.

"Who won?" he asked somebody who was clearing up the salon of discarded race cards and empty glasses. The man stopped what he was doing and leaned on his broom.

"Why, Priam, Mr. Chifney's colt, by two clear lengths. And he got left behind a hundred yards at the start."

"Thank you." Drawing on his gloves, he made his way to the staircase. Strange, that the Derby winner had been the dark bay colt that Anna had stood beside in the Warren. Somehow, it seemed like an omen.

Seeing him had ruined everything for her. His face, his voice. They brought back every bitter, painful memory that she had striven to rid herself of. Like a ghost, he had come back, still not exorcised. She felt tainted, unclean. As if by breathing the same air she had somehow become contaminated by his presence.

The rain lashed down, harder than before. As she battled her way through the gaping hordes of men to seek refuge in the grandstand, someone stepped forward, frowning, and barred her path.

"No unescorted ladies are permitted anywhere on the course or in the grandstand. And only ladies whose escorts are either members of the aristocracy or gentlemen of the Jockey Club are even permitted in the ladies' salon there."

There was rainwater in her eyes. She screwed them up, trying to make out the face of the man who was barring her path, but they were smarting and stinging. It was then that she heard another voice, somewhere from behind her.

"This lady is with me. Now go about your business."

"Why, my lord Russell. I had no idea. I beg your pardon."

"It would be more appropriate, don't you think, if you begged the pardon of this lady."

She could see clearly now. The man in front of her, cringing, obsequious. At her side stood Ralph Russell. She was vaguely aware of other people, staring their way, but she was so stunned that for a moment only he seemed real to her.

"There was no need for you to interfere."

"No." He laughed softly, infuriating her. "I thought I was doing a service to a lady in distress."

"You flatter yourself."

"But he was right. You have no right to be here. Escorted or not. A racecourse is no place for any female. Respectable or otherwise." She glared at him. "What in God's name are you doing here, in this pouring rain?"

"I came to see Priam win the Derby."

"Then I wish I'd met you earlier. You could have saved me two thousand guineas."

"Two thousand guineas?"

"I backed the favorite, Red Rover."

"More fool you. Next to Priam he looks like a cart horse!"

"You have an interest in him?"

"I saw him, when he was being walked from Newmarket, at the inn yard at Epping."

Around them, the vast grandstand was beginning to empty of its occupants.

"You're soaked through," he said, drawing her to one side. "How do you intend to get home through this crush?"

"The same way as I got here. I have a horse tethered at the milestone by Walton Parish."

"That's more than half a mile's walk across country. I'll have a groom ride over and pick it up. You'd best come back with me, and get into some dry clothes before you catch your death of cold."

"I'd rather walk back than ride with you." She drew away from him defiantly, almost savagely. But as she began to walk away he came after her. He put his hand on her arm. She shook it off.

"You still hate me, don't you? For what happened that morning, when I caught you on my land." She walked on, without speaking, dashing away the rain with the back of her hand. Her long gown was saturated, clinging to her legs as she went. Her boots were caked with mud. "I thought so. Well, I don't blame you. I was at fault, not you. I'd been traveling for five days and nights, almost without a stop. I'd eaten little and drunk too much. I behaved badly. If you've ever done anything that you were sorry for afterward, maybe you can forgive me for what I did." She still walked on, but her step was slower. "But if you're so perfect that you've never made any mistakes, then perhaps I'm asking too much of you."

She stopped walking, and looked up at him from beneath the dripping crown of her velvet bonnet.

"I don't need your charity, Ralph Russell."

"It's a long walk back to Walton Parish in a wet gown."

She wiped the rain from the tip of her nose roughly, on the back of her sleeve. "I'll survive."

He watched her as she made her way through the dispersing crowds on the opposite side of the course, then disappeared from sight. For a while he stood there, wondering if she would change her mind and come back. When she did not, he turned away and made his way back to his carriage.

His coachman sat on the box, greatcoat drawn up to his chin to keep out the rain, gloved hands folded on his lap. At the sight of Russell he stiffened, cleared his throat, and tucked away the gin flask that he always carried with him on a journey, long or short. The footman, also muffled against the driving rain, jumped down from the seat and opened the carriage door.

"Wicked day for any race to be run, milord," he said, pulling down the folded steps. "Let alone the Derby. Another hour and I reckon the nags could've swum past the post." Russell laughed, good-humoredly, clapping him on the shoulder.

"Red Rover wouldn't have passed the post first if he'd been carried there on a stretcher. This year the Chifney brothers have cleaned up." He got into the coach and put his head out of the window. "Take the Walton Parish road, will you? And don't drive too fast."

"Go by Walton Parish, milord? But that's five or six miles out of our way. And it's no proper road, neither, begging your lordship's pardon. It's a track, more like. With this weather we might even get bogged down, halfway."

Russell lay back against the soft upholstery of the carriage seat, a smile playing at the corners of his lips. In his hands he held a soggy, crumpled copy of Henry Dorling's official race card, especially printed for that afternoon. "Jeremiah, I said we'll go home by the Walton Parish road. Be a good fellow and do as I say."

He caught sight of her, suddenly, on the winding, narrow road ahead of them, leading her limping horse, head bowed against the wind and rain. Ordering his driver to slow down, he waited until the carriage was almost level with her before he pushed down the window and looked out. She went on walking, holding her sodden hemline above her ankles with her free hand.

"I see your horse has gone lame."

"He'll live."

"He'd do better spending the night in my stables and having my groom take a look at that foreleg."

"He doesn't belong to me. I only borrowed him."

"I can send someone over to his owner with a message; or would you rather make him walk an extra five miles in pain because you're too cussed to take help when you need it?" She stopped walking, abruptly, and stared up at him, stung by his words. In spite of her tangled, wet hair and sodden clothes, he had never seen anyone more beautiful, and somehow that disturbed him without his fully understanding why.

"All right," she said, without gratitude. "I'll tie him to the back of the carriage." Unwillingly she climbed inside, the rain from her clothes dripping over the floor. She looked at it, but without being sorry.

"It's all right," he said, with that same mocking smile she detested and remembered from their first meeting. "Rainwater dries."

Uncomfortably, Anna settled back into her seat, watching his face without speaking.

She remembered the long, winding drive, lined with shrubbery, and the great house at the end of it. The massive gates that she and Clara had stood staring through were wide open, and the carriage passed through, trundling over the stones. Water dripped from the overhanging branches of trees, making strange sounds on the carriage roof; the courtyard was full of swirling puddles and rivulets. She got out without a word and followed him up the flight of wide stone steps that led to the front door. In the porchway she hesitated, looking anxiously toward her lame horse, which a groom was untying and leading away.

"Don't worry," Russell said, seeing her expression. "He'll be well taken care of. Young ladies who get soaked to the skin on racecourses are much more fragile."

She stood in the drawing room, looking around her, aware at once of the strange, musty odor of disuse. So he was away from home often. She went on looking. The walls were lined with paintings, books; statues of horses stood about on tables and cabinets. Suddenly, she realized how wet through she was, and went over to the roaring fire. For the first time, she shivered.

"First you must get out of those wet clothes." He went to the bell rope and pulled it, hard. "Then we must try to find you some others." She went on holding her hands out toward the blaze.

"Take hot towels up to the yellow bedroom," he said to a manservant who answered the bell, "and find this lady a change of clothes. There should be something left in one of the wardrobes, if one of the maids looks hard enough. Then organize something hot to eat."

"Yes, milord."

Russell turned to Anna. "I'll show you the way upstairs."

He stopped, outside a door on the second landing. "This is it. I'll wait for you downstairs, if you can find your way back again."

She looked at him suspiciously.

"Whose room is this?"

"My sister last used it, on one of her rare visits. I believe she left some clothes behind. Can you manage?"

She gave him a cold glance and went in, slamming the door behind her. To his amusement he heard her lock it from the other side.

Sam Loam reined in his horse, jumped down from the saddle, and tied his horse securely to a tree near the old cottage. Then he stood for a moment or two, looking at it. It was years since he'd ridden up this way, and longer since he'd seen the inside of the old place. But he had a good memory, he reckoned, and he couldn't recall when last anyone had lived in it, or whom it belonged to, either. Wasn't any Epsom landlord, as far as he knew. Still, he was here to do what good he could, not to poke his nose where it had no business to be. A bottle of good brandy in his hand, he pushed open the broken, rickety little gate and went up to the front door. Then he knocked, loudly, several times, and called out before anybody answered him.

Slowly, the door creaked back a few inches, and a face stared around it at him, so like young Anna's that he knew instinctively it was her mother.

"Yes?" she said, in a voice that held fear.

He took off his hat and smiled at her; then explained who he was and why he was here. The hunted look in her blue eyes vanished, and she stepped back and opened the door for him to pass through.

"It's kind of you to call, Mr. Loam. Please sit down." Yes, she was afraid of something. Flustered. Ill at ease. Sam remembered what Anna had said about the bailiffs, and understood. "I'm grateful for the kindness you've shown to Anna, giving her work. She loves the horses. She's always had a way with horses." She fidgeted with her pale, slender hands as if she was at a loss as to what to do with them. "She's gone off, with one of Ephraim Troggle's lads, to watch the crowds up on Epsom Downs." The little bitch, after he'd told her not to! "She said you never work on Derby Day."

"That's right, ma'am. I never do. Reckon that's one day me and my men deserve to have off. I'll be making my way down to the course, presently. When you've lived up here long enough, like me, you know all the short cuts off by heart." He smiled. "But this place isn't far out of me way, and young Anna mentioned that you'd been feeling poorly, so I reckoned I'd be a bit neighborly and drop by with this." He put the bottle on the table. "A glassful of this'll do more than any doctor's medicine. I swear by it." So much he wanted to know. So many things he would have liked to ask her; but he had no right. It wasn't his business to pry, whether she had things she wanted hidden, or not. She talked rapidly, too quickly, about trivial, mundane things, while he sat there, half-listening and studying her face.

Yes, there was great beauty beneath the fine lines of ill health and suffering; he could see where the girls got their looks from. She never mentioned a husband. But she had a servant, and only lords and gentry had servants; she was a lady come down in the world and that to him was one of the saddest things of all to behold.

It was different with folk born poor, born into the working classes. It was bred in their bones, being hungry, cold, going without; they were born into it and they accepted it because they didn't know any different. It was like being born with a harelip or twisted foot; you were stuck with it and there was nothing you could do about it. Turn a rough, wild pony out on the freezing moors with nothing better than some poor, rank grass and a few bushes to feed on, and it'd survive; turn out a high-bred blood horse that had been coddled from birth and given everything of the best, and in a week it'd be on its knees. Stood to reason.

"Now, if there's ever anything that wants doing, ma'am," he said, at length, trying to make conversation, "you just send word by Anna, and I'll send one of my men up to tend to it, straightaway." He hoped that she wouldn't think he was offering charity. "I'd be right glad to oblige a lady like yourself . . . and it's no trouble. No trouble at all."

She thanked him again. She repeated that she feared he'd ridden out of his way, and that she didn't want to keep him any longer from his journey, the crowds being what they were because of the Derby. And she smiled, with increasing difficulty. The sharp, gnawing pain that had racked her body for months on end had suddenly come back again and she had been in some discomfort for several minutes. In a few more she would be in agony.

"Yes," he said, unaware that anything was wrong. "The crowds are always bad, even a week before the big race. Roads are all but blocked, for miles around; folk on the Downs thicker than flies round a jampot." Mercifully, at last, he stood up, holding his hat, ready to go. "Well, I reckon I'll be on my way, Mrs. Brodie." He nodded at the door. "A privilege to have made your acquaintance, ma'am."

"Good day to you, Mr. Loam. And my thanks once more."

The moment the door closed behind him she sank down, bent double with the searing pain. The bottle of brandy he had brought was several feet away, at the end of the table. Pulling herself up, she edged along toward it, then grasped it with both shaking hands. Jessie had left a cup conveniently near. Tortuously slowly, Anna Maria managed to half-fill it and gulp down the liquid.

It was years since she had tasted any spirits, even wine. The strong, dark brandy burned her mouth and her gullet and made her eyes water. She felt dizzy and sick. Clutching the nearest stool, she lowered herself onto it, resting her head on the table with her eyes closed. That was how Jessie found her, half an hour later, when Jeremiah Troggle dropped her off at the gate on his way to deliver corn in Walton Parish.

She dumped her basket of shopping on the floor.

"Merciful 'eaven, what's wrong?" She rushed over to Anna Maria as fast as her bulk would let her. "Lassie! Lassie, what's wrong? What is it?"

"I'm all right, Jessie." She raised her glassy eyes to Jessie's broad, anxious face. "It's only a headache, a sick headache. I'll be all right later, when I've slept." She swallowed, wincing at the agony in her chest. "I didn't sleep well last night."

"It's the pain again, isn't it? You can't fool me!"

"It will pass."

"Ay, and be back tomorrow, twice as bad. Lassie, you can't go on like this, in agony, pretending nothing's amiss . . . you must see a doctor—"

"And pay him with what?" In spite of how ill she felt, her voice was vehement, almost shrill. "I swore when we left Saffron Walden that we'd never get into debt again, no matter what. I'd starve sooner."

"Lassie . . ."

"And you're to say nothing to the girls, do you understand? Nothing, Jessie. I don't want either of them to know." She put a hand to her chest where the pain was, and held it there, as if touching it would somehow make it go away. "I'll be all right, when the warm weather comes." She rose to her feet, unsteadily, and walked to the staircase. The brandy had made her giddy and she clung to the rope rail to steady herself. She glanced up at the steep, winding little staircase with trepidation, as if it was a mountain to climb. "Mr. Loam called today, while you were out. The man Anna works for. He seemed a kindly man."

"Oh, ay, young Anna's told me that."

"He left me the bottle of brandy." Jessie noticed it for the first time. "Well, I must go upstairs now. There are some old gowns of mine in one of the trunks that need sorting. I can make skirts from them for the girls." That was it. That was what she must do. Keep occupied. Keep her hands busy. Her mind off the searing pain. When she'd gone Jessie wearily took out the provisions from her basket and set them on the table. New loaf, a pound of cheese. A piece of mutton. Only scrag end, but the butcher had been kindly and given her nearly double weight for the price of one. And Mrs. Troggle, the corn chandler's wife, had given her four pounds of apples from her apple store. A bit shriveled, but they'd bake well with some treacle or honey. Thank the good Lord young Anna was bringing some money in, to eke out what little they'd brought with them. And there'd been precious little of that, when that bitch Edith Flood had put a stop to the allowance Edmund had given his niece.

After a while there were no longer any sounds coming from Anna Maria's bedroom upstairs. Jessie bustled over to the hearth and busied herself with making up the little fire.

Left alone, Anna undressed and laid her soaking gown on a stool beside the bed. Then she rubbed herself all over vigorously with the hot towels until her skin was dry and tingling. Dressed in the borrowed gown, she went over to the mirror and stared at her reflection, turning this way, then that. She touched the rich material with one hand, trying to imagine the girl who had last worn it. A peculiar scent hung about it, something that she could not identify. She walked around the room, touching things. The satin canopy of the bed, the fringed curtains, an embroidered cushion on the chair. She opened the wardrobe and looked at the row of gowns hanging inside. In a drawer of the dressing table she found a single pair of gloves, their color faded on one side. Then she went to the window and pulled back the drapes, staring out into the wild night. It was still raining, steadily, and the rain trickled down the windows like tears and splashed upon the sills outside. For a moment she saw her father's face reflected in the glass, then it faded, leaving only her own image.

She let go the drape and went back downstairs, rubbing her wet hair with one of the towels.

"I must go," she said, sitting on a stool beside the fire. "When my hair is dry, I must go."

"Of course. You'll be missed at home. Won't you eat with me first?"

"I'm not hungry." She lied.

"Will you not have something to drink, then? To warm you?"

"No." Slowly, she went on rubbing her hair with the towel.

He fell silent. Then he went across to his desk and sat on the edge of it, still watching her by the fireside, but taking something out of his pocket. He saw her looking at it.

"Henry Dorling's official race card." He smiled, and held it up. "A little battered, and very wet. But perhaps you would like it as a souvenir." Slowly, he turned over the pages. "What a shame one of the runners was scratched from the Derby because it went lame on the gallops." He was watching her face carefully. "And the talk in the grandstand was that Edward Brodie had bred a Derby winner at last." She got to her feet and half-turned away from him toward the fire. He watched the light of the leaping flames, flickering on her face. "Why didn't you tell me that he was your father?"

She swung round, flinging down the towel.

"How dare you! Who told you that lie?"

"No one did. Except you. I saw you on the course today with him. I watched you. You have the same features, the same gestures. He tried to speak with you and you snubbed him . . . then you turned and walked away. Your name is Brodie too. That was when I understood."

"You have a lively imagination."

"You've inherited his passion for horses."

"I told you that he isn't my father."

"Do you hate him that much, Anna?" She paused, harnessing her shock and anger that he had guessed. It was the first time he had ever used her name, and something about the way he spoke it made her feel oddly vulnerable.

"My mother will be worried about me," she said, in a cold, stiff voice. "Will you please lend me one of your horses so that I can go home?"

"My coachman will drive you back in the post chaise."

"Thank you." The words stuck in her throat as she spoke them. "I'll give you back these clothes as soon as my own are dry."

He came toward her and looked down into her face. Yes, he had been drinking when he'd kissed her that day outside the doors of his coach house. But he had not touched a drop of liquor all day and the desire to kiss her now almost overwhelmed him; but he fought against it. No, he must never let himself fall under the spell of another woman, not even this one.

"I'm sorry," he said, turning away from her and going toward the bell rope, which he tugged hard. "I made a mistake. I hope you can forgive me."

"A mistake? About what?"

"When I thought that you were Edward Brodie's daughter."

In the icy little attic bedroom, Anna Maria lay in the growing darkness, listening to the last patterings of rain against the windows and against the roof. From the straw pallet she could see the night sky, and the stars that had already begun to appear, twinkling dimly, in the heavens. Midnight blue, with silver spangles, so like a gown she'd once worn, in the days of happiness and plenty. So many gowns, so many days and nights had passed, vanished into the world she had once been a part of, but was part of no longer. She closed her tired eyes and there before her, suddenly, but out of reach, she could see her beloved rosewood piano. Standing in a beautiful room, a room with real pale gold silk upon the walls, and lit by a crystal chandelier that jingled, softly, when people passed beneath it. Her hands stretched out and touched the keys, and the sweet, strong sound of her voice rose up like the crest of a wave until the piano, and the room, and the blurred faces behind her disappeared like a cloud, and there she was, half-sitting, half-lying, in the great curtained bed, her dark hair spread about her shoulders like a cape.

She heard the footsteps as they halted outside her door, and then the handle turned; slowly, softly. Edward Brodie came smiling toward her, his arms outstretched, and then as he knelt beside the bed she heard him whisper her name. When she opened her eyes, suddenly, as the cruel pain gripped her once more, his face was still there, hovering above hers, but blurred and indistinct, like the reflection in a pool.

Edward. Edward. She had always known that he would come for her. He was here, at last.

PART III
April 1833

William Hubbard dismounted, tethered his horse to a nearby tree, then opened the little lych-gate that led into the churchyard. Almost at once he caught sight of the solitary figure of a girl, standing beside the headstone of one of the graves. She wore no bonnet. Her long, dark hair blew about her face, and the breeze ruffled her cloak so that it fluttered out behind her.

In her hands she held a small posy of wild flowers. As Hubbard watched, without moving, he saw her lean forward and lay them on the grave below the headstone. Then she stepped back and stood, looking at it. Removing his tall hat, he began to walk toward her.

The sun was bright overhead. As his shadow fell across the headstone she spun round, startled, anger and suspicion in her face.

"Who are you? What are you doing here, spying on me?" My God, she was beautiful, Edward Brodie's bastard daughter! For a moment he was as startled as she was. Then the cool, efficient clerklike Hubbard took over, and he rapidly composed himself.

"Forgive me, if I took you by surprise. I didn't mean to. But I've been seeking a lady by the name of Anna Maria Rowe . . . or Brodie, whichever name she was accustomed to using; my name is William Hubbard, of Tuke, Benet, and Tuke, the Newmarket lawyers."

"Well, you've found her," the girl said, with heavy irony. He looked beyond the little posy of flowers to the inscription on the headstone, then understood.

ANNA MARIA BRODIE,
LATE ROWE, NEE FLOOD.
BORN 1793. DIED 1831

"She was my mother. She's been dead for two years." Anna's voice was harsh, concealing her own deep-rooted pain. "What did you want with her and how did you find us?"

"I can explain everything to you, if there is some place where we could speak privately." He could see that she was still suspicious of him. "I was asked to find her by a client of my firm . . . with the greatest discretion, of course." He glanced beyond her. Two other mourners had entered the churchyard by the lych-gate. "The information I was given brought me to Epsom, then to your cottage on Mickleham Downs. An old woman told me that I would find you here." Jessie, no doubt. In her mind's eye Anna could picture her, glowering at him suspiciously from a half-opened door, thinking he was a debt collector, after money.

"The church is empty at this time of day," she said, turning to follow his eyes and catching sight of the two mourners who were now bending down, in prayer, beside one of the other graves. No one she knew. "We can speak in there." She glanced once more at the headstone. For a brief, painful moment she remembered her mother's laughing face, her voice, in the far-off days before illness, tragedy, and ill luck had changed her to a pale, thin, haunted shadow of what she had once been; then the ugliness of the darkened attic bedroom, where her sightless blue eyes had stared upward toward the damp, peeling roof, sightless in death, rose up and vanquished it. Then as now, cold anger smoldered, lingeringly. How much he had to answer for, her father. How much he had to repay.

She turned away and walked into the little church in silence, Hubbard at her side.

They sat down in one of the wooden pews.

"Miss Brodie, your father is a sick man. Were you aware of his ill health?"

So, he had sent Hubbard! His image came to her, the face she had glimpsed in the midst of the crowd on Derby Day, three years ago. She stiffened, enraged.

"I neither knew nor care. Didn't he have the guts to come himself? No, of course not. Somebody might recognize him and find out the truth!"

"Please, hear me out. I can understand your bitterness." Yes, bitterness was something that he understood only too well. Gnawing, haunting him, worming its insidious way into him as he sat, day after long, weary day, crouched over a desk at Tuke, Benet, and Tuke. Ignored, overlooked. His skill and industry unappreciated and unrewarded. "I understand your feelings toward him. Believe me, I am on your side." She glanced at him sharply. "Because of his decline in health over the past few months, he realizes that he may not be long for this world. He has expressed a deep desire to see your mother again. And you, of course. He had no idea that she was already dead."

"He's afraid of dying with what he has on his conscience!" said the mocking voice at his side.

"Yes, if you put it like that." He turned to her and looked into her face. "As you must know, he is a very wealthy man." He paused, letting his meaning sink in. "Too discreet, however, to leave you or yours anything in his will. As I am one of the witnesses . . . indeed, as I was delegated the task of drawing it up, I happen to know its exact content."

"Why are you telling me?"

"Because I think you have a right to know. Because I think he has treated you and your mother badly, and you deserve justice." Careful, now, he cautioned himself. Best not overdo it. "From what I glimpsed of the inside of your cottage on the Downs, I can hazard a guess as to what kind of life you've led, and your mother. When I think of your father's magnificent house . . ." He paused, watching her face carefully for the expected reaction. "He has behaved badly."

"He is your firm's client. He has sent you to come here and find me. Why should you care about how I feel, how my mother suffered?"

Yes, she was still half-suspicious of him. He glanced down at his smooth, well-kept hands. He must be careful, for she was nobody's fool.

"If I told you that we are . . . kindred spirits . . . would you understand then? I, too, have suffered from bad treatment and injustice. Oh, nothing like so severe as you have, I grant you. Many would say I should count myself fortunate. I have never been without shelter. Subsistence of a sort . . ." Suddenly he leaped to his feet, agitatedly, and seized her by both hands. "Oh, for God's sake, Anna! Can't you see what I'm trying to say to you? Let's be done with all this formality, all this polite pretense! Your father should rot in hell for what he's done to you. All of you. He thinks he can buy salvation, like all rich men do, now, when it's too late to make amends, when your mother's dead, when nothing he can do or give will ever bring her back again or wipe out all the suffering and humiliation that she went through! No, he didn't have the guts to come here himself. He couldn't have, even if he wanted to, even if he wasn't afraid of being recognized, even if he wasn't too ill to make the journey. Men like Edward Brodie don't do things like that. They pay someone else to." She, too, had risen to her feet. He almost smiled. The narrowed eyes, the suspicious look she'd had when he first came into the churchyard and approached her, had gone now. Exactly what he wanted.

"All right. I'll be honest with you. I've spent the last ten years with Tuke, Benet, and Tuke. I started as a clerk. I'm still a clerk now. Can you imagine what it's like, bent double over a desk for ten years? Ten wasted, weary, monotonous years, waiting to be recognized, waiting for my work and abilities to be rewarded? Can you understand what it feels like when after all that, you're passed over for somebody else, somebody just down from Cambridge, somebody who doesn't know a will from a litigation, just because he's Benjamin Tuke's nephew and I'm a nobody?" Despite the chill inside the church, beads of perspiration had broken out along his forehead.

"What do you want from me, Hubbard?"

"Let us both take what we deserve, Anna. What is ours by right. I came here to do your father's bidding, yes. But I had plenty of time on the way to think about how we've been treated . . . and I offer you my help in gaining what is yours. All I ask in return is a sum of money from your father's estate—when he dies—for, shall we say, services rendered?"

She stayed there, as if rooted to the spot, stunned by the enormity of what he was suggesting. To forge the will. To leave her almost everything of the Brodie fortune, her and Clara. There was no danger in it, he said, confidently. Old Tuke, one of the original witnesses to the will, had been dead for more than a year. A new one could be made out and no one the wiser. He, Hubbard, had a score of documents bearing the old man's signature, easily forged. And so, too, could Edward Brodie's be. Hold the parchment up to a fire and it would turn yellow, giving it the appearance of age.

There, he had said it, out loud. Everything that had teemed wildly, inside his head. His heart was pounding with excitement.

He held his breath as she moved slowly away from him and began to walk about the church. Her eyes stared at the ground. She clenched and unclenched her fists. She was no longer with him, she was somewhere else, far back in time, trudging across the frost-covered Downs with Clara, blowing on her freezing fingers, pulling her ragged cloak further about her body to ward off the bitter cold. She was remembering the humiliation she had shared with her mother that day in the town square at Bury Saint Edmunds, when her father, riding by in his ornate carriage and four, had averted his eyes from them as if they were strangers, ashamed to acknowledge them. And she recalled her own secret, determined vow to avenge that insult. As she paced, all the bitter grievances of the past years came flooding. Her own wild longing, the dreams she'd nurtured within her like an unborn child, when she'd first glimpsed Priam outside the inn at Epping.

At last, she stopped pacing and turned to him. If she had believed in God she would have believed He had sent Hubbard to her in answer to her prayers.

"Do you know the penalty for the forging of a will?" She knew it was not what he had expected her to say. But she had already thought of it, and it had made her blood run cold. "Forgery is a crime punishable by transportation for life. To return from a sentence of transportation, the penalty is the gallows." She thought, with a shiver, of the ghoulish tales Jessie had often told of a winter's night, of felons and highwaymen swinging from a squeaking gibbet, their flesh dried out on their bleached bones. Invisible cold fingers reached out and touched her spine.

"Then you're afraid to do it?"

"I'm afraid of nothing!" Inwardly, Hubbard sighed with relief. He had thought, for one terrible moment as she hesitated, that he had fatally miscalculated her reaction and completely misjudged her. Now he could breathe again. Slowly, deliberately, he rose to his feet.

"Your father sent me to find you and bring you back to Mildenhall. He needs to see you, to explain certain things to you that you cannot understand now . . . his exact words. When I left, he was very sick . . . though he refused to go to bed . . . we have little time to lose. If you could make ready to leave with me at once, there is a fast mail coach leaving . . ."

"What about her?" He caught the bitterness in her voice and knew she was talking of Brodie's wife.

"Safely out of the way, with her sons, visiting her father at his house near Ipswich. And not expected back for at least two weeks."

"She left him there, knowing how ill he is? What wifely devotion." Contempt in her voice now.

"She has no idea how ill he really is. He's hidden it from her, deliberately, to make certain she went ahead with her visit."

"Am I supposed to be grateful?"

"Guilt does strange things to dying men."

Anna leaned against the pew and looked at him, searchingly. "No man is rich enough to buy back his past."

The mail coach had reached Bishop's Stortford before the last passenger had alighted, leaving them completely alone. It was the first opportunity they'd had, other than snatched pieces of conversation in the taprooms of inns along the way, to speak without fear of being overheard.

"Was he very ill when you left him?"

"Yes."

"How long do you think he can last?" There was an anxious note in Anna's voice. How unthinkable to come so far and be cheated, at the last moment, of telling him to his face how much she hated him, should he die before they reached their destination.

"I don't know. It could be months or weeks. Perhaps much less. His physician says that he has a weakened heart and should take no strenuous exercise, nor travel long distances. An unexpected upset, a shock, anything could trigger a serious attack." Was that why he had never come back to Epsom, and not because he feared to face her? Why he'd sent Hubbard to find her, and not made the long journey himself? Both unacceptable thoughts. He had only sent for her now because he was afraid to die with all he had on his conscience.

For the rest of the journey they discussed how and when Hubbard would forge the will, and how much he expected her to give him from the estate when at last it belonged to her. Ten thousand pounds! Five hundred pounds a year for the next twenty years of his life, to spend as he wished; in a lump sum, a fortune. More than he'd ever dreamed of, crouched over his tall desk in a bad light day after long, dreary day in Tuke's office, getting nowhere, for fifteen shillings a week.

"We must take care," he said, at length. "As much as I would wish to, I cannot rewrite the will leaving everything to you . . . that would only invite suspicion and lead to its being closely scrutinized. We must avoid that happening at all costs." There was a pause while they both braced themselves as the mail coach swerved around a sharp bend in the road.

"Give me his horses and his money and she can do what she likes with all the rest."

*   *   *

She caught sight of the house, suddenly, through a line of trees, as the driver of the hired post chaise slowed the horses to take a wide, sharp bend in the drive. Her eyes clung to it, just as they had many times before when she'd stared, hungrily, from the back of the blacksmith's cart on its way to Newmarket Heath, thinking, bitterly, *This is my father's house.* Then she would picture him, as she was doing now, sitting at the head of his table, his family and friends around him, smoking a cigar, drinking vintage wine, boasting of his bloodstock and his ambition to breed a Derby winner. In her mind's eye Anna had seen the magnificent furniture in the room, and the oil paintings that hung upon the silk-lined walls. And beside him, in satin or in velvet, his wife would sit. Her unknown face was blurred, as it always was when Anna thought of her, it was a thing without shape or form. But about her neck there would be a necklace of diamonds, or sapphires, and as the stones caught the light from the lamps and candles on the long table they would glitter, like stars.

As a child Anna had woven fantasies, fantasies of how one day she would ride up that long, winding drive and demand admission at the door, and when they asked her who she was she would reply, boldly, defiantly, *I am Anna Brodie, your master's bastard daughter.* But it was no longer a dream. No longer a child's fantasy. For here she was, traveling along that same winding drive, at the end of it his house, and Edward Brodie himself. Beside her in the post chaise William Hubbard had fallen silent, as if he knew what she was thinking and understood her need to retreat into herself. He spoke only when the post chaise clattered to a halt at the front of the house.

"The servants were told to expect us," he said, climbing down and offering her his hand. "Will you wait here while I ring the bell, or will you come now?"

Her eyes went beyond his face, searching every window. No drapes were drawn. He still lived. She was not too late.

"I'll come with you to the door." A pause. "Do they know who I really am?"

"No. No one has been told."

Her lips curled into a mocking smile. "Of course. He would never have told them."

Inside the vast marble hall lay a different world, the world of her angry dreams and imagination. The world of the rich, the privileged, the powerful. For a moment she thought of Ralph Russell. Wealth and opulence surrounded her, encompassed her, looked down on her, from the huge glass chandelier overhead to the giant statues mounted on white marble plinths and set back in the niches of the wall. She looked around her, with growing rage, comparing what she saw to the hovels in which she and her mother had been forced to live because the man who owned all this was too much of a coward to acknowledge them. This was the house where her mother should have lived, the house that was rightfully hers alone.

"Mr. Brodie is expecting you," said the manservant who had let them in, and led them to the door of his drawing room.

Their eyes met instantly across the space of the room. It was three years since they had set eyes on each other, that Derby Day at Epsom when she had cut him dead. Priam's Derby. All the bitterness that had fermented inside her since her mother's death and before it was resurrected at the very sight of him, seeing him here among all the trappings of the wealth and position that she both envied and despised. Her sharp eyes took in at once the paintings of his blood horses, the silver cups and trophies they had won him scattered about the room. And there, above the mantlepiece, was a lifesize portrait of his wife, in her wedding gown. The sight of it, dominating the entire room, enraged her.

"You waited until she was out of the way before you sent for me, Father." The final word, with mocking emphasis. "Are you so afraid of her . . . or is this her house and not yours?"

Hubbard had not exaggerated his illness. If she had felt anything toward him but hatred she could not have failed to be moved by the deep-etched suffering in his face, which he was trying to pretend was not there. But it would have been madness to feel pity for him. Visions of her mother, bent double in the bad light over the piles of sewing she'd been forced to take in to keep them out of the workhouse, the attic bedroom, the grave in Epsom churchyard, all rose up and made the final, insuperable barrier between them.

He glanced past her to where Hubbard stood.

"Mr. Hubbard, if you would be kind enough to leave us for a few moments I would be most grateful."

"Hubbard, stay where you are!"

"I think under the circumstances it would be more proper for me to wait outside." He left the room so quietly she did not even hear the door close behind him, and they were alone.

"Anna, where is your mother? Did she refuse to see me?"

"My mother died two years ago." For a moment she was back in the little windswept churchyard, standing beside the grave with its single posy of flowers and reading the stark, simple inscription on the headstone: "She died of the consumption."

He stared back at her for a moment in disbelief; then his face crumpled like a child's and he sat down, heavily, clutching the arms of the chair for support. For him, too, the vision of Anna Maria rose up, the Anna Maria he had lost. Coupled with his feelings of guilt and anguish, the thought of her ill and dying before he could find her again to say what he had for so long wanted to say to her momentarily overwhelmed him, and he could not speak.

"She died of consumption brought on by living in damp hovels. By years of poverty. By going without food herself so that we might not go hungry. Running from the bailiffs, living in fear of the debtors' prison. Trying to make one day's money stretch into three. Sitting up, night after night by the light of a single candle, sewing for other people until her fingers were raw so that we might have proper boots on our feet to keep out the wet and cold." She planted her final dart with care. "She might still be alive, despite all that, if she could have had a doctor's care when she first became ill. But she couldn't have a doctor because there was no money to pay his fee."

He struggled forward in the chair, his face suddenly drained of color. In his chest, the ominous pain hovered; not agony, not yet. But, like a distant thunderstorm it gathered momentum, ready to strike. "Anna, in God's name. Why didn't she come to me for help if she needed it? Did she think I'd stand by and see her destitute?"

"Isn't that exactly what you did, eighteen years ago? Stood by and saw her destitute? When she needed you most you turned your back on her!"

"That isn't true!"

"You used her and threw her aside!"

"I loved her. As I've never loved."

"You never loved anyone but yourself. And your reputation. All you cared about was that nobody should ever find out what you really were. Or that Edward Brodie, that esteemed member of the Jockey Club, that respectable pillar of society, had a mistress and two bastard daughters!"

"Anna, you don't know the truth."

"The truth?" Her voice mocked him now. "From you? Do you really think I would believe anything you say?"

There was no answer to that. Of course, he deserved it. Her hate, her anger, her contempt. Yes, she was right. He had been a hypocrite, was one still. Then he had been terrified of so many things; discovery, ruin, disgrace. He had lain awake, sweating, at nights, afraid of discovery and everything that would mean to him. Scandal. The meaningful glances. The whispering behind hands. Expulsion from the company that his wife's father had in his power. But Anna Maria had become a drug that he could not exist without, survive without; he had continued walking the tightrope of danger until she herself, realizing they could never be openly together, had disappeared, without trace, taking both of his daughters with her. He no longer had the note she had left for him, but the words were engraved on his memory. *There is no future for us. For your sake and my own I must leave. Do not try to find me. Anna Maria.* And he had respected her wishes until now, when he knew he was dying. When he had sent Hubbard to find her. Too late.

Slowly, he looked up into Anna's face. She bore such a striking resemblance to her mother that it almost hurt him to look at her. But he could see part of himself in her, too. There was a strength, a resilience, a determination about her that her mother had never possessed; in Anna

Maria's place eighteen years ago he sensed that she would never have written that note, never given up quietly and gone away. She would have stayed and fought tooth and nail to be with him, no matter what the odds were against her. Suddenly, to his own consternation and to Anna's amazement, his eyes filled with tears.

"For pity's sake, do you think I wanted her to go out of my life? Do you think I felt nothing?" The scene that had haunted him, pursued him, tortured him, came back, vivid and alive. "That day in the market place at Bury Saint Edmunds. That day you saw me with my wife and sons in the carriage and I passed you by as if you were strangers. I sat there, watching her looking at me, holding each of you by the hand. All I wanted was to jump out of that carriage and go to her, but I couldn't. I couldn't even acknowledge my own flesh and blood; can you ever understand how I felt?" Into the sudden silence that had fallen between them came the sound of wheels and hoofbeats on the stones outside. A moment later, the door of the room was flung open without warning, and a woman stood there, staring at them.

Anna knew her at once; the face was older, thinner, her hair was grayer than in the portrait that hung over the fireplace, but her identity was beyond doubt. She looked at Anna, then at her husband.

"Edward? I had a message sent to me at Father's house . . . it said you were ill . . . that I was needed. I packed my things and came back at once." Again, she stared at Anna. "Who is this?"

"Who would have sent you such a message? Where are the boys? Did you leave them at Ipswich?"

"Edward, who is this person?"

"Lilly, will you sit down; there is something I have to tell you."

"I'll not sit down nor leave this room till I have an explanation." There was anger and suspicion in her voice. "You never spoke of being ill. You let me go off to Ipswich without a word. Was that because you wanted me and the boys out of the way for some reason of your own?" Her pale eyes stared from their sockets, like those of a dead fish. "Oh, I see now. I see it all very clearly! You're not ill at all. You couldn't wait for my back to be turned before you started amusing yourself with other women . . . and you have the gall to bring this creature into my house, a girl young enough to be your daughter!"

There was a pause. "She is my daughter. That is what I wanted to tell you." She stared at him, as if she was in a trance. "I'm sorry. I should have told you a long time ago."

On the wall opposite hung a large mirror, and she caught sight of her own reflection in it. Middle-aged, unlovely and unloved, no man had ever looked upon it with desire; what was it like, she wondered, fleetingly, to possess a face that had the power to turn men from their rightful path, their wives, their duty? A face such as this girl had, such as her mother would have had, too, when Edward Brodie had first looked upon it. The very thought of him, the husband she'd loved and trusted, in another woman's bed, the father of her bastard child, shocked and disgusted her so much that for a moment she could not speak. Then, suddenly, when the full enormity of what he had said got through to her, she began to cry and shout.

"I'll never forgive you for this! Not for as long as I live, I swear it! Now get her out of this house. Get her out before I have her thrown out!"

"You'll not lay a finger on her . . ."

"I'll do as I please!"

"This is my father's house." Anna looked at her with cold anger. "He asked me here. When he asks me to leave I shall go. But I'll do nothing at your bidding." Her voice was bitter. This was the woman she had seen that day in her father's carriage as they'd stood alone in the market square. The woman who had sat in her mother's place. She remembered the mud that had been thrown up from the wheels as they'd driven by, nearly knocking them aside, and splashing against her mother's gown. And, more than anything else, she remembered her own impotent, childish hatred.

"You'll go this instant!" Lilly flung open the door and called to William Hubbard. "And you'll go back from where you came and tell your slut of a mother that she'll never get a farthing from him, do you hear me? Not a brass farthing!" Her hands shook, as if she had palsy. "Do you think I'd stand idly by and see a penny of his money go to some whore and the bastard who was fathered when he was drunk?"

She was standing within reach. Anna lifted her hand and slapped her so hard across the face that she cried out and reeled backward from the blow.

"You can take that lie and put it back in the cesspit that it came from!"

Without warning, Lilly Brodie staggered to her feet and lunged at her, screaming abuse. But she never reached her. Edward Brodie pulled her roughly away from Anna, and shook her. He could not stop shaking her. Her stared into her face, round-eyed, like a madman. He was filled with a sudden revulsion for her. He wanted to shake her until all the pain and anguish had gone out of him. Then the agony in his chest welled up and exploded, without warning, and the last thing he saw was Anna's face. Swimming, blurred, indistinct, like the ruffled reflection in a pool.

Stony-eyed with misery, Lilly Brodie sat in the middle of the small drawing room, staring down at her hands, which lay folded in her lap. She sat apart from the others, the small gathering of far-flung relations, acquaintances, friends, who had come to hear the will read. Her two sons stood behind her chair, like sentries, one on either side. Every now and then one of them would stoop forward and put a hand on her shoulder, but she could not speak even to them because she was afraid that if she did she would burst into tears, and she could not bear to humiliate herself in public. Her grief was as much from the discovery of her husband's infidelity and the shameless way he had deceived her for so long as from his sudden death. Last night, alone in the big bed they had shared, she had sobbed into the pillow until she was exhausted, tormented by grief and guilt, guilt because she would always wonder whether it was her fault that he had collapsed and died when he did, trying to protect his bastard daughter from her fury. But she would never know, and that thought continued to haunt her without pity.

The will, she already knew, was only a formality. She could already guess what it said. A few small bequests, for past kindnesses and favors, to friends and loyal, long-serving servants; the mills to go to their elder son; a handsome settlement on their younger, put in trust till he came of age. The house and the rest of the estate, to her. Samuel Tuke had ridden over from Newmarket to read it, and she watched him now as he sat down behind the table and took the document from his clerk. Hubbard, who had been thoughtful enough to send her the message when she was at her father's house, at Ipswich. For some reason she did not understand she disliked Benjamin Tuke's young nephew; all her dealings had been with his uncle and the very unfamiliarity of his successor made her faintly uneasy. But seeing Hubbard, sitting there beside him, a face she knew, made her feel oddly comforted in some way she did not understand.

Then Samuel Tuke cleared his throat and began to read, and silence fell on the little gathering.

"*I, Edward Brodie, Esquire, Gentleman of the parish of Mildenhall in the county of Suffolk, being of sound mind do, this seventh day of January in the Year of Our Lord Eighteen Hundred and Thirty-three, hereby make this, my last will and testament . . .*"

Her heart began to beat faster, all at once. January 1833, only three months before? But he had made out his will more than twenty years ago, when they were first married . . . what reasons could he possibly have had for writing out another one? Her common sense came to her rescue, chasing out a darker, more fearful suspicion. Of course, it was clear now. When he had married her he had only a fraction of the wealth and property that he had possessed three months before his death. Relieved, she settled back into her chair.

"*. . . I hereby assign and bequeath all my personal estate, to wit, my house and all its adjacent lands and contents in entirety, together with my properties outside of this county and all monies deposited in my name at the Newmarket Bank in the county of Suffolk, to my dearest and most beloved Anna Maria Brodie, late Rowe, now or late of Saffron Walden in the county of Essex, and to my natural daughters, Anna and Clara Brodie if she predecease me . . .*"

A gasp went up among everyone present. At the same moment the door at the far end of the room suddenly opened, and in walked Anna Brodie with a younger girl so like her that Lilly knew instinctively they were sisters. His bastards. Anna's cold, bright blue eyes looked at her from beneath the rim of her black hat. They were both dressed in black velvet from head to toe, but they were so cursedly beautiful that the mourning garb only made them appear more striking. Everyone in the room turned to stare at them.

"... *I bequeath to my wife, Lillian Mary Brodie, the sum of five thousand pounds held in government stocks and bonds in my name, her personal jewelry and my bloodstock, to be maintained or disposed of at her pleasure. To my sons, John and William Brodie, I bequeath the equal sums of one hundred pounds only, by reason that they will in due course benefit from the aforesaid bequest to their mother, Lillian Mary Brodie.*" Amid whisperings and exclamations of dismay, Samuel Tuke went on.

"There is a codicil to this will."

Again, he cleared his throat. "*I, the within-named Testator Edward Brodie, do make and publish this codicil to my written will, and that is that should any of the benefactors named herein dispute in any manner any legacy assigned and willed by me the said Testator, they shall forfeit their said portion in entirety, and the said portion so forfeited shall be distributed to the poor of this parish.*"

Across the room, Anna's eyes met Lilly Brodie's, then moved on swiftly to the face of William Hubbard. And there was fury in them.

Lilly Brodie's face was drained of all color. On each side of her, her two sons tried to bear her up. It had to be a mistake. This was someone else's will, not Edward's.

Slowly, unsteadily, she got to her feet and went over to the table where Samuel Tuke and young Hubbard sat. At the disbelief in her face, he handed the document to her without a word, unable to meet her eyes. There, at the bottom of the single page, was his signature, the handwriting she knew so well. Only pride saved her legs from giving way beneath her.

But it was the truth that hurt; that her beloved, trusted Edward had done this to her. It was the final betrayal. She had brought him her father's wealth and her father's influence and her own good name, and he had sullied it. In return for her love and trust he had cheated her. He'd gone sneaking behind her back into another woman's bed, knowing that she'd never suspect him. And he'd left her home, and their sons' inheritance, to his mistress's bastard daughters.

She looked at them now with hatred. But she wouldn't cry, she couldn't. Not here, in front of everyone. If there were any tears to be shed she'd shed them later, when she was safe under her father's roof and on her own where she could let out the great wave of anger and grief. In a moment, when the shaking in her arms and legs had stopped, she'd turn round, with dignity, and walk out.

When she reached the door Edward's bastards were still standing there, blocking her way. How young and beautiful they were. Had their harlot of a mother looked as they did, when Edward had first looked upon her face? Anger flared up in her.

"Well, where is your mother, the Anna Maria Rowe who dared use the name of Brodie as if she was his true wedded wife? Is she too ashamed to walk over the threshold of my house and meet me, face to face?"

Anna understood her humiliation and rage, feelings that were nothing new to her. But the picture of her mother lying on the dirty straw pallet in the freezing room, side by side with the vision of this woman, lying with her father in the ornate bed on the floor above, rose up and washed away the vestiges of a grudging sympathy.

"My mother died, two years ago. And she is buried in a pauper's grave."

It was twilight when she left the inn at Newmarket and made her way to the town's livery stable where she had hired a horse for seven o'clock. The night was chilly, and she wore a long, sweeping cloak, her face half-hidden by its enormous hood. Beneath it she had concealed two heavy leather bags, firmly attached to her belt.

She had sent a boy from the inn to hire the horse, and the groom was clearly astonished to see that it had been reserved for a young woman.

"Lad never said 'orse was to be for a lady, ma'am." He touched his forelock. "Ain't got no sidesaddles 'ere, 'fraid."

"That doesn't matter. I never ride sidesaddle." Ignoring his open mouth and rounded eyes she hoisted herself expertly into the saddle, and gave him a sovereign, taking little notice of his advice that it was highly dangerous for lone travelers, at this time of night, to be venturing more than half a mile out of the town. Inside her cloak was a loaded pistol.

She turned the horse's head in the direction of the Cheveley road, and was soon out of sight in the growing mist.

When she reached the milestone, she drew rein and slowed the horse to a walk. Fifty yards past it, she halted him. Her ears and eyes straining in the darkness, she could neither see nor hear anything. Then, without warning, something rustled in the undergrowth and she pulled out the pistol, holding it ready. Suddenly, a few feet ahead of her the bushes parted and William Hubbard, riding a black horse, appeared from the darkness. Her heart stopped hammering.

"You don't take any chances, do you?" He had a soft, low laugh. He was wearing a Venetian mask, the kind highwaymen often wore, and he pulled it from his face as she edged her horse close to his.

"You bloody, blundering fool!" Earlier, back at the house after the will had been read, she'd slipped him a note telling him to meet her, at this time and at this place.

His smile vanished instantly.

"What is it? What's wrong?"

"I told you what I wanted from him. His money and his horses! I might have known better than to trust you to rewrite his will. I should have stood over you, and dictated it myself!"

He was stupefied by her anger.

"But you have everything worth having. The house and land. His business. His money. What use are a few horses to you, why do you want them? With the assets you gain you can buy any horse that you want to."

"Money can't buy the kind of bloodstock he had, don't you understand that?" Her throat was tight with rage. "And if it could do you think that she'd sell them to *me*? That bitch'd have them shot, rather than let me get my hands on them. God's truth, Hubbard, don't you understand what you've done?"

"Anna, I'm sorry."

For a moment she was silent. She gathered her temper and harnessed it. Then she untied the two leather bags from her waist belt and handed them to him. They were so heavy that he almost dropped them. "Each one contains five hundred pounds in gold. Inside one of the bags you'll find a letter of credit, for four thousand pounds, made out to the name you wanted. William Crossdill." Crossdill, his mother's maiden name. Perfect. "Well, I've kept my part of the bargain. You've still to keep yours." She held out her black gloved hand. "The real will. The original will. Where is it?"

"Why, don't you trust me?" She had never quite liked the way he smiled. Nor how casually he used her first name, on their first meeting. But she could not afford to make an enemy of him by offending him. He reached into his pocket, pulled out a rolled document, and gave it to her. When she got back to her room at the inn she would burn it on the fire.

"Farewell then, Hubbard." But he hesitated.

"There is . . . just one question that I always meant to ask you . . . before we part company for good." He shifted himself in the saddle. "What do you intend to do with your share of the inheritance?"

Despite her anger at his stupidity, the question made Anna smile. How could she possibly explain to someone like Hubbard, in a few words, about the dream she'd carried with her for so long, born outside the inn at Epping, the dream that had sustained her on the long, freezing walk from the miserable little cottage to Sam Loam's yard, her feet so numb with the cold that she could scarcely put one foot before the other? No one, least of all him whose carelessness had signed away the one thing of her father's she had really craved, would ever understand.

"I'll make a wish come true with it."

PART IV
May 1833

❄ 6 ❄

Anna slid down from the saddle of the hired horse and looked around her with narrowed, searching eyes. There was no need to shade them from the sun now; it had vanished, gone, behind the clouds of the oncoming evening. But it was still light enough for her to see what she had come to see. It would still be light when Clara reached home, in the hired post chaise with all their luggage, and Anna pictured her, still in the black velvet mourning gown, sitting on the edge of one of the hard kitchen chairs, her blue eyes animated, telling Jessie what had happened to them, what had been left them in the will. She could picture Jessie's face, pale with disbelief, and then her throwing up her big hands, astonished, when Clara started to unwrap the parcels and beribboned boxes full of the finery they had bought in London. Poor Jessie. Dear Jessie. "Where's Anna?" the first thing she'd say. "Why isn't she with you? What's wrong?" And Clara would tell her that Anna had business in Epsom and would be late back for supper, and Jessie would grumble, as she always did. Then, together, Clara still excited, Jessie still asking countless questions, they would take the parcels and the boxes upstairs to lay away.

Anna was three miles from Epsom now, standing here, on the brow of the small rise, looking downward through the trees where she could see the tall gabled chimneys of the empty house. She stood for a few moments looking at it, then took up the horse's loose rein and led him forward. It took her ten minutes to reach the big iron wrought gates, and there she stopped, and stood, gazing through them, while the horse grazed beside her, unaware of anything but the thick, lush grass that covered the rising bank.

It was so like that other time, when she and Clara had stood like this, gazing through the gates of Ralph Russell's mansion, staring at the vastness and splendor they could only glimpse through the trees at the end of the long, winding drive. She could smile now. Wryly. Bitterly. But with a dark, ruthless satisfaction.

She had waited so long for this moment. Ached for it. Hungered for it. The moment when she, too, would have wealth and power. She had never doubted that she would find herself standing here, now, like this, with almost everything that she had ever wanted to happen to her within her grasp; she had only been marking time, waiting, like a child who counts each month and week and day to her birthday. And now it was here. Anna Brodie could buy anything she wanted because at last she, too, had wealth; and wealth could buy power.

She gazed through the rusted gates to the drive beyond, choked with weeds and nettles, taken over by a sprawling army of neglected bushes and towering, spreading shrubs that had spilled from the banks of the drive and had encroached like rushes growing in a pond, upon the courtyard and the garden.

There was no way that Anna could pass through the tall gates and walk through the tangled foliage and evergreens to the house itself. A huge chain hung about them, fastened with a massive padlock. She already knew what she wanted. For two years or more she'd ridden down here, on the Sundays when Sam Loam closed his yard, and stared along that wild, weed-strewn drive to the empty house beyond it. Thinking. Hoping. Longing to take a scythe to those weeds and nettles, to walk up that flight of steps to the front door and open it, then go inside and search every secret nook and cranny, every room, every stairway, every passage, and as she did so wipe away lovingly all the dust and cobwebs of the years.

She remounted the hired horse and turned its head in the direction of Epsom.

Frederick Nubbles had been about to take down his hat and cane from the cloak stand when the door of his office in the high street opened, setting off the loud tinkling of a bell. It was gone half past six, he knew; only five minutes ago, tidying away his papers, he had glanced methodically, as he always did, at his gold pocket watch suspended from its narrow chain. His partner and his clerks had already left, as they always did, at six o'clock. He was not expecting any of them to return, or any visitors to arrive, after hours. When he looked up at the cause of the disturbance, surprise, a rare visitor to his calm, wizened features, spread across his face and into his watery, birdlike eyes.

A young woman stood in front of the now closed door, leaning against it. A young woman dressed all in black. The mourning gown was not the first thing that he noticed, but the beauty of her face. It was a striking face, but of great strength and character. He stood up at once.

He glanced beyond her to the street outside and saw no one waiting. She was clearly a lady. But ladies did not go out unaccompanied. His initial surprise changed to intrigue.

"Madam?"

She told him her name. She apologized for calling on him so late, when she could see he was about to go home. But a lawyer in Newmarket had recommended his name to her in all matters relating to the law of land and property, and she needed his help.

"Ah," he said, pulling out a chair for her to sit on. "You are from Suffolk, then?"

"No. I live here now." She did not sit down on the chair. "I came back today, after my father's will was read there." She watched his sharp, sharply chiseled weasel's face crease in a look of sympathy. "I'll come directly to the point, and save my time and yours. There is a house, a big house, about three miles from here. It's stood empty for as long as I can remember. The grounds are half-hidden by trees, wild, and overgrown. No one ever goes there. Do you know the place I mean?" The specter of it rose up in front of her again, as if it was not in her mind but a painting, framed and hung on the bare office wall behind him.

"Yes. The Old Brew House."

"I made inquiries about it and I was told it is for sale." She paused. "I want to buy it."

Only a faint rising of his white, straggly eyebrows betrayed his surprise.

"Unfortunately, I do not think that would be possible."

"Why not?"

"Because a sale has already been agreed upon . . . in principle at least, between the owner and a local buyer."

Her heart fell. So it was gone then, this part of her burning ambition, cut from her before she could reach out and touch it. The vision of the house came back, inviting, beckoning her through the wild tangle of trees and untended shrubbery, then disappeared, like a white, silent ghost. She felt sick, as if she had not eaten in a long while.

"But nothing has been signed?"

"Not yet. But it will be, within the month."

"Can I ask you how much the owner is selling for?"

He hesitated, momentarily. Strictly, it was a confidence. But it could not matter now.

"Five thousand guineas."

"I'll give him ten if he sells to me." Yes, that had startled him. She let her mouth turn up, slightly, at the corners, in a ghost of a smile. "I can have the money ready tomorrow, as soon as the bank is open for business."

"Ten thousand guineas is a great deal of money."

"And five thousand guineas is a pittance. The house, even in the state it is, is worth that much alone, without the grounds and land. Can you tell me why the owner is selling it far below its real market value?"

She could sense him hesitating, as if he was uncertain whether it was right for him to tell her.

"I can tell you that at one time he was a wealthy man. But he lost everything, and he was compelled to move to London and live in much more modest circumstances."

"But why had no one made an offer for it before now? There are plenty of wealthy men around here." She thought of Ralph Russell, Sir Gilbert Heathcote, Edward Randyll. "It doesn't make sense."

He shrugged his narrow shoulders.

"A man can live in a mansion and employ many servants; everything about him—the state he keeps, his style of living—can give the illusion of great wealth. In truth his real wealth is in his land and his family name, and in the credit with tradesmen his good name commands. It does not always follow that he can produce large sums of money at will."

"But I can. And I want the Old Brew House. Will you contact the owner and ask him if he'll accept my offer?"

"I shall inform him, of course. But if you are prepared to pay double the sum he expects to get from Mr. Hindley, then the property is yours tomorrow. I was given full responsibility for the sale, and my duty is to obtain the best possible price for my client. There is no way Mr. Hindley can outbid you, particularly if you have the ready cash at hand. On the contrary, it has taken him some months to raise the five thousand guineas he is putting up now." She smiled her gratitude at the little man, deciding that she both liked and trusted him, the latter a gut feeling that rarely led her astray. "I should warn you, however, that Mr. Hindley will be most displeased."

"Is he a racing man?"

"Yes, one of Epsom's leading owners. And a gambler for high stakes."

"Then he should learn to be a good loser." She smiled, mischievously, and he had the vague impression that she meant something other than losing the Old Brew House. "One more favor, Mr. Nubbles. Can you let me see over the house tonight, while there is still daylight left?"

To anyone else he would have declined, politely, pleading another appointment. It was nearing dusk. He was tired. And the road from Epsom to the Old Brew House was rough and uncomfortable.

But there was something about her that fascinated and charmed him, so that he did not mind going out of his way to oblige her. Fetching the keys he said, genially, "Of course. It is no trouble at all."

The tall, rusted gates creaked as they were swung to, and the long, winding, weed-infested drive wound away before them. Anna stood there for a moment, on the other side of the gates, looking at it. Then she took her horse's bridle and led the way without a word, as if she had walked along the drive a hundred times before, and knew every bend and twist by heart. Now she stood there, looking across the courtyard to the front of the house. Since they had entered the gates she had not spoken a word, and still she was silent.

"Are you disappointed?" Frederick Nubbles asked, at her side. "I told you that the only part of the old house you can see from the road is the north side, and part of the roof. As you can see for yourself, three years of neglect have taken their toll." He sighed, remembering it as it had once been before its owner's downfall on the turf. "I am afraid it will need a great deal of money spent on it to make it fit for habitation." Still, she continued to stare at it as if she could not take her eyes away. "You are still free, of course, to withdraw your offer to purchase."

She turned to him, her eyes alight with excitement.

"Never. I wanted it the moment I saw it. I haven't changed my mind. Can we go in now?"

Inside they found an old lantern, and some candles. Following the wizened little man, Anna gazed silently about her, feeling a strange upsurge of joy and power. This would be it, her home. The first home she'd ever had, in the whole of her life. The dampness and the cracks in the walls and the thick cobwebs that hung from the beams and the ceilings meant nothing to her; in her imagination she knew exactly how it would be when she had finished with it. Nobody else would understand; only she could see the picture in her mind. Moving like a sleepwalker, she went in and out of every room, the wizened, crooked little man behind her, holding the lantern.

"Of course, the Tudor interior is very unfashionable, as you may know," he said, looking up at the thick, dark beams and apex roof above the landing.

"I want it just the way it is." No, Anna wanted nothing changed in the house, nothing stripped from its mellow, ancient beauty. She stretched out her hand, reverently, and touched the exquisite carving on the balustrade of the staircase. "This is what a house should be. The warmth of oak, the haven of a beamed room. It is a thing of timeless beauty."

He looked at her without answering, his silence meaning his agreement. Yes, she had an eye for beauty.

"Can I see the stables?"

"As you wish." He followed her back down the staircase and into the hall, where he set down the lantern on an old table and fiddled with the ring of keys, faintly surprised. It was unusual for a lady to display any interest in the stables of a house. "They, at least, I believe," he said, "are quite sound. Some repairs are needed to the coach house roof, however."

He watched her as she walked in and out of every stall, bending to examine things, testing the wood for splinters, her long gown sweeping the old pieces of straw that had been left behind.

She said, suddenly, taking him completely by surprise, "They'd do, certainly, for ordinary carriage horses. But not mine." She laughed, seeing the expression on his face, and her laughter filled the dim little stall. "I intend to breed and race my own blood horses." There, she had put it into words at last, the ambition she'd carried with her for so long, so secretly that she'd never hinted at it, even to those closest to her that she could trust: Jessie, Clara, Sam Loam. It seemed odd to her now that she had kept it from them and yet was telling this strange, crooked little man, a perfect stranger. Perhaps it was easier to confide in someone you didn't know because he would not criticize, raise objections, place obstacles in your path.

He said, with no emotion in his voice whatsoever, "You will find that a most difficult task."

"But not impossible."

"Few things are truly impossible. But I would say that trying to enter into the men's world of the turf is one of them."

"Because I'm a woman?"

"Because you are a woman and because you are an outsider." He hesitated, momentarily, before going on. "And there are other considerations. Do you really know what manner of people are part of the turf? I understand that villainy, poisoning of horses, and bribing of jockeys are commonplace; that certain bookmakers will stop at nothing to insure the result of a race is the result they want . . . and I've no doubt that the same applies for many of the more unscrupulous owners as well."

"I already know all that."

"But the hardest part of all is being accepted and acceptable." He smiled. "Many gentlemen have found it impossible to get onto the turf. Do you think for one moment that the Jockey Club and the clique of owners who are part of it would allow a lady to succeed where they have failed?"

"You're trying to make me change my mind."

"I do not think that anyone could make you do that." Again, he smiled at her. "You are a lady who is a law unto herself."

A silence fell between them while they walked from the stable block and back through the wild grounds toward the house.

"There is something else, also, which we haven't yet discussed. Something I wonder if you are aware of?"

She glanced up at him through the fading daylight.

"In law a young woman is at a great disadvantage. A married woman, for instance, can own no property of her own. When she marries it automatically becomes her husband's."

"How unfortunate for married women."

"Unmarried girls are the chattels of their fathers."

"My father is dead."

"In your circumstances it is usual for the testator to either appoint a legal guardian or create a trust if there is no living relative, to manage and administer the estate until the young woman marries."

"My father did neither. And I'm of age. I don't need a guardian or a trustee to meddle in my affairs. I can handle them myself." Her self-confidence was both admirable and exasperating.

"A young woman such as yourself, with considerable means," he said, gravely, "is at a special disadvantage. You have nobody to guide or advise you that you can trust to be impartial and hold your interests at heart."

"I have you." They stopped walking.

"I am flattered," he said, simply.

"Will you handle my affairs for me? Advise me? Tell me if I go wrong? Most things I know I can do for myself, for, as they say, no man is an island. But I don't know the law as you do. No one can know everything. Two heads are better than one."

He smiled, and she knew she had made the right decision in trusting him.

"I shall go back to my office and collect the materials I need to make out the document of sale tonight. I am authorized to act as proxy for my client. Then, if you will call by my office in the morning, you can sign and I can witness your signature."

"And this Hindley? What will you tell him?"

"I shall call at his house on my way home. It is not far out of my way."

"Will you tell him who has outbid him?"

They had reached the horses now, tethered on the inside of the rusted gates.

"It is not his business to know. And he will find out soon enough. But I fear you will have made an enemy of him."

"No doubt he'll be one of many." She smiled. "Can I have the keys to the gates, before you leave? I should like to walk around alone, for a while."

"But it will be dark soon." There was anxiety in his voice. He looked down at the winding drive, made darker still by the thick, wild trees that had grown across to meet one another, forming an arch that kept out the light, and then at Anna. It was not a place where he would care to linger, alone, even in daylight.

She smiled as she took the keys from him.

"I can take care of myself."

She walked slowly back to the house, leading her horse by the bridle. Then she left him to crop the overgrown grass while she let herself back into the hall, and relit one of the candles. How quiet it seemed, so still, so peaceful. The ghostly light flickered high upon the ceiling, casting long shadows along the walls. She climbed the staircase for a second time, noticing things that she had missed before.

But it was growing dark outside the dusty windows and she must ride back now, before Jessie and Clara began to worry. It was then, as she was making her way downstairs, that she heard the sound of another rider in the weed-strewn courtyard outside. Horse's hooves upon the stones. The neigh of greeting from her own horse tethered at the front of the house. As she reached the foot of the staircase the front door creaked open, letting in the last rays of light from the fading day, and the silhouette of a man appeared outlined by the sky outside.

A stab of fear, then anger followed by surprise, as she raised the candle above her head and recognized the intruder.

"You're trespassing," she said, in a voice of stone.

Ralph Russell came further into the dingy hall, his feet treading on twigs and leaves that had been blown in from the grounds outside.

"And you?"

"I have a right to be here." He fancied he saw a look of triumph—and devilry?—in her eyes . . . or was it just his imagination? They glowed, like a cat's, in the darkness around them. "This estate is mine." Yes, that had stunned him. She smiled, without warmth.

"Since when has it been yours?" As quickly, he recovered from his own astonishment.

"Since when has that been any of your business?"

"Since you told me I was trespassing."

Slowly, Anna walked down the remainder of the staircase, the solitary candle spluttering in the draft. She paused on the last step, so that she still appeared taller than he was. She said, in the kind of voice any other woman might use to dismiss a servant, "You can close the gates on your way out."

For a moment he hesitated. He had noticed that she was dressed in a somber velvet gown . . . not black, surely? Dark green? Dark crimson? In the bad light he could not be sure.

"It's growing dark outside; in half an hour you won't be able to see your own hand in front of you. And the Epsom road is no place for a lady to travel alone, not after dusk. When you've finished here you'll find me waiting outside the gates."

"But I'm not riding your way."

"But I'm riding yours."

Despite herself, despite her determined efforts to be hostile to him, she almost smiled. For a moment the tone in his voice reminded her of Jessie, in one of her bullying moods. Come on, do as I tell you; I know what's best. I know what's good for you. So he cared, or pretended to care, what happened to her. For his own reasons, of course. If he accompanied her on the long ride back he could get her to talk and find out what he was clearly itching to find out: how could poor Anna Brodie afford to buy an estate like this one? She shrugged her shoulders, carelessly, showing her indifference whether he came with her. "Suit yourself. If you want to ride ten miles out of your way or not."

"If anything happened to you, I'd blame myself. And I have enough on my conscience already." God knew, that was true enough.

She gazed at him through the dim, fading light. For the first time and almost against her will she realized that she liked him, and remembering her mother's weakness she was angry with herself and wanted to fight against it. He was a man, and therefore she could never allow herself to trust him. Not now. Not ever. She swept past him and opened the door that led to the courtyard outside, letting in a single, last ray of the fading daylight. As it flickered weakly across her gown, Russell could see that the material was neither dark green nor crimson, but black.

"Why are you dressed all in black, Anna?" It was the first time he had used her first name, and she was startled by it.

"Isn't black the color people usually wear when somebody dies?"

He stared at her, with clear, honest eyes. "I'm sorry. I should have realized." He glanced down at his hat for a moment, angry at his own unaccustomed clumsiness, turning the thing over awkwardly in his thick, strong hands. "Was it . . . someone close to you?"

"No, it was no one close to me." Abruptly, she turned away and walked back into the leaf-strewn courtyard while he followed behind her in silence. She locked the door herself, then still without speaking to him, untethered her horse and led it back along the overgrown drive. Only when they had reached the tall gates at the other end did she break the silence between them.

"What were you doing at the house? Why were you there?"

"It isn't important now, is it?"

"That isn't an answer to my question."

After a pause he said, "I was riding by and noticed these gates were unlocked, and half-open. My curiosity was aroused; the house has been empty for years."

"You're a long way from home," she answered, in an accusing voice.

"Yes, I am. I was riding over by Woodcote Park to pay somebody a visit. The road past the Old Brew House is the quickest route, that's all."

"Woodcote Park is in the opposite direction to the way I'm going."

"So it is. But no matter. The . . . person I was on my way to see can wait until tomorrow." He thought, then, briefly and unwillingly, of that hard, veined, scarlet face that he disliked so much. The pale, bloodshot, bulging eyes, waiting, staring from some window in the house. Waiting, impatiently. Then, realizing he would not come, impatience turning to fury. In the same way that he might slam shut a door or a window to keep out an unpleasant draft, Russell slammed shut his mind on Hindley. Yes, let him wait. They rode on for a long while before she spoke again. Then, when they had neared the familiar sweep of ground that suddenly began to rise steeply toward where the track that led to Mickleham Downs began and the Epsom road ceased, Anna reined in her horse and turned to him, her face pale and proud in the moonlight.

"Thank you for your escort." Did her voice hold that same touch of mockery that it had back at the Old Brew House, or was it again just his imagination? "I think I can manage to find my home from here."

"I'll not be content until I've seen you safely to your front door."

For a moment they stared at each other through the darkness. Then she nodded, and turned her mount's head in the direction of the old cottage, and he followed beside her, in silence. Suddenly, through the black all around them, he saw the distant glow of light from a lamp that stood on the ledge of the downstairs window.

When they reached the gate, she dismounted.

"You're shocked," she said as he continued to stare toward the ramshackle building, without speaking. It was a statement, and not a question. "No; don't bother denying it. I can see it in your face." There was no rancor in her voice. "So was Sam Loam, when we first came to Epsom and I told him we were living here. That was when my mother was alive. We were poor then. But no longer." She paused. "Not that it makes any difference now to her. She'll never know we got the better of him in the end." She stopped speaking abruptly, as if she had said too much and instantly regretted it.

Russell had gotten down from his horse, and stood beside her, his hand on the gate. He looked down into her face, the face that had haunted him since he first saw it, more than three years ago. It swam before his eyes, like her so near and yet so far away, and untouchable. He did not expect her to invite him inside, and she did not. Without looking behind them, he felt that he was being watched from behind the curtained windows.

"Goodnight," she said, with a faint smile.

"Goodnight."

He took up his horse's reins, and prepared to hoist himself back into the saddle.

"One thing I haven't asked you. And forgive me for it, but my curiosity outruns my mannerliness."

"Oh?"

"The Old Brew House and the estate that goes with it. I happen to know what price was being asked on the market." He hesitated, trying to find the right words so that his question did not seem offensive. "To be able to pay that kind of money, somebody must recently have left you a small fortune. Have they?"

She smiled, and the same wicked look and tone that he'd seen and heard back at the old house came into her eyes and voice.

"Let's just say that somebody was repaying a debt."

She disappeared into the darkness of the ramshackle little hut at the side of the cottage that served as a stable, without saying goodbye.

For a few moments Russell stayed where he was, mounted, staring at the decaying woodwork and crumbling stone. He thought of his own house, not without a stab of shame. *Rich man,* she'd called him, derisively, that time when their paths had first crossed more than three years ago. He remembered her anger clearly, sharply, as if it had happened only yesterday. But only now, seeing where she lived and where her mother had died, did he truly understand why she had been so bitter. Slowly, reluctantly, he took up his reins again and spurred his horse back along the little track that led to the road.

Jessie and Clara were all over her the moment she got inside.

"Thank the Lord you're back, lassie, we was worried sick!"

"I've got back from Sam's later than this and you've not worried."

"Ay, but it's pitch dark now!"

"I had things to see to in Epsom. I told Clara to tell you I'd be late back . . ."

"Ay, lass, but . . ."

"Anna, who was that man you were with outside?"

"Ralph Russell. Him who's got the big house and stables over Durdans Park way." She threw herself on the settle and began pulling off her boots.

"But that's *Lord Russell*, Anna!"

"All right. So he's Lord Russell. That doesn't make him God, does it?"

"Lassie, come to the table and sit yourself down. Eat your supper and tell me all about this will . . ."

"Anna, we've hung all the gowns we bought in London away . . . I was extra careful with yours . . ."

". . . you too, miss. You've both 'ad a long ride back and nought inside you but taproom rubbish. Get this down you and you'll be fit for anything!" She began ladling the steaming mutton broth from a pot on the stove into their basins, grumbling that she'd had to keep it hot for hours. But Anna had gone over to where her baggage lay, propped up against the settle, and pulled out a bottle.

"I've got nothing against your cooking, Jessie. But a glass of this is what I need first." She took a cup down from the dresser and poured herself a measure, while they both watched her, round-eyed.

"Anna, that's brandy!"

"Where you get that from? It's spirits!"

"From the Crown at Epsom. Cheers!" She drank the cupful in one draft and dumped the bottle on the table, ignoring their shocked looks. "It's all right. I've not taken to drink."

"How long you bin drinking that stuff? Why, your ma'd turn in 'er grave . . ."

"All right, Jessie! Save the lecture for another time. Open your ears, both of you, and listen." She sat down, while the pair of them continued to stare at her, all attention. Steadily, she gazed at Jessie across the table.

"I suppose Clara's told you it all. About what he left us."

"Ay, and no more'n the pair of you deserve, the way 'e's treated you and your poor ma all these years, God rot 'im!" Jessie busied herself with the serving of their supper.

"Lilly was scarcely left penniless." Anna's voice was bitter. "The blood-stock that I didn't get was worth more than the house and everything else he had put together."

"Nay, lassie. There's no bunch of 'orses bred what are worth more than that big 'ouse and all that land . . . and that's not counting what 'e 'ad stowed away in the bank!"

Anna fell silent, brooding almost, only picking at her meal, although it was hours since any food had passed her lips. Jessie didn't realize. She didn't know. She couldn't even begin to understand. Anna stared at her plate and thought of the colt that had gone lame on that Derby Day, three years ago; Priam's Derby. Her father could have, might have, won the coveted race, the greatest prize the turf had to offer, if the horse had stayed sound. What could she not have done with an animal like that? Six years old now, perfect for breeding. But for Hubbard's blunder the horse would have been hers, and from the raw material her father had had but failed with, she would have bred her own Derby colt. To better him, to succeed where he had failed, that was the ambition that burned in her and would never be quenched. How could she possibly expect Jessie or her sister or William Hubbard to understand that?

Later, when the meal was finished and Clara had rushed upstairs again to pore over all her new clothes, Anna went over and stared at the moon from the little mullioned window, still brooding, even her excitement and pleasure at the thought of the Old Brew House dimmed by the rekindling of her bitter disappointment.

"Something's troubling you, girl," Jessie said, putting down her stack of soiled dishes and looking at her. "I can tell. You scarce touched your dinner. Want to talk about it?"

"It's nothing you'd understand." Anna remained where she was, without turning round.

"If something's making you miserable you'll feel a deal better if you get it off your chest." No answer from the window. "Is it that Ralph Russell fellah?"

Anna wheeled round, suddenly.

"Christ, no! I never think about him, even!" A half-truth. "I just met him on the road, that's all. No, Jessie, it's something else. Nothing you can help me with."

"Try me."

Slowly, Anna walked away from the moonlit window and sank into a chair. "I was thinking about my father's horses. His running horses. What I could have done with them. Done what he couldn't, with all his money and power." Jessie saw the way her eyes gleamed, with a strange, far-seeing look, as they always did when she talked about horses. "That was what he wanted most of all, didn't you know . . . more than anything else in his life. To breed a horse that could win the Derby. He never did it. I could." Her blue eyes burned into Jessie's dim gray ones. "And I will. I mean to. I'll show them all."

"Oh, lassie . . ."

". . . I've bought a house, Jessie. And all the land that goes with it, to do just that. That's why I stayed behind in Epsom. That's why I was so late back." She got up and began to pace the floor. She'd told her that much. She might as well tell her the rest. And now was as good a time as any. "So tomorrow you can start packing. We're moving on to better things."

"Anna!"

". . . it's the Old Brew House, over Woodcote Park way. You know, the one that's stood empty for years." For a moment she stopped pacing, a curious little secret smile playing about her lips. "When we first came here, I used to walked over that way and stare through the railings to look at it. Pretend it was mine, that it was waiting for me to pass through the locked gates and go along the drive in my carriage. I used to ask Sam questions about it; why it was empty, who lived there, why they left, why nobody had bought it. And then I'd think about the empty stables, and the land all around, filled with horses. My horses. And doing what he did, my father, but doing it better. Succeeding where he couldn't. Breed a Derby winner. I'll start from nothing, I'll start from scratch . . . and I'll do it. I'll do it, Jessie."

"But, lassie, what are you saying? That's not a lady's place to be, near running 'orses and racegrounds. Why, there'd be such a scandal you'd not dare show your face ten miles 'round Epsom!"

"I'm sorry, Jessie. My mind is made up. Nothing anyone can say will ever change it, not even you. I've waited too long."

"But you can't do it, Anna. Think of your sister, if you won't think of yourself. What decent folks'll be wanting to invite you or her into their 'omes, meet their sons and all? Nobody. They'll turn the other cheek and shun the both of you. Is that what you want?"

"Meet their sons? In Christ's name, is that all you can think about? Being married to some man, bored out of my mind, handing over to him on a plate everything we've been left between us? A married woman doesn't own anything, Jessie. The law says so. Not even the clothes she wears. Everything belongs to her husband, and he can spend every penny, gamble it away or drink it away, and there's nothing in hell she can do about it! Is that what you want for both of us? Well, Clara will have her share—she can do what she likes with it, when she comes of age. But I know exactly what I want. I've lived with it too long for me ever to forget it. I mean to buy that house and the land that goes with it, and I mean to breed and race my own horses. Nobody will stand in my way. I don't give a damn what anyone says or what they think. And if they think that because I'm a woman I can't do better than they can then they're in for the shock of their lives."

She looked up. Clara was standing in the doorway, at the foot of the narrow flight of stairs, one of the London-bought gowns draped over one arm. Her face was white.

"Jessie's right. You can't do it, Anna. You can't. No one will want to know us. We'll be shunned, never invited anywhere." Tears came quickly to Clara and they came now, glistening but not yet falling. They were petulant tears, the tears of a child who cannot have its own way. "Because of the money he left us we'll be able to have what Mama always wanted for us, a decent life. We'll be accepted anywhere, by everyone. But not if you do this. Anna, please, don't spoil everything for me. Please don't!"

"Spoil *what* for you?"

"The chance to be what I've always wanted to be, a lady. To do the things I've always wanted to do, longed for. You know. Don't you understand?" Hampered by her inborn inability to express herself, Clara became frustrated and then angry. "I want to be invited into houses . . . big houses, gentry's houses, like Durdans and Chilworth Manor. I want to be treated like Mama was, when she was young. We missed all that, what we should have had if Father had married her, we always had to live like poor folk, wearing shabby clothes and going to bed hungry and cold." A tear welled up in the corner of her eye and then rolled down her cheek. "It was bad enough you having to go rough riding for a living at Sam Loam's yard . . . but if you start behaving like a man we'll both be outcasts!"

"God forbid I should ever behave like a man!" Anna shouted, furiously, shaking off Jessie's hand. "Or turn into what you want, a spoiled, idle bitch with nothing better to think on than licking the boots of the local gentry, your tongue hanging out for them to pat you on the head and accept you as one of them because you've suddenly got more money than they have! My God, is that what you call living?" She wrenched the gown from Clara's hands and flung it on the floor. "And don't ever speak to me about being ashamed of what I do for a living! The work I did for Sam Loam put clothes on your back and food in your mouth, Clara Brodie . . . and don't you ever forget it!"

For a moment Clara stared at her, like a dumb thing. Then she burst into tears and turned and fled up the stairs. Anna heard the sound of her footsteps on the bare floor, then the slamming of her bedroom door.

"Oh, lassie, you shouldn't 'ave spoke to 'er like that, really you shouldn't," Jessie spoke, after a short silence.

"Why not? It was all true, wasn't it?"

"Two wrongs don't make a right."

"Don't lecture me, Jessie, I've had enough for one day. And don't talk to me in riddles."

Without speaking, Jessie got up and began clearing away the rest of the supper things in silence, while Anna went back and stood against the window, staring out into the night, still smoldering with anger. This wasn't what she wanted, it wasn't what she'd planned, riding back on the mail coach to Epsom, the secret happiness warming her, the thought of the house, her horses, everything she'd longed for and dreamed of ahead, within reach at last. She'd thought of how the evening would be; the three of them, sitting around the fire after supper; she would tell them about the house, and they would smile and laugh and ask her questions. Without a word to Jessie she turned away from the window and went upstairs.

She could hear her sister's sobbing through the thin walls, muffled by her pillow. She knocked on the door and there was a sudden silence from the other side. When there was no answer she went in.

"Don't let him do this, Clara. Don't let Father drive a wedge between us with his damned money, not now, not after everything we've all been through. He destroyed Mama when he was alive. Don't let him destroy us now that he's dead." Anna stretched out one hand and laid it stiffly on her sister's shoulder. Gestures of affection did not come easily to her. "Clara?"

Slowly, Clara rolled over on the little bed and hauled herself up into a sitting position. She wiped her nose on the back of her sleeve. "You better not do that when they invite you to Durdans," Anna said, with a ghost of a smile. Clara half-smiled at the wry joke, then began to cry again, but in silence. She covered her face with her hands, as if she could not bear Anna to see her.

Anna sat down beside her on the bed.

"Clara, listen to me." She hesitated, searching for the right words. "I know we don't want the same things. What you want . . . that kind of life isn't for me. And I don't expect you to ever understand why I want to breed and race my own running horses . . . maybe I don't even understand myself." She got up and walked across the tiny room to the casement window. It was half-open and she reached out and shut it, against the chill night air. "I want to breed a Derby winner. Father failed and I want to do better. I want to do what he couldn't, with all his money. But it's much more than that. In any case, he won't ever know. Horses have always been in my blood, you know that. I can only be what I am. And I didn't go begging Sam Loam for a job in his yard rough riding just because we needed the money, though God knows we did. I did it because I longed to do it." She turned back to Clara, looking at her hopelessly. How could she ever hope to make her understand? "It's like a fever, Clara. It rages. It's part of me, don't you see?"

"I've tried to, Anna."

"No one here knows yet who we really are, have you thought of that? But news travels fast, especially scandal. And that's what they'll call it, a scandal: Edward Brodie leaving a fortune to his two bastard daughters."

"What are you trying to say, Anna?"

"That you'll have to be ready for anything that happens, that's what I'm trying to say. You're not tough enough, Clara. You proved that when you burst into tears downstairs, just because I told you something you didn't want to hear. Outside, you'll hear plenty. People staring at you when you walk into a crowded room. They'll smile at you to your face and then call you a rich man's bastard behind your back. They'll do it because of jealousy . . . women because you're more beautiful, men because you've got more money than they have. But you mustn't ever show that it hurts. Because that's what they'll be waiting for." Silence from the huddled figure on the bed. "I know we don't want the same things, you and me. But I'm trying to be fair. You can go to London when you want to, take Jessie. You can have the best clothes money can buy. And when you're twenty-one you'll have your share from the will and you can do what you like with it.

Till then you'll just have to trust my judgment about what's best for you."
She went to the door and lifted the latch. "It's cold in here. Do you want a
fire lit?"

"No. No, Anna, I'll get undressed now and go to bed. I feel tired, after
the traveling." She found her handkerchief and blew her nose loudly.

"Anna? I'm sorry about what I said. About you working in Sam Loam's
yard."

"I'd already forgotten it," Anna said. "Goodnight Clara."

❋ 7 ❋

Ralph Russell eased his gelding down to a steady pace as they reached the
tall gates of the hall, beyond which wound the long, curving drive, and
beyond that, the house itself. It was curious how darkness changed things,
he was thinking; how it tricked the eye, how it made a place that in daylight
was bright and happy with dappled sunlight and the chatter of the gardeners as they worked, sinister and melancholy when night had fallen. Not
a place to linger. She would walk in the grounds, he remembered, unwillingly. He could almost see her, her pale gown trailing behind her on the
leaf-strewn grass, a parasol in that white, waxlike hand, the fair curls
blowing softly across her brow. And in the rooms of the house where she
had been, the sickly sweet scent of her perfume.

He closed his eyes, willing the picture of her away, and in her place the
face of Anna Brodie came to him, with the cloud of dark hair and the
glittering, bright blue eyes, and cheeks full of color from the wind, and he
no longer shivered. He thought of her, and he smiled.

The house loomed suddenly, through the screen of trees, lights streaming from some of the downstairs windows. It was late, past eleven, and
most of his servants would have gone to bed, except Jason, his butler, and
Robert, the head manservant. When he dismounted in front of the house a
groom appeared to lead away his horse, and bidding the boy goodnight he
strode into the hallway, where Jason was already waiting for him.

"A good evening, milord. A pleasant ride back from Mr. Hindley's,
milord?" He took his hat, helped him out of his greatcoat. It was warm in
the hallway, after the chill night air.

"Fair to middling, Jason. I'm later than I expected to be." He handed
him his riding crop. "I'll have a glass of brandy in the library before I go up.
No need for you to stay, though. You and Robert can go to bed."

"Milord," Jason said as though it was his fault, "you have an unexpected visitor in the library . . ."

"What? But there was no carriage outside when I arrived just now! Who the devil . . ."

"Sir Gilbert Heathcote, milord. He came on horseback." Deftly, from years of practice, he folded the greatcoat over one arm. "And from the look of his horse it seemed to me he'd ridden over here in a great hurry. All lathered up, it was. The groom took it to the stables to water it and give it a rubdown."

"All right, Jason. That'll be all."

"Goodnight, milord."

With a sigh, Russell went into the library, anger mixed with his weariness. He wanted to be alone, to sit in one of the great scarlet wing chairs and sip his brandy. He wanted to think about the past few hours of the day; he wanted to think about Anna Brodie. Now it was not to be. He strode into the room and shut the door loudly, not bothering even to wear a false smile for his unwanted guest.

"Russell! Forgive me for calling on you at this hour. I arrived before eleven, but your man said he didn't know when to expect you back."

"That's right." Still curt, he went over to the little table that housed a decanter of brandy and glasses, and poured himself one. "Will you join me?"

"Thank you, yes."

"Well, what news have you that couldn't wait till tomorrow morning?" He drained the glass in one gulp and went over to stand beside the fire.

"Edward Brodie's dead."

He swung round, both his tiredness and annoyance gone together.

"What?"

"I only heard the news myself early tonight. My cousin, who's come from Newmarket for the next spring meeting, was full of it. I was stunned, I can tell you . . . why, I never knew he was ill, even. They say it was his heart. But that isn't all . . . when his will was read he'd left everything but his bloodstock to his two illegitimate daughters! What do you think of that, eh, Russell? One in the eye for his widow and sons, I can tell you. My cousin has it from a first-class source that the poor woman well-nigh collapsed when she heard . . . what a shock for her! What a shock for us all! Why, I never so much as suspected that Brodie had ever kept a woman . . ." He was so intent on relating his news that he did not notice how quiet Russell had become. His face was half turned away, staring at the remains of the fire. A nerve twitched in his cheek. "It'll be all over Epsom, I'll warrant, by noon tomorrow. Some woman in Saffron Walden, I think it was. Dead now, of course, but the two girls would be old enough to inherit . . . and both of them, my dear Russell, arrived to hear the will read, after everyone else was there, my cousin heard, as bold as you please! Why, apparently, they were both so handsome, particularly the

eldest, that black mourning garb became them more than a ball gown
would become any other young woman . . ."

Russell turned, slowly, from the flickering flames of the dying fire, and
went back slowly to where the decanter stood. He lifted it, still without
speaking, and poured another measure into his empty glass. Gilbert
Heathcote had still not touched his. Yes, it was her, it had to be her. So she
had lied to him. She was Edward Brodie's daughter.

"Russell? Are you all right?" Gilbert Heathcote's voice seemed a long
way away, like an echo. Muffled and indistinct.

"Yes. Yes, I'm all right. It was a shock, that's all. As you say, I never had
any suspicion that Brodie might be ill."

"The widow will want to dispose of the bloodstock, no doubt," Heathcote
went on, relentlessly. "And there's more than one or two animals among
them that will interest me. Why, that colt of his, Firestone, that went lame
on Derby Day three years ago . . . think of the stallion prospects of a horse
like that! If I could get him I'd willingly pay two thousand guineas."

Russell had gone back to the fireplace. He stood there, leaning against
the mantle, sipping the brandy. His voice, when he spoke, seemed strange
even to his own ears; strained, husky, as if he was recovering from the cold.

"Did . . . your cousin say anything more? About Brodie's daughters?
Where they might be, now?"

"He could find out no more than what I've told you . . . but all Newmarket's talking of nothing else. Why, Brodie was worth a fortune, not
counting his bloodstock. Whatever state they kept before he died, those
two bastards of his will want for nothing now."

The word hit him, sharply, painfully, as if it had been directed at him and not
the girls. It made him angry, more angry than he had felt in a long while.

"It isn't their fault what they are. Would anyone be a bastard from
choice? Even a rich man's bastard? No doubt Brodie left them his money
because of his guilty conscience. Because he should have married their
mother and didn't." Gilbert Heathcote stared at him in surprise.

"But how could he, my dear Russell, when he was already married to
someone else, with two legitimate sons?"

"If a man wants something badly enough he'll move heaven and earth to
get it."

Into the sudden silence, the clock on the mantle chimed midnight.
"Twelve already!" Heathcote said, putting down his empty glass. "Why,
I've kept you up too long, my dear fellow. Again, you must forgive me for
calling on you at this unsociable hour . . . but I knew you would want to hear
the news, if only because of the dispersal of his bloodstock. I reckon his
widow'll be putting the whole lot of 'em up for bids at the Newmarket sales."

"Yes . . . I'm grateful for your call." He went over to the bell rope and
pulled it. "I'll have Robert get the groom to bring your horse 'round to the
front of the house."

Heathcote regarded him more clearly for the first time since his arrival.

There was something remote about Russell tonight, something uncharacteristic, curiously detached, as if his mind was not on the subject of conversation.

"Your man mentioned, when I asked, that you'd ridden over to Hindley's earlier. I trust you found him well?"

"I . . . no. I intended to ride over, but I had other business on the way, which took longer than I thought." It was impossible to put her out of his mind. Slowly, unwillingly, he came back to the present. Heathcote was looking at him, waiting for him to speak. "I shall see Hindley presently, no doubt," he said, hoping not to be pressed further.

"He'll not have heard the news, then. About Edward Brodie."

"No, he'll not have heard it."

There was an interruption when Robert came into the room to say that Heathcote's mount was ready, and waiting outside.

"Well, you'll both be our guests at Durdans after the King's Plate on Saturday; I shall introduce you to my cousin and you shall both hear about it from him, firsthand."

When he had gone Russell went back to the fire and sat down. The last log had almost been consumed by the flames, and was now charred and smoldering. He took up the poker and prodded it, and sparks flew from its underside, red and glowing.

He wished she were here, now, in this room. He felt a sudden, pressing need for her presence. But above all he wanted to ask her why she had lied to him.

❋ 8 ❋

She was awake long before daylight, long before even the birds began their dawn chorus. She pulled on a gray velvet wrap that had been bought four days before in London and went downstairs. Even Jessie was still asleep. She got wood for the kitchen fire and lit it, and filled the kettle with water from the well outside. While it whistled and hummed on the stove she crept back upstairs and began to go through the pile of clothes left out from the night before, old, well-worn gowns and patched linen that would not be going with them to the Old Brew House. Each one held a memory. The sight of Anna Maria's tiny, neat stitching brought a lump to her throat. She put out a hand and picked up an old chemise and held it to her cheek. The white had faded into dull patches of yellow, in places, and there was a strange, musty smell to it.

She held it to her for only a moment; on the landing outside she heard heavy, slow footsteps, then Jessie's voice.

"Why, you up already, lass? And it not light yet, neither!"

"I wanted to start packing up, Jessie. That's all."

"But we're not leaving today, are we?"

Briskly, Anna folded the chemise and put it with the other things. "Why not?"

"But this big 'ouse, what you was talking about last night . . . why, it's bin empty for years! It'll be as damp as the grave, for one thing, and filthy with dust and cobwebs, for another. It'll be weeks afore anyone can go there, maybe longer. As it is it ain't fit to live in!"

"And was this place when we came here? Jessie, we're paying other people to clean it for us . . . Mr. Nubbles is seeing to everything. You won't have to lift as much as a finger. Now, how does that suit you?"

"*Mr. Nubbles?* And who might 'e be?"

Anna smiled, pressing down the pile of discarded clothes in the old trunk.

"Come downstairs and I'll tell you over a mug of tea."

Jacob Hindley stood at the window of his small dressing room, staring down into the little rose garden below. But the beauty of last summer was far from his thoughts now as he stood there, his hands gripping the window ledge so tightly that his knuckles showed white. All he could see before him was the narrow, wizened face of Frederick Nubbles, and his voice saying, placatingly, "*I regret to inform you, Mr. Hindley, that another buyer has purchased the Old Brew House . . .*" and the same hot, red mist of impotent rage rose up again as it had last night, choking him, stinging at the backs of his eyes. All his scheming, his patient waiting till the right moment to place his bid, were all for nothing; an outsider, an interloper, had walked into Nubbles's office and upstaged him. His fury knew no bounds.

Into the early hours, he'd tossed and turned, unable to sleep. And, when sleep had come, finally, as the harsh dawn light began to streak the sky, he had fallen into a fitful, uneasy slumber, dreaming of Frederick Nubbles's clever, weasel-like face, the thin lips saying over and over again to him the same words. ". . . *ah, no. I regret that I cannot reveal to you the name of the buyer . . . it is not my business . . .*"

Neither of them heard the approach of a rider until the banging on the front door startled them; then Clara, still in her nightgown, shouted down the stairs, "Anna! It's him! That Lord Russell who came back with you last night. He's outside, knocking on the door!"

Jessie heaved her bulk off the bench with a speed Anna had never seen, her face white as flour.

"Dear God, and neither of you decent! Quick, get upstairs an' I'll answer the door!"

Anna looked at her defiantly, without moving an inch.

"If he comes calling at this time in the morning he can take me as he finds me."

"But you're undressed, you're in night things! You can't let 'im see you like that!"

"Jessie, for Christ's sake open the door before he breaks it down."

He stood there on the threshold, framed in the little doorway, dwarfing the tiny kitchen in his greatcoat and top hat. He gave Jessie a small, informal bow of the head, apologizing for his early call. Then he caught sight of Anna. For a moment their eyes met and held, then Anna gave Jessie a single look and she disappeared instantly, muttering something about Clara's tea.

"Is this your usual visiting hour?" she said, sarcastically, without any greeting.

"I'm sorry, I apologize. I hope you can forgive me. But I heard some news last night when I got back to the hall, and I had to see you."

"Oh?"

He stood there awkwardly, waiting for her to invite him to sit down, but she did not. Slowly, she reached out across the table for the teapot and refilled her pewter mug. The tea gushed out, dark and strong. "And what news would that be?"

"Edward Brodie died ten days ago." He watched the expression on her face carefully. "In his will he left everything to his natural daughters, cutting out his widow and sons . . . and you and your sister have just come back to Epsom, worth enough to purchase an estate as large as the Old Brew House. That's more than a strange coincidence. Why did you lie to me, Anna? Why did you deny that Brodie was your father?"

She got up suddenly from the bench, her dark, waist-length hair a shining, tangled cape about her shoulders. Her eyes were hard and cold, like the sky outside.

"Who the hell do you think you are, coming here and questioning me, as if I was on trial? Who gave you the right to poke and pry into my affairs? Is it because you're a big name in these parts, because you've got a big house on the other side of the Downs and a title? Or is it because you pretended to play the good Samaritan yesterday?"

"There was no pretending. And I don't give a damn where you got the money from . . . I came back with you because I cared about what happened to you. Believe me or not, that's your choice. All I want to know is why you lied to me when you didn't have to."

"I didn't lie to you. Edward Brodie has never been a father to me. Or to my sister. No more a father than any prize stallion that's led to a mare in season. He begot us, that's all. And left my mother to struggle to bring us up, to clothe and feed us, to make one day's money stretch into seven, taking in other people's sewing to keep a roof over our heads. He never went hungry so that we could eat, he never sat up, without sleep, night after night, nursing us when we were sick. He wouldn't have known what the word *father* ever meant. Yes, he left us his house and his money, a sop to his guilty conscience at the way he treated her! But none of that could ever make things right. As long as I live I shall never forgive him."

"I'm sorry, I never knew."

"My mother was a lady. She was gentry. She was brought up sheltered, not bred for the degradation he dragged her down to, lower than a peasant. Scrubbing floors and plying needles until her hands bled. Her beautiful hands." She looked at him, harshly, the way she would have looked at her father. "He never heard her, crying herself to sleep. He never saw her bent double with pain because she was always in debt and couldn't pay to see a doctor. He never saw her handkerchiefs, the handkerchiefs she used to hide from us, all spotted with the blood she used to cough up from the disease that was killing her. I watched my mother die. I watched and there was nothing I could do. Can you ever understand how I felt?" He could not speak. He felt stupid, tongue-tied, useless. "That's what my father did to her. I survived because I was stronger than she was. My hate for him kept me alive." She had forgotten Jessie, forgotten Clara, waiting upstairs for Russell to go; forgotten that she meant to ride over to Sam Loam's, to pack, to ride into Epsom and meet Frederick Nubbles. "Oh, I know what they'll all be saying in Newmarket and Epsom, when the news gets out about Brodie's daughters! I can hear them now, picking it over as they would a fowl's carcass at dinner. Have you heard, did you know, Edward Brodie left a fortune to his bastards and nothing to his poor grieving widow and sons! Why, there ought to be laws against it!"

"It's none of their business," he said, quietly.

"Nothing! He only left her the finest collection of bloodstock in the country, the best anyone could ever hope to own! The one thing he had that I wanted and didn't get." There was a long silence, broken only by the wind rattling against the window. "Well," she said at last, "you've said what you came to say, haven't you? I should like you to go now. I have a lot of work to do."

He felt like an intruder, like someone who had inadvertently wandered into a confessional, and had heard what he had no business to hear.

"If I had known you when you first came to Epsom, I could have done something to help your mother."

She laughed, suddenly, with sour humor.

"You did know me when I first came to Epsom . . . remember? You threw me off your land." He said nothing. "Well, at least you have the grace to look ashamed."

"I am ashamed." He fingered his hat awkwardly, as he'd done yesterday at the Old Brew House. "And I think I'd best be on my way, if I can be of no help to you."

"Help to me? What help to me could you be?"

"If you need any advice about the estate, or any assistance on any matter, you know where I am. Don't be too proud to ask for it."

As soon as he'd ridden away Anna went over to the foot of the stairs and shouted at the top of her voice, "It's all right, he's gone! You can both come down now!"

Clara came down first, already dressed, Jessie behind her.

"What in Heaven's name did he want, Anna? And so early, too! We tried to listen, but you were too far away for us to hear anything."

Anna held up her hands in exasperation.

"All right! All right. He heard about Father's death. From someone, last night. He knows I've bought the Old Brew House and the estate, that my name's Brodie, that I must have come into money to enable me to pay for it. He's put two and two together and made four, just as I said someone would, sooner or later." She sat down, cross-legged, on the pine bench. "He asked me once if I was Edward Brodie's daughter . . . a long time ago. I don't know what it was that made him suspect . . . Father's name was printed on a race card he had, and he saw me on the course. He could see I loved the horses, that I had a special interest in being there . . . I suppose that's why he linked us together . . . and then my name being Brodie . . ."

"You never said anything to us about it before."

"Does it matter?" She took the mug of scalding tea from Jessie and sipped it. "He asked me and I said no. I said I wasn't his daughter. He wanted to know why. That's the reason he came."

"'E seems a good man to me; a real gentleman. Different from the run of the mill. I get a feeling about folks, and what little I seen of 'im, I like. Didn't 'e ride all the way back with you last night, out of the goodness of 'is heart to make sure you got here safe and sound? Well, you can't tell me a man rides ten miles out of 'is way for nothing! And he's not married, neither, is he? A widower, isn't that right?"

Anna gave Jessie a ferocious look.

"No, he's not married. And for all I care he can stay that way." She slammed down her half-drunk mug of tea, got up, and ran upstairs two steps at a time, her long hair flowing behind her.

Sam Loam was with his blacksmith in the shoeing shed when Anna rode into the yard not long after nine o'clock. He noticed at once that she was not dressed for working: she wore a tailored black grosgrain habit he had never seen before, and a silk riding hat with a short lawn veil. She had changed her hair style, too. Each long braid, brushed until it shone, had been wound and looped in the French fashion. When he called out to her and waved his hand, she dismounted and led her horse over to where he was. The horse was new, too, he noticed.

"So you're back?" he said, simply.

"Yes, I'm back."

"Fine-looking animal, that." He walked around it, stooping now and then to run a hand over its points. "Good hocks. Plenty of bone. You hired 'im or bought 'im?"

"Neither." Her eyes darted toward the smithy, busy with his hammer and nails. "Someone gave him to me . . . along with a few other things."

Sam raised his eyebrows.

"Oh? Somebody generous, then? He's worth a couple of hundred guineas if he's worth a pound."

"Not generous at all." Her eyes went back to the smithy. Sam could tell by the short, clipped answers that she was waiting for them to be alone.

"Got a fresh batch of colts and fillies ready for breaking while you was away. Fancy a stroll up to the meadow to run your eye over 'em?"

"Yes, I'd like that."

He spoke a few words to the blacksmith about where to put the horse when it was shod, then joined Anna outside. They strolled toward the top meadow, Anna leading her mount.

"So, what's new?"

"Oh, nothing's happened much in the yard while you've been away." He paused. "Well, there was some news from Newmarket this morning," he said at length. "One of the big owners over at Mildenhall, Edward Brodie, died about ten days ago. Left a fortune, they said. Shame, that. Three years ago 'e might 'ave 'ad Priam beat in the Derby with that colt of his, but it went lame on the gallops before the race. A real sporting gentleman, he was." Anna had gone very quiet. They had reached the meadow where the new, unbroken horses were kept, before going to the breaking paddocks. "Of course, you may 'ave heard the news before we did, coming from that part of the world."

"Yes," she said, in a strange, subdued voice, not like her own, "yes, I already knew." They stopped walking. For a moment she leaned against the fence, gazing across at the grazing animals. Then she turned her face toward him. "Haven't you left out a piece of your news, Sam? About Edward Brodie? Hadn't you heard, he left most of what he had to his two bastard daughters . . . all except his bloodstock, which his grieving widow is too stupid to realize the value of?" There was a long pause, while he stared at her. "I'm the eldest of those bastard daughters, Sam." She half-laughed, bitterly. "Don't tell me you never guessed. My name is Brodie, and horses are in my blood, too. I must get it from him, don't you think? The only worthwhile thing he was born with."

"You told me you didn't have any father." If he was shocked, taken aback, there was no sign in his face. "The first time I met you, when you walked in here with Mattie Troggle. That's what you said."

"I didn't lie to you, Sam. He was never my father." She turned her head away, abruptly, and stared toward the horses in the meadow. "You remember that day, Derby Day, when you rode over and gave my mother a bottle of brandy? A few months later, she was dead. What you saw her reduced to, that was his doing. Since the day that she met him, he dragged her down until he couldn't drag her down anymore."

It came, then, the torrent of words. The hatred, the lifelong grudge. Part of what she had let herself say to Hubbard, to Ralph Russell; but much more because with Sam there was no need for the same careful weighing of words, the guardedness, the hiding of how her father's neglect had hurt her that had become almost second nature. And, as she'd known that he would, he understood it all. When she had finished, he put one gnarled hand firmly on her shoulder and patted it, much as he would have done to a restive filly.

Neither of them said anything for a long while. Then Sam spoke.

"Well, I reckon we'd best get down to brass tacks, don't you? About what this means to both of us."

She turned her head toward him sharply.

"What do you mean, Sam?"

He laughed, a little wryly.

"Well, now. If I was in your shoes, I'd be thinking on what I was planning to do. You'll not be working for me no more, now there's no need. I mean, that'd be a fool thing to do, wouldn't it?"

"Do you really think I did it just for the money?"

He smiled.

"No. No, I don't reckon I do. But let's have it straight, Anna. Tell me how long I've got you for because when you leave the yard, I'll need to find someone to take your job over. I was going to say, someone to take your place. But they're not the right words, are they, because there's nobody ever could." He was silent again. It was the closest he had ever been to telling her that she was the finest rider and handler of horses he had ever seen, including himself.

"Sam, you should know me better than that. Do you think I'd up and walk out on you after everything you've done?"

"So now. Are you going to give me a straight answer to my question or not?" They had reached the smithy, now empty. Anna could feel the heat from the furnace.

"I've made a bid for the Old Brew House estate, Sam. I aim to start up on my own . . . breeding and racing my own blood horses. That'll take time, I know that. I know there'll be resentment. I know there'll be opposition. But I can overcome that because I intend to succeed. As far as working for you is concerned, I'll still break in any horses you want me to, except that I'll be doing it at my yard instead of yours."

"You can't be serious," he said, simply.

"I don't know what you mean."

"Don't know what I mean? For Christ's sake, Anna! You can't go onto the turf, like a man does. You just can't buy or breed horses and enter 'em for any race you fancy! Do you think that clique at the Jockey Club would let a woman inside the saddling ring, let alone compete against 'em? They've got a set of rules to keep out anyone they don't want joining their act so tight that a nit from a dog's ear wouldn't squeeze its way in!"

"When I first came into this yard *you* wouldn't let me in. But I didn't take no for an answer. I knew I could do the job and that you'd hire me if I could get the chance to prove to you what I could do. And you did."

"This is different. I took you on because what you could do with a half-tamed horse was good for my business. They won't let you in, Anna. Hear me out, and listen to a good piece of advice for once in your life. I know you're clever. I know you're headstrong. I know you've got guts. But this time the odds are too high. There's too much and too many stacked against you."

"Sam!"

". . . them in the Jockey Club, let alone them that'll try to cut your throat out of it, are a law unto themselves, believe me. You can't even get the toe of your shoe inside the door." He waited for her to lose her temper. To shout, to argue with him. But to his surprise her face showed only calm.

"I've made a special study of their rules, Sam. There's nothing in them to say in black and white that a woman can't enter a horse for any race she pleases, provided she complies with the ordinary rules of racing."

"That's because no other woman would ever think of doing it. It's unheard of. And whether letting a woman onto the raceground is written into their rules or not, all they got to do if there isn't a rule is to make one."

"Thanks for the encouragement, Sam."

"Look. You should know me by now; I don't mess around covering the truth with fancy words and phrases; if a spade's a spade, I call it one. And the truth is, whether you like it or not, that no woman has ever bin mixed up with the turf before and is never likely to be. Not even you."

"You care to take a bet on that?"

They stopped, beside Anna's horse. She was in the saddle before he could move to help her. "Listen, girl. About this racing nonsense. Put it out of your mind, ay?" The light, casual tone had gone from his voice. He was no longer smiling. "No good can come of it, believe me. And I don't want to see you hurt. I don't want to see you broken by what it can do to you. It's broke plenty of men, I can tell you. Rich men. Strong men. Men that knew how to hold their own. You'd stand no chance against the muck and the filth and the rats that live off what goes on underneath. It's no place for a woman, Anna. You don't belong there."

"I'll be seeing you on the course at the spring meeting, Sam." She turned the horse's head and moved away, leaning out of the saddle on the other side of the yard to let herself out of the gate. He stood there, on the steps of his house, watching her as she rode away toward Epsom. No, she would never listen to him. And he feared for her.

Nathaniel Street whistled a tune beneath his breath as he left Ralph Russell's stableyard by the back entrance and set off on his long walk home through Walton Spinney. It was a distance of some three miles or more, and by the time he had reached that part of the road that veered sharply to the right and descended into a wooded lane, it was growing dark. A thick mist lay upon the ground and already there was a sharp chill in the late evening air. But no matter about that. In another half-hour the boy would be warming himself in front of the little cottage fire, spilling out the news that he himself had only been told of that afternoon by Mr. Inchcape, his lordship's head groom.

Halfway along the little narrow leafy lane he stopped, and climbed across the stile that led into a small copse. By walking through the copse instead of continuing along the lane he could cut the rest of his journey home by half.

But he never reached the road on the other side. All at once, so silently that he never heard them coming at him, four ruffians sprang out of the thick bushes and set upon him, throwing a sack over his head and binding him hand and foot so that his useless cries for help were drowned, unheard. His arms flailing blindly around him, he felt himself being dragged across rough grass; then he was hoisted up in the air and tossed, like a piece of baggage, into a waiting carriage. Fear, then anger seized him, and he kicked out as hard as he could with his ankles lashed together by a rope. One of his attackers gave out a cry of pain and rage, followed by a string of filthy oaths. Then something hard and heavy crashed down upon the top of his head, and he remembered no more.

The first sensation he was aware of when he came to was a crushing pain across the breadth of his skull. Through the thick, musty-smelling sack he could hear whispered voices and the sound of wheels and horses' hooves clip-clopping along the uneven road. Then the vehicle turned sharply right, paused briefly before it lurched forward again, and finally halted. Still covered by the sack, and still bound at ankles and wrists, he was pulled roughly from the cart and dragged several yards across a granite path to a flight of steps. Then one of his attackers cut loose his wrists and ankles and bundled him through a door.

When they pulled the sack from his head and shoulders, he screwed up his eyes painfully against the light that flooded the room. Slowly, dazedly, he looked around him.

Everything he could see was costly, sumptuous, almost to the point of vulgarity. Crystal chandelier; silver; plate; rich brocade fabrics hung at the windows, covered the walls and furniture. But after a few moments the boy did not see them at all. His eyes were fixed on the face of the big, gout-ridden man behind the desk at the far end of the room.

A lamp glowed softly upon the desk, throwing his ugly, red-veined skin into sharp relief. It was a revolting face, a face he knew. The small, wicked, piglike eyes of Tobias Slout glinted at him like chinks of colored glass, and his own flesh crept. Behind him, Slout's ruffians hovered, barring the door.

"Well, well, now," Slout said, at length, looking him up and down as a man might look over a horse or a cow for sale. "So you're young Nat Street, the 'prentice jockey 'is lordship's putting up on Eagle in the King's Plate Saturday?" There was a coarse guffaw from the ruffians behind him. "Reckon you can do as well with the nag as young Chifney, then?"

Nat's bruised head reeled. Jeremiah Chifney, Lord Russell's new jockey, had hurt his arm and couldn't take the ride. He was being given the chance and the honor of riding the colt in Chifney's place. But Russell had only told him the news, via Mr. Inchcape, that very afternoon; no one else knew. How had Tobias Slout come by the same knowledge so swiftly? And, more important, how had he, an outsider, come by it at all?

"Who told you Lord Russell gave me the ride on Eagle?"

Behind him, two of the ruffians grabbed him by the arms and pinioned him. Slout lurched to his feet with amazing speed for so big and ungainly a man; he struck the boy so savagely across the face that he fell backward, only kept on his feet by the two men who had hold of him at either side.

"You're not 'ere to ask *me* questions, you scrawny little runt!" He struck him again, across the other side of his face. "You're 'ere to listen, boy. *Listen.* You hear me?" He stepped back, but the pig's eyes never left Nat's face. "And you call me *sir,* you understand? *Sir.*"

"What do you want, why have you had me brought here? Sir."

"All right. That's better." Slout went back to the desk and sank his bulk into the chair behind it. "You've got the ride on Russell's colt. With Chifney up it'd be odds-on to win, right? Even when it gets round tomorrow that he can't ride and 'is lordship's put a 'prentice jockey up, it'll still be odds-on, won't it? Stands to reason. Not a nag in the race what can touch it, with the form it's bin showing." He was watching the boy's face carefully. Yes, this one was scared all right. Just the way he liked them. Too scared even to open his trap anymore, in case he got another fist in it. "If I go and take a lot of bets on Eagle and the nag runs away with it, I'm out of pocket, as you might say. A lot out of pocket. Now, if a nag like

Phoebe got to come in first, at ten to one, that'd suit me much better . . . if you take my meaning?"

"Mr. Hindley's filly? But I don't understand . . ."

Slout gave a nod to the ruffians over Nat's shoulder and one of them suddenly jerked his arm backward, behind him, until he screamed out in agony.

"Why, you do disappoint me, young Nat Street! And me thinking you was a bright young lad! Not very quick on the uptake, is 'e, boys, this young spark what 'is lordship thinks so 'ighly of?"

"Please; please, I beg of you, let go my arm!" The pain was taking him over, crowding out everything else. Dear God, if they broke his arm! Slout gave another nod and they released it.

"All right, you bloody little weasel, you. That's a sample of what you'll get if you don't take my advice. So listen. You hold Eagle back enough to let Phoebe win the race on Saturday . . . make it close. A short head, a neck. Whatever you like. Just make sure the filly comes home before Russell's nag." He paused, letting the words sink in. "If she don't, Nat Street, what my boys 'ave done to you just now is just a sample of what you'll get . . . and you won't be riding no more nags for Russell or anyone else." He grinned, showing a mouth of rotten teeth. "Now, I can see you've got a bit of sense. You know what's good for a young 'prentice, trying to make 'is way of the turf. Not easy, with all the competition for patrons and good rides." He smiled. "Smart lads know there're times when it's better to lose a race than win it. Unpleasant things can 'appen to them what choose to ignore my advice." He had gotten up again and come across to where the boy stood. He was so close to him that Nat could see the ugly, bloodshot flecks that stained the dull whites of his eyes, the pores in the skin that hung in folds about his chin. "No one ever crosses me and gets away with it, you understand that, boy?"

Pull Eagle. Cheat Lord Russell. Betray the man who was giving him his first chance to make a success, to put his head above the water, where just yesterday he'd been nothing more than another eager, struggling apprentice, yearning for a good ride to show what he could do. Slout was ordering him to ride a crooked race. Desperately he tried to think, pray, but his mind was frozen. Sweat stood out in little beads across his forehead and on his neck. The palms of his hands were sticky, clammy.

"I can't do it, sir. Not take a pull." One of the roughs hit him a stinging blow across the ear. "Please, leave me be! Get somebody else to do it. I'll stand down. I'll tell Lord Russell I feel ill and he'll find another jockey to take the ride . . ."

"Want us to rough 'im up a bit, Mr. Slout?"

"Not now, Billy boy. Not two days before the race. Use your 'ead, won't you? If the little bastard turns up on the course full of cuts and bruises, then Eagle don't win, people'll start talking." He reached out one huge, hairy hand and took the boy by the scruff of the neck and shook him, so violently that his teeth chattered. "Now you listen to me and you listen good! I'm a patient man, but my patience is wearing thin. You'll take the bloody ride and you'll see to it that Eagle comes in behind the filly. And if you think you can get clever by running to 'is lordship and telling 'im about this, forget it." He let him go, suddenly, and walked to the other side of the room. He sat down. "All right, Billy boy. You tell this little runt what 'appened to the last lad who thought 'e'd get clever with me. Go on. Tell 'im!"

"Up at York, Mr. Slout, weren't it? That apprentice who didn't do what you wanted 'im to? Knavesmire Plate, if I remember right." He prodded Nat in the ribs, savagely, with his fist. "Found 'im a couple of days later, trussed up like a fowl for the oven, floating face down in the river. Heard 'is face was so battered, not even 'is own kin could say it was 'im for sure."

Slout opened an ornate box on the desk and took out a cigar. One of the lackeys rushed to light it for him, and he rose, slowly, holding it between his gross, bloated fingers.

Slout inhaled the smoke from the cigar, then blew it out into the boy's ashen face. He was bent double in a paroxysm of coughing. His eyes streamed. If only he could have water. He hung his head. It was enough. He understood now. Slout smiled, satisfied. He'd seen that look many times before. White, yellowy, sick with fear. What would happen to him or his if he disobeyed had sunk in. They could take him back in the cart now and dump him on the road just outside Epsom. He gave the orders and stood for a while at the window watching them. Then he drew the curtains, shutting out the gathering dusk.

"He's gone," Slout said, into the empty room. Behind him, a little door in the wainscoting creaked open, and another man appeared. He was shorter than Slout, younger. Fair, florid, thickset; dressed as a prosperous member of the county gentry would be. Attached to his waistcoat there hung a fine gold watch, with scrivening on the outer case; on the little finger of his right hand, he wore a gold ring set with a single pearl. "Hear all that, did you?"

"Will he do what you want? How can you be sure you can trust him?" Unconcerned, Slout poured brandy into two glasses.

"The little bastard'll do it because he's scared. That's why. When you've got 'em scared, sick scared, they're like clay in the palm of your 'and." He gave him the glass of brandy and took a noisy swig of his own. "Don't worry. You can lay Russell's nag and put as much brass as you like on the filly. She'll fly it."

"There's one thing that still worries me. If Russell suspects . . . he's no fool. If he questions the boy and he breaks down and tells him, we're done for."

"Don't talk stupid! How many lads and grooms has Russell got working in 'is yard? Any one of 'em could 'ave put it about that Chifney couldn't ride and Nat Street was being put up in 'is place. Besides, Russell won't be surprised when 'is colt just fails to get 'is 'ead in front. Stands to reason. Give a ride like that to a green young apprentice, never bin in a big race before in 'is life. 'E'll 'ave nerves, shakes in 'is wrists. Sure, the boy's up on a fast colt, but 'is inexperience lets 'im down at the crucial moment. Russell won't think twice about it."

"This time you're wrong. He's put two thousand guineas on the nag and he expects it to win . . . even with Street up. He reckons the boy's his best apprentice yet. I know; he told me as much only this afternoon."

Slout drained his glass of the remaining brandy.

"Well, that's just too bad, ain't it? 'Cause the little runt won't be riding up to 'is lordship's expectations. Besides, what's two thousand to 'im? 'E's got plenty of brass to throw around."

The other man finished his brandy in silence. He went over to the window and stood there, holding the drapes aside. A nerve twitched in his cheek. "You don't understand. I can't run the risk of having him suspect me. Not now. Not yet. I have a hold over him, yes . . . but it won't last forever." He still held his empty glass. Nervously, he turned it over and over again in his hands. "Nothing lasts forever. Nothing." Almost reluctantly, he turned back to face Slout. "Did you know that the Old Brew House estate has been snatched right from under my nose? By an outsider." A red, angry flush spread from his thick neck to his cheeks. "After everything we had to do to force Dewar to sell up, after all the risks I took. Just when I had him right where I wanted him, just as his tongue was hanging out, ready to sell to me, some Johnny-jump-up straight out of trade comes down here and snatches it right out of my hand!"

"Trade? Rich London trash?"

"I'd bet my stables on it. That little weasel Nubbles rode in from Epsom, made a special journey to break the news to me . . . oh, he's wily, that one. Wouldn't give me any names; wouldn't even tell me what price they'd offered Dewar. A confidential matter, he said, between Mr. Dewar and his client. All he'd let on was that the offer was 'substantially greater' than mine. And more than I could ever hope to raise. If that doesn't smack of rich London trade I don't know what does." His eyes had become slits, glinting like small chinks of glass in the redness of his face. "And I'd swear he was enjoying it, telling me. He was glad I'd lost the estate. The little bastard. For twopence I'd wring his neck like a chicken's!"

"It's bad news," Slout said. "But maybe not so bad as it seems."

"Oh? And what does that mean?"

"Ask yourself . . . what does rich London trade know about racing blood 'orses, ay? Nothing. It's some mercer, or butcher, or goldsmith got rich, wants to buy 'imself a big place in the country to show off to 'is friends, pretending 'e's made 'imself into a gentleman. 'E's made a pile of brass and 'e thinks 'e can buy 'imself into the gentry. Well, 'ow long's someone like that going to last down 'ere? For a start off, 'e'll get sold a string of nags that couldn't go no faster than a plow 'orse, and lose 'is shirt on 'em. Then when 'e tries getting a toe into the Jockey Club, them snotty blue-bloods'll kick 'is arse out faster'n Eclipse could run a mile. Stands to reason. All 'is brass'll be gone, 'e'll resell the estate for whatever 'e can get for it and run back to the City quicker'n what he run out of it. And you'll be ready and waiting."

The other man's face brightened, the flush gradually drained away, leaving only two round spots of color in the middle of his heavy-jowled cheeks. "You reckon?"

"Couldn't be otherwise, could it? I seen it too often to be wrong. Buying their way into earls' and dukes' company with their common brass is one thing . . . but tryin' to buy their way onto the turf . . . well, that's a different kettle of fish altogether. And you know it." There was a sudden, brief silence, broken only by the sound of Slout refilling both glasses with brandy. "Nobody can play at making a living out of blood 'orses; even them with the real know 'ow sink more often than they swim . . . what chance 'as them that don't 'ave it got? Ask yerself that, friend Jack."

"Yes. Yes, you're right. You always are." He took the glass from Slout's hand, and drank. "To success . . . for both of us."

"I'll drink to that, right enough." He laughed; a coarse, vulgar laugh, the laugh of the East End gutter from which he came, the only one from a family of thirteen who lived past the age of nine.

It was almost dark now. Thin, dismal clouds had begun to streak the evening sky like skeins of smoke from a dying fire.

"It's safe for me to leave now, without being seen," the other man said. He set down his glass, his thick lips wet from the brandy. "We'll talk again, later. After the race." He let himself out. Not by the study door that Slout's ruffians had used but by a smaller one, its edges concealed in the paneling, that opened in the wall and led to a narrow tunnel. At the end of the tunnel, more than a hundred yards from the house, there was a carefully camouflaged door that opened into a thickly wooded copse, beyond which lay the London-to-Epsom road.

A hunter, lazily cropping the grass, was tethered to a tree nearby. Slout's visitor untied the reins, led him into the clearing, then mounted and rode off briskly; not along the highway but across a field that skirted part of Walton Parish and the woods.

He was all but in his own territory now; no one would think it strange, even at this hour, to see someone so familiar riding near Epsom Downs. His face was well-known, it was respected in these parts.

The hired gardeners had already cut back the tangled overgrowth that had spilled out from the banks onto the weed-choked drive. With scythes, they had cut away the army of tall nettles and dead cow parsley that had encroached on the flagstones of the courtyard, and the house had been opened up with its windows flung wide to let in fresh air and light. No longer was it a silent, empty shell, lying forlorn and neglected within its prison of weeds, but a living, breathing thing. Women from the estate and the surrounding villages had been brought in to clean and sweep. Carpenters were busy looking over the woodwork for repairs.

Anna's keen eyes moved rapidly over the walls and ceiling, stopping at the foot of the staircase. Here, yesterday, she had stood with Ralph Russell. She remembered what words they had spoken; she remembered the look in his eyes. When the house was polished, and furnished and bright with light again, she would always pause and look at the staircase and remember it just as it had been yesterday, dark and coated with dust, and see his face looking at her by the dim light of her lantern.

Without speaking, she passed on.

In a small antechamber, once used for hats and cloaks, Frederick Nubbles took out the documents he had brought with him from his office in Epsom.

"This is a legal bill of sale to the property, the estate, and the adjacent land. It requires only your signature and mine, acting as proxy for Mr. Dewar, and that of an independent witness." He turned to his clerk. "I brought my clerk Monson with me in case you preferred to sign the papers here rather than make another trip into Epsom."

"That was thoughtful of you." She took the pen from him and put her signature at the foot of the document, using the windowsill as a desk. She handed him the pen, and stepped back while he, too, put his signature to the paper, followed by the clerk, Monson. "I shall need your advice . . . upon another matter." She glanced up and caught his eye. He understood. He invented an errand for Monson. In a minute, they were alone in the little dusty anteroom.

"I am here to help you in any way I can."

"I explained last night the terms of my father's will . . . that his widow and sons inherited the whole of his bloodstock and I got no part of it."

"Yes."

"She'd never sell to me, whatever price I offered. She hates us, Clara and me. But she'll have to sell, to somebody. The sons have no interest in the turf and a hundred blood horses eating their heads off with no income coming in is a liability she'll want to be rid of as soon as she can. He had horses in training at Newmarket, all of them entered for big races they could well win, except that the moment he died their entries would be forfeit, under Jockey Club rules."

"And how can I be of help in this?"

"Three years ago he had a colt entered for the Derby. The Derby Priam won. That was his ambition, his dream . . . to win the Derby with a horse he'd bred himself. It went lame on the gallops before the race, so no one ever knew if it could have beaten Priam or not." She looked into the cadaverous, clever face. "I want that horse. Any way I can get him."

"That might prove difficult."

"Not if Lilly Brodie doesn't find out whose money is being offered for him."

"It isn't as simple as that. With another animal, of little or no importance, I could arrange for a third party to make the purchase and then resell immediately afterward, to you. But with an animal of this value, a great deal of interest among the racing fraternity would be generated by its sale, the price being asked for it would be high. Only a buyer in a high social position would be likely to be wealthy enough to afford it; an unknown third party, however respectable, would be regarded with suspicion if he was able to put forward such a large cash sum as the animal would command. Questions would no doubt be asked, inquiries made . . ." he spread his thin, skeletonlike hands wide in a gesture that she understood only too well. "There is a great deal of jealousy and vindictiveness among the gentlemen of the racing fraternity . . . as Mr. Dewar found to his cost."

She raised her eyebrows.

"That I already know. But he went broke because of his own gambling excesses, didn't he? At least that's what I heard." (She had, from Sam Loam. "Any man who bets more brass 'n he can afford to lose, deserves what 'e gets, Anna. That's the quickest road to ruin I know.")

"On the contrary, Mr. Dewar was regarded as reserved in his betting habits, compared to some of his . . . acquaintances." Deliberately he did not use the word *friends*. "He gambled for high stakes, occasionally . . . when he felt as sure as any man in his position might be of one of his own horses' winning. As you yourself know, even if it isn't a one hundred percent certainty in a race, it can often be ninety-nine."

Anna's eyes narrowed. "Is there something you're trying to tell me?"

He hesitated momentarily, held back by his habitual caution.

"His filly Gadfly was entered for the Princess of Wales Stakes; those that knew what they were talking about backed her heavily . . . it was being said she was the fastest filly since Eleanor. John Dewar backed her more heavily than all the rest put together. He thought he had reason. On the morning of the race she was odds-on and the bookmakers on the course were refusing to take any more bets on her. Because the odds were so short, he needed to put far more on her than he would have done had they been longer . . . and in a great error of judgment let himself be persuaded to use all the capital he had."

Anna thought she knew what came next.

"Don't tell me. The filly was got at in the night? On the morning of the race?"

"No. But either the jockey was or she was beaten fairly and squarely by a better horse."

"What?"

"She was beaten by a short head and Dewar lost everything. He was penniless. To meet his debts and losses he sold all his stable off at whatever he could get for them, and put the estate up for sale."

"That's a tale of woe, and I've often heard others like it. But there's something you're still not telling me."

"This is confidential, of course . . ." he glanced out of the little window, at the trees and shrubs in the overgrown garden outside. "But I always thought that Mr. Hindley came very well out of his friend's misfortune. He was given first refusal of all the bloodstock; the prices he offered were accepted without demur because of his long-standing friendship, and had you not come along with your much larger offer he would have had the whole estate as well at a price far below its real market value."

Anna smiled.

"Do I detect a note of distrust?"

"Distrust? Yes, perhaps that would not be too strong a word."

"And you said nothing of this to John Dewar?"

"It was hardly my place to offer such a criticism of one of my client's oldest friends, and I had no proof that he could have been involved in any way in Mr. Dewar's misfortune. Indeed, anyone could have answered that it was merely coincidence that had the best of the bloodstock and the pick of his racing stable fall into Mr. Hindley's lap."

"Yet you were still suspicious?"

"A feeling, no more."

"The estate has been empty for more than three years, the grounds overgrown, the house falling into ruin. Why did Hindley wait this long before making an offer for it?"

"Dewar's asking price three years ago was more than he wanted to pay. The longer it was left unlived-in and neglected, the less anyone could be expected to pay for it."

"So Hindley waited until the property was run down enough and Dewar hard up enough to accept his offer?"

The little man smiled. The weasel face gave away nothing.

"That is only a private supposition."

"And how did Hindley take the news that someone else had beat him to the post?"

"As I would have expected him to take it . . . with a bad grace." He glanced again out of the little window. "Ah, the post chaise from Epsom has arrived with your sister and your woman. Shall we walk outside to meet them?"

When they reached the front door Anna could see the driver, helping Clara and Jessie down. They had not caught sight of her, watching them. They both stood, side by side, staring up at the house.

"I should warn you about something. Jacob Hindley is a prominent member of society in these parts, and no mean power in the Jockey Club. I fear you have already made an enemy of him. And if you mean to carry out the plans you outlined to me yesterday, he will do everything he can to bring you down." His faded, watery eyes twinkled behind the pince-nez. "I should not like to see that happen."

She put her hand on his arm as they walked out together into the sunshine.

"Nobody ever crosses me and gets away with it."

He eased his gelding's reins gently backward and brought him to a halt outside the rusted gates. They were slightly open, the huge chain and padlock dangling idly to one side. Beyond it in the drive and on the banks he could see the workmen, busy at chopping down the unruly overgrowth, the sounds of their voices as they talked echoing in the still air. As he dismounted and led his horse forward, one of them turned, caught sight of him, and rushed to swing wide the gate.

"G'morning, Lord Russell."

"Good morning to you. Is Miss Brodie up at the house?"

"Why, yes, milord. With Mr. Nubbles from Epsom. Over first thing, they was. And a post chaise come, not fifteen minute ago, with 'er sister and their woman." He touched his forelock and went on with his work.

Russell remounted and trotted the gelding along the long, twisting drive, acknowledging the workmen as he rode by. He was well-liked around Epsom. He had the common touch the laboring men liked. When he reached the flagged courtyard he saw the post chaise at the door, the driver chattering to one of the gardeners as he heaped the piles of cut weeds and dead leaves from last winter into a wheelbarrow. They stopped talking as they caught sight of him.

"Morning, milord. And a fine morning. With luck, it'll hold for the meeting tomorrow."

"With luck, it will." He dismounted and the driver of the post chaise took the reins from him. "I'm looking for Miss Brodie . . . is she still in the house?"

"As far as I know, milord."

Ralph Russell thanked him and strode inside, and then stopped, abruptly. Standing with her back to him, she spun round when she heard his footsteps. Clara, not Anna.

"Oh!" she said, in surprise and embarrassment. She recognized him from the one time she had seen him, hidden behind the curtain with Jessie back at the cottage.

He removed his tall hat.

"Miss Brodie. I'm sorry if I startled you." He introduced himself and shook her outstretched hand. Yes, they were alike, the sisters. But the striking face with the same blue eyes and dark, lustrous hair beneath the fashionable bonnet lacked Anna's strong, purposeful look, the look that fascinated him.

"I was looking for your sister."

"She's gone round to look over the stables, with the head carpenter," Clara said. She twisted her gloves in her hands, nervously.

"Would you care to walk with me?" He smiled, to put her at her ease. But she continued to twist the gloves into a ball in her hands.

"I couldn't tell you where it is."

"Then come with me. I was a regular caller here, in the old days. Before the owner went broke." Together, they walked out into the sunlit courtyard. "It's a fine house. A big estate." He looked up at it as it towered above them, dwarfing them with its height. "Your sister has good taste."

"Anna always knows what she wants," Clara said, with the same ill-at-ease smile, not realizing that she had made a perfect judgment.

As they approached the dilapidated stable block Russell saw the carpenter emerge, a sheaf of papers in his hand, then disappear behind the other side of the house. It was more than three years since he had walked inside the grounds, and their sad, stark neglect shocked him. The gardeners had not yet reached this part, and the grass grew in thick, uneven clumps, high as a man's waist. The stone path that had once led from the rose gardens into the orchard beyond it was drenched in moss, weeds growing in profusion between the slabs. Wild and unpruned for so long, the climbing roses had outgrown their strength, stretching long, uncared-for tendrils outward like a skeleton's hands.

It was darker and cool inside the stable block. She was there, alone, examining the long line of loose boxes with her sharp eyes. The old, musty straw crackled beneath their feet, and she turned and saw them.

She invented a message for Jessie to get rid of Clara, and in less than a minute they were alone.

"What do you want, Russell?"

"I rode over to see if you could use any help."

"That's what you said last time we met. And my answer's the same now as it was then. I don't need any."

"You will to get this house back to the way it used to be."

"I don't want it the way it used to be. I want it the way I plan it to be."

He looked around him, slowly, smelling the neglect, the odor of stale hay. "You'll have this demolished, I suppose. And a smaller one built on the site."

"A smaller one? I shall need stables twice as big as this one."

"To house your carriage horses and two or three hacks?"

"To house the bloodstock I mean to breed and race with."

He stared at her, momentarily at a loss for words. For an instant he wondered if the outrageousness of what she said was her idea of a joke; but she did not smile.

"You can't be serious."

"What's the matter? Are you afraid of the competition?"

"You can't do it. They'd never let a woman onto the course. Not in a hundred years. Not ever."

"They don't have any choice." Her voice was touched with anger now.

Sharp, and lashing, like a whip. "I have the money and the means, just as my father had. The only difference will be that I intend to do better than he did."

"They'll break you, Anna. And I won't stand by and watch you destroy yourself." They looked at each other for a moment in silence. "This is just a game to you, isn't it? A diversion, a kind of new amusement. You can't settle for what other women settle for, you want to be different, you want to shock people."

"That's a lie and you know it."

"I've seen men with more money and more sense than you broken on the turf. Not because of gambling. Not because of bad luck. Because someone else wanted to get rid of them. They don't care how they do it, Anna. Poison the horse, nobble the jockey, hold a knife at the stableboy's throat. Have you ever seen an animal, writhing in agony from a mercury ball stuffed into its guts, and stood by helpless, knowing that all you can do is just stay there and watch it die? Can you imagine what a man's face looks like, when he's just killed himself by sticking the barrel of a pistol down his throat and pulling the trigger, because some crooked owner or blackleg who'd stab his own mother in the back for a shilling has bribed his jockey to lose the race, and he's lost a fortune on it that he'll never get back again? The raceground isn't just about horses, Anna; it's about jealousy, and corruption, and dirt and filth, too. No lady should ever have to see some of the things I've seen in my time. Least of all you."

"My stomach's as strong as yours could ever be. I had to stand by and watch my own mother die, remember? Because for the last fifteen years of her life there was never enough food to eat, because there was no money to pay a doctor who might have been able to save her. Don't preach to me about suffering, you don't know the meaning of the word. And I've already had one lecture today from Sam Loam . . . I don't intend to listen to another one from you."

He looked at her. Color had come into her cheeks. Her eyes were like a cat's eyes, two slits of vivid blue. She wore no bonnet. Pieces of blossom from the fruit trees in the orchard had blown down, lodging themselves in her hair. He reached out and caught hold of her wrist, and shook her.

"You bloody little fool! What do I have to do to make you listen?"

Angrily, she shook him off.

"Get out of this stable and get off of my property before I have you thrown off."

"I wouldn't stop another minute where I wasn't wanted. Especially to be insulted by a girl who's spent so long working among foul-mouthed men that she's turned into one."

"You bastard!"

She moved so quickly that he was caught before he could duck out of her way; she raised her riding whip and slashed it across his sleeve, severing the cuff-button and cutting the skin of his hand. The blood oozed out, in red, glistening globules, from the long red weal.

For a moment neither of them spoke. Then he slowly reached into his pocket for a handkerchief and held it over the injured hand.

"I could answer that, but I have better manners." He turned on his heel and strode out. Pushing through the tangle of the wild garden, kicking the twigs and last year's leaves beneath his feet. He did not stop at the front door. He did not look back. When he reached the place where his horse was tethered in the courtyard he mounted it and rode off.

When Anna had given him enough time to be gone, she came out of the stable and made her way back to the house. The men had stopped work in the grounds and had gone to eat their makeshift lunch under the giant chestnut tree on the lawn. Clara was wandering about the rooms upstairs. Jessie was in the big kitchen, her sleeves rolled up, polishing the stove.

"You shouldn't be in here, down on your knees, doing a kitchen maid's work."

"This is going to be my kitchen; it might as well be me what takes 'and in getting it to rights."

"I've already told you, you don't have to. Someone else can do it."

"Ay, that's as may be. But they won't do it as thorough as what I will." She glanced over her shoulder to where Anna stood, whip in hand, leaning against the doorway. "'Ere, there's blood on that crop!"

"Yes. It's Lord Russell's."

"What?" Awkwardly, hampered by her bulk and her bad leg, Jessie heaved herself off her knees. "Anna, you never 'it 'im with it?"

"He asked for it and I gave it to him. And I don't want to talk about it." Abruptly, she turned round and went out, the sound of her footsteps echoing on the bare stairs. Jessie heard her walk across the landing, then call Clara's name. A door opened and shut, and then there was silence once more. Behind her there was an old stool somebody had left, and she sank down on it. The fool of a girl! Her and her cursed, wild temper. And after all he'd done to try and help her, too. And he was a lord, a big name in these parts. She waited until she heard them coming down again, and went outside into the hallway.

"Anna, you should send 'im a note. Apologize. It don't do to fall out with your neighbors. Now, you know that's plain common sense."

"What's wrong, Jessie?" Clara asked, not understanding.

Anna ignored both questions, as if neither of them had spoken.

"Nubbles has invited us to dinner with him tonight. And offered to let us spend the next three days as his guests until the furniture I ordered for the house comes down from London. I said that we'd accept, gratefully."

"Why, that was right kind of 'im, I'm sure." A sudden thought struck Jessie. "But the furniture. 'Ow come you knew when you bought it that you'd be able to buy this 'ouse . . . didn't you say there was some other gentleman, wanting it?"

Anna smiled.

"But he didn't get it, did he?"

The hired post chaise had taken Jessie and Clara on to Epsom. The workmen had finished for the day. As dusk fell, Anna wandered alone through the deserted garden, past the piles of cut grass and weeds that the gardeners had left for taking away in the wheelbarrows tomorrow, the sacks of twigs and dead leaves. She walked slowly, looking about her, seeing for the first time the beauty and subtle color of the shrubs and flowers that had been released, suddenly, from their prison of nettles and weeds.

There were flowers and shrubs that were strangers to her, whose names she did not know, their deep mauves and carmines restful in the stillness and tranquillity of the oncoming evening. Her mother would have known their names. Their habitats, their different colors, the soil in which they needed to be planted to survive and bear flower. Anna could see her in the tiny cottage garden long ago at Saffron Walden, leaning forward to cut the long-stemmed roses and foxgloves, laying them side by side in the basket that she carried gracefully on one arm, a straw bonnet tied under her chin with ribbon to shield her from the hot June sun.

But Anna Maria was gone, she would never walk in this garden. She would never see it in its glory, a riot of scent and color; she would never come along the twisting, steep-banked drive and look up, in pride and wonder, at the brick and beam of the house. For her there would be no new life. For her it was too late.

Anna came to a massive, gnarled oak, magnificent in its loneliness, and leaned against it. Thoughts of her mother tore at her, tortured her, giving her no peace. Anna Maria would not have spurned the friendship of Ralph Russell. She would not have struck him with her whip. She would not have been too proud to admit that she was sorry. She was both stronger and weaker than Anna, and both her strength and her weaknesses had conspired to destroy her. All Anna knew was that she would never make any of her mother's mistakes.

When the dusk deepened, she got slowly to her feet and walked back through the gardens. She crossed the courtyard, and inside the house stood without moving in the quietness of the hall. The stair banisters and the rich dark paneling gleamed in the last rays of the day's light, from the kitchen she could smell the whitewash, not yet dry.

This was her house. The first home she had ever had. It was not leased, it was not given in grace and favor, it did not belong to anyone but herself. A sudden feeling of peace and happiness that she had not often felt in her life settled upon her, like a mantel. Smiling, she came out and locked the door.

*   *   *

There was a short cut back onto the Epsom road that Sam had shown her, three years ago, and she used it often. She had been longer than she expected back at the house, and it was still not dark enough to be wary. With a pistol in the reticule that hung from her waist, she turned her horse into the narrow opening in the bushes, and set off down the track that would bring her out near the crossroads. From that point into Epsom was a matter only of little over a mile. At a canter, she had reached the gulley in twenty minutes, and dismounted so that she could lead her horse up the steep sloping bank to the road. Then she paused, at the sound of wheels somewhere beyond the dense thicket that hid her from view.

A cart came trundling along the lonely stretch of road, two men up on the driving seat and two more lolling inside. But they did not go on along it into the village. Her curiosity aroused, Anna tethered her horse to the branch of a tree and climbed up the slope, on hands and knees, peering through the undergrowth when she reached the top of the bank.

Two of the men had gotten down from the cart and were pulling something roughly from it, laughing, jeering. It was then that Anna could see it was not a sack, as she had thought, but a boy. Thin, white-faced, he struggled to his feet from the place where they had thrown him in the road, and stumbled away from them, then ran, as fast as he could, in the direction of the small lane opposite, which she knew led to a small row of cottages. The men shouted something after him that even her sharp ears could not hear, got back onto the cart, turned it around, and headed back in the direction from which it had come.

The boy had disappeared by now. Anna slid back down the bank, untied her horse, and led it forward, then she mounted it and made off along the last stretch of Epsom road.

Later that night after dinner, when Clara and Jessie had gone to bed, she sat alone with Frederick Nubbles in his parlor.

"The stretch of road between Epsom and Egham," she said, into the easy silence that had fallen between them. "Are there any farms or houses along there that collect their workers and then bring them back again at the end of the day?"

"There's one farm, Pond End, about four miles from Epsom." He lay back in his winged chair, the flames from the small fire flickering across his thin, clever face. He laughed. A short, clipped laugh that ended in a cough. "But old Ned Warlow that owns it wouldn't give one of his farmhands a lift back home unless they'd lost both arms and a leg. Oh, he's mean, that one!"

"And there's nowhere else, no other farms, that hire anyone for a day's work and fetch them back again, at night?"

"Why, no. Most of the hands live on the farms, or within walking distance from them. Why do you ask?"

She decided to say nothing for the moment.

"Oh, no reason." There was a pause. Both felt comfortable, they were at ease with each other. Against the quiet of the evening there was only the distant sound of the servants, clattering with dishes in the kitchen, and the peaceful ticking of the mantle clock. Anna stretched in her chair, her hands spread out toward the fire. It was chilly for the month of May, the coldest she could remember.

"Have you never been married?" she said, in idle curiosity.

"More than thirty years ago, yes. But my wife, God rest her soul, has been dead these past eighteen years."

"I'm sorry."

"We had a happy life together." He smiled. "There is no need for you to be."

"And you don't mind living alone?"

"I am rarely alone, with my housekeeper, my cook, my manservant, and two others in the kitchen. This is a small household, but a happy one, I like to think."

She warmed toward him, this old, bent, wizened little man, in a way that she could not explain. He told her the truth; without criticizing, without trying to belittle her judgment, without Sam's and Russell's impatience or Jessie's hysteria. She felt, instinctively, as she had before, that she could tell him anything, even the incident back in the stables at the Old Brew House when she had argued with Ralph Russell and then struck him. But she would not tell him now. She would wait until another time. He was old, and tired, and she could see that it was long past his usual time for bed.

"I've kept you up too late," she said, rising to her feet.

"By no means. I often work in my office late into the night. It is easy to forget the time."

"But it isn't night anymore. It's morning."

"Ah, so it is." He smiled his thin, weasel-like smile. "And I never noticed it." It was a compliment to her, and she realized it. At the foot of the staircase she paused, and turned to him, her hand on the rail.

"Ralph Russell. Would you say I could trust him?" The longcase clock in the hall began to strike, solemnly, and he waited for the chimes to die away before he answered her.

"I would say that indeed you could."

❋ 10 ❋

"I don't want to come with you, Anna."

"Oh, why not? You think it'll spoil your chance of making a brilliant match, being seen with me on Epsom racecourse?" Anna was already dressed for the day, in one of the austere, highly fashionable French riding gowns she had bought in London on their way through, striking by its very plainness. Clara was still in her petticoat and chemise.

"It isn't funny, Anna."

"Of course not. Racing is a very serious business. *Business,* Clara. I mean to make my living by it, just as Father did. Only I shall do better."

"He didn't make his living by it, he had the mills. That's where all his money came from."

"Rubbish. The brass he made from his bloodstock made the profit from the mills look like duck corn. And the mills weren't his, not to begin with. They came into his hands when he married that farmyard bailiff's daughter."

"But you don't intend to keep them, for safety's sake?"

"For safety's sake?"

"In case what you plan with the horses doesn't work. In case something goes wrong. Then you'll need another source to fall back on."

"It won't go wrong. I won't let it." Anna took a dark-gray silk and velvet bonnet gently from its box and lay it at a perfect angle on her head. Her reflection beneath the spray of plumes that adorned it stared back at her, from the little swivel mirror, supremely confident. "I've talked everything over with Nubbles, especially the question of the mills. They don't interest me. They mean nothing to me. There's no point in keeping them and being an absentee owner, not knowing what's going on and who's milking what part of the business, leaving everything to managers and foremen I don't know and can't trust. I don't know anything about mills and I don't want to learn. What I want is here, right where I can see it."

"But it won't be as easy as you think, Anna."

"I never said I thought it would be easy at all." She looked back at her reflection in the mirror, then turned away, satisfied. "If you don't want to come with me, I won't force you. Make yourself useful to Jessie instead." She went to the door, where Clara's voice halted her.

"What shall I say to Lord Russell if he comes back and asks for you?"

"He won't come back."

Ralph Russell had arrived on the racegrounds long before necessary, and made his way quickly to the private boxes in the new grandstand. It was almost deserted. Not for another two hours or more would it begin to fill, slowly and then with increasing numbers, with local gentry, aristocracy and their ladies, the only females allowed entry. He wanted to be alone. He did not want to be recognized by anyone he knew, be drawn into their meaningless, idle conversation. He felt restless, tormented. In a different way almost the same torment that he had gone through before, with her, she who had occupied and slept in that hated room, the room he had unmercifully stripped bare, whose hangings and drapes he had had burned so that the memories might be destroyed in the flames. From that day he had kept the room locked, but still there was no peace for him.

He closed the door of his private box and leaned against it. Even here he could not be alone. Even here he could not hide. In a little while, some official would come and tap on the door, and tell him that it was time to go down to the paddock.

Half an hour passed; a full hour; two. The quiet had been superseded by bustle, and noise, and the shouting, raucous voices of bookmakers, assembled down at the betting stand. Behind the closed door of his box he could hear the grandstand filling up, the opening and closing of the private boxes on each side of his. Voices, women's laughter. Outside, the Warren began to fill with horses for the first race of the afternoon. He leaned on the edge of the balcony and stared down into the teeming mass of humanity below him.

There were faces that he recognized. Edward Randyll from Chilworth Manor was in the enclosure, with his groom and jockey, a stable lad holding his Sultan filly while another pulled off her rugs. There was Sir Gilbert Heathcote from Durdans, without a horse in the first race but standing in animated conversation with his neighbor, pointing to the other runners. Not all the horses would come into the Warren to be saddled. It was not compulsory. Some would be saddled and mounted in the racecourse stables, others outside the fence.

Still he sat waiting; tense, restless. Any moment the official he knew would come for him, would walk up to the private box and tap on the door. And then he must leave this temporary haven, he must go down among the crowds he detested, and act out his part. He stared down again into the teeming, noisy masses, then saw that many of them were stopping, and staring to a point beyond which he could not see. Suddenly there was less noise, conversation and bookmakers' shouting at the betting stands began to die away on the air. Suddenly, there was almost a hush. And then he saw why.

She came into sight from the side of the grandstand, walking side by side with the little wizened Epsom lawyer, Frederick Nubbles. She was dressed in sober gray. No jewelry, no adornments, immaculate as a fashion plate; her one extravagance the spray of plumes that decorated her silk and velvet bonnet. He saw their mouths fall open, heads turn in dozens. Shock, astonishment, outrage. Words and sentences flew upward toward him, shattering the still air.

"A woman on the course!"

"She'll have to leave . . ."

". . . they won't allow it!"

"In God's name who is she?"

"I've never seen anyone so beautiful!"

"Fetch the clerk of the course!"

"It's scandalous!"

"It's an outrage!"

"Doesn't she know the ruling?"

"Isn't that Frederick Nubbles?"

"He knows no women are permitted here!"

She had done it again; she had walked onto men's hallowed ground and created a sensation. But it was more shocking now than it had been before, three years ago. Then it had been less noticeable. Because of the lashing rain. The vast, impenetrable crowds. Because it had been Derby Day, and because of her own bedraggled, weather-beaten youth. Only a small group of people about the entrance to the grandstand had seen her then. Now she stood out vividly, a forbidden intruder. He caught a glimpse of officials swarming round her, closing her in. Then he rushed from his box so quickly that he overturned his chair and did not even stop to close the door.

"No ladies permitted anywhere on the course or in the grandstand unless escorted by a member of the Jockey Club?" There was no rancor in her voice, no annoyance. "Then your rules will have to be revised." She smiled, but the smile was not a part of her; it hung there, about her lips, like a false, unreal thing. "My father owned a private box in the grandstand and when he died a short time ago he left it to me. I am Anna Brodie." There were gasps from the crowd that had gathered around her, then murmurs, muffled and low. "Now will you be good enough to get out of my way . . . if you please." It was then that she looked up and saw Russell, standing in the doorway of the grandstand entrance. No smile passed between them.

"Madam, have you verification of this?"

"I don't carry a copy of my father's will around in my pocket!"

Russell came forward and lay his hand on the other man's arm. "Do you doubt Miss Brodie's word in this?"

The man turned round, startled, and recognized Russell at once. "Why, no, my lord . . ."

"Then be good enough to show her the way to her father's box." He had removed his tall hat and inclined his head toward her, still not smiling. He greeted Nubbles, then replaced his hat.

"I wish you a pleasant afternoon's sport, Miss Brodie. You must excuse me, I have a horse in the next race." He turned away and the crowd parted for him, respectfully. When he reached the fence at the Warren, he stopped and glanced back over his shoulder. But she was gone.

He pictured her inside, sweeping up the grand staircase, walking through the private gallery with as much ease as if she did it every day, impervious to the whisperings and stares. Then she would pause, at the door of Edward Brodie's box, and turn and look at them, the hordes of the shocked and the curious. She would not look or feel discomfited. She would not allow them to stare her down. Then she would turn and go into the box, as if it had always belonged to her.

He looked down at his hand, half-healed now from the cut of her whip. His anger had passed. He could not hold it against her.

Then he glanced up and saw his head groom running toward him through the crowd.

"It's young Nat Street, milord! 'E's not turned up."

"There's no need to panic." Russell took out his gold fob watch and flipped open the lid. "The runners for this race haven't gone to post, and there's a King's Plate to be run before the Queen Adelaide."

"I told 'im to get 'ere by three, milord."

"It's too early yet to start worrying." He snapped the watch-case shut and put it back inside his coat. "Sir Gilbert Heathcote's caught sight of me, I shall have to speak with him." He saw Heathcote standing in the Warren with his training groom and another man, and they were both looking his way. The cousin from Newmarket, no doubt, who had regaled Heathcote with details of Edward Brodie's will. "Come to me as soon as the boy arrives. He'll have to put on his silks and weigh in before I speak with him about the race." The groom touched his forelock.

"I'll see 'e does, milord."

Heathcote came toward him, hand outstretched.

"Russell, did you see her? There, at the entrance to the grandstand demanding to be let in?" Hastily, almost perfunctorily, he introduced his cousin. "It's her, Brodie's byblow! Why, the news is all over the course! She came in a post chaise, with that lawyer, Nubbles, right onto the raceground, as bold as you please. Everyone I've spoken to is too shocked for words . . ." Russell looked back steadily at him, without answering. "And that isn't all, we've been told. There's a rumor that she's been living here, in Epsom, for the past few years, working as a rough rider for Sam Loam . . ."

"Yes, I know," he said simply. Heathcote and his cousin stared at him.

"You know?"

"Three years ago I had a Selim colt that was sent to Loam's yard for breaking. But nobody there could break it. Yes, I see that astonishes you. If Sam Loam can't do anything with a horse, no one can. He told me later he was on the point of sending it back to me as a bad job . . . but one day a young girl turned up at his yard, begging for work. He felt sorry for her but sent her away with a flea in her ear. He treated it as a great joke. She came back when he was asleep and took the colt out of his stable and up onto the Downs. She rode him all night. When she brought him back to Sam's yard the next morning, he was eating out of her hand. That's when Sam hired her." He paused, a tight smile playing about his lips, enjoying their outrage and surprise. "She said to him, 'I have a way with horses, that's all.' That's what he told me. But it was more than that. She needed the money. Brodie never did her mother any favors, not while she was alive . . . he never gave her a penny. She died three years ago, with consumption of the lungs." He looked from one to the other. "Whatever his conscience made him leave the two girls, in my opinion, can never be enough to make up for the way all of them suffered. Remember that, before you make any more judgments." A great, pressing weight had lifted from his chest as he spoke. "Will you please excuse me, I have to find my head groom."

He turned and began to walk away from them, but Heathcote followed him and lay a hand on his sleeve.

"Russell . . . we'll talk later, if you will." He was confused, embarrassed. "You're still coming to Durdans, after the meeting, for dinner?"

"You may have to make my apologies to your wife. I can't promise." With that he strode off toward the racecourse stables. He wanted to get away. He wanted to be rid of them. In the distance he could see Inchcape, his head groom, deep in conversation with the clerk of the course. His face was anxious, he waved his arms wildly, gesticulating.

"Lord Russell," Henry Dorling said as he reached them, "it seems the young apprentice given the ride on your colt in the Queen Adelaide has gone missing . . . as time is so short I would strongly advise you to engage another jockey."

"If he was ill, milord," Inchcape was wringing his hands in agitation, "he would have sent a message, I'm sure of it. This is most unlike him, I can vouch for that."

"Ask about the stables, and on the course. Have word put about that when he makes an appearance he must come directly to me."

"Yes, milord." Inchcape hurried off in the opposite direction.

"He can still have the ride, if he gets weighed in on time."

Dorling's bland face darkened with disapproval.

"If you will pardon my outspokenness, milord, in my opinion the boy has forfeited your trust by his flippant behavior. Why, there are experienced jockeys here without a ride in the Queen Adelaide who would jump at the opportunity to ride the favorite in a race of this importance . . ."

"I'm willing to give the boy the benefit of the doubt . . . if he gives me an adequate explanation of his conduct."

"As you will, milord."

Russell walked off, between the groups of people, nodding to those he knew, otherwise looking straight ahead. He stopped stable lads and grooms, asking questions. None of them had seen Nat Street. On and on he went, threading a path through the swarms of people, pausing now and then, moving on as head after head was shaken. It was then that he looked up and saw her. Their eyes met above the moving crowds, and suddenly he felt himself pushing through them, thrusting the anonymous black-coated bodies from his own, desperately, almost rudely. He saw the heads turning toward her in their dozens, the expressions of outrage and dismay plain upon their faces.

"Can I escort you somewhere?" he said, when they had reached the same spot. Nubbles was still behind her, a small, shrunken little caricature of a man, with his skeletal hands and bright, clever eyes.

She looked up into his face.

"I've heard your apprentice hasn't turned up to weigh in. Is that true?"

"So the news has reached the grandstand already?" There was a trace of cynicism in his voice, but he smiled. "Yes, it's true."

"Do you want us to help you look for him?"

"If he's anywhere on the raceground he'll be found. But I should be glad of your company, yes." He offered her his arm, but she did not take it. They walked on, side by side.

"Has he ridden for you before, this apprentice?"

"Not in a race, no. But he has great promise. Genius, even. When young Chifney injured his arm in the Queen's Cup at Egham I had no hesitation in offering him the ride."

"Maybe he wasn't ready for it."

They made their way back toward the stables, ignoring the stares at Anna as they passed. Some men stepped back, smiling, removing their tall hats, others scowled, some were too shocked at the sight of a woman on the course to say or do anything. Those that acknowledged her she inclined her head toward, with a ghost of a smile.

"You don't give a damn about any of them, do you?" She stopped, and looked at him.

"I was always taught that a lady acknowledges courtesy. And I won't ever let anyone say that I'm lacking in it."

Beyond them, in the Warren, more horses and jockeys had gathered, ready for the next race. One horse plunged and kicked, alarmingly, as the groom tried to remove its layers of rugs and hood; the air was rent with men's raised voices and the neighing of horses. Then, from the door of the weighing shed Anna caught sight of Heathcote's groom, shaking his head.

"The boy's not there," Russell said. "I'm going to search the stables and outbuildings behind the grandstand. He must be somewhere."

"I'll come with you."

"The stables are no place for a lady." He stopped, abruptly, having realized what he had said; for most of her life she had lived in poverty, for the past three years she had made her living from working in stables. He suddenly felt foolish and absurd. But she looked at him with a half-amused expression in her eyes.

"I think I can get used to them," she answered, with heavy irony. "Shall we go now . . . there isn't much time."

The racecourse stable was a long, high-ceiling building divided into fifty or more stalls, three quarters of them filled with animals. They were cold and crowded, a constant source of the coming and going of grooms and animals. But there was no sign of Nat Street. Lads sat on stools polishing saddles and tack; others were busy giving their masters' animals a last-minute grooming with the dandy brush and hoof cloth. They looked up, their mouths gaping, when Russell and Anna came in.

"'E might of got lost on the course, milord," one of them said, his eyes on Anna.

"If he comes by here, tell him to go to Mr. Dorling's office straight-away."

"Will do, milord."

"Devil take the boy! What in hell's the matter with him? He knows that jockeys have to be on hand at least an hour before any race to make ready! I should have listened to Inchcape when he told me it was too much responsibility for an apprentice, a race like the Queen Adelaide." His face was white, the pallor of candle wax. "It's my own fault. I have nobody to blame but myself."

"You still have time to engage another jockey."

"Yes. But Street knows Eagle like the inside of his hand. He isn't an easy ride. He's unreliable, temperamental in the wrong hands. That's why there's so much at stake."

They walked away from the bustle of the stables, past the rubbing house, the weighing shed. In the distance there was a tall, narrow brick shed, used for storing tools and old tack.

"He wouldn't be in there. He'd have no reason to be," he said.

"You never know." They exchanged glances. "Maybe someone else has made him disappear. Maybe someone doesn't want him to ride Eagle. Maybe some of your other apprentices are jealous that you chose him above them, and have tied him up till after the race. It's possible, isn't it?"

"They wouldn't dare!"

"You'd never prove it. It'd be their word against his. Release him after the race is run and he'd never be able to prove who did it to him. Why not?"

"Nat's one of the most popular lads in my yard. Everyone likes him."

"Nobody likes anyone when it comes to prime rides in big races." He stared into her vivid eyes and saw wisdom in them. Without speaking he began to walk toward the outbuilding; then his walk broke into a run.

There was no lock on the door, there was never anything of value left inside. He pushed it open impatiently. Then he turned away so swiftly that he almost knocked her aside.

"No! Anna, don't look!"

But she had already seen what lay beyond the half-open door. From the apex of the ceiling beam was a hook; and, on the end of the thick rope that had been slung through it dangled the hideous, swollen-tongued body of what had been Nat Street. The sightless eyes bulged from their sockets, obscenely, like a gargoyle's, the sticklike arms and hands hung limply at his sides. Never again would they hold the reins of a horse, urging and coaxing it to victory, never again weave their magic; those cold, dead things would never realize their promise now, and it was the wanton waste that infuri-ated her. Pushing past Russell she grasped a blade that had been left lying on the floor, and hacked through the rope.

"Anna, for Christ's sake!"

Roughly, she shook her arm free.

"Anna, don't touch him!"

"Do you want to leave him hanging there, poor little bastard!"

At the sound of Russell's shouting others had come running. Some craned their necks round the edge of the narrow to peer inside. Someone had gone to fetch the clerk of the course. The rope cut through, the body slumped to the floor. Anna took hold of an empty grain sack and draped it over it, a makeshift shroud.

She stood up and stepped back. She looked at Russell.

"You'd better find another jockey to take the ride."

"There'll be no need. I shall withdraw Eagle from the race."

"What?"

"How can I let the horse run now? Go on, as if nothing has happened? The boy hung himself, Anna!"

"That's just what they want you to do, don't you know that? If you pull out now he'll have killed himself for nothing!"

They were in Henry Dorling's small office on the ground floor of the grandstand.

"They? Who in God's name are *they?* What are you talking about?" He could no longer think properly, or feel. Beyond the office windows, the noise of the crowd outside was a dulled, distant hum of humanity.

"I've seen that boy before. Only yesterday. Despite how grotesque he looked when we found him, I still recognized his face."

"You saw young Nat Street? Where? What time?"

"It was getting dark. I stayed late at the house and I took the short cut home, through the wooded lane that leads out onto the crossroads about a mile from Epsom. I stopped, when I heard the sound of the cart. There were four men in it; rough men, working men . . . they looked like laborers. When they threw him out into the road I thought they might be farm workers, bringing the boy home and rough-handling him for some reason of their own."

"But there's only one farm in these parts, near enough. Pond End. And all their laborers live on the estate."

"That's what Nubbles said when I asked him." She paused for a moment. "There's only one answer, isn't there?" He turned away from her and went over to the window.

"You think he was nobbled, don't you?"

"There's no other answer, Russell. He had the guts scared out of him. Rather than pull the favorite after you'd given him the chance to ride in his first big race, he took the only way out that he knew."

"But no one knew I'd given him the ride." He spun away from the window, his face haggard with emotion. "There was nobody left in the stableyard when Inchcape told him the news."

"Do you trust Inchcape?"

He looked outraged.

"He's worked for me for seven years!"

"That doesn't answer my question."

"Yes, I trust him, damn you!" She made no answer to his outburst. "I'm sorry. I'm sorry, Anna. I shouldn't have said that."

"No, you shouldn't have."

"If you'd known Inchcape and worked with him as long as I have you'd never ask that question." There was a silence of several minutes.

"And what time did the boy leave the yard?"

"Half past six. His walk home would take him no more than an hour." He glanced up at her. "You saw the cart at nine o'clock . . ."

"Where was he for two and a half hours?"

Russell put his hand to his forehead and closed his eyes as if he was in pain. "I don't know."

"Are you going to let them get away with it? Let them think that any time they want to they can stop your jockeys and your horses with impunity? If you scratch Eagle from the Queen Adelaide now you'll be playing right into their hands . . . it's just what they want you to do. And when they've cleaned up from the bookmakers Nat Street will have hanged himself for nothing." There was a haranguing note in her voice and it found its mark. He looked up sharply.

"No, I won't let them get away with it."

"Then tell that to Dorling. He's coming across now from the Warren."

"My lord," Henry Dorling said gravely, "what are your instructions regarding your colt Eagle? The other horses are ready to go to post."

For a moment he hesitated, then glanced sideways at Anna. Almost imperceptibly, she nodded her head.

"Eagle will run as planned. I'm on my way now to engage another jockey." He turned to Anna, lowering his voice. "You must excuse me if I leave you with Nubbles."

"Of course: I was going anyway."

Yesterday was still between them, unspoken of. If she had glanced down she knew she would still see the mark on his hand where her whip had cut the skin. But she could not apologize.

"I left you hastily yesterday," he said at length. "And I am sorry for it."

"No doubt you thought you had reason." She moved away from him, beckoning to Nubbles on the fringe of the crowd. "I wish your colt good fortune, for Nat Street's sake." She turned away and moved imperiously through the thick crowds of men, the weasel-faced little lawyer at her side. Russell watched her for a few moments, then she was swallowed up and disappeared from sight.

"A tragic business," Nubbles said, as they walked back toward the grandstand. "An appalling tragedy. And a waste, too. A great waste."

"And when I see Sam Loam he'll say the same. Lie down with dogs and you get up with fleas."

"It was not a sight that any young woman should ever have to look upon."

"For three years I watched my mother dying. No one should ever have to look upon that, either."

They walked on in step. For a few moments there was silence between them.

"Perhaps what you were forced to witness today will change your mind about the turf."

"No, it hasn't changed my mind. On the contrary, it's made me more determined." He smiled, and his face held no surprise, as if that was the answer he had expected her to give him. They reached the entrance to the grandstand.

A group of men directly in their path turned, and catching sight of Anna, removed their top hats and stepped back to let her pass, whispering among themselves; all but one. He stared at her sullenly from small, ill-natured, bloodshot eyes, unmoved by her striking looks. Instinctively, she disliked and distrusted him.

"Ah, Mr. Hindley," Frederick Nubbles said, to her surprise, "good afternoon to you." He turned to Anna, a question in his bright, alert little eyes that she understood. Almost imperceptibly, she nodded. "May I present Mr. Jacob Hindley, of Roos Lodge. Mr. Hindley, this lady is Miss Anna Brodie, the new owner of the Old Brew House estate." They both saw the heavy, thick-jowled face grow deeper crimson; an ugly scarlet flush spread from his bull neck to his temples. His small eyes twinkled maliciously with barely suppressed rage that he was fighting to control in front of his friends.

"Miss Brodie." Slowly, reluctantly, he removed his top hat. He tried to smile at her to cover his true feelings, but failed. "It surprises me, and many people here, I should think, that any lady should want not only a house as large as the Old Brew, but also all the acreage that goes with it. You intend the land for leasing, no doubt?"

"By no means. I intend to breed and race my own blood horses."

There was a shocked silence. "You must forgive us if we leave you in a hurry, gentlemen." Was there a mocking tone to her voice? "But I must get to my box in time to see Eagle win the Queen Adelaide. Because he will." She walked on by, Nubbles by her side.

"The bitch!" Hindley whispered, between clenched teeth.

Anna got up and went downstairs.

Frederick Nubbles was in his study, writing.

"Excuse me from taking dinner with you, will you?" She stood at the door without coming inside. "I want to ride over and see Sam Loam."

He looked up from his papers, pen in hand.

"I would feel better if you took one of my menservants with you. Or my groom. They would be glad to accompany you."

Anna smiled.

"He who travels alone travels fastest."

"I was thinking of your safety."

"That was kind of you. But I can take care of myself." She did not mention the loaded pistol that she always carried with her. "I shan't be late."

"If you are I shall send out a search party."

"That won't be necessary."

When she had gone he found it difficult to continue with his work. He got up and paced the little room. He sat down again. Outside, the late afternoon was turning into evening, and he felt disturbed, unhappy that she was out there, somewhere, alone on the Downs. She had shown her face today. She had revealed her identity. She had made faceless enemies because she had walked where no one else had ever dared to tread. He admired her. He recognized her courage. She was a mythical niece, the daughter he would never have. And he wanted to protect her.

The little study seemed strangely empty and deserted when she had gone, like his dining room, after dinner. She cast a spell, something he could not quite describe to himself, brilliant though he was with words.

All evening while he waited for her return he tried to put a name to it, and failed.

The house seemed deathly quiet to Ralph Russell on his return. The servants moved about him silently, unobtrusively, like ghosts. News of the tragedy had already spread beyond the course and traveled before him, casting an aura of gloom. He sat morosely at one end of the enormous dining table, staring at the food it was laden with, the exquisite glass, the ornate silver, but touched nothing. No one dared offer congratulations on Eagle's victory, no one spoke its name. Down in the stableyard the colt was being put away in its stall for the night, rubbed down and given water and feed, just as if the race had never happened, the lad who looked after it as miserable as if it had lost the race, or had broken a leg and was about to be shot.

The tick of the clock seemed louder than ever, something he had never noticed before. The noise and bustle of the servants bringing in and taking away the succession of dishes irked and irritated him as it had never done before. When he could bear it no longer he went into the library and shut the door, then sat down heavily in one of the great wing chairs, staring into the unlit fire, trying to retrace in his mind every detail of yesterday that he could remember. If only young Chifney had not injured his arm. If only he had not given the boy the ride. Eagle would still have won. The boy would still be alive. It was his fault, he was to blame.

Chifney. Inchcape. He trusted them as he would have trusted his own brother. Neither of them could have betrayed him, he felt certain of it.

But there had been one other who had known that Nat Street had been given the ride on Eagle, someone who would have had time to pass on the information to those that had a special interest in stopping him, or stopping Nat Street. But he was beyond reach.

PART V
July 1833

❋ 11 ❋

In the dusty heat of midsummer Anna traveled to Newmarket with Frederick Nubbles and Sam Loam, using the brougham she had inherited from her father. His coat of arms painted on the side caused heads to turn as they clattered at last into the crowded high street, the town being full to overflowing for the horse sales at Tattersall's Corner.

"Do you think it wise to attend the sale in person?" Nubbles said, as they lunched on cold beef and apple tart in the taproom of the inn where they'd gotten rooms for the night. "I ask for two reasons. The first is that it isn't usual for any lady to be seen round the selling ring, the second . . . well, your presence would be greatly talked about and remarked on; the shock of your father's will would still be a big talking point hereabouts, and if Mrs. Brodie got to hear about your visit . . ." he spread his hands wide.

"Oh? It isn't any of her business, is it?"

She felt Sam looking at her.

"No. But if you want to bid for any of your father's bloodstock and her agent recognized you, he might withdraw the horses from the sale." He had scarcely touched any of the food on his plate, Anna noticed, or his glass of wine. "After traveling all this way, it would be madness to jeopardize your chances of buying the bloodstock you want just for the sake of making your own bids instead of doing it by proxy."

"But I won't know what I want until I see it." He smiled; the little weasel's eyes twinkled. Only a woman would make such a remark.

"You have the lists already."

"They're just names on a piece of paper. I can't judge any animal from one line telling me who its sire and dam were and what color it is."

"But Mr. Loam here can. You said yourself there's no better judge of horseflesh than he is . . . look the animals over yourself before the sale begins and he can make the bids on your behalf. Nobody will ever be the wiser, until it's too late."

Sam looked up from his almost-empty plate. He wiped his lips on his napkin. "I'll do whatever Anna wants me to."

"I'll be there this afternoon and I'll do my own bidding. No offense, Sam."

"None taken."

"The bidding on Firestone will be fierce," Nubbles said, and she noticed how rarely it was that he used such extreme words. Fierce. Yes, the bidding would be fierce. "If you want him you'll have to be prepared to bid high. Or for the Brodies' agent to withdraw him from the sale if you happen to be recognized."

"You really think she'd do it, don't you? Just to spite me?"

"You also are a woman. You would know the answer to that far better than I would."

Among the swarms of top-hatted men that choked the precincts of the auction ring, the unprecedented appearance of any woman would have been regarded with stupefaction. But Anna's striking looks, which turned heads by the dozen, and her arrival in a brougham stamped with Edward Brodie's coat of arms, caused nothing less than a sensation. Scandalized onlookers stared at her from buildings, from the windows of carriages, from the crowded balcony over Tattersall's office. Word spread like wildfire that Brodie's bastard daughter had come into town and was brazenly rubbing elbows with gentry and aristocracy around the selling ring. When the sale began, at two o'clock, there was more interest and craning of necks to get a glimpse of her than there was interest in the horses for sale.

She took no notice. She glanced to neither left nor right except to speak to one or other of her companions, now and then. She stared straight ahead of her into the auction ring, as horse after horse was brought out and led round by a groom and paraded in front of the crowd. By looking at her, her face calm and almost expressionless under her wide-brimmed satin bonnet, no one would ever guess that inwardly she seethed with rage. How dare they turn and stare, whispering behind their hands. How dare they judge her.

"This one you'll fancy." It was Sam Loam, whispering in her ear. "A Sultan colt, two years old, not even come to hand. And out of a fast half-sister to Turquoise. She walked the Oaks in '28, remember? See the interest in him around the ring." She watched him, her blue eyes narrowed, while his groom paraded him round and round. Slowly, she shook her head.

"He's good to look at, yes. But I wouldn't touch him with a barge pole. Turquoise was by Selim and so was Sultan; that makes this colt double inbred by any standard. Too much concentration of blood, Sam."

"You know what you're looking for," he said, as the hammer came down and Tattersall closed the bidding at nine hundred guineas.

"Yes, Firestone. But they'll bring him out at the end, with the other six-year-olds. You'll see."

"A bay filly, three years old," Tattersall's voice rang out above the top-hatted heads of the crowd, "winner of the Newmarket Town Plate and three King's Cups, by Cadland, out of Arab. Her sire, the 1828 Derby and

Two Thousand Guineas winner, her dam winner of the One Thousand Guineas in the same year. Gentlemen, the bidding will start at three hundred guineas."

All around the bidding was fierce. It was as she glanced up and looked across the ring at the crowd along the other side that she suddenly caught sight of Ralph Russell, and their eyes met and held across the back of the Cadland filly in a long, unsmiling look. It was then that she saw he was not alone. Beside him, his hands resting lightly on the ring rail, stood Jacob Hindley and another man whose face she did not know.

"One thousand and fifty guineas once," called Tattersall above the heads of the crowd, "one thousand and fifty guineas twice. One thousand and fifty guineas three times." He banged down his hammer. "Sold to Mr. Hindley of Epsom for one thousand and fifty guineas." The groom led the filly away and another came in, and as it did so Hindley turned from his companion and glanced across the space of the ring. When he caught sight of Anna his smile faded. She could see the small, flinty eyes, bright with hostility, and the red, ugly flush that stained the skin of his bull neck and thick-jowled cheeks. But the young man beside him had also seen her, and he was smiling toward her, ogling her, almost. As she looked back at him, wondering who he was, he slowly and deliberately removed his top hat and bowed in her direction. Hindley scowled.

"Who's that with Hindley, Sam?"

"Lionel Tollemache . . . he comes from around these parts. But I've seen 'im at big meetings at Ascot and Epsom often enough. The family's got connections at court, so they say."

"He's a gambler, then?"

"If 'e is then I don't know where 'e keeps getting 'is brass from. Like I said, the family's well-to-do, but 'is old man won't throw any of it 'is way . . . goes through 'is fingers like water, so I've bin told."

"Oh?"

"Not a racing family, the Tollemaches. More your landed gentry, into prize cattle and new breeds of sheep. There's an older brother, apple of the old man's eye; and a younger one, got sent down from Oxford for something or other." He glanced over his shoulder and lowered his voice further still. "Reckons 'is only chance of gettin' 'is 'ands on any real brass is to marry for it."

"Then he's wasting his time with me!"

"Now, you can't blame 'im for looking . . . and they do reckon Lionel's one for the ladies, so I've 'eard . . ."

"Then what's he doing in Hindley's company?"

"What the likes of 'im does with any of that set. Lives off 'em."

Tollemache was still watching her. Ignoring him completely, Anna turned her eyes now toward the entrance of the auction ring where a groom was about to lead in another horse; and all at once her pulses began to race, her heart began to hammer wildly just as it had that day more than three long years ago when as a girl of fifteen she'd first set eyes on Priam in the inn yard at Epping and wanted him more than she had ever wanted anything in her life. Between the thin, pale girl with tangled hair and shabby clothes and the poised, striking young woman in the finest garb that money could buy was an unrecognizable gulf; but the ambition that had been born in her then had remained the same raging fire that poverty, misery, and hopelessness had never managed to put out. This was a horse that she had to have, no matter what.

"A black filly, two years old," shouted Tattersall, "by Glenartney out of Dragonfly, by Dr. Syntax. Unraced as yet, but has plenty of time to come to hand. A fine-shaped, strong filly. Gentlemen, the bidding starts at thirty guineas."

"Fifty guineas!" said Anna in her strong, clear voice. The crowd about her rumbled, heads turned her way. There were gasps. Whispers. Without looking back across the auction ring she could feel the searching eyes of Russell, Tollemache, and Hindley. But she kept her own fixed steadfastly on the black filly.

"Fifty guineas I'm bid," Tattersall looked to his left and then his right, concealing his astonishment that a woman should not only be among the crowd of men, but also bid with them. "Fifty guineas for this daughter of Glenartney. Fifty guineas, gentlemen. Do I hear fifty-five? Fifty-five guineas?" A voice from somewhere at the back of the crowd called fifty-five.

"Seventy-five guineas," said Anna.

"It's your brass," whispered Sam in her ear, "but I wouldn't touch that nag with a barge pole."

"She's the best lot, colt or filly, that we've seen yet!"

"You don't pick a horse and pay good brass for it just 'cos you fancy the color of its coat. It's the breeding that counts."

"Glenartney as good as won the Derby in '27 . . . if his jockey hadn't been bribed to pull him and backed Mameluke to win, he'd have been first past the post and you know it."

"Ay, but he's done done nothing yet to prove that he'll amount to anything as a sire . . . and the filly's dam, Dragonfly, was never raced in her life. Keep your brass in your pocket, Anna, and save it for something better."

"Seventy-five guineas I'm bid. Seventy-five guineas for the Glenartney filly."

"One hundred guineas!" called Jacob Hindley from the other side of the ring. His small, light eyes, full of malice, rested on Anna's face for a moment, a barely concealed grin played at the corners of his mouth.

"One hundred and fifty!"

"Two hundred guineas!"

"Two hundred and fifty!"

"Three hundred guineas!"

"Four hundred guineas!"

"He's doing it on purpose!" Sam grasped her arm so tightly that it hurt. "Anna, don't bid any more. Hindley's got no more intention of buying that nag than I 'ave! 'E's waiting for you to overreach yourself so you have to pay through the nose for the bloody horse!"

Almost angrily, she turned to him.

"And what am I supposed to do about it except keep bidding if I want the filly?"

"Raise your bids in tens, not hundreds!"

"Five hundred guineas!" called Hindley from the other side of the auction ring.

"Bid five 'undred and ten guineas," whispered Sam.

But Anna paid no attention. An idea had suddenly come to her. "Wait, Sam, I'll call his bluff." She made no bid.

"Five hundred guineas I'm bid," shouted Tattersall. "Five hundred guineas for the Glenartney filly. Do I hear an increase on Mr. Hindley's bid?" Anna remained motionless. "Do I hear an increase on five hundred guineas?" There was a pause, while Tattersall looked over the heads of the crowd. Utter silence. "Five hundred guineas once. Five hundred guineas twice . . ." Anna glanced at Hindley, and he was no longer smiling. The scarlet flush had stained the coarse skin of his neck and face, his forehead glistened with sweat.

"Five hundred guineas three ti—"

"Six hundred guineas!" said Anna, her eyes still on Hindley's panic-stricken face.

"You scared the guts out of 'im . . . and serve 'im right!" laughed Sam against her ear. "My, you ran that one close as a barber's blade!"

"Six hundred guineas I'm bid," went on Tattersall. "Six hundred guineas for the Glenartney filly. Six hundred guineas, gentlemen!" He looked around and over the top-hatted heads of the crowd, but there were no takers. "Six hundred guineas once. Six hundred guineas twice. Six hundred guineas three times. Sold, to the lady, for six hundred guineas." Excited as a child, Anna turned to her companions.

"She's mine, Sam. She's all mine."

Nubbles was smiling, but said nothing.

Sam said, "Like I said, it's your brass."

"And what exactly does that mean?"

"You must 'ave noticed that Hindley was the only one from this lot to oppose you in the bidding . . . and he only did it to make you pay three times over what the filly was worth. 'E didn't want the nag."

"So? If this bunch of fools don't know a bargain when they see it, that's their loss."

"This bunch of fools comes from the four corners of England and 'ave as likely seen more auctions than you've 'ad 'ot dinners; they know a piece of class 'orseflesh when they see it."

"Sam, this time next year you'll be eating your words."

"For your sake I 'ope I am!"

Anna turned back to the auction ring, suddenly, as the next lot number was announced.

"A fine brood mare by Prince Leopold out of Filligree, five years old with foal at foot by Turcoman, from the estate of the late Mr. Edward Brodie at Mildenhall . . ."

"This is it, Sam."

"Ay, so it is. And there's Mrs. Brodie's agent next to Tattersall, looking your way." Sam nodded toward the far end of the ring. "If you make any bidding I'll lay you two to one that he'll withdraw the lot."

Anna followed his eyes. There, standing a few feet away from Tattersall's dais, stood a small, thin man whose face she vaguely recognized, and with him another whose face she knew instantly.

"He was there, that day when the will was read. The one with him is my half-brother. Damnation." She saw her high hopes of buying Firestone, the Prince Leopold mare, the pick of Edward Brodie's bloodstock, dashed into the ground. "Wait. I'll call their bluff and bid."

"Two hundred guineas I'm bid," said Tattersall. "Do I hear an advance on two hundred guineas, gentlemen?"

"Two hundred and fifty!" shouted a voice from the side of the ring.

"Two hundred and fifty-five!"

"Two hundred and eighty guineas!"

"Three hundred."

"Three hundred and forty guineas."

"Three hundred and seventy-five guineas!"

"Three hundred and seventy-five guineas, gentlemen, for this fine mare bred by Mr. Brodie. Sired by a royal Derby winner, out of a champion mare. Her foal at foot by Turcoman, winner of the 1827 Two Thousand Guineas . . ."

"Four hundred guineas," said Anna, into the rising noise around the ring. Without looking at them, she could feel the eyes of Lilly Brodie's agent and her half-brother turned hostilely her way. Then the agent leaned toward Tattersall and whispered something in his ear.

"Gentlemen, may I have your attention, please." He looked down and made a signal to the groom. "The Prince Leopold mare with foal at foot has been withdrawn from the sale."

There were rumblings among the crowd. Exclamations of surprise and anger around the ring. The groom, slightly bemused, led the mare and foal away and for several moments no other animal was brought into the sale ring.

"That bitch!" said Anna, between clenched teeth. All the joy of buying the Glenartney filly was momentarily swamped by her bitter disappointment. She had imagined herself, at the end of the sale, leading away the pick of her father's stock, the priceless Firestone. Now it was not to be. "Are they allowed to withdraw in the middle of legal bidding?"

"The nag's their property till the hammer comes down on the last bid."

"Nubbles?"

"Yes, I fear so." He glanced down the ring to where Lilly Brodie's agent and her son stood, watching Anna with suspicion. "Will you leave the sale or stay and watch the bidding?"

"What point is there in staying if I can't bid?"

"One. You could wait and see who does. Then approach the new owner after the sale with a substantially higher offer than the price he paid for the animal. It might work."

"Not for Firestone it won't. I came here especially to buy him and so did three quarters of the other bidders. Do you think whoever gets their hands on a horse like that is going to hand him over to me at any price?"

"You can but try."

"I'll stay," Sam Loam said. "You go back to the inn with the filly when you've settled with Tattersall's clerk for 'er, and get 'er stabled for the night. It'll be an early start tomorrow. I'll keep me eyes and ears open and send word when the bidding for the Brodies' stock is over. You never know . . . there might be something else worth bidding for."

Dejectedly, Anna turned away and walked back through the crowd with Nubbles, men standing aside for her and removing their hats as she passed. "We'll settle for the filly and then get a groom to walk her back to the inn yard."

"Just as you wish."

"I'm not a bad loser; don't think that. It only galls me to lose something when the odds don't start fair and square." She thought of Lilly Brodie, back at her father's house in Ipswich, contented and smug. "Why should she care whose brass it is that buys the nag?"

"I did warn you, before we set out, what the consequences of Mrs. Brodie's grievance against you might be."

"Yes, you did warn me. But I didn't think she'd be so petty-minded." She stopped, abruptly, as a small group of men blocked her path. As they turned around suddenly she recognized them. Gilbert Heathcote, from Durdans; Edward Randyll, from Chilworth Manor. Hindley. And Lionel Tollemache. All four removed their hats at once.

"Why, Miss Brodie," said Tollemache, without waiting for the formal courtesy of an introduction, "I am honored to make your acquaintance." His impudent light eyes moved quickly over her face. "Lionel Tollemache, very much at your service."

Her response was cold and brief, almost to the point of snubbing him. "Goodbye, Mr. Tollemache." She nodded toward the other three.

"If his head grew any bigger he'd need two necks to carry it," she said as soon as they were out of earshot.

"As far as ladies are concerned I believe he thinks it has good reason to be."

"Yes, Sam already told me. But I'm one lady who isn't impressed."

"It would seem you are in a minority, then. I have heard that Mr. Tollemache is very partial to the ladies . . . and that society hostesses never fail to put his presence at the top of their guest lists."

"He wouldn't be on mine if he was wearing a halo. I wouldn't trust any friend of Hindley's further than I could throw Epsom grandstand."

When they had paid for the Glenartney filly Anna walked round to the stalls and had a groom bring her out.

"Walk her round for me . . . up and down." She stood watching for a moment. "Now hold her still." She bent down and ran expert hands over the filly's withers, flanks, legs. "She's money well spent all right. I can't find a fault in her."

She opened her reticule and took out a sovereign. "Here. Take her round to the stables at the inn and see that she's taken care of. And mind they give her a bed of good, clean straw."

"Ay, ma'am, that I will right away, ma'am." His eyes shone and his grubby fingers closed like a trap over the coin. "Thank you kindly, ma'am."

As they turned to go Anna caught sight of Sam Loam, edging his way through the crowd. He reached them, out of breath.

"What is it, Sam? Has she gone and withdrawn the whole lot?"

"Firestone's just been knocked down for three thousand guineas! It was pandemonium in there. Every buyer from York to Exeter was after getting the nag!"

She shaded her eyes from the late, strong afternoon sun and stared at him.

"Who got him?"

"Ralph Russell."

"What the devil are you laughing at?"

"Your face. When Brodie's bastard called your bluff over the black filly."

"That jumped-up bitch! One day I'll teach her a lesson she won't be likely to forget!" Hindley's lantern-jawed face turned a deep, ugly crimson. He stood, his back toward Lionel Tollemache, staring from the tiny inn window. "Brodie must have been off his head when he left that bastard all his brass!"

"But he left it to her, nonetheless." Tollemache lay back in his chair, a glass of claret in his hand. Every now and again he took a sip of it. "You don't like her, do you?"

"*Nouveau riche.* She's got no right to all that brass. It's too much for any woman to handle. And she could do a lot of damage with it!"

"Like buy and sell you seven times over!"

"She's not entitled! She wasn't born to it!"

"She's better born than Brodie's sons are. Brodie's widow is common farm stock, a bailiff's daughter . . . his mistress was gentry."

"Mistress! Whore, more like!"

"By all accounts she was nothing of the kind. A real lady, so I've heard. Lived all those years like a pauper rather than let him know she was desperate for money. Never made any claim on him, either. She could have done, got herself and her girls set up, and exposed him at the same time. You couldn't have blamed her for it."

"She had her reasons, doubtless!" Hindley's voice was bitter. He came across to where Tollemache sat and poured himself a glass of claret.

"Don't you ever give any woman the benefit of the doubt?"

"Where women are concerned there's always doubt. They're all bitches. Scheming bitches all of them." He drained the glass in one swig and put it down, angrily. "And Brodie's bastard is the biggest bitch of all. She outbid me over the Old Brew House estate, she thinks she can stand equal with men and breed and race horses on the course at Epsom. Well, they'll never let her. Women on the turf! It'll never happen."

"Are you sure about that?"

"There's not an owner within thirty miles of Epsom or Newmarket that'll stomach a woman running horses against theirs. It's not heard of."

"If there's no ruling against women in the Jockey Club rules then you can't stop her."

"If there isn't any ruling then they'll make one."

"But there isn't one now?"

"How the hell do I know? I didn't write the rules! If there isn't a rule stopping women it's because nobody ever considered that one was needed. No woman would ever think of competing with men on the turf!"

Tollemache settled himself more comfortably in his chair. He lit a cigar, slowly. "I hear you had bad losses on your filly Phoebe in the Queen Adelaide Stakes two months ago."

"I stood them."

"A bad business . . . about Russell's apprentice. Foolish of Russell, don't you think, to have put him up on the favorite. Too much responsibility for a lad that's more used to sweeping out stables than riding in big races."

"You try and tell that to Russell."

"I s'ppose the pressure made the boy go off his head . . . and do what he did to himself. But there's some talk of foul play . . ."

Hindley rounded on him, his face and neck scarlet.

"By who? Russell himself saw the body swinging. And that Brodie bitch. The boy hanged himself, no question about it!"

Tollemache shrugged.

"There was some talk that Tobias Slout might have had something to do with it. You've heard of Slout, the bookmaker?"

"I've heard of him, yes. His name is common knowledge around Epsom. But I've never had any bets with him . . . nor would anyone who called himself a gentleman!"

"Of course." Tollemache leaned across to the little table beside his chair and refilled his empty glass with the rich, dark claret. "By the way, I must introduce you to my younger brother . . ."

Some of the angry flush had gone from Hindley's neck and face. His eyes held interest.

"Yes, I should like that. A good-looking boy, from all I've heard."

"Would that his behavior matched his face!"

"Oh?"

"He was sent down . . . from Oxford. Father was not amused when he heard."

"Young men have high spirits. I should have thought that was to be encouraged rather than dampened down."

"My father was never famed for either his generosity or his understanding . . . as we've both discovered to our cost." He drew slowly on his cigar, sending a thin column of smoke into the air. "Now, if I could be sure of a good, long-priced winner at the next Epsom meeting . . ." he smiled, calculatingly, "I daresay I could scrape up some brass to put on it . . ."

At last Hindley sat down.

"I think I might be in a position to put a good tip your way."

It was dusk when the three of them arrived back at the high street inn after the close of the sales at Tattersall's Corner. Nubbles and Sam Loam went straight into the taproom to order supper, Anna walked round to the stables to look over her purchase. To her dismay, in the stall next to the filly's was Firestone, eating oats from his manager.

She went outside and found a groom.

"Is Lord Russell putting up at the inn?"

"Why, no, ma'am . . . 'is lordship left Newmarket, straight after the sales."

"Then why is the horse he bought there tied up in your stables?"

"The big light bay with the blaze and one white pastern? 'Is lordship brought it by this afternoon, on 'is way out . . . said it was being left 'ere for a Miss Brodie."

"I am Anna Brodie."

"Then 'e must of meant you, then, ma'am." Fumbling inside his jerkin, he brought out a sealed letter and handed it to her. "'Is lordship left this, miss. Reckon it's yourn."

She took it from him, stunned, in a daze. Yes, it bore her name upon the outside, in a firm, clear hand. She tore it open.

There was no letter, only a bill of sale. And where the words *Sold to Ralph, Viscount Russell, for the sum of three thousand guineas* had been written, his name had been crossed out. In its place, he had written *Anna Brodie.*

At the foot of the bill the words *By rights he is yours, anyway.*

✳ 12 ✳

Anna stood at the open window of the library watching the shadows grow longer upon the freshly cut lawn.

She turned away and looked back into the room, only half-finished. Crates of books lay upon the floor unopened. Her desk, set in the recess of another window, was laden with papers and packages, waiting for her attention. She passed by them on her way to the kitchen, feeling guilty that there was still so much to do and since she had come back from Newmarket she had scarcely done anything at all. But they would have to wait.

"You gone and unpacked them boxes, then?" Jessie said as she walked in, glancing up from making an apple pie.

"No, I haven't done anything." Broodingly, she sat down, cheeks cradled in hands. "It's no good. I can't keep that horse in my stable any longer. I'll get one of the grooms to take it back to him."

"But 'e ain't there . . . isn't that what Mr. Nubbles told you?"

"He left Newmarket and went on somewhere or other. Nobody seems to know where." She began to bite her nails, something she often did in moments of stress. "But that won't stop me from returning the horse."

"Then you want your 'ead examining. If 'e wants to spend three thousand guineas on some nag and then 'and it over to you, that's 'is business. You keep the brute if you got any sense . . . which sometimes I doubt!"

"You don't understand, Jessie. I can't take anything from Ralph Russell."

"Why not? Because 'e's a man? They're not all tarred with the same brush . . . and you bear that in mind, me girl."

"There are other reasons why I can't." Agitatedly, she got up and went to stand by the stove. She took one of Jessie's wooden spoons and began to stir the contents of the cooking pot, as if she could not bear to be idle. "I won't take presents from any man, least of all him."

"You read 'is note. 'E reckoned the 'orse was yours by rights . . . it belonged to your father, God rot 'im."

"It still puts me under an obligation."

"All right then, if you want to be stubborn . . . wait till 'e comes back and then offer to give 'im what 'e paid for it."

"He wouldn't take the money."

"That'd be up to 'im, then, wouldn't it?"

"Even if he did, I'd still be under an obligation. If it hadn't been for Russell bidding for Firestone in the first place, he wouldn't be in my stable now." She dropped the spoon in the pot and began to pace the flagstones, clenching and unclenching her fists. "I have no way of knowing if he bid for the horse just to get him for me. And that he let the bidding go so high because he was determined to get him at all costs. I don't want him to do me any favors. But he must have known that I went to Newmarket specifically to try to get Firestone, and that I couldn't bid because of that bitch Lilly Brodie's agent being there, and the son, who recognized me."

"Much good it did 'em," Jessie said. She trimmed the pastry round the pie dish and pushed it into the stove to cook. "Now you listen to me a minute. You got what you went up there for . . . no matter 'ow you got it, you got it. And don't folk say the ends justifies the means? Well. You offer 'im the money when 'e comes back from wherever it is 'e's gone to, and get that Mr. Nubbles to make 'im take it. That way you'll feel better about it and you won't owe 'im nothing."

"He still did me a favor."

"Oh, for mercy's sake! You never asked and 'e never offered. You got the nag, and when 'e comes back to Epsom 'e'll 'ave 'is three thousand guineas . . . and nobody owes anything to the other."

Anna left the house and walked through the gardens, peaceful in the gathering evening after the heat of the day. She wanted to think. She wanted to be alone. She went to the stables and saddled Firestone.

He was a superb animal, faultless in make and shape, just as she would have expected any full-brother of the Derby winner Priam to be, different only in color and markings. His true potential had never been realized; he had beaten all the best horses of his day but missed the classics because three times he had gone lame; only her father's death and the automatic cancellation of his racing engagements had prevented him from a sparkling career as a five-year-old; for thirteen months he had not been in a race. The sheer waste appalled her, the unrealized potential. His name would not go down in the annals of the Derby; history would never remember him. If his name was to be salvaged from utter anonymity it would have to be as the spectacular victor of every race left to a six-year-old, and as the sire of champions. She had no doubt in her mind that he could do it, because he belonged to her now, not her father. And where her father had failed she would succeed.

She led him through the sweet-smelling garden and beyond it to the orchard. At the far end, on the other side of the high yew hedge, lay the acres she had bought, rising steeply to the line of trees in the distance. She mounted him and set him off at a steady canter until they had reached more even ground. Then she urged him into a fast gallop.

No horse she had ever sat on had given her a more beautiful ride. And his speed took her breath away.

"I'm entering him for the King's Cup two weeks on Saturday. I decided last night, after I'd ridden him. He hasn't been raced for over a year . . . but my father's training groom must have kept him in peak fitness right up until the moment of the sale. He'll fly it, Sam."

"Not if the Jockey Club don't accept your entry, he won't."

"What the hell do you mean? Why shouldn't they accept it?"

"Anna, we've been through all this before. You're treading on hallowed ground, where only men tread. You're an outsider. You're a woman. One or the other alone would be enough to keep the gates shut to you; together they're a mountain you can't hope to climb."

"You're a miserable pessimist, Sam."

"I'm just calling a spade a spade. I know that coterie, inside out. If you're not one of them, they don't want to know you, and they'll move heaven and earth to stop you getting so much as the toe of your boot inside their door."

"You mean that they're afraid to let anyone outside their narrow little circle come in, just in case their horses happen to be better than theirs are?"

"In a lot of cases, yes."

"Oh, for God's sake!"

"You won't listen. You just won't get it through that stubborn head of yours, will you? Not until it 'its you in the face. Do you 'ave any idea of the uproar you'll cause when you enter that colt for a race under your own name? It's never been done."

"Then it's time it was." His dogged attitude irked her, irritated her. "I won't let them dictate to me. I won't stand by and see everything I've worked for and sweated for trampled in the dirt, just because some insignificant little clique of men want to play at being God. That colt runs in the King's Cup whether they like it or not."

"You 'aven't listened to a word I've said. If they want to stop you coming onto the turf, all they 'ave to do is pass a resolution—if one doesn't exisit already—barring all animals entered by a woman. And if you enter the nag under a *nom de plume,* making out you're a man, they 'ave their ways and means of finding out . . . they'll make it their business to stop any professional jockey from taking your rides . . . they'll squeeze you out by one means if they can't do it by another."

"Racing's supposed to be a sport, Sam. Open to all. Not a petty vendetta launched by one party against another."

"You're telling me. It's *supposed* to be, like a lot of other things in this world. But it ain't."

"So what do you expect me to do, Sam? Go back home and spend the rest of my life in a rocking chair, embroidering altar cloths for charity?"

For the first time he laughed. Tears came into his eyes.

"You couldn't do it if you tried to."

"And Firestone runs in the King's Cup."

"If you can find a jockey that'll risk defying the Jockey Club when they come out against you, he'll run. But I wouldn't count on it."

"No? I've already got somebody in mind." The same sly, mischievous look she'd had when he'd come down that morning and found her on the back of his Selim colt came into her eyes now. "And I think I can persuade him to take the ride. You just be there, Sam, on King's Cup day. You'll see my colt leave the rest of the field behind and me rub the Jockey Club's noses in their own dirt."

He watched her ride away, disappearing beyond the trees up ahead. And he never doubted her.

Jeremiah Chifney dismounted and led Lord Russell's colt in from the bright sunlight outside to the cool and dimness of the rubbing house, then unbuckled his girths while a lad held his head. He was sweating a little along his flanks and neck. Chifney put down the saddle, sent the boy off to bring in a halter and a light rug, while he stood with a handful of straw, wisping the animal down.

The report on the fast gallop that he'd taken half an hour before in the company of some very smart animals—one of whom had twice beaten last year's Two Thousand Guineas winner, Archibald—and which he'd give his new patron when he came back to Epsom, would be both good and bad . . . but completely honest. He would say in the forthright manner that had helped him get the valuable retainer in the first place that although he'd rarely ridden a colt with such acceleration and speed, he'd not stay a yard beyond a mile.

"You can give him just a drop of water," he said to the lad as he heard the sound of footsteps behind him. He was intent on what he was doing and did not turn round. "But not a bloody bucketful, mind. And not ice cold, either."

"If I were you I'd give him a bottle of port in his bucket," said a stranger's voice, "or better still, brandy."

Chifney spun round. His mouth fell open with surprise. There, in the doorway, stood a young woman in a black grosgrain riding habit, with startling blue eyes, the most beautiful girl Chifney had ever seen in his life. For a moment he was rendered speechless.

"My name is Anna Brodie," she said, when he made no answer. "You may have heard of me."

Heard of her! When the whole of Epsom from the lowest groom to the highest members of the gentry and aristocracy had talked of nothing else since the sensational news of Edward Brodie's will had become common knowledge more than two months' ago. At last, he managed to find his tongue.

"Yes, Miss Brodie . . . I have heard of you. And I'm honored to make your acquaintance." He could not offer her his hand; he was not her social equal. He wore no riding cap; therefore he could not remove it as a mark of respect. Not knowing quite what he should do or what on earth she could possibly want here, in a rubbing house strewn with straw and horse droppings, he just stood there, awkwardly, feeling more foolish than he looked.

"I'm afraid Lord Russell is away from Epsom. When he left the New-market sales he went on to wherever it is that he has some business or other. He could be away for days yet; even weeks."

"I didn't come here to see Russell, I came to see you."

"Me? I'm Jeremiah Chifney, his lordship's jockey."

"Are you the same Chifney that rode Electress in the Queen's Cup at Newmarket, who beat Galata by a short head at Egham on a colt that everyone said couldn't stay beyond a mile and a quarter, and who got Sorcery first past the post in the strongest Princess Royal Stakes field for thirteen years?"

"Yes."

"Then you're the same Chifney I want."

"I'm sorry, I don't understand."

"It's very simple, Mr. Chifney. And I'm a blunt speaker so I'll come directly to the point. I've got the fastest six-year-old you'll ever sit on entered for the King's Cup two weeks from Saturday. I want you to ride him."

"I . . . I couldn't do that."

"Oh? Why not?"

"I'm under retainer to Lord Russell."

"Russell isn't here and he doesn't have a horse entered in the race, anyway. That makes you free to take on any other rides you choose to. That wouldn't be construed as disloyal, would it?"

"No, of course not."

"You don't like the idea of riding for a woman?"

"No," he said at once, in a firm voice that matched the honesty in his eyes. "No, that isn't true. The fact is, an aquaintance of his lordship's has asked me to ride his horse in the King's Cup . . . and I haven't yet had time to send him an answer. But he did imply that since he was a friend of Lord Russell's, he should have first claim on my services in his lordship's absence."

Her sharp ears detected a note of resentment.

"And who is this friend of Russell's?"

"Mr. Hindley, miss."

"Ah. You don't surprise me." She smiled, a little wickedly. "Mr. Hindley has a habit of expecting to get his own way. Well, the decision is yours. You can ride his horse or mine. But you'll only win on one of them." She turned to leave. "Let me know what you've decided by this time tomorrow."

He took a few steps toward her.

"There are plenty of other good jockeys you could have asked, who would give anything for the chance to ride your horse. Can I ask you why you want me?"

"Because you're honest, Chifney. And I can count on the fingers of one hand the number of jockeys that have never taken a pull or a bribe in their lives. And you're brilliant, as well. Brilliance and honesty . . . how many jockeys could I find that match up to that?"

"You flatter me."

"I told you, I'm a blunt speaker."

He was totally unused to being in the society of women. Especially ladies of quality. More especially any as striking as this one. Already he was remembering all the countless stories he had heard about her: secondhand, thirdhand, on the stable grapevine. Never had he expected to meet her, to have her walk casually into his life, and to make him an offer that only a fool would ever refuse. She was fondling the chestnut colt's ears now, and patting its neck, oblivious to dirt and the soiled straw that had already ruined the hem of her gown.

"With these markings he must be one of Selim's stock," she said, looking him over, nodding when Chifney told her she was right. "Yes, Russell always had a passion for Selim's stock . . . the first colt I ever broke to saddle for Sam Loam was one of his. Myself, I never rated them as true stayers. Does this one?"

"Not a yard over a mile. Under that, I'd say he was well-nigh unbeatable."

"Then when Russell comes back you can tell him to enter it for next year's Guineas. Has it got a name?"

"Not yet, miss."

She glanced over the bright, glossy coat, at the vivid markings that reached from the middle of his tendons right down to the top of his hooves.

"Tell him to call it White Stockings," she said. And laughed.

A few miles away across the Downs Tobias Slout strolled musingly in the grounds of his house, one of his paid cronies by his side. In his younger days One-eyed Bill had been an unsuccessful pugilist, and then, later, an arranger of crooked contests, until he by chance made the acquaintance of Slout and quickly discovered that there was more profit to be made in running horses than in prizefighters. He was a useful acolyte. By reason of his intimidating size and hideous, pockmarked face, he was the perfect righthand man: One threatening word in the ear of a terrified stableboy was always enough to get a bucketful of cold water administered to a hot favorite before a race, and where that was impossible—which wasn't often—there was always somebody frightened enough or greedy enough in the stable to take a bribe.

Slout was anything but satisfied with his spoils of the last few months. After nearly a year of scheming to insure that that year's Derby would be won by a hundred-to-one outsider, Mr. Sadler's colt, Dangerous—lame both before and after the race—had forgotten its affliction while running and stormed home to win at thirty to one, leaving Slout to recover enormous losses, not half of which he had managed to make up. His one big chance to reverse his fortunes had not long after presented itself when Ralph Russell's new stable jockey, a nephew of the Newmarket Chifney brothers, had injured his arm and his lordship had put young Nat Street up on his colt instead . . . the aftermath of that plan he didn't even want to think about, except for the hole that it had made in his pocket, even deeper than before. For the past two weeks, his mood had been black and his temper vile.

"No need to think twice on it, Gov'nor," One-eyed Bill said, kidding to him in a manner that had brought toadyism to a fine art. "We'll fix Coquetry in the Surrey Stakes, no question. I've 'ad me ear laid about for near two month or more . . . everyone's brass'll be on that filly." He made a pretense at laughing, showing a mouth of half-missing, half-rotted teeth. "That Edward Randyll's 'ad 'is training groom up on the Downs with 'er, these past three weeks . . . I bin watching, I 'ave . . . and she's a fast nag all right. Pity their wasting all that time and effort, ay, Gov'nor?" He scratched his unshaven chin with nails that were thickly embedded with dirt. "But I tell you this . . . it'll take more'n a bucketful of cold water in 'er guts to stop 'er beating Thrush, and that's the truth of it."

"I know that, I know that. Just do your usual scouting job, then come back later and I'll decide on what I want doing to stop 'er. You won't get a nose inside Randyll's yard, so the only way is to wait till I get me 'ands on the plans of the place from the usual source . . ."

"You can always count on 'im, ay, Gov'nor?"

"Nobody's placed better to get the inside information!" He chuckled, then paused while he took out his snuff box and inhaled a pinch. "If only them blue-blood swells 'ad an inkling . . ." the end of his words were swallowed up in a bout of crude laughter, which turned into coughing. When he got his breath back he let out a string of foul oaths. "Better find out if young Chifney's got a mount at the meeting, while we're about it. Russell's away and 'e won't be back till afterward, and 'e ain't got nothing entered for any of the races that day, so far as I know. At least Chifney's under retainer to Russell's yard, which means 'e won't be let loose to ride anyone else's 'orses. And that suits me. You'd never get 'im to take a pull, not for a cartload of gold bars."

"You 'eard anything on the grapevine about the bastard, Gov'nor? She's back from the sales with some black filly or other. That's what I 'eard at the ale'ouse in Epsom, night before last."

"That jumped-up bitch of Brodie's! What does she think she knows about 'orseflesh? A bloody woman trying to stick 'er nose in the turf!" He spat on the path. "They'll be trying to get into parliament next! And I thought I seen everything. But she'll disappear quicker than what she came, One-eye, you'll see. More brass than sense. Some rich man's bastard what thinks she's going to breed another Eclipse! Well, let 'er waste 'er brass on what she likes, so long as she don't get in my way."

"Local swells won't let 'er get 'er toe in, Gov'nor!"

"I give the girl a year. Eighteen month at most. She'll throw all 'er brass away on a string of useless beasts that wouldn't outrun a cart'orse if they 'ad gunpowder up their arses, marry some squire or lord what cares more about getting 'er in 'is bed than that she's Brodie's byblow, and that's the last we'll ever 'ear of 'er."

"You're right Gov'nor. You're always right."

"Now, back to the matter in 'and. Coquetry and the Surrey Stakes. You come inside with me and I'll cast an eye over me notes on the other runners."

"Just as you say, Gov'nor." The two men went into the house together, Slout's dogs running at their heels. They walked along a little paneled corridor until they reached the room that Slout used as a study, the room into which, two months before, Nat Street had been dragged, a prisoner. Neither of them so much as spared a thought for him now. Slout sat down behind his desk and One-eyed Bill drew up a chair and sat down beside him, but his interest in the plans of stables and other documents that Slout had taken out of one of the drawers was only a pretense; he could neither read nor write.

One-eyed Bill chewed on his filthy nails. Then he and Slout let out a simultaneous cry of surprise. Behind them, the concealed door in the paneling came open, and Jacob Hindley almost stumbled into the room from the dark passage behind him.

"That bastard bitch of Brodie's! That fool Russell bought her father's prize horse Firestone at Tattersall's Corner and made her a present of it, and she's gone and entered the nag for the King's Cup!" He pushed back the door, and ran a hand across his red, sweating face. "I've just come from a meeting of the stewards . . . the madmen are arguing that they can't stop her running the horse without a definite ruling against it from the Jockey Club in Newmarket!"

"But women are banned from going on the course . . ."

"She's already been on the course! Brodie bequeathed her all his property and that included his private box in the grandstand. Nobody can stop her having access to it, or to any other of the privileges members are granted. The bitch has got Henry Dorling and all the rest of them eating out of her hand! And that isn't all." The red, angry flush had already dyed his thick neck scarlet and was spreading to his face. "Since Russell's got nothing running at the King's Cup meeting, I asked his jockey Chifney to ride my horse in the big race. Just before I left, he came riding up to my front door himself, to tell me that he couldn't take the ride . . . he's promised to ride Firestone for the Brodie bastard!"

"Firestone!" Slout was out of his chair in an instant. "That bloody nag's a full-brother to Priam! 'E'd 'ave like as not won the Derby in '30 if 'e 'adn't gone lame on the gallops the morning before the race! With Chifney up, 'e'll walk the King's Cup!"

"'Struth, Gov'nor!"

"I stand to lose more than five thousand if that horse runs and wins," Hindley said, ignoring One-eyed Bill's outburst. "Chifney can't be bribed and Firestone can't be nobbled. You've got to think of some way to stop that bitch running him in that race, or I'll never make up those losses. I'm already in debt over wagers that I've had with Heathcote and Randyll; I can't afford to let go any more brass." He began to pace the room, agitatedly, mopping his face with a handkerchief. "I need one big win. And it's got to be at that Cup meeting."

"All right. All right." Slout made a sign with his hand and One-eyed Bill left the room. He poured two glasses of brandy. "Don't panic. There's ways and means of doing everything. It's a matter of finding the right one, that's all. Now, as I see it, you got the means in your own 'ands. You're a big local name, you're a member of the Jockey Club. What you say carries weight around 'ere. Just go back and tell the stewards that there's no precedent for a woman being allowed to enter a nag in any race under club rules, and that the whole matter will 'ave to be referred to Newmarket. That'll stop the bastard running Firestone, Chifney'll be free to ride your horse, and as soon as they get wind at Newmarket that Brodie's bastard is trying to get 'er foot in the door of their precious little clique, they'll shut it so fast she'll get 'er meddling little toes cut off!"

"Don't you think I've already done that? It was the first thing I said! Gilbert Heathcote and Randyll had the rest of them agreeing that although there was no precedent for a woman to enter a horse for a race under Jockey Club rules, there was no definite ruling against it, and that while they'd contact Newmarket for a proper ruling for or against, she should be allowed to run the horse in the King's Cup!" The hand holding the brandy glass shook with rage. "All the others agreed with me. John Walters and Colonel Anson told Heathcote that if Brodie's daughter was allowed to enter Firestone they'd withdraw their animals in protest. They can afford to make gestures like that! Neither of their colts could win the race if they were given two hundred yards' start!"

"Cheap talk, all right!"

"Ay. And you were wrong about the girl. She's no weak, empty-headed ninny playing at getting heads turned on the turf. She means business. And trouble for us."

"You've still got nearly two weeks. Go back to the stewards and make 'em consult with Newmarket over a woman being allowed to enter a nag for the King's Cup. If they shift their arses, you can get a decision against Brodie's bastard before the meeting starts."

"That's easier said than done. By the time the Jockey Club finds out and gets down to sitting around a table and discussing it, the race will be over and won. That scheming bitch!" He got up, his fists clenched in anger. "I'd give half my stable to be able to get my hands round her neck!"

"You give up too easy. So she runs the nag. So maybe she wins. As soon as them snotty-nosed swells at Newmarket get wind that a woman's trying to invade their pitch, all 'ell will be let loose. She'll be drummed out, you mark my words, and kept out. And you know the Jockey Club better than I do."

Hindley was silent for a moment; then he walked over to the concealed door in the paneling, at the back of the room.

"They'll drum the bitch out. I must go. We have guests in the house." He opened the door, and the little passage behind it loomed narrow and dark. "I'll get you those plans. And find out how Randyll intends to protect his yard." His mouth turned up at the corners, in a leer rather than a smile. "He's invited us to his prerace dinner on Friday night. That's when I shall pick his brains."

"Good 'unting," Slout said, as Hindley disappeared behind the door and it swung back into place. He went over to the fireplace and rang the bell, and One-eyed Bill came back into the room.

"Mr. 'Indley gone, then, Gov'nor?"

Slout sat down again.

"Yes . . . and 'e didn't 'ave very good news for us, Billy boy. Seems that Brodie bastard is getting too big for 'er boots. Got to be taught a little lesson . . . if you take my meaning?"

"What you want us to do, Mr. Slout?"

"Draw up that stool there, and we'll talk about it."

❋ 13 ❋

Hat in hand, Chifney strolled with Anna through the garden and orchard at the Old Brew House, his first awkwardness in her company swiftly subsiding as they talked. She did not talk down to him, as many in her position would have, rating him only a little higher in the social scale than a servant.

She did not patronize him. Her knowledge of horses astonished him and her plans left his head spinning. One thing was certain. She was no ordinary young woman. And he was more glad than anything in his life that he had turned down Jacob Hindley and had promised to ride her horse instead.

"What did you say to him?" A smile, a little wicked, played at the corners of her lips.

"I said that since I had been asked by a lady to take the ride on her horse, he as a gentleman would understand that I had to decline his offer."

She hooted with laughter.

"My God, you'll have made a bigger enemy of him than I have."

"He was hard-pressed to hide his anger, it's true. But he can find another jockey to take the ride."

"But it's you he wanted." She could picture the thick-jowled face, the ugly red flush that spread from the neck to the cheeks. The bloodshot eyes, the tight-lipped mouth. "It seems you can make more enemies by being honest than by being dishonest in this place."

"Perhaps that's true." He was thinking of himself, of how he had left his home in Newmarket and come south because his grandfather and his uncle had gotten themselves bad names for stopping horses, and if anyone ever bothered to distinguish between him and them it was to think that the nephew and the grandson of a Chifney must needs be dishonest too. He had fought a long hard battle to disprove this, and he looked like winning. He'd worked his way steadily and honestly to the top, or very near it, never straying from the straight and narrow path, whatever the temptations to do otherwise, and he reckoned he'd proved that whatever Old Sam Chifney had done in the past to blacken the family name, or whatever Young Sam was doing in the present—and that, by all accounts, was plenty—he was a Chifney who was different.

He had already explained why he had come to Epsom to her. And she had understood.

"Did you ever ride any of my uncle's horses? He'd often stable them at Lord Foley's, when his own yard was full."

"If ever I'd ridden Priam I'd never have forgotten it." A gleam came into her eyes; a warm, far-seeing look that he'd not noticed before. She turned to him. "You must have seen him many times at your uncle's stables, and working on the heath. Tell me about him."

"My uncles heard that there was a wonderfully fine colt by Emilius out of Cressida among a new batch of unbroken yearlings from Sir John Shelley's one day, that were taking their airings at the foot of Warren Hill. When they sauntered up to look them over, they were instantly struck by him, and swore to have him at any price . . . they got him for a thousand guineas. There was no room at either my uncle Will's stables, nor Sam's, so he stood for a few days at Sam Day's, where Sam's groom Martin Starling put him through his first paces."

"You were there?"

"It was the year before I left home, yes. They never ran him as a two-year-old, neither in public nor in private . . . but he took his first gallop with Flacrow, out there on the heath, and my uncle Will says that he never saw any young thing run so raw, or get beaten off so far. He was the most perfect blood horse I think I ever saw, without exception; he had a look about him, something special, as if he had been fashioned for great things. I never doubted that he'd win the Derby. The biggest mistake my uncle made was when he sold him to Lord Chesterfield, but he badly needed money and the Jockey Club had brought in their new ruling that stopped ordinary gentlemen from entering their horses in certain important races—like the Ascot Gold Cup—unless they were members of it themselves." He sighed. They had reached the big oak tree and sat down on the seat in front of it. "Maybe that was the only unselfish act my uncle ever did . . . releasing Priam so that he could run in the races he'd have been barred from had he kept him."

"I was fifteen when I first saw him. Outside the Cock Inn, in Epping high street. Our stagecoach had stopped there to change teams on the way to Epsom, and I caught sight of him with his groom at the water trough." A wistful note crept into her voice. "That's when I knew what I wanted to do. Breed and race blood horses."

"Did your father know what you wanted to do? Did you ever tell him?"

"He never knew anything about us at all."

For a moment Chifney fell silent. There was a hard, angry edge to her voice, and he shrewdly guessed that Edward Brodie was a subject that was painful to her. He had had no right to ask her, he could not intrude upon that part of her past. Instinctively, he sensed her bitterness and understood it. As instinctively, sensing his sudden awkwardness, Anna turned to him.

"It's all right. You don't have to feel sorry for me. My sister and I are his bastards and there's nothing I can do to change it. For myself, I curse every rotten drop of his blood that I have in me." Chifney stared down at his hands, not knowing how to answer her. "I suppose you've heard plenty of rumors about me, here in Epsom. And in Newmarket, too, I shouldn't wonder. That will he left set them all by the ears!"

"I never listen to gossip."

"Which means you've heard plenty." She laughed when he did not answer. "I've only myself to blame, haven't I? Not just him. I could have stayed what I was, what he made me. A nobody. Anonymous. Taken his money and gone away, abroad maybe, never to be heard of again. No more scandal, no gossip. They would have approved of that, wouldn't they? They could have lived with it. But instead I've moved right up into their territory, a woman who's dared to set foot on ground where only men are free to tread; a rich man's bastard who means to outbid, outbuy, and outrace all the holier-than-thou's in the big country houses and in the

Jockey Club. If they can't find any dirt to dig up and throw at me, they'll make some."

"What your father left you in his will and what you do with it is no business of anyone's. And you could never have been a nobody if you'd tried to." There was real feeling in his voice, a tone that almost startled her.

"Thank you for saying that," she said, simply. For a brief moment, she lay her hand on his arm, in a gesture of appreciation and friendship. She felt comfortable with Chifney. He was no threat to be kept at arm's length. From the moment she had met him she had felt the same trust, a gut feeling, that she had felt with Sam Loam, with Frederick Nubbles. He did not arouse strange emotions in her, like Ralph Russell. "Can I ask you how long you mean to stay with Ralph Russell, as his jockey?"

There was a pause before he answered, almost as if her familiarity with him had taken his breath away.

"The retainer is for one year."

"After that year would you consider riding for me instead?" He stared at her. "I know what you're thinking. That I might not even have a stable by then; that the Jockey Club will have banded together and stopped me from racing my horses. They won't. If they want a fight then I'll give them one. And whatever I have to do to outwit and outmaneuver them, I'll do it."

"They have only to declare a ban on women entering their own horses for races and there would be nothing you could do. They're despotic. They're all-powerful. And I should hate . . . I should hate to see anything happen to you . . ."

She smiled, and took his arm.

"I think I can take care of myself." Slowly, they began to walk back toward the house.

Much later, riding back, riding home, Chifney could still feel the touch of her hand on his wrist, almost as if she still held it there.

"You're senior steward. It's your duty to show an example. If you just sit idly by and let her run the horse, you'll be opening the floodgates for any riffraff who think they have a right to race with gentlemen!"

"But she isn't any riffraff. She's Brodie's daughter."

"His bastard. And she's a woman. Women have never been permitted to race with men in the past, and you should see to it that they never are in the future. Stop her. Refuse to allow her to race the animal in the King's Cup on the grounds that there is no official sanction from Newmarket. As soon as you send word to the Jockey Club there that she's trying to compete with men on equal terms, they'll squash her underfoot like a beetle." Hindley's voice shook slightly. He could not control his anger. "I consider it an outrage that you can even consider permitting her to be present on the course, let alone race with gentlemen as if she were their equal!"

"My dear Hindley, let's not turn this after-dinner discussion into an argument. I can scarcely stop her from making use of her own box in the private grandstand, when it was left to her by her father . . . and the only way she can reach it is by walking across the course."

"On the day the Queen Adelaide Stakes was run she spent no more than a quarter of an hour in the grandstand," said Colonel Anson, supporting Hindley's arguments. "She walked about the course and the Warren as bold as brass, as if she owned the place!"

"No lady careful of her reputation would have dared to be seen in public on a racecourse, mixing with the men!" said someone else.

Gilbert Heathcote bowed before the onslaught of hostility and opposition. For years he had held the position of senior steward on the course at Epsom; his ancestral home, Durdans, was adjacent to the raceground and had always been a center where the local racing gentry and aristocracy would gather, before important meetings, to discuss their horses and make wagers with one another on the outcome of the races. He had always been a mediator; fair-minded, disliking quarrels and friction of any kind. Although he had never known Edward Brodie well, he had nonetheless liked and respected him, and the revelations about his private life—which would have ruined him had they become public while he lived—then the sensational contents of his will, had shocked him as much as they had anyone. But the whole matter now of Anna Brodie made him prey to a conflict of feelings. He did not approve of ladies' being given the freedom of the course, and never would; everyone had their place and women had theirs. Nor did he think for one moment that the Jockey Club at Newmarket would ever give its consent to a woman's being involved with horses or racing in any way, competing as an equal with men. But he found it difficult not to admire the girl. Whatever else they said about Anna Brodie, no one could deny that she had guts.

But clearly he was in a minority. Ever since it had become common knowledge that she intended to breed and race her own horses the idea had been met with outrage from every quarter.

"A letter should be sent to her from the stewards," Colonel Anson said, amid a chorus of agreement, "stating that until a clear directive has been received from the Jockey Club on whether or not women might be permitted to enter a horse, she is forbidden to do so under pain of being warned off."

"Hear hear!" shouted Hindley, and most of the room with him.

"Of course your determination to stop her running the horse in the King's Cup has nothing whatever to do with the fact that you want her jockey freed to ride yours?" Everyone turned in surprise in the direction of the speaker. Lionel Tollemache lounged nonchalantly on the edge of a chair, smiling, a glass of port in his hand. He had not spoken a word since the arguing had begun, and since he and his half-brother were guests of the Hindleys, Heathcote was astonished at what he said.

Hindley's face flushed scarlet.

"That has nothing at all to do with it!"

Tollemache continued to smile.

"And the rest of you sporting gentlemen, naturally, only wish to stop her horse starting for the race because she's a woman . . . and not because you're all afraid that if it does run, your animals don't have a hope in hell of winning?"

"That isn't true!"

"I resent your implications!"

"And I."

"And me, too!"

"Then if you have nothing to fear, why not let the lady run her horse? Since you're all so confident that when the Jockey Club is asked to adjudicate the matter, they'll ban her anyway, it seems to me only an act of courtesy to permit her horse to run. What can be the harm in that?"

"I suspect that my brother's support for the lady is motivated more by his admiration of her physical attributes than by his principles," said James Tollemache, sarcastically. Hindley beamed at him.

"Only a person of unnatural inclinations would be likely to be unaware of them," Lionel Tollemache answered, with a sting in his voice that his brother recognized.

James scowled, and fell silent.

"Gentlemen, please." Heathcote held up his hands. "Can we not discuss this matter in a calm, civilized manner, as befits gentlemen? If we take a vote on the matter, informally, no doubt we shall find that the vast majority are against the lady's being permitted to start her horse for the race. Very well. But I bring one fact to your attention . . . we can scarcely talk of threatening to ban her from the course under pain of warning off. For one thing, to be warned off, she would have to have committed some serious offense, such as dishonesty or worse. This is not the case. For another, only the Jockey Club itself, as you all know," he glanced at Hindley, "can issue such an edict. In the circumstances I suggest that we accept her entry for the King's Cup, after asking the Jockey Club to make an official ruling on the matter of women owners. When they give us their ruling, then we can act upon it. To ban her before receiving their ruling would only look as if we were acting out of malice."

"I agree with that," said Edward Randyll, from his place near the window, but Hindley was furious.

"You would agree with it, Randyll; you have nothing to lose. You have no horse entered for the bloody King's Cup!"

"Gentlemen, please . . ."

". . . if the bi— if the Brodie girl was running Firestone in the Surrey Stakes, you'd soon change your tune!"

"She could hardly run him in the Surrey Stakes, a race for fillies."

"Don't get clever with me. You know damn well what I mean. If she was

running against you with a horse that would probably have won the Derby
if it hadn't gone lame the morning before, you'd have a different song to
sing!"

"You're only against her because you wanted Chifney to ride your horse,
and he chose to accept the mount on hers instead!"

"That's a bloody lie!"

"Hindley . . . Randyll, please! Gentlemen . . ."

Lionel Tollemache, at the back of the room, finished his port in silence,
then got up and left, unobtrusively. Outside in the vestibule he stood for a
moment looking around. Then he found his way to the drawing room and
took a cigar from one of the ornate boxes on the table. There was a portrait
of Lady Heathcote over the fireplace, and he went over and stood in front
of it, looking at it for several minutes. Then he rang the bell and a servant
appeared almost immediately.

"Give me a light for this, will you?" His manner toward underlings was
much like his manner toward women, genial and familiar. Puffing the
cigar, he strolled back outside and went into the gardens, where he sat for a
while on one of the wooden seats cloistered by a rose arbor.

"G'day, sir," said one of the gardeners in passing, touching his forelock.

"Good day." Tollemache stood up, exhaling a cloud of smoke from the
cigar. "Perhaps you can do something for me, while you're here." The man
stopped. "Cut me a large bunch of your best roses. The strongly scented
kind." He smiled. "And remove the thorns from the lower stems." The
man looked astonished.

"Yes, sir. Of course, sir. But I should mention that Lady 'Eathcote don't
usually 'ave the flowers cut for the 'ouse from this part of the garden."

Tollemache leaned forward and patted him on the shoulder. "I'm sure
that her ladyship won't miss a single bunch from among all these. And
particularly if we keep the matter between ourselves." He fished in his
pocket and brought out a guinea.

"Why, thank you kindly, Mr. Tollemache, sir." The man stared open-
mouthed at the coin, more money than he had ever had at one time in his
life. " 'Ave you got any preference for what color you'd like me to pick; or
don't it matter?"

He stroked his chin thoughtfully.

"Perhaps deep pink would be best. And when you've cut them, maybe
you'd have one of those grooms saddle me up a horse."

"Right away, Mr. Tollemache, sir."

Tollemache strolled back along the path he'd come, glancing up at the
windows of the house. Heathcote's wife and daughters would be somewhere upstairs, dressing for dinner. The room full of male guests that he
had left not long before was on the other side of the house, and the heated
exchanges over Anna Brodie would in all likelihood go on for some time.
He would not be missed until they sat down for dinner.

While he waited on the steps of the house for the groom, he finished Heathcote's cigar. Then he flung the stub upon the ground.

As Anna sat at her desk in the half-finished library, two of the dogs that Sam Loam had sent over as a present several days before sprang up and began to growl and bark. For a few minutes she ignored them and went on with what she was doing. Then she got up and went over to the window.

A strange horse was tethered some way from the house. Then she heard Ellen Troggle's voice, talking to Jessie in the hall. She opened the library door.

"Is that Chifney come back again?"

"No, miss. Another gentleman, real gentry by 'is clothes. I showed 'im into the drawing room."

"And who is he?"

"I forgot to ask 'is name, miss."

With a sigh of impatience Anna brushed past her and went into the room opposite, the dogs at her heels. She stopped abruptly in the open doorway.

"You!"

"Why, Miss Brodie," Tollemache said, in his most ingratiating manner, "I trust I haven't called at an inconvenient moment." He held out the bouquet of pink roses. "For you."

"You have called at an inconvenient moment. And I don't accept gifts from strangers." Beside her, sensing her hostility, the dogs began to growl, low and menacingly. Tollemache stepped back and looked at them uncertainly.

"They won't bite, will they?"

"Not unless I tell them to."

"Do you always make your visitors feel so welcome?"

"Visitors usually come because they've been invited. You are just an intruder."

"Please . . ." he glanced around him for a place to put down the bunch of roses. "I have to talk to you. In your own interests I would advise you to hear me out."

"I'm listening."

"I've just ridden over from Durdans, where the local racing fraternity are holding a meeting on whether you should be allowed to run your horse Firestone in the King's Cup next Saturday." He smiled, in a way that would have been irresistible to any woman but Anna. "Ah, I see that does interest you. I thought it would also interest you to know that Gilbert Heathcote and Edward Randyll disagree with the majority. They're on your side. As I am, of course . . . but then I hardly count. I'm neither a steward nor a member of the Jockey Club. Heathcote is both."

"What are you trying to tell me?"

"To be forewarned is to be forearmed, don't they say? From the way the argument is going, I should expect Heathcote to insist, as senior steward, that you be allowed to run your horse in the King's Cup pending official ruling on women owners from the Jockey Club."

"You're saying that all the others want to see me barred?"

"Almost to a man. I can see through them all, as a neutral observer. For one thing, they're afraid that if your horse is allowed to run, especially ridden by a jockey like Chifney, their horses stands no chance. After all, it's common knowledge that Firestone's a full-brother to Priam and that if he'd not gone lame before the Derby three years ago, he stood an odds-on chance of winning it. For another, none of them can stomach the idea of being beaten by a woman. Especially one of your . . . background."

Anna gave him a scathing glance.

"Why don't you come right out and say it? They resent me because I'm Edward Brodie's bastard and he left me almost everything. And money means power. Is that what they're afraid of?"

"You've already bought the Old Brew estate right from under the nose of one of them. And he isn't one to forgive or forget."

"Hindley! I might have guessed he'd be behind this!"

"You outbid him and humiliated him in one. Believe me, he'll move heaven and earth to stop you running that horse in that race."

"I outbid him fair and square. He couldn't raise the purchase price and I could. That was just his hard luck."

"I doubt if he saw it like that."

Anna began to pace the room, her gown swishing behind her like the tail of an angry cat.

"Why are you here, Tollemache? What have you got to gain by telling me what's going on in the enemy camp?" Her blue eyes narrowed as she looked at him. "You were in Hindley's company at Tattersall's. You're a guest at his house now. Does he know that you're here, or why?"

"No." His eyes gleamed as they rested on her. "He doesn't know." For a moment there was a brief silence between them. "That you saw me with him in Newmarket and that I'm a guest in his house now doesn't mean that I care for his company or his friendship. Staying with the Hindleys is merely an ideal and inexpensive way to enjoy a comfortable mode of existence."

"I see. When you tire of their hospitality you move on to someone else?"

"Exactly."

"You still haven't answered my question. The real reason you're here."

"Oh? I thought that would have been obvious to you."

He wore the same over-familiar smile she remembered from their first meeting, the smile she had never quite liked.

He took a step toward her but the dogs were up in an instant, growling and snapping. She rested her hands on their collars to quieten them.

"I think perhaps you had better leave."

"Yes, I think perhaps I had." He picked up the bouquet of roses and held it out to her. "I left Durdans without telling anyone where I was going. No doubt I shall be missed and awkward questions asked if I fail to make an appearance at dinner. But please . . . take these; I had them picked especially for you."

"From Gilbert Heathcote's garden?" she asked, mockingly.

"His gardeners grow the finest roses in Epsom. I could scarcely bring you anything but the best."

She looked at them. If she refused to take them he would no doubt throw them away; and it seemed a sacrilege, a wanton waste. She could not bear to think of them, beautiful and fragrant, lying by the roadside or in some muddy ditch, trampled and rotting. Reluctantly, she took them from him. She went to the door and held it open for him herself. He paused in the hallway outside.

"You realize that the Jockey Club will never sanction women competing in races on a par with men? It's completely unknown."

"There's more ways than one to skin a cat."

He moved closer to her; so close that she could feel his warm breath upon her face. She could not deny that he was handsome. His thick, dark hair waved richly into the nape of his neck; his features were so perfect that they might have been sculpted. She could guess that most women he met would find him irresistibly attractive; and he was very well aware of it. But it was his own barely veiled vanity that made her detest him.

He picked up his hat and cane.

"Please remember, Miss Brodie. If you ever have need of my assistance, you have only to call on me."

"At Jacob Hindley's house?"

"Wherever I am when you need me."

After Tollemache had gone, she went into the kitchen and found a vase for the roses. Then she went upstairs. Outside her sister's bedroom she hesitated, hearing the laughter and whispering coming from the part-open door.

"It was 'im, I swear, miss. Could never forget 'is face! Was the afternoon I went 'ome to see me ma, and Mr. 'Indley's carriage was in the inn yard, having a change of 'orses. The three of 'em come out the taproom, together . . . Mr. 'Indley, Mr. Tollemache, an' 'is brother. Oh, the dead spit of 'im, is Mr. James!"

"But why should he call here, Ellen? My sister doesn't know him." Clara's voice.

"Why, I reckon she gone and met 'im when she went to them sales at Newmarket . . . the Tollemaches got a big 'ouse out that way." More laughter and giggling. Through the crack in the door, Anna saw Ellen Troggle lean closer to Clara. "Four years ago, mind, afore you and Miss Anna came to Epsom, there was a big party, some down from London for the racing, two earls' daughters among 'em. All the ladies fair fell over 'emselves for Mr. Tollemache. And one of the earls' daughters . . . well, it was said that she and 'im . . . now don't breathe a word of what I'm saying, Miss Clara . . ."

"What, Ellen? What? Tell me!"

". . . 'appens she was betrothed to some viscount or other in London. And word come down from the 'ouse . . . well, you know 'ow these things get about; there ain't no privacy in gib 'ouses. Too many people in 'em for that. Well . . . she was seen, coming out of Mr. Tollemache's bedroom, at two o'clock in the morning!" She broke off and both girls burst into muffled laughter for several minutes. "She was whisked off, back to London. Never stopped to see the week out. It was all 'ushed up, according to Mrs. Dewar's maid, who 'ad it from the maid of another lady staying in the 'ouse. *But that ain't all,* Miss Clara . . ."

"Go on, then, Ellen, go on! Tell me the rest . . ."

"Well, miss, she married this viscount not long after. Big wedding it was, up at St. Paul's. Nine month after, she 'as a baby boy . . ." She lowered her voice but Anna could still hear every word. "And some people reckoned it looked more like Lionel Tollemache than 'is lordship 'er 'usband!"

"Ellen!"

At that point, Anna walked unannounced into the room.

"If you spent more time doing what I pay you to do than sitting gossiping about people you've never met and are never likely to, we might get the sheets on our beds by tonight."

They both turned and saw her at the same time, their faces red with guilt. Ellen sprang up, and bobbed a curtsy.

"Yes, Miss Anna. Right away Miss Anna." She scurried away, so quickly and so quietly that Anna did not even hear her close the door.

Slowly, a little defiantly, Clara got to her feet. She raised her chin, as she always did when she was preparing to defend herself.

"Ellen had nearly finished the linen. She only came in here to talk for a moment or two."

"I don't begrudge either of you doing that. What I don't like is what and who you were talking about."

"So it was Lionel Tollemache who came to the house?"

"Whether he did or not is no business of Ellen's. Or yours."

"You were listening to what we said!"

"With your door half-open and the pair of you clacking like a couple of hens in a chicken run, I couldn't very well avoid it."

"You were eavesdropping on me!"

"When I walk past a door and somebody is talking about me and what should be my business, I have a right to eavesdrop. In my place you'd do exactly the same. And while we're on the subject of listening to other people's conversations, might I remind you of the morning when Ralph Russell came to the cottage. Who was eavesdropping then?" Clara opened her mouth to make some retort, but Anna forestalled her. "Let's close the subject, shall we? I'm tired and I'm hungry and the last thing I want at the end of the day is an argument over anyone as worthless as Lionel Tolle-mache."

"So you do know him?"

"If catching sight of someone across the auction ring of Tattersall's is knowing them, then I know him. And he made a special point of introducing himself to me as we were about to leave, for reasons best known to himself." She sat down on Clara's bed. "He was with Hindley. I didn't trust him then and I don't trust him now. He's a guest at the Hindleys' house, for God knows how long."

"But what did he want?"

"He rode over from Gilbert Heathcote's place where they're having a meeting . . . about whether or not I should be permitted to enter Firestone for the King's Cup next Saturday."

"But if Lionel Tollemache came here to tell you what they were doing, he can't be on their side."

"That's what he implied. But how do I know that he acted purely out of sincerity? I didn't believe a word of his story. For all I know Hindley could have sent him over here himself."

"To find out what you're doing?"

"Exactly. As they say in military parlance . . . one spy within the walls is worth an army outside. Before I came on the scene Hindley stood a two-to-one chance of taking the King's Cup; especially if Chifney was in the saddle. Now he's got a horse like Firestone up against him, and Chifney's riding for me instead of him. You can bet that rankles."

Although all the scheming and subterfuge were quite beyond Clara's understanding, she tried to make an effort.

"What can Lionel Tollemache gain by coming to tell you what the others are doing?"

Anna smiled.

"What indeed."

The heat of the day had lessened by the time Tollemache arrived back at Durdans, taking the roundabout route that traversed the racecourse. This lessened his chances of being seen by anyone from the first or second floor of the house.

He was generous with the groom who came at a run to take his horse, tipping him two sovereigns. Pocketing the coins, the groom led away the horse, and Tollemache made his way back into the house.

The vestibule was deserted. No sound of voices came from the library on the opposite side of the hall. Mounting the staircase he went directly to his room and opened the door, where he stopped, abruptly, in surprise. There, lounging in the middle of his bed with her fair hair loose about her shoulders, was Lady Helen Gordon, one of the Heathcotes' guests. She was the only child of a Scottish duke, unmarried at twenty-four, and because of her father's power and position at court she spent her entire idle

life either there or as the guest of her many wealthy and aristocratic acquaintances. In her own opinion she was a court beauty; and Tollemache
had already heard that she was reputed to be the mistress of both Viscount
Northropp and the Earl of Leopardstown, the latter due to arrive at Durdans in the morning in time for the King's Cup meeting at the end of the
week. Intrigued as to why she had let herself into his bedroom, he closed
the door quietly behind him and waited for her to speak first. On the floor
lay her discarded satin slippers. Draped carelessly over one of the chairs he
caught sight of her gown. She wore only a flimsy silk bedrobe, undone to
the waist. Her pale eyes gleamed at him.

"Where *have* you been, Mr. Tollemache? Didn't anyone ever tell you
that a gentleman should never keep a lady waiting."

"I wasn't aware that I'd made any assignations with a lady. And is it any
business of yours where I've been?" he said, but he was smiling at her.

"I was watching on the landing when the gentlemen quit the library after
their discussions about the race . . . and you weren't among them." A sly
note came into her voice. "And as I was waiting for you particularly, I was
most vexed to find you gone."

"You flatter me." She got up from the bed and came slowly and lan-
guorously toward him; then she reached out her arms and put them about
his neck. "But do you not think it a trifle indiscreet to come into my
bedroom like this and lie on my bed in a state of undress? Anyone could
come in and find you. Someone wishing to speak with me; one of Lady
Heathcote's servants, wanting to turn down the bed . . ."

"Nobody could get in because I locked the door from the inside."

"But it was unlocked when I came in."

"Only because I unlocked it again when I saw you come into the house."

"I dislike being spied upon . . . even by a beautiful lady."

"You should have been here when I wanted you," she said, moving
closer to him and lifting her face up to his. When he kissed her she hung on
to him, digging her long nails into his back so savagely that he could feel
them through the thickness of his coat. She threw back her head and
laughed. "If you go back and relock your door, I can promise you enter-
tainment of a kind you've never dreamed of . . . and we have more than an
hour before we must go down to dinner."

He looked at her, thinking how cheap and vulgar she was beside Anna
Brodie, like base metal compared to gold.

"How much I would like to accept your irresistible invitation. But I have
to speak to Jacob Hindley on a matter that cannot wait."

She narrowed her eyes. She let her arms fall to her sides, and moved
away from him.

"My favors are much sought after, Mr. Tollemache. And I know no man
who would give up the opportunity of having me as his bedfellow even if
the king himself wished to speak with him."

"I beg you to forgive me. What man in his right mind would choose to talk business with another in preference to the enjoyment of your incomparable charms? I'm merely postponing our . . . assignation. Until later." Her very coarseness excited him, even though he despised her for offering herself with no more subtlety than the lowest streetwalker in London. Tonight he would go to her bedroom when the rest of the house was asleep and he would use her as he used every other woman he slept with. But he did not consider her a conquest because she was not really worth having. She turned away and picked up her gown from the chair, then let the bedrobe drop to the floor and stood naked.

"For punishment, you can do my maid's work and help me to dress. Then I shall go back to my room and don my evening gown, in readiness for dinner."

"I'm honored to serve you." He stepped forward, and lifted the gown above her head. As he spoke there was a sudden tap on the door, and they both held their breath. "Yes, who is it?"

"Mr. Hindley's valet, sir. Mr. Hindley is about to dress for dinner, and asks if you would have the goodness to go to his room at your convenience, so that he may speak with you."

Helen Gordon began to laugh, but Tollemache grabbed her and put a finger to her lips. "Very well. Tell Mr. Hindley that as soon as I can I shall be with him."

"Yes, sir." The man's footsteps died away and Tollemache breathed a sigh. "You must leave here at once and go back to your room. If Lady Heathcote should see you . . ."

"That scrag-necked old hag!"

"It is your reputation that I'm thinking of," lied Tollemache, averting his face so that she would not see the expression on it.

"No one would dare to cast a slur on it! They would have my father to reckon with if they did!"

"Of course." Already, he had tired of her. "How shall I know your room?"

She was sitting on the edge of the bed now, pulling on her satin slippers.

"I shall leave my shoes outside the door, pointing to the west. As if they were left there for my maid to clean." She smiled. "But she will be told not to do so."

He smiled back.

"You trust her?"

"She's afraid of me." As she passed by him he took her hand and pressed the palm to his lips.

"How much I envy her. To be with you all day. Every day. My very beautiful Lady Helen."

So great was her vanity that she believed every word.

Hindley's back was turned toward him when he knocked and came into his room, and found his valet helping him on with his dinner jacket. But their eyes met and held in the long mirror.

As soon as the manservant had gone, Hindley rounded on him.
"Were you drunk this afternoon?"
"For Christ's sake!"
"You took the part of that low-born bastard against your own kind!"
Tollemache's nonchalance enraged him further. "You, a guest in my own
house . . ."
Tollemache sat down without being asked.
"Oh, come, Hindley, it was only a joke."
"A joke? Don't think I don't know why you took the bitch's part. Ever
since you set eyes on her at Tattersall's you've been drooling over her, like
a dog in rut. Much good it'll do you. You go on sniffing round her skirts
and making a fool of yourself; you'll never get inside her bed in a hundred
years."
"Would you care to take a bet on that?"
"Don't go flattering yourself that the bitch is interested in an idle ne'er-
do-well like you. She's got bigger fish to fry."
For the first time, Tollemache's forehead creased in the beginnings of a
frown. "Do you begrudge her winning it so much?"
"The bitch hasn't won it yet!"
"But you think she will . . . and so does every other noble owner who
has a horse entered in the race. That's why you're all against her."
Hindley's face flushed fiery red. Tollemache's smile baited him further.
"For my part I'll see her in hell before she makes a fool of me again."
Irritably, he glanced at his pocket watch. "It's almost the hour. We'd best
go down for dinner."
Together, they went into the drawing room, which was already filled
with Heathcote's guests. Tollemache's eyes roved at once over the female
company; there were one or two who mildly attracted him, but beside
Anna Brodie they looked ordinary and dull. There was no sign of Lady
Helen Gordon; no doubt she hoped to make a late, grand entrance, as
women of her type were wont to do. As soon as Hindley had become
engrossed in conversation with Colonel Anson and several other guests,
Tollemache unobtrusively slipped out of the room. Unobserved, he made
his way quickly to Heathcote's study and tried the door. He smiled when it
opened easily, and he slipped inside.
The letter to the stewards at Newmarket lay, as Tollemache had expected it to, on Heathcote's desk. With nimble fingers he broke the seal
and read it. Then, glancing out of the window to make certain he was still
unobserved, he took another sheet of paper from the drawer and folded it
in exactly the same way as the letter addressed to the Jockey Club. Finally,
with great care, he sat down and copied Heathcote's handwriting, so
cleverly that only Heathcote himself, or someone very familiar with his
hand, would be able to detect a difference. Stuffing the original letter into
his pocket, Tollemache slipped out of the study and went back toward the
drawing room. Helen Gordon had come down during his absence, and he

went across to her at once, bowing extravagantly over her outstretched hand. But as she talked and flirted with him, he was only half-listening to what she said. For presently, Gilbert Heathcote went to the door and called to one of his passing menservants to fetch the letter that lay on his desk in the study, and take it to the coaching inn at Epsom in time to catch the fast mail to Newmarket.

For a moment Tollemache held his breath, while keeping his face perfectly normal and composed.

"Just the one letter, Sir Gilbert?"

"Yes. You will see that it is addressed to the president of the Jockey Club. Be certain it is delivered to the mailcoach before nine. They will depart promptly."

"Yes, sir." The manservant went away and Heathcote closed the door, going back among his guests. Inwardly Tollemache breathed a sigh of relief.

"Is something wrong?" said Helen Gordon, narrowing her sharp, light eyes.

"By no means. If I seem bereft of speech, I assure you that it is merely because your beauty has temporarily overwhelmed me." Inwardly, he laughed at his own duplicity, and her colossal vanity that made her believe what he said.

✳ 14 ✳

It was growing dark as Anna walked her horse slowly along the little track that led to the road, and from there branched off directly to the Old Brew estate. It had been raining steadily during the afternoon and early evening, and because underfoot the ground had turned to mud, she did not want to risk cantering the horse and having him slip, and maybe incur an injury. It took a horse and rider three quarters of an hour to reach the Old Brew House from Sam Loam's yard—which Anna had left more than twenty minutes before—and she wanted to reach home before the rain returned in force. Jessie's warm, cozy kitchen, and the fire she would have already lit in the bedrooms and the library, occupied her thinking as much as the King's Cup meeting, only two days away.

Halfway along the track the trees overhead met in an arch, and their thick branches made the ground below less wet than before. Seeing this, she set the horse into a trot, and went on for several more minutes before she noticed that up ahead a large tree trunk and several logs had been dragged across the track. She pulled the horses up instantly, sensing danger.

There was no way that the tree trunk could have fallen there by itself. There had been no high winds. It had not been there earlier, when she had ridden in the opposite direction. Instinctively, she reached for the pistol that she always carried with her when she was traveling alone, and held it ready, but low enough to conceal it from sight. She slowed her horse to a walk, and advanced, little by little. Suddenly, as she had almost reached the tree trunk, three roughly dressed men, ragged kerchiefs tied around the lower half of their faces, sprang from the dense thicket, and her horse reared in terror as one of them tried to grab her reins.

Her reflexes were instantaneous. Kicking one of them in the face with the full force of her booted foot, she slashed at another with her whip until with a shout of pain he fell away. In the sudden respite she leveled her pistol at the third assailant and fired without hesitating.

The shot hit him in the shoulder and he lurched backward, screaming, clutching at his bloodsoaked shirt.

"Run! Run! The bitch 'as got me!"

Before either of the other two could make a second lunge toward her, Anna spurred her horse forward, jumped him over the logs, and galloped him forward without looking back. But one of the ruffians shouted after her.

"Take your horse out the King's Cup or you'll end up like Nat Street!"

The horse was sweating badly when she reached the gate of the Old Brew House. When she had gotten him into the stable she unfastened his reins and unbuckled his girths, then began rubbing him down herself, without calling one of her grooms. Her legs felt like water. Her hands shook. To give herself something to do while she composed herself she gave him his feed, then went outside to draw him a bucket of water from the well.

Inside the house, Jessie came out of the kitchen to greet her.

"Why, there you are! You've got a vis—"

"Not now, Jessie. Just leave me alone for a while, will you?" She went straight to the library and closed the door. Then she received her second shock of the evening. Ralph Russell was sitting by the fire in one of the great wing chairs, and he rose at the sight of her.

For a moment she was still too stunned by the attack on her to wonder why he was here, why he had returned to Epsom more than two weeks early. All she wanted to do was to stop the shaking in her legs and hands. She went over to the little table where she kept the spirits and poured herself a measure of neat brandy. Then she swigged back the lot.

"Anna! What is it?"

"I'm all right now." She turned around, leaning for support against the table. Drinking the full glass on an empty stomach made her throat burn, and her head go round and round.

"What's happened?" She felt him take hold of her by the arms. Through the daze she could feel the strength in his fingers.

"For Christ's sake, tell me!"

She told him, in as few words as possible.

"In God's name, they'll pay for this! I'm going straight back to rouse twenty of my best men, and we'll comb every inch of that track for ten miles around till we find something!"

"You'll do nothing of the sort. I forbid it. I want this kept between the two of us until I say otherwise." She sank into the chair he had just left, and lay back, closing her eyes. For a moment she felt weak, helpless, totally at variance to the strength and presence of mind she'd felt less than an hour before, when she'd been attacked. "If you do that the whole of Epsom will know what happened by morning . . . and any chance I have of finding out who waylaid me and who paid them to do it will go up in smoke. I don't want that to happen."

He stared at her.

"They could have killed you, Anna! Do you mean you want me to stand by and do nothing?"

"What they did was meant as a warning. Whoever sent them wants me out of Epsom. If they'd wanted to kill me they could have done it, easily."

"And if you don't heed their warning, next time they will kill you. You don't seem to realize how serious this is. I should be riding into Epsom now to report it to the constable, not standing here arguing with you!"

"No!" Unsteadily, she got to her feet. "I won't let you. Mind your own business, will you? I'll deal with it in my own way."

"I told you what would happen if you went ahead and tried to force yourself onto the course . . ."

"All right. You told me. Nubbles told me. Sam told me. Now you can all have the satisfaction of saying I told you so. I expected to make enemies and I have . . . that's all. If I turn tail and run when the going gets rough I'll be doing just what they all expect me to do. And I won't give in to threats."

"Then at least let me do everything I can to try to find out who was responsible for this, before it happens again!"

She sank into the security of the chair.

"Why don't you let me deal with things in my own way?"

"Because I care what happens to you."

For a moment Anna made no reply.

"All right. Meet me tomorrow at six in the morning on the north side of Durdans Wood. I can show you where it happened. They must have had horses waiting in the thicket so that they could escape, quickly. They'll have left tracks in the soft ground. Even if we rode back there now it'd be too dark by the time we got there to see anything."

"Very well. But I don't want you riding out there alone. There's too much risk. We won't meet at Durdans Wood. I'll meet you here, outside your gates." He poured her another glass of brandy and pressed it gently into her hands. "Here, drink this. Have a light dinner and go straight up to bed. And bring a couple of your dogs with you tomorrow. Don't forget."

"Wait a minute." She put her hand on his sleeve. "There are things I must talk to you about before you go. My father's horse . . . you paid three thousand guineas for it . . ." The brandy was acting on her mind like a drug. She closed her eyes and passed her hand across them. "You just disappeared after Tattersall's. I didn't know where to find you. Then the groom at the inn said that you'd left Firestone for me, and gave me your note. Nobody knew where you'd gone, so I couldn't send on the money."

"I don't want any money from you. The horse was meant as a gift."

"I can't take him unless you let me pay you."

"Because you think it places you in my debt?"

"Yes."

"Can't you just accept him in the spirit that he was given? As any other woman would?"

"You already know the answer to that."

"All right. Have it your way." He picked up his hat and riding crop and went to the door. "Tomorrow then. At six. Goodnight and sleep well."

"Wait. There's something else I haven't told you. About Chifney."

"Chifney?" Russell hesitated at the door.

"Yes. Since you didn't have anything entered in the King's Cup, I asked him if he'd ride Firestone. Do you mind?"

"Not at all. It's his decision. I made it clear to him when I offered him the retainer that he was free to ride for other owners if I had nothing running in a particular race."

"That's what I thought. But your friend Hindley asked him first."

"Hindley's no friend of mine. He's just an acquaintance." Something in the too-emphatic tone of his voice made her sit up, and take notice, fighting a battle with her spinning head. "If you both wanted Chifney, it's his decision whose mount he rides. Not mine."

"Hindley was more than put out. He reckoned that Chifney had a duty to ride his horse because of his long-standing friendship with you." She watched his reaction carefully.

"Did he say that? Did he use those words?"

"To Chifney, yes. Chifney told me later."

"You can leave Hindley to me."

When he had left Anna fell asleep in the chair until Jessie came to waken her, just before eleven o'clock. The dogs had come into the library in search of the fire and lain down on the rug in front of the blaze, and she stretched out her hand and stroked their massive heads.

"Devil take this topsy-turvy weather," Jessie grumbled, stabbing at the fire with the poker, "fires in the middle of July! Why, two weeks ago we couldn't bear ourselves, with the heat!"

"At least it's stopped raining," Anna said.

Then, a little unsteadily still, Anna got to her feet.

"I'll have some supper in the kitchen, then I'll go on up to bed as well. Let the dogs out into the yard when you lock up, will you?" She paused at the door. "Jessie? I'm sorry I was short with you when I came back tonight. I had a lot on my mind."

She went out before Jessie could answer her.

She did not sleep well. She tossed and turned, this way and that. Then, finally, when she drifted fitfully into an exhausted slumber, it was to become an unwilling prisoner of a nightmarish dream. In her dream she rode again down the wooded, lonely track. She heard the sinister rustling of the leaves, the crackling of fallen twigs beneath the unseen feet. Then as the three ruffians sprang out upon her, she felt her heart thud and lurch as her terrified horse reared and plunged.

The felled logs and massive tree trunk ahead barred her way. Her assailants' ugly faces, half-shrouded by filthy rags, leaped up at her in her dream, ten times their ordinary size. Their dirty gnarled hands, the nails thick with filth, pawed at her, reaching out like claws. Then as she made her escape through the rough, a savage voice shrieked after her.

"Take your horse out the King's Cup, or you'll end up like Nat Street!"

The dead boy's image rose before her in the dream, the body twisting obscenely upon the rope that hung from the hook in the ceiling, its features bloated and horrible.

She awoke minutes later, still screaming.

Nobody had heard. She pushed back the bedclothes, hauled herself from the bed. She pulled aside the bed curtains and struggled into her night robe. As she went over to the window and peered out at the sky, her mantle clock chimed four.

She could not sleep again. For if she went back and lay down in the bed she would drift back into unconsciousness and the nightmare would come back to imprison her.

She sat in a chair beside the dead fire until the dawn.

He had already been waiting outside the gates for more than half an hour when she arrived, leading her horse and with two of her dogs following at her heels.

"You're early," she said simply, no trace of the weariness and fear of the night before about her. Her face was a mask.

"Yes, I'm early. Did you sleep well?"

"I've slept better," she answered, shortly, and he did not pursue the subject. She had climbed into the saddle before he had the chance to dismount and help her. "There's been no more rain. They could well have left a trail."

"And if they have and we can follow it, you'll agree to ride over with me to the constable?"

"He'll do nothing without proof."

"But he has the authority to ask questions, and ask questions he will."

"If he hasn't already been bought and sold!" Her tone was cynical. "Haven't you ever heard of crooked judges and magistrates? They have crooked law officers as well, didn't you know?"

"Not Amyas Stoat . . . as he's as straight as a die."

"One man alone can't do much against the forces of evil. Otherwise he'd have cleaned up certain parts of Epsom long ago."

"You mean men like Tobias Slout and the professional nobblers?"

"According to Sam Loam Slout's been behind every bit of turf villainy for the past ten years. Grooms bribed, jockeys in his pocket, horses poisoned in their stables. But he's still here. Still thriving. Still sitting like a great, ugly, bloated spider, spinning his web of dirt and corruption. Everyone's afraid of him and nobody does anything. Most of all the law."

"To even begin to know how to fight them you have to use their own weapons. And you know what they are as well as I do."

"Don't worry. If I'm forced to it I can fight just as dirty as they can."

When they reached the other end of the track Anna noticed at once that an attempt had been made to drag back the tree trunk and logs from the path, but they had only been dragged back a little way, roughly, as if whoever had done it had done it in a hurry. By the place where she had shot the third attacker, there were bloodstains on the grass. They both dismounted. At once, Anna's dogs began to circle the spot, sniffing and whining.

"Was he badly hit?"

"I didn't stop to find out. When I'd beaten the others off I just pointed my pistol at him and pulled the trigger."

Russell knelt down by the logs.

"See, here, where the bushes are crushed. This is where he fell. And if you look you can make out where the heels of his boots have been dragged. No doubt he was too badly wounded to walk . . . or at least the others might have thought that you'd ride to the nearest place for help, and they dragged him away to where their horses were hidden, because he would have slowed them up if they'd just helped him struggle back on his own two feet."

Anna grasped the collars of her dogs and thrust their noses at the blood. "Seek!" As they began to bark and wag their tails, she and Russell led their horses through the dense thicket, until they reached a tiny clearing not more than fifty yards away from the track. There, in the soft ground, were the hoofprints they had hoped to find.

"The branches are too low for them to have ridden here by this way,"

Anna said. "They would have led the horses in from whichever direction they came. Follow the dogs!"

It took them more than half an hour before the trail came to an abrupt end, at the side of the Epsom road.

"The scent's gone stale. And they could have ridden to this spot from any direction. They most likely wouldn't have ridden along together, in case the sight of them aroused suspicion. Ruffians mounted on good horses. What working man owns his own horse, except a small farmer . . . and there aren't any around these parts."

"Wait a minute." Anna walked back to the edge of the woods, retracing their steps. "Come here, will you?"

"What is it?"

"Look. Here, beside the hoofprints. These foot marks. Can you see how the footprints on the right sink lower into the earth than those on the left? That means that one of them must walk with a limp."

Russell stood, looking at the footprints.

"None of the roughs that tag onto Slout that I've ever seen walk with a limp. But it's a clue and the only one we've got. Other than the fact that one of them was wounded. You can be sure that whoever he works for would never risk calling a doctor. If they can't get the shot out of him by themselves, they'll just leave him to get by the best he can."

"Or finish him off."

"Life is cheap to men like Slout . . . whether it's a horse's or a man's."

They walked slowly back toward the track, then remounted and made toward the open road, the dogs running along behind.

"If you still mean to run that horse in the King's Cup tomorrow, and I reckon nothing will stop you, I'd feel better if you let me send over half a dozen of my men, just to make sure there's no last-minute attempt to get at him in his stable."

"I'd kill the first bastard who put his foot over my wall!"

"What worries me is that I don't think for one moment you realize just what you're up against."

Her blue eyes lit with anger.

"You're wrong. It's the others who don't realize what they're up against." She turned her mount's head and spurred him into a gallop, not slowing down until they came within sight of her gates. She drew rein and let him catch up with her. "All right. Send your men over to me. I'll be glad of any help I can get. Tell them to come armed with blunderbusses and pistols. By the end of next week I should have had time to take on enough men of my own."

Russell lay his hand on her horse's bridle.

"Wait a moment."

"What is it?"

"After the King's Cup I usually hold a dinner at the house, whether I've

had a runner in the race or not. If I send you and your sister an invitation
. . . will you come?"

"We have no jewelry suitable for an occasion like that."

"I can remedy that."

"I won't accept any gifts and I won't let Clara accept any."

"As you will. But I have the collection of Russell jewels that have been
wrapped away in velvet and gathering dust for the last fifteen years . . .
ever since my mother died. Surely you can wear something from it for one
evening without it offending your principles?" There was an almost imper-
ceptible note of innocent mockery in his voice, and her sharp ears caught
it. She frowned.

"I shall accept, more for my sister's sake than for my own. She complains
that we never go anywhere where she can show off the gowns we bought in
London."

He smiled, and let go his hold on her bridle.

"Come early. An hour before the time on the invitation."

"And you'll send your men over tonight?"

"Long before darkness. I'll give them their orders as soon as I get back
to the house."

She dismounted and led her horse along the drive, to give herself time to
become composed. She was grateful to him, but something within her
would not let her admit her gratitude. She liked him, but all the old caution
and misgivings rose up, threatening her peace of mind. Russell disturbed
that peace of mind and her very awareness of this disquieted and angered
her, because it was half beyond her control. She felt like someone wading
out into the sea; certain at first where the water was shallow, then less and
less sure as the swirling waves threatened to engulf her, bringing her further and more dangerously out of her depth. Before it was too late she
must turn back, and reach the safety of the shore.

Halfway along the drive, Russell caught sight of a post chaise and recognized it at once. A feeling of outrage swept through him. Deliberately, he
rode on to the stables to give his orders to the men before going back into
the house, where his butler was already waiting for him. He opened his
mouth to speak but Russell irritably forestalled him.

"I know Mr. Hindley is here. I saw his post chaise as I came up the
drive."

"I showed him into the drawing room, my lord. He insisted upon waiting
for you, no matter how long you might be."

"Doubtless." Angrily, he went into the room to confront his unwelcome
visitor, slamming the door behind him with such force that Hindley jumped
in surprise. "How did you know that I was back?" he asked roughly,
without greeting.

"You were seen in Epsom, when you stopped to rest and water your
horses."

"How fast news travels!"

"Why did you come back before you were supposed to? Are you so devoid of any vestige of duty that you can't wait to be quit of your responsibilities?"

"Get out of my house!" Russell strode across to the spirits table and poured himself a full glass of brandy, downing it in one long gulp. He did not pour any for Hindley.

"You seem to forget . . ."

"How can I ever forget anything with you to remind me of it?" His voice was bitter. "Well, if all you came for was to find out why I'm back, you can leave."

"I'm here on even weightier matters."

Russell turned round and looked at him.

"What is it now? No, let me guess." Suddenly, he recalled what Anna had told him about Chifney. "In my absence you thought you'd help yourself to the services of my stable jockey, and when he told you he was riding Anna Brodie's horse in the King's Cup, you took it as a personal affront."

"Then you can do something about it, now you're back. You can instruct Chifney to take the ride on my horse, and that Brodie bitch can go whistle for another jockey to ride her ill-gotten nag. If she can find one to ride for her."

"I shall do nothing of the sort. I have no runner in the race and Chifney's free to ride for any other owner of his choice."

Hindley's eyes bulged from his head.

"Are you telling me that you won't instruct him to ride my horse?"

"That's what I'm telling you."

For a moment they looked at each other, in hard, mutual dislike. "You're doing this to try to get even, aren't you?" Hindley fumed. "Well, you won't. Not in a hundred years. With one word I could ruin you and you know it."

"Likewise. So we have a stalemate, don't we?" Slowly, harnessing his anger, Russell put down his empty glass. "Chifney rides Firestone in the King's Cup . . . and that's my last word on it."

"That isn't all I came about."

"For Christ's bloody sake!"

"Before the whole grandstand hears, Russell." He moved closer to him. "In your absence, there's been a full-scale meeting of local Jockey Club members at Durdans, to discuss what's to be done about that upstart Brodie bastard . . . and despite Randyll and Heathcote prevaricating like a pair of old women, we've forced Heathcote, as chief steward, to write to the Jockey Club at Newmarket and insist on a ruling directive that'll put a stop once and for all to this nonsense of letting a woman race horses on the course . . ."

". . . and no doubt you suggested the wording!"

". . . everyone present, with the exception of one or two abstainers who were too stupid to see reason, put their signatures to a petition demanding that, if she wins the King's Cup tomorrow before the Jockey Club has had sufficient time to answer us, all honors attendant to the race shall be declared null and void."

Russell looked at him as he might have at a beetle, crushed underfoot.

"You stink, Hindley! You'd really do that to her, wouldn't you? You can't leave her be. All she wants is to race horses. Not because of the money. The prize money, what a horse is worth after he wins a big race . . . to her, that's less than nothing. She wants to race horses because she loves them. You've never seen her with them. She's a genius."

"That bastard outbid me for the Old Brew est—"

"Oh, for God's sake get out of my sight! You make me sick. Anna Brodie came to Epsom and gave Dewar what the estate was really worth. And you got your long-deserved comeuppance."

"Then you refuse to add your name to the Jockey Club petition?"

"Go wipe your arse on it!"

"I warn you. You'll be sorry for this."

"I'm already sorry. That I ever set eyes upon you and all your cursed brood." Savagely, he rang the servants' bell. "Mr. Hindley is leaving," he said, when his butler came to answer it, and walked out of the room and out of the house even before Hindley had been shown to the door. He went back to the stables where Chifney and his head groom had just returned, bringing the horses from exercise. They both doffed their caps.

"You're back early, milord," Inchcape said, surprised.

"Yes. Since the running of the King's Cup this year promises to be fraught with so much bitterness and controversy, I reckoned it would be better for Miss Brodie if I was there to back her up against the hostility, if need be."

"When I'd agreed to take the ride on Firestone, I went over to Mr. Hindley's myself and told him. He was none too pleased with me."

"Doubtless he wasn't."

"They mean to get her out," Inchcape said.

"And don't much care for how they do it, either. Chifney, I warned her that there might be some attempt to get at the horse in the night . . . and something that happened yesterday only strengthens my belief . . . the feeling against her is so strong that she herself might possibly be in no small danger. I've promised to send half a dozen of my best men over to keep watch in her yard, and I want you to go with them."

Chifney stared at him.

"But surely nobody would lay hands on a woman?"

"She's made enemies and they want to see her hounded out of Epsom. How far some of them would go to achieve that is something we can only guess at. But there's no sense in taking chances. I put you in charge. Pick your six men and have them come to the gun room in half an hour. They'll need to be well armed."

"No one could hate her that much!"

"Someone already does."

"You bloody fools! Three of you, against one girl, and still you bungle the job!"

"She 'ad a pistol, Mr. Slout! She could 'ave shot us all dead!"

"She'd 'ave done me a favor!" Tobias Slout looked down in disgust at one of his men, his jerkin bloodsoaked, writhing in agony on the straw. Pouring with sweat, half delirious, he clutched at the pistol wound in his shoulder with filthy hands.

"'E needs a doctor, Mr. Slout . . ."

"Doctor my arse! What do you think I am, ay? Mad? Bring a doctor 'ere, and let 'im see this? One look and it'd all be up for the lot of us. Go down to the kitchens and get some 'ot water. Bathe it for 'im. And give 'im a glass of gin. That'll ease 'im."

"But if the shot's not dug out, it'll turn poisonous!"

"That's 'is 'ard luck. If 'e 'adn't bin so stupid, 'e'd 'ave made sure 'e kept all in one piece!" Slout turned on his heel and stamped out of the room.

"'E's out of 'is mind with the pain, Gov'nor," said One-eyed Bill, outside in the passage. "What'll we do? 'Ave a go at digging out the shot?"

"Do what you can. I got business to see to."

"What if 'e croaks it, Gov'nor, while you're gone?"

"Bury 'im in the yard. Away from the 'orses, mind. And if the wound turns septic, and 'e starts being a nuisance, give 'im a little something to 'elp 'im on 'is way . . . you know what I mean. I don't want no millstones round my neck."

"You can leave it to me, Mr. Slout."

At the front of the house, Slout got into a closed carriage and pulled down the window blinds. Then he banged on the roof with his walking stick and the driver whipped up the horses.

The journey reached its end outside the lych-gate of Epsom churchyard.

The driver jumped down, tapped on the window, and from inside Slout whispered a few words. Going through the lych-gate, the lackey made his way among the tombstones, until he came to a solitary grave set apart from the others, its headstone covered with lichen and moss. At the foot of the grave stood an urn, the tiny posy of flowers someone had placed there long ago dead and shriveled. He thrust his hand inside the urn, and drew out a folded piece of paper. Tucking it away inside his coat, he made his way back to the carriage.

Slout lowered the window enough to take it, then signaled for him to drive back in the direction they came.

The note was unsigned, but he knew the small, slanting hand only too well. Inside it was a detailed plan of Edward Randyll's stableyard at Chilworth Manor. Beneath it, someone had written, *Tonight. Half past eleven.*

Coquetry in coach horses' box away from main block. Two guards and dogs.

A postscript was scrawled at the bottom, written so hastily that it was almost illegible.

Cannot move Russell. But the bastard must be stopped.

❊ 15 ❊

Downstairs the hall clock struck midnight, then the last great chiming clang shivered on the air, and was still. From her place on the end of her sister's bed, Anna pulled a shawl a little closer around her shoulders. It was chilly in the early hours, and her gown was only thin muslin. She got up and went over to the window, which had been left half-open, so that she could look down into the courtyard below them.

"Are the men still there?" asked Clara's sleepy voice from the curtained bed.

"I thought you were asleep." Anna turned, and went back to sit beside her. She pulled back the curtains at the head of the bed. "Yes, they're still there. They'll be there all night, and they'll be riding with us when we walk Firestone to the raceground."

Clara struggled up and sank back against her pillows.

"But no one would really break into the stables and hurt any of the horses, would they? Do you really think anyone would come?"

"What a child you still are!" Anna was half-laughing. She reached out and patted her sister's hand. "The same men who drove Nat Street to hang himself wouldn't let their consciences be worried by what happened to a horse. Life's cheap to them. Only money matters. They use any means they can to get what they want." She got up, and went back to look down into the courtyard from the window. "Firestone's the favorite to win tomorrow's race and if there was some way they could stop him, they'd try it. So far they haven't made the attempt."

"Maybe it's got about that Lord Russell's sent over Chifney and six of his men to guard the yard. Maybe they're too scared to try anything."

"Maybe." Anna looked round at her. "I should lie down and try to get some sleep. I'm going down to find Chifney."

He was sitting on an upturned bucket near the entrance to the stables, a blunderbuss slung across his knees. He jumped up at the sight of her but she waved him to sit down again.

"Isn't it time you went into the house and got some sleep?"

"Thank you, but I'm all right."

"Don't fall asleep in the saddle tomorrow." She smiled, and he smiled back.

"I won't, you can depend on it. One of the others will be along in half an hour to relieve me for a while. I reckon I can stay awake until then."

"You're on my land now and you'll do as you're told. So give me that blunderbuss and go and get yourself something to eat in the kitchen. There's plenty of bedrooms upstairs, you can take your pick. As long as it isn't my sister's or Jessie's." They both laughed.

"I'm grateful, don't think I'm not. But I daren't eat. For the past ten days I've been trying to waste off an extra two pounds I shouldn't have."

"Two pounds extra won't worry Firestone. And Jessie's broth won't put on an ounce. You can piddle it out before you're weighed in for the race."

"You're very confident."

"You've tried him out, too."

"It's always different on the course to what it is in a trial gallop. He hasn't had a race in a long while."

"He's never lost one, either."

"All right. I'll take a little of the broth and have a few hours' sleep. But I'll call Rush to take over before I go."

"What's wrong with me taking over?"

He looked at her in dismay.

"Ladies don't handle guns."

"They do when they have to. Didn't Russell tell you what happened yesterday?"

"No."

"Of course, he wouldn't have. I told him not to tell anyone. But I trust you." For a moment they looked at each other. "I was riding back through Walton's Spinney and three men jumped out and tried to drag me off my horse. I kicked one in the face and knocked another away with my whip. The third one was waiting up ahead, barring my way. So I took out the pistol that I always carry with me and shot him."

"Jesus Christ, you could have been murdered!"

"If they'd meant to kill me then they could have. They had the chance. But my guess is that they were sent to warn me off . . . by whom? Well, your guess is as good as mine. As I rode away one of them shouted after me, 'Take your horse out the King's Cup or you'll end up like Nat Street.'"

"The bastards!" Chifney blurted, enraged.

"Suddenly I don't feel much like sleeping, not after what you've told me." The very softness of his voice only underlined the anger that lay beneath it. "Why in God's name didn't you go straight to the constable and tell him? If respectable women can't ride along minding their own business without being attacked and threatened . . ."

"I would have gone to him, if I'd thought it would have done any good.

But he would only have seen what happened on the face of it . . . three ruffians, up to no good, laying in wait for the first lone rider that came along, intending to rob him of his purse. He wouldn't have believed me if I'd said that I suspected that someone else, someone maybe of great importance in Epsom, had hired them to scare me so much I sold up and moved out."

"But you could tell him all your suspicions."

"How could he act on them? Nearly every owner in Epsom would give his right arm to see me back out . . . and every crooked bookmaker within fifty miles."

"If you hadn't been the rider you are you could have been thrown to the ground and maybe mortally injured. Whoever sent them has got more than just an interest in the result of the big race. They want you out. And at any cost." He caught her sudden expression. "Do you have any suspicions in your own mind who that might be?"

"Maybe. But so far I've got no proof."

At that point they were interrupted by one of Ralph Russell's men, gun under his arm, coming toward them from the opposite end of the yard, two of Anna's dogs trailing at his heels. They ran toward her, wagging their tails, thrusting their damp noses into her hands. She knelt and made a fuss of them.

"Quiet as a graveyard, Miss Brodie. Not so much as a whisper."

"What's the time now?"

"Gone half past twelve." He fished in his pocket for a fob watch, and held it up in the light of his lantern. "There, not a bad guess, ay?" Anna looked and saw that it was ten minutes past the half hour.

"If they mean to come, they have another five hours." She turned back to Chifney. "Go on, go into the house and get some sleep. You're riding tomorrow." He protested but she made him go.

"You can go to bed and rest easy yourself, miss," Russell's man said, his narrowed eyes moving agilely about the deserted yard, "there's no one'll get 'is foot over your wall while we're 'ere. If anything 'appens, we'll rouse you, depend on it."

"Yes, I know. And I'm grateful for your help." She passed a hand across her tired eyes. "But I'll be sleeping in Firestone's stall tonight. There's blankets already there." The man looked stunned, but she simply smiled. "I wouldn't feel happy about sleeping in a comfortable bed in the house, while you men were outside in the cold. I'll be all right."

"But it isn't a lady's place to be sleeping in stables, not in where the 'orses are!"

"I've slept in worse. And if it's good enough for my horses then it's good enough for me. Goodnight." She walked off, leaving him to stare after her.

There was no moon, but the cloudless night blazed with stars. On the other side of the Downs, nestling in a wide hollow like a jewel in the palm of a hand, Chilworth Manor lay sleeping.

Edward Randyll had taken a last walk around his stableyard just before midnight, in the company of his head groom, satisfied that all was well. Every door in the yard had been fitted out with new locks, and the keys lay in the drawer of the clothes press in his own dressing room. In an empty stall next to the hayloft two of his grooms had been stationed, giving them a view of the whole yard that stretched from the stables to the main gate. At the slightest suspicion of any intruders, they would take only a minute to raise the alarm. And, most ingenious of all, his prize-winning filly was not in her usual loose box with his other running horses, but had been led out as soon as it was dark and taken into the stable where his carriage horses were kept. With a peaceful mind, he had fallen asleep almost as soon as his head had touched the pillow.

Somewhere beyond the house, in the thick shrubbery of the grounds, someone stirred, rustling the leaves. For a moment there was silence again, then two pairs of noiseless feet crept from the expanse of bushes and made their way toward the wall. For another moment they paused. Then one of the shadowy figures clasped his hands together, and the other stepped onto them, hoisting himself onto the top of the wall. He hesitated before helping his companion up beside him, his ears strained toward the quiet yard. Within a few minutes, both of them had leaped noiselessly from the wall to the soft earth beneath, and on hands and knees began to traverse the ground in the direction of the stables.

Not the stable block where Edward Randyll's running horses were kept. But those beyond it, where on any night but this, he kept only his carriage horses and hacks.

The first voice Anna heard on waking was Sam Loam's, and she leaped up at once with a start, her heart beating wildly, wondering what he was doing here. Beside her Firestone munched contentedly at his hay, and with a sigh of relief she leaned back against the solid wood of his stall. It was then that Sam burst in on her, Chifney a few paces behind.

"They didn't come, Sam! The men waited up all night and it was quieter than Epsom churchyard."

"The nobblers didn't try and break in 'ere, but they got in Edward Randyll's place. Found 'is filly dead in 'er stall at five this morning . . . arsenic in 'er water."

"No, Sam!" She stared at him wild-eyed, pieces of straw sticking to her loose, unkempt hair.

"This'll finish Randyll."

"For Christ's sake, didn't he have guards in the yard, as we did? That animal must have died in agony!" She sank onto a wooden stool and buried her head in her hands. "He knew what was at stake. He knew he couldn't take risks with his security." There was a break in her voice. Chifney went over and lay his hand on her shoulder.

"He stationed two grooms as lookouts, sat up in the hayloft of the barn

. . . but they both fell asleep in the early hours, just before the nobblers must have struck."

"Two grooms, with no guns or dogs, when a horse's life was at stake? They could have poisoned his whole stable!"

"They might just 'as well 'ave done. This is the end for Randyll. Talk is that he's bin losing so 'eavily over the past few months, 'e raised big brass to put on the Surrey using Chilworth as security. And you know what that means."

"He'll have to sell up and move out."

"Just like John Dewar did."

Anna looked at Sam, then at Chifney.

"Doesn't that strike you as too much of a coincidence?"

"Maybe. But if you've got the sense that I think you 'ave, you'd best keep it to yourself."

"Keep what to myself? That I reckon they were both inside jobs?"

"Whether they were or not, nobody can ever prove it. And you can't do nothing without proof."

"Sam, I think you and I are at cross purposes. When I say I reckon they were both inside jobs, I don't mean I think anyone working in the yard had anything to do with it . . . it goes a lot higher than that. Think about it. I got every bit of information I could out of Nubbles about how Dewar went down; none of his stable benefited from what happened to his horse. Only his Jockey Club friends. To meet his losses he had to sell everything he could lay his hands on, and he let all his best horses go for a fraction of what they were really worth . . . he didn't have time to sent them to auction. Now Randyll's been hit the same way." She paused for a moment, letting her words sink in. "I'd stake everything I have that the same man's responsible for the ruin of both of them. And that he's someone that they both knew and trusted. No one else was in a position to know what measures they planned to assure nothing happened to their horses. And no one else profited by it."

Sam looked grave.

"You'd best not repeat any of this, if you know what's good for you."

"I'll repeat it when I'm good and ready, Sam. On the day of reckoning. And there'll be one."

Beside her Chifney smiled.

"Mr. Loam, that leaves the Surrey as being a three-horse race. Between Thrush, Ambush, and Fidelia. It could go to any of them. The nobblers wanted Coquetry out of the way to leave the field clear for their runner; which one of those three we don't know. I reckon that their brass is going to be on Thrush, and that Edwards will take a pull to make sure Ambush comes in a hair's-breadth second."

"Only time'll tell," Sam said, soberly. "Well, I'd best be on me way again. I'll see you on the course." He nodded toward Firestone. "And don't let that bloody nag out of your sight!"

"Don't worry. I won't." As soon as he had gone, Anna closed the stable door and lay back against it. "What do you know about Jacob Hindley?"

"Hindley?" There was surprise in Chifney's face. "He's one of the biggest owners in Epsom, a big name in the local Jockey Club. And he usually bets heavy, so I've heard. But that's just stable talk. Show me an owner around here who doesn't when he thinks he's sure of what he's backing."

"Is that all?"

"He's a frequent visitor of Lord Russell. But between you and me I don't think there's any love lost between them. Maybe that's something to do with you. Russell can't see any reason why a woman shouldn't be allowed to run horses on the turf, but Hindley's dead set against it. He was there at the house, only yesterday."

"Oh?"

"Inchcape and I were bringing the horses back from exercise, and we noticed Hindley's post chaise in the drive . . . how he knew Russell had come back early God only knows. But he was there. From the way Russell was afterward when he came into the yard to give us orders about coming over here, I reckoned they'd been arguing. His face was like thunder."

"What made you think they'd been arguing about me?"

"Because Russell's one hundred percent behind you and Hindley one hundred percent against; but then so are most of the big owners around these parts. They all see you as an intrusion and a threat. That's no secret to anyone."

"But Hindley stands to lose the most if Firestone runs?"

"Yes, but . . ." he stared at her, sudden realization dawning on him. "You don't think he had anything to do with the nobbling of Randyll's filly?"

"I can't prove it. But look at the facts. First there was Dewar. I know from Frederick Nubbles that the man to gain most when he went down was Jacob Hindley. Only me giving him a fair price for the Old Brew estate when I did prevented Hindley from getting it for next to nothing because Dewar was desperate for money. Before I came on the scene it was Hindley that stood to gain enormous profit from the King's Cup because his horse was reckoned to have been odds-on to win it. All that's changed. To cover the big losses in wagers he needs another big win, at the same meeting. With Randyll's filly nobbled, he can bribe Edwards to take a pull on Ambush and clean up. Then he hopes that the Jockey Club at Newmarket will outlaw women from the course, and put paid to me."

"But that's all guesswork! There's never been a whisper against Hindley . . . I can't believe it, not of him."

"Why not? He has the motive. He's a prominent member of the local Jockey Club, his friends trust him, he's in the perfect position to abuse their confidences."

"But I just can't believe . . ."

"Don't take my word for it. Wait and see. See if Ambush goes down in the Surrey and Hindley makes a big killing. Ambush will be hot favorite now that Randyll's filly isn't in it . . . anyone who bets big brass against her is taking one hell of a risk, unless they're in the know that she isn't going to win."

"Even if you're right about Hindley, how can you ever hope to prove it?"

"I don't know how I can. Only that I will."

"You bloody poxy pair of fools! Didn't I tell you no arsenic? Just a few grains of the powder I give you, enough to make 'er sick. But oh, no! You got to go and panic when you think you 'ear a noise in the yard, and dose the nag with the whole bloody lot! Do you know 'ow much brass that nag would fetch at auction?"

"But you told us to stop 'er no matter what, Gov'nor!"

"Stop 'er from winning the bloody Surrey Stakes, yes. Not stop 'er stone dead. And this is the second job I give you that you've bungled. First the Brodie bitch . . . now this. One more thing fouled up and the pair of you'll be out on your bloody ear!"

"But Mr. Slout!"

"No one saw us, Gov'nor! We made sure!"

"Don't argue with me. I said lay low of a while and that's just what you'll do." Slowly, he lowered himself back into his chair. "You can get drunk 'ere just the same as in Epsom." He picked up his fallen glass and poured himself another drink of gin. "All right. You can get out." After they had gone he sat for some time, rubbing his chin thoughtfully, then he got up and went along the passage to the back door of the house. One of his men was outside, about to come in.

"Just on me way in to tell you, Mr. Slout. 'E's got worse in the night. Billy don't reckon on 'im lasting till tomorrow."

"Pox on it!"

"Even if 'e could 'ave a doctor, it wouldn't 'elp 'im none, not now. Wound's gone poisoned, like I said it would."

"If that bloody fool had done what I paid 'im for, 'e'd be in one piece. It's 'is lookout, if 'e's stupid enough to get shot. All right. Let's 'ave a look at 'im." They walked across the yard together, and into one of the outhouses. Lying on a rough makeshift bed among the straw, the same ruffian that Anna had shot two days before writhed and mumbled in his agony, plucking at the horse blanket draped over him with dirt-encrusted hands. He did not recognize any of them as they stared down at him. Too far gone, he gazed up at the cobwebbed ceiling with bloodshot eyes, the pus and gore from his wound black against his filthy shirt.

Slout stepped back quickly and wrinkled up his nose.

"Christ . . . 'e stinks! And I don't want 'im left in 'ere, attracting vermin and flies. 'E's a goner anyway. Might as well put 'im out of 'is misery."

"What you mean, Gov'nor? Give 'im a drop of something to knock 'im out?"

"The state 'e's in, 'e won't keep nothing down. Get some old sacks and 'old 'em over 'is face till 'e stops breathing. Then as soon as it's dark you can get rid of the body. Just let the bitch enjoy watching 'er nag in the King's Cup. For the first and last time."

"What you got in mind for 'er, Gov'nor?"

❄ 16 ❄

Hours before the first race was even run the crowd began to converge on the course, wending their way on foot and horseback across the Downs, or coming by road in carriages, post chaises, and even carts. They massed along the far side of the racecourse from the start to the judge's chair beside the winning post; they stood on the tops of their carriages and the seats of their carts and any wooden edifice that could be climbed for a better view. The aristocracy and gentry filled the grandstand and private boxes, craning their necks toward the Warren to catch a glimpse of Anna when she appeared, for word had spread all over Epsom faster than a forest fire that no move had yet been made to stop her from running Firestone in her own name. The nobbling of Randyll's filly and his inevitable ruin were almost ignored in the excitement and speculation.

"She's Edward Brodie's bastard daughter!"

"Firestone was his horse!"

"They say he left everything to her and her sister . . ."

". . . but not the bloodstock. His wife and sons got that . . ."

". . . I heard that Russell bought the horse in Newmarket, and then sold it straight to her!"

"I heard differently . . . there's some say it was a gift . . ."

"What does any woman know about blood horses?"

"They tried to stop her running the nag, but the Jockey Club hasn't put a ban on her in time . . ."

They waited for her to appear on the course from the Warren in vain. She came from the opposite direction, leading Firestone on foot, Chifney beside her, Ralph Russell's men mounted and armed, to her left and right and behind. The moment the crowd caught sight of her, there was a tremendous roar as their cheers rose on the air and burst into a crescendo, reaching to the furthest corners of the grandstand far back on the other side. Smiling, Anna acknowledged the cheering from the common people with a casual wave of the hand.

"They're one hundred percent behind you even if the local hierarchy and the Jockey Club are one hundred percent against," Chifney said, as they walked Firestone across the course at Tattenham Corner. "Or, rather I should say, ninety-nine percent against. Russell's been for you every inch of the way."

"Maybe he just feels sorry for me," Anna commented wryly, as they reached the other side.

There was no cheering here. The lines of peering, avid faces held only curiosity as they jostled and pushed to get a glimpse of her. As they walked by the silent, sullen groups of top-hatted men she saw only animosity, outrage, prejudice. She was an outsider, a woman, a threat to everything they represented, and what they thought and felt about her she could see reflected in their faces. Behind her, Russell's men pressed their horses in close.

High up in the private boxes in the grandstand, some of the men and all of the ladies from the Durdans house party crowded to the front of the balconies to get a better view as she led Firestone past. Lady Helen Gordon had elbowed her way to the best place in Heathcote's own box and watched from above with narrowed, spiteful eyes.

"Look at her, the brazen bitch!" Not hearing, the men swarmed around her, passing their telescopes from hand to hand.

"There she is!"

"Where? I can't see!"

"Leading the horse through the Warren with Chifney beside her!"

"Jesus, she's a real beauty."

"Ay, I'll second that." The speaker was Helen Gordon's lover, the earl of Leopardstown, and she glared at him in a jealous fury.

"Fine feathers make fine birds!"

"Fine feathers are nothing to do with it," he answered without looking at her, still staring intently through his telescope. "If you dressed her in a corn sack she'd still be more beautiful than any other woman here. There she goes . . . look. They're making their way toward the racecourse stables. Let's go down and get a closer look at her!"

"I'm all for that!"

"And me!" shouted a chorus of voices. Beside Leopardstown, Helen Gordon's face turned white with rage. She grasped roughly his sleeve.

"You're not going anywhere without me."

"You can't come down into the Warren. You know that. No lady would dare to."

"Then what does that make her?"

"Helen, for God's sake . . ."

"Don't you dare turn your back on me! You'll take me down to the Warren with you or you won't go at all!"

"I said that I can't take you. She's different. She has her own stables and she isn't from the court. And because she's got a runner in the King's Cup under her own name she's entitled to all the concessions and privileges of any other owner, until the Jockey Club takes them away from her. She can do things you can't and get away with them."

"She looks like a harlot to me."

Leopardstown looked down into her face, with growing anger. She was not really beautiful at all; not pretty, even. It was the powder and rouge, cunningly applied, that made her look so attractive by candlelight. Here, in the merciless sunshine, he could see at close quarters the small, hair-fine lines in her skin, the coarse pores, all the flaws in her face that he had never noticed. For the first time, he felt a flicker of distaste.

"A jealous woman is never a pleasant sight. Now please let go my sleeve and stop making an exhibition of yourself before the grandstand hears." Slowly, her eyes still on his face, she let go and stepped back. Then he moved away and was swallowed up in the crowd behind.

She stood there, looking down below her but seeing nothing through her rage; a nerve beat furiously in her temple, and she could feel the hot, sticky sweat in the palms of her hands as she clutched at the edge of the balcony. Behind her, people were whispering and tittering, and her cheeks began to burn like fire. How dare he do this to her, Helen Gordon, the court beauty whose favors men begged for. But she would pay him back. She would get even. Nobody ever slighted her and got away with it. Turning abruptly on her heel she pushed her way from the crowded box and went out into the ladies' gallery, where she caught sight of a liveried doorman.

"Is Mr. Lionel Tollemache in the building?"

"'Aven't seen 'im for more than 'alf an 'our, milady. Think I last saw 'im on 'is way to the betting stand, with the rest of the gentlemen."

"Send someone to find him for me."

Anna was helping her groom to unrug Firestone in the racecourse stables when Tollemache walked in.

"All right. I can manage now." She invented an errand for the boy and in a minute they were alone.

"Get out of here."

"It's taken me all of twenty minutes to push my way through the crowd to find you."

"Then you can spend the next twenty pushing your way back again. I'm busy." She took the last rug from the horse's back and folded it in two. Tollemache stepped nearer and patted its neck. "Take your hands off him."

"I like horses. Especially when they're a certainty to double my money."

Anna stopped what she was doing and folded her arms.

"What do you want, Tollemache?"

"When we last met I said that I'd keep you informed about what went on at Durdans. Don't you want to hear what they all decided?"

"I'm listening."

"You already know that they're all against you, almost to a man. One less now that Edward Randyll's finished. After I'd left they took a vote and the result was that Heathcote, as chief steward, was made to write a letter to the Jockey Club at Newmarket, demanding a ruling against you as soon as possible. They all put their names to it. Except Edward Randyll, Heathcote and me. But then neither of us are of any consequence because he's ruined, and I'm not a Jockey Club member."

"I might have guessed what they'd do!"

"Wait a minute. I said Heathcote had written the letter. I didn't say it was going to reach its destination."

She stared at him searchingly.

"What do you mean?"

He stood there smiling at her for a moment. Then he reached into his coat and pulled out a folded paper.

"Here you are."

Slowly, she took it from him and unfolded it. Then her eyes scanned the writing and she looked up, astonished.

"How did you get this?"

He was still smiling.

"Do you really want me to tell you?"

"You know what would happen to you if they found out?"

"They won't. Unless you tell them."

"When Heathcote doesn't get an answer to his letter, he'll send another one. And the Jockey Club will want to know what happened to the first."

He shrugged his shoulders.

"It got lost along the way to Newmarket. Such things have been known to happen. But the delay will give you valuable time, time you need. You can petition the stewards of the Jockey Club yourself to be allowed the same privileges and rights as any other owner."

"And you really think they'd give them to me?" she asked, cynically.

"What will you do if they don't?"

"I don't for one minute think they will. But I anticipated that. I'm ready to fight them, if that's what they want. In the law courts if need be."

"You really mean business, don't you?"

"If you knew anything about me that's a question that you'd never ask."

"I know enough to wish I knew more."

They were interrupted, suddenly, by a surge of people coming in and out of the stables; grooms leading in horses for the first race; lads carrying piles of rugs and tack. The brief moment of privacy was gone.

"I shall see you again," Tollemache said, replacing his top hat, and went out. She stopped what she was doing and counted the signatures, and there were more than forty. Forty men against one woman. Shrewdly, she guessed why Tollemache had taken it; but because if she was right he would be wasting his time she dismissed the thought, and turned back to Firestone.

He looked magnificent, her lads had done him proud. His bay coat had been brushed until it gleamed; beneath his coat, his muscles rippled hard and strong, and she had worked him so thoroughly, all over the Downs every day since she had brought him back to Epsom, that he was at the very peak of fitness. As she turned round she caught sight of Ralph Russell.

"You've heard about Randy's filly?"

"I rode straight over there the moment I knew," he said, coming into Firestone's stall. He lay a hand on his bridle and stroked his nose. "Not that it did much good. Nothing would have done. He was so stricken that he could scarcely string two words together."

She looked at him searchingly across the horse's gleaming back, thinking how different he was from the suave, shallow Tollemache; instinctively she trusted one and mistrusted the other.

"You won't go ahead with the dinner tonight, not after what happened?"

"I can do nothing else. All the invitations have been sent and the acceptances received, it's too late to cancel it now. Besides which, nobbling racehorses is a cruel fact of life, as even Randyll would be the first to admit." He saw the expression on her face. "But you'll still come?"

"For Clara's sake, yes."

"Not a little for your own?"

All around them the bustle of a busy stable racecourse went on. Russell looked back at Anna.

"Will you come to watch the race with me?"

"The only race I'll be watching is the King's Cup. And I'll watch that from the edge of the course, not my box."

"But you won't have as good a view as you would from the grandstand."

"It's not the same from up there. It's not close enough to what's happening, not near enough to the horses. I want to feel the ground trembling as they come by, with the rush of horses and the clods of turf flying in the air as they fly past." Her blue eyes gleamed. "You can't feel anything just watching from the boxes. No more than you could feel the heat of a fire if you stood on the other side of a great room."

He smiled his rare smile. Beneath the new, elegant Anna, with the exquisite veiled hat and fashion-plate clothes, was the Anna of long ago. He remembered the wild, tangled hair, dripping with rainwater, and the dirty, mud-caked hem of her gown, as she pushed her way through the milling crowds, her blue eyes searching for a sight of the horses as a hungry man's might search for a sight of food. Nothing about her had changed. Except that she was more beautiful.

"I understand," he said. He looked from one to the other of them. "Good luck."

"Thank you, milord," Chifney said.

A little smile played about the corners of her lips.

"Luck has nothing to do with it."

Suddenly, from outside, they heard a voice shouting wildly,

"Thrush 'as won the Surrey! She got 'er nose in front of Ambush on the line!"

Anna and Chifney exchanged glances. Neither of them spoke.

"Tobias Slout is down with the other blacklegs at the betting stand. He's made a killing on Thrush's win."

"Did anyone see how Edwards rode?"

"If you mean did anyone see him take a pull, the answer's no. He's too clever to be caught out. If he held back Ambush deliberately on the line you can be sure that nobody watching would ever see him do it."

"Has Edwards got a mount in the King's Cup?"

"On a no-hoper called Otho. It's a brilliant miler, by all accounts, but most reckon the Cup distance is too far for it to be a danger to the favorites. But don't worry. I know what you're thinking. If Edwards tries to bump and bore me, or box me in, he'll get more than he bargains for."

"Watch him, that's all. I don't trust him."

"If that horse starts away half as fast here as he did on the gallops, he'll leave all the others behind in a cloud of dust."

Anna smiled.

"It helps to have the best jockey riding him, too."

She made her way down to the very edge of the course with Firestone's lad, as soon as the first of the field had gone to post, groups of top-hatted gentlemen and their training grooms turning to gape at her as she passed. Some of them took off their hats and bowed toward her; others stood sullenly, whispering to one another as she went by. Acknowledging the first and ignoring the second, Anna found her way to a place near the judge's chair, where she had a clear view of the course right up to the turn at Tattenham Corner.

Leaning forward, she dug her nails into the hot, sweating palms of her hands. She felt sick, light-headed, her legs had turned to water. Inside, beneath the cool, elegant veneer her stomach twisted and turned, fears and doubts that she'd never expected to even think about all rose up and took their place. Firestone was a six-year-old, unraced for more than two years; maybe he was finished as a racehorse, maybe the breathtaking speed he'd shown her on the gallops was a sham, something that he'd never produce again. Maybe he'd jump off in front and shoot his bolt before the straight was reached; maybe the deafening roar of the Epsom crowds would upset him, and he'd fade away, a spent force, behind the leaders. Maybe the lameness that had dogged him all his life would suddenly come back, now, and render him useless forevermore. She sighed. She swallowed, her throat and mouth as dry as tinder. In her nervousness and agitation she began to bite her nails, a long-vanished habit of childhood that her mother and Jessie had always scolded her for. It seemed as long since the last of the field had gone down to post . . . where were they now? Was something wrong, had the race already started more than a mile away, would there be a countless succession of delays and false starts, like those that had marred the beginning of Priam's Derby on the same course three years ago? Suddenly, the press of people and the heat became unbearable coupled with her anguish, and she untied the strings of her bonnet and took it off, using it as a gigantic fan, her eyes closed against the tumult and the noise. Then, all at once, she heard the roar of the great crowd around them and the boy beside her both together.

"They're coming 'round Tattenham, miss! By Christ it's like a bloody cavalry charge!" In his excitement he grasped her sleeve with shaking fingers. "Look, miss, look! Firestone's laying third, on the inside!"

Trembling like a leaf she rushed forward on legs that scarcely bore her up. In the maze of horses and men all she could make out was Chifney in her pale blue silks, leaning forward in the saddle, his grip on the reins as light as air. Half a length in front of him raced Hindley's Prince Llewelyn and Carey's Otho, galloping neck and neck at the zenith of their strength. For a moment she held her breath. Then as Otho began to tire and rapidly fall away she saw Chifney urge her horse forward, and to the wild cheering of the crowd he drew level with Prince Llewelyn, then swiftly outpaced him.

Suddenly, from the packed masses of the crowd that lined the course, a man sprang out into Firestone's path, and Anna felt her voice rise up from her throat in a half-strangled cry of shock and rage as he lunged wildly at the horse's bridle. In a split second of lightning-quick thinking, Chifney drew his whip and knocked the man away, at the same time turning Firestone swiftly out of reach. For a moment he lost ground to Prince Llewelyn as Chifney fought to get him back into his stride; then he recovered himself, and surged ahead into the final furlong, two lengths clear of his nearest rivals. Behind them his attacker tried desperately to rise and throw himself out of the path of the oncoming horses, but he was too late. As they trampled over him Anna heard his screams of agony; then he rolled over and over and lay still. As the crowd began to surge onto the course, she saw Firestone streak further and further away from the rest of the field, and as he reached the winning post she let out a shriek of triumph that carried far above the heads of the crowd about them. Half-crazed with relief and joy, she grasped the lad's hand and pushed him behind her as she broke into a run.

All around them, people stepped back quickly to get out of her path.

Helen Gordon stood staring from her window back at Durdans, seething with rage. There was still no sign of any of the party returning.

For ten minutes more she paced up and down her room, her hands clawing at her loose, tangled hair. The house was as silent as the grave. Only the slow, rhythmic ticking of the clock on her mantlepiece broke the stillness. Suddenly she could bear it no longer. Taking off one of her high-heeled slippers, she threw it at the clock with all her might and it toppled from its place and crashed onto the floor.

She stood there for a moment, listening to the silence. Then she rushed over to the bed and began tearing off the covers, throwing them to the floor and trampling on them. She grasped the pillows and flung them in all directions. She ran over to her wardrobe and began pulling out the gowns inside, ripping them from end to end, her breathing labored, heavy, coming in gasps as if she were drowning. When there were no gowns left she grasped hold of the nearest pillow and clawed at it like a wild animal, and a shower of feathers billowed out in a cloud. Covered in them, wading through the pile of bedclothes and torn gowns, she dragged herself over to the tallboy and rummaged through one of the drawers until she found what she was looking for, a hipflask of gin. Sinking to a heap on the floor she put the rim to her lips and swigged it all.

Then the door opened and Leopardstown stood there.

For a moment he was too shocked to speak. He looked around the wreckage of the room, then back at her, sitting there half-naked in the middle of it, feathers sticking to her hair and skin. Disgust held him speechless.

"Well? What are you gawping at?" she said, unsteadily. She hiccuped. "Haven't you ever seen anyone drunk before?"

"I've never seen a lady drunk, no." He closed the door behind him. "But then a real lady would never get drunk, would she? She'd have too much self-respect."

Maddened, she flung the empty gin flask at him, missing his head by inches. "Like that common little horse-breaker you've been running after?"

"Anna Brodie's more a lady than you'd ever know how to be."

"I'm lady enough to be the next countess of Leopardstown!"

He looked at her with distaste, as if she were something that he'd trampled on, underfoot. He wondered how he could ever have thought her beautiful; she wasn't pretty, even. In the strong late afternoon sunlight that bathed the room he could see the lines of debauchery on her face, and he felt sickened by her. Even from where he was standing he could smell the gin on her breath.

"You, countess of Leopardstown?" He gave a short, bitter laugh. "I might have been fool enough to go to bed with a whore; but not stupid enough to marry one."

"Bastard!"

"We won't meet again." He turned back to the door and opened it. "Tonight I shall be at Ralph Russell's place, for the King's Cup dinner; after that I shall go on to my estates at Blairruarchdar." He let his eyes run meaningfully over the sea of mutilated gowns. "Since you have nothing left in one piece to wear, clearly you won't be among the company."

She struggled up, her pale eyes blazing.

"Get out! Get out of here!"

In a cool, calm voice that only enraged her more, he said, as he went out, "I'll send your maid to you to clear up this mess."

"Bastard! Lecher!" She grabbed an ornament and hurled it at the wall, where it shattered into pieces that flew in all directions. "Go on, get out! Go sniffing round that Brodie bitch, like a dog in heat! Do you think I care?" She staggered to her feet and ran after him, shouting abuse. As he walked down the staircase, she hung over the banisters, calling after him.

"I hate you! Hate you, do you hear me?" Coldly he ignored her and went on down the stairs. "But you'll be back, you'll come crawling on your hands and knees! And then I'll make you beg for it!"

He stopped at the foot of the staircase. Then he turned and glanced up. He gave her one last look of disgust and contempt. Then he walked out. Through the closed door, he could hear her screaming.

❋ 17 ❋

Ralph Russell stood at his window looking down across the courtyard, then the grounds beyond. At seven o'clock it was still light and the courtyard deserted. In an hour it would be dusk and the emptiness filled with post chaises, barouches, and private carriages. He took out his pocket watch and flicked open the lid. She had promised to come an hour before anyone else, and there were only five minutes left if she was to keep her promise. He wondered if she would.

Another minute ticked by. Then another. He continued to stand there, staring along the empty drive. Then he turned away and made his way slowly downstairs. As he reached the last few steps he heard the sound of horses and wheels crunching on the gravel of the courtyard, and below him his butler was standing ready at the door. As she stepped through into the hallway she glanced up and saw him at once and their eyes met and held in one long, unsmiling look.

"Good evening," he heard himself say, unable to drag his eyes from her. A few steps behind her stood her sister. They were both in white; Clara's gown was of organzine and Anna's of tarlatan. With their dark hair and vivid blue eyes neither of them could have worn a color that would have provided such a startling contrast. For a moment he could not make himself speak.

"You asked us to come an hour early," Anna said, breaking the silence.

"Yes, of course. Please come into the drawing room." At the flick of an eyebrow Jason faded away and he opened the door for them himself. As they walked into the room and stood there, he noticed that Clara's eyes went straight to the ornate piano that stood in the corner of the room. "Please," he said, indicating the settee and chairs. "Will you sit down? Can I offer you something in the way of refreshment?"

"Nothing for either of us," Anna said, taking a chair. Clara sat down on another, staring about her in wonderment, her eyes straying every few moments back to the piano, and lingering on it, almost hungrily. He sat down himself. He felt foolish, awkward. He wished he and Anna were alone so that he could say what he wanted to say.

"The jewelry is kept locked up in another room," he said, getting to his feet. "If you care to come with me I can show it to you." He turned to Clara. "Do you play, Miss Brodie?"

She looked back at him nervously. He noticed how she fiddled with her hands in her lap. "Why, yes, I do. Mama taught me. But we have no piano yet, though Anna has promised me one."

He smiled at her.

"Mine is suffering from acute neglect." He pointed to it. "Please, use it whenever you wish to. I love music almost as much as I love my horses."

She stammered words of thanks, and went over to it while they watched her. Slowly she sat down upon the stool, and raised the lid to reveal the keys. She sat there, staring at it almost as if it was something unreal. She touched the keys with her outstretched fingers, almost reverently.

"Let me give you the necklace," Russell said to Anna, and she followed him from the room into another. He closed the door and went over to a casket that stood upon a table. He opened it and took out something sparkling and light that winked and shone brilliantly as he turned it over in his hands. She had never seen anything so beautiful.

"This necklace is the centerpiece of the Russell diamonds," he said, coming toward her. "It was last worn by my mother and has been in my family for almost a hundred years." She was standing in front of a great mirror, watching him. Gently, he led her closer to the mirror and turned her round so that she was facing her own reflection. For a moment they both stood there, looking at it; then he raised his arms and lay the diamonds about her throat. She could feel the warmth of his fingers as he fastened the clasp behind her neck. Then he stepped backward and she was left alone, staring at her own face.

"They're very beautiful," she said, simply.

"This once they've been outmatched by their wearer."

Their eyes met in the mirror.

"But no doubt many of your guests will say that I've no right to wear them. I'm not a Russell."

"That isn't any of their business."

She turned round to face him.

"Most of the men you've invited here tonight are the same men that voted to petition the Jockey Club in Newmarket to blackball me. They think of you as one of them. When they see me, and Clara, wearing the Russell jewels, they'll accuse you of giving succor to the common enemy."

He looked outraged.

"Whom I choose to invite into my house is no concern of theirs or anyone's. Less still who wears something that is my property." His eyes narrowed, in sudden realization. "How did you know that they'd petitioned the Jockey Club to blackball you?"

"I prefer to keep that to myself." She walked away from him, over to the window. "But I know a letter is on its way to the Newmarket stewards urging them to make an official ruling against women's being permitted to go anywhere near the course, much less race horses on it."

His mind was racing, wondering how she could possibly have come by such knowledge. There was only one answer. Somebody at that meeting held at Durdans had told her. But he could not imagine who that might be. They were completely hostile to her, almost to a man; only two that he knew of besides himself—Heathcote and Edward Randyll—had been opposed to keeping her out. Maybe there was another, anonymous as yet, who found himself in sympathy with her ambitions, but if there was then his identity was a mystery. Only Anna herself could tell him. And he knew better than to ask.

"Why are you looking at me like that?" Anna said. Her eyes glowed. The diamonds at her neck sparkled as they reflected the rays of light.

"I was thinking that you should be painted. Just like that. In that gown. Exactly as you look now."

She allowed herself to smile. If Tollemache had told her that, she would have dismissed it with a shrug, as lip-service flattery. But she knew that Russell meant everything he said.

"I'd rather be painted on a horse."

He laughed; she laughed with him. Just then came the sound of Clara's playing from the other room, and her face changed instantly.

"What is it?" he asked, frowning. "What's the matter?"

"She plays beautifully. Just like our mother used to." She turned away, toward the door. She lay her hand upon the handle, and then opened it, slowly, just a few inches. Suddenly, high above the notes of the piano, came a voice. Sweet and powerful, it rose up to unbelievable heights, then dropped again, in perfect timing. It rang out, filling her ears, dwarfing even the perfection and beauty of her playing. Against her will, Anna felt her throat tighten, as it always had whenever she had heard her mother play, in another world. "There was a piano in my uncle's house, at Saffron Walden. She played upon that. The servants would sneak up from the kitchens to hide on the downstairs steps, just to listen to her." She was not looking at him. "She had a piano of her own, one that her father had given her when she was fifteen. However long she played on it, it was never long enough. The bailiffs took it." Now she glanced up at him. He saw both pain and bitterness in her eyes. "I remember the morning that they came. There were four of them. We all stood there, Clara and I holding my mother's hands, watching them while they loaded it onto their cart. I always swore that one day I'd buy her another one. Now I can, now that it's too late."

He still looked at her. He tried to think of the right words to say, but none came. To cover his awkwardness he walked back to the table and took a small box from the casket.

"I think this would suit your sister," he said, holding it out to her. "Shall we take it to her?"

She made no reply. She glanced once at her reflection in the mirror, then went back to the room where Clara still played.

All the reception rooms were crowded with people, laughing, talking, standing together in groups, seated around the silk-hung walls on brocade sofas and elaborately carved chairs. Satin and taffeta, lace-paneled ball gowns swept against each other, fans waved, footmen in immaculate livery moved with unobtrusive, polished expertise among the vast swarming throng, balancing glasses of wine and champagne on silver trays with one hand, never spilling a single drop.

Music from the hired string ensemble in one corner of the great room drifted above the moving heads of the guests, voices rose louder and were swelled by those still arriving, the clatter of carriages and barouches in the courtyard outside sounding every now and then above the noise. As a fresh party arrived on the threshold of the drawing room, James Leopardstown glanced up, glass in hand, and his wrist froze halfway to his lips in midair. Even blindfolded he would have recognized her shrill, raucous laugh at once. There, thrusting herself forward, in an ill-fitting, borrowed red gown that was almost indecently low-cut falling carelessly from her bare shoulders, was Helen Gordon. Moving backward into the press of guests so that she would not catch sight of him, he saw her narrowed, sharp eyes rapidly rove about the crowded room, searching. He put down his half-finished glass of wine. He turned away, partly obscured by a pillar. With a swift glance backward to see where she was now, he let himself be drawn into conversation by a group of Russell's guests. Then behind him he heard the chattering voices suddenly fall silent, broken only by one or two isolated whispers, and slowly, still half-hidden by the pillar, he glanced over his shoulder.

"It's her. It's Anna Brodie!" he heard another startled voice say.

*   *   *

Her eyes met Hindley's across the crowded room. Instinctively she knew what he and almost everyone else was thinking. In the sudden moment of stunned silence that had fallen as she came into the room, she caught sight of his party, one of the last to arrive; she saw Gilbert and Lady Heathcote, two or three unknown faces. The smiling eyes of men around the room; the cold, staring eyes of the women. Some curious. Some shocked. Some hostile. Then, a smirk playing at the corners of his lips, Lionel Tollemache. Every pair of eyes had fallen on her as she walked further into the room, her white tarlatan gown trailing after her, the Russell diamonds glittering at her throat. A sense of triumph pervaded her. She had beaten them on the racecourse today; she had beaten them here. It was clear to all of them without a word being spoken that she was Russell's guest of honor, and there was nothing they could do about it. As she walked among them with Clara, smiling and talking, her sharp eyes saw Hindley motion Russell toward the door. And she knew why.

"You'll be sorry for this!"

"Don't threaten me in my own house!"

"I'm not threatening you, I'm telling you. If you support that Brodie bastard once more against the interests of your friends, you'll live to regret it."

"And if I hear you call her a bastard just one more time in my hearing, I'll thrash you till you can neither sit nor stand."

"She's using you, can't you see that? She knows she can twist you around her little finger. She's been dragged up from the gutter, and her kind know all the weaknesses in others that they can exploit for their own scheming ends. She knows full well that all of Epsom's against her, that it's only a matter of time before the Jockey Club bans her horses from the course. Ordinarily she'd be finished then. But she thinks that if she can get you where she wants you, you'll find a way out for her." Russell stared at him, bitterness in his eyes. "Your uncle is one of the big guns over at Newmarket . . . put her case to him through you, and she gets a reprieve, maybe an indefinite stay of execution. That what she wants, that's what she's hoping for. Don't tell me you never realized that."

"She doesn't even know that my uncle is the chief steward at Newmarket."

"Would you care to take a bet on that?"

"I only bet with gentlemen." They glared at each other from opposite sides of the room. "And for as long as I've known her, she's never once tried to get anything out of me. Quite the contrary. When I offered her any help she might need, she told me that she didn't want it."

"She's just playing you on the end of her line!"

Russell's voice rose in anger.

"All the overtures of friendship have been from my side. Not hers."

"So I can see. As everyone else that you've asked here tonight can. Have you gone mad, loading that bitch and her sister with the Russell jewels? Jewels that you wouldn't even let your own lawful wife wear, jewels that she had a right to!"

Russell came toward him, slowly. Instinctively, he stepped back. When Russell spoke his voice was so soft that Hindley barely heard what he said. "Get out of this room. Now. Get out before I strike you down."

When he was alone he went over to his brandy and poured some. He drank it down, then poured another. From outside he could hear the sounds of his guests, of laughter and the loud, disjointed clamor of conversation. He put down the glass. He must go back to them.

His eyes traveled swiftly over the groups of people in the room, looking for her; the men laughing and talking together, discussing the afternoon's racing; the hovering footmen, the chattering ladies in their bright gowns; young, shallow, too-immaculate James Tollemache; charming, pretty, naive Clara Brodie. But she was not there.

Anna paused at the foot of the staircase as someone called her name. *"Miss Brodie?"*

She turned, glancing over her shoulder, and looked into a strong, clean-shaven, dark-eyed face, somehow vaguely familiar to her.

"I'm Anna Brodie, yes." He smiled but she did not.

"Allow me to present myself, if I might take the liberty. James Leopardstown. Your servant."

A wry smile curled her lips.

"An expensively dressed servant, Lord Leopardstown." Yes, she remembered the face now. She could see it, among a cluster of others, ensconced in the comfort of Sir Gilbert Heathcote's grandstand box. Sam had once mentioned him in passing. Rich, Scottish. With a castle and acres somewhere in the Highlands. Because of who he was and what he was, the mothers of every marriageable girl of standing were falling over one another to interest him in their wares. Anna's eyes held a wariness that he was too shrewd not to recognize.

"I wanted to offer my congratulations on your horse winning the King's Cup. It was a splendid achievement."

The wry smile curled her lips even further.

"The horse's achievement, not mine."

"I realize that. But I wanted you to know that I was delighted he won the race. I can think of nobody who deserves success more than you do."

"Then you must be in a minority, my lord." Was it his imagination or were those last two words spoken with a lacing of scorn? "Please excuse me." Before he could say another word she had lifted the hem of her ball gown and was halfway up the stairs.

He stood there for a moment or two, until she had vanished out of sight, listening to the rustling of tarlatan as it became fainter and fainter. She had not offered him her hand to kiss. Her blue eyes had been as cold as ice. But standing closer to her than he had ever been before he had been struck by her beauty and the power of her presence.

Slowly, half-elated, half-disappointed, he turned away to go back into the crowded drawing room, and came face to face with a wild-eyed Helen Gordon.

"You!"

"You stinking jackal!" Savagely, she tugged at the shoulder of her borrowed, ill-fitting gown. "You thought you'd be rid of me, didn't you, so that you'd be free to lust after that common little horse-breaker!" Spittle, from rage, came out of a corner of her mouth. "Panting after her, like a dog in heat. You didn't waste any time, did you?" She was inches away from him now. "Well, I foiled you. I borrowed this gown from Charlotte Heathcote and followed on as soon as I could! And I wasn't wrong, was I? That's the only reason you're here, to sniff round that bitch Anna Brodie!"

He stared down at her in cold anger. Under the lights of the chandelier, he saw with distaste the blemishes in her complexion from her way of life, emphasized rather than concealed by the white paste she had smothered her skin with. A stark contrast to the flawless skin of Anna Brodie. The expression on his face infuriated her far more than any spoken insult could have done.

"I have nothing else to say to you, Helen."

"Don't you dare turn your back on me!"

"Take your hand off my sleeve before I throw it off!" For a few seconds they glared at each other. "If you want to make a public spectacle of yourself, do so. But don't include me in your shame."

Slowly, her hand dropped away from him, like a limp, lifeless thing. She stepped back. Behind them, the door of the drawing room opened and a bevy of guests, laughing, chattering, spilled out, on their way to the cold buffet laid out in the adjoining room. Leopardstown made perfect use of their sudden appearance to make his escape.

As he passed by her she gave him one last, bitter, parting look.

"Don't ever think you'll get away with this."

Anna stopped halfway up the staircase and looked around her. Portraits hung upon the walls of every floor, below and above her as far as she could see. She paused every now and then, admiring one. There was a Stubbs. Several Old Masters. Lely, Kneller. Great canvasses of unknown horses, being exercised on Epsom Downs. At the top of the staircase on the first landing there was a magnificent painting of Herring's, of Russell's Selim colt, Levethian, entered for the Hambletonian Stakes. She stopped in front of it for several minutes, then turned away and glanced at the row of doors. They all looked alike to her. She tried several, but they were only disused bedrooms. The last one was locked.

"Can I be of any help, madam?" said a manservant's voice from behind her, at the turn of the stairs. Startled, she spun round. Robert stood there, a tray in his hands.

"I was looking for the ladies' cloakroom."

"The door at the far end of the landing, madam." He started to go on down the stairs.

"Just a moment." He glanced back up at her. "Why is this door kept locked? None of the others are."

"It always has been, madam. For as long as I can remember. Lord Russell's orders."

She nodded. "Thank you." She made her way to the cloakroom and went inside.

It was a beautiful room, like all the rooms in the house. She looked around her. Gold and white satin drapes, the upholstery trimmed with rich gold fringing and braid. Huge vases filled with summer flowers stood on every surface. She sat down on a chair and eased her satin shoes from her feet. She was not used to wearing them, and they had rubbed against her heels and across her insteps, making sore, angry patches that would be blisters by tomorrow.

She sat there for what seemed to her a long while, listening to the slow, methodical, peaceful ticking of the clock that stood in the middle of the mantlepiece, faint sounds of the celebrations below drifting to her ears.

Her eyes wandered over the contents of the room, over the cloaks and capes laid carefully side by side. There were several fur mantelets, and some in velvet edged with fringe. Long satin capes, cloaks in rich brocade, exquisitely embroidered, and taffeta and lace pelerines, Lady Heathcote's with its stiffened collar and beaded edges lying next to Clara's and her own. Then the clock struck the hour and she realized that she had been here for more than twenty minutes. Too long. She got up, the satin shoes in her hand, and went out again. At the top of the staircase she paused, distracted by muffled voices and strange sounds that seemed to come from within the locked room. She frowned and turned back.

No light came from beneath the door. For a moment she stood outside, listening. Then her curiosity got the better of her and she placed her hand upon the knob and turned it. It was no longer locked.

She opened it only a few inches, enough to see inside. There was no lamp burning in the room, but the drapes had not been drawn. From outside the moonlight shone brightly through the window, casting silver rays that fell gently across the big, canopied bed. The bed was not empty. For there, sprawled across the rumpled coverlet, their naked limbs grotesquely entwined, lay two men. And both she recognized.

She fled back along the landing to the cloakroom, fighting back the wave of nausea. She grasped her cloak and Clara's, and ran back downstairs without a glance behind, back into the noisy, crowded room. Swiftly her eyes searched above the milling heads for Clara, and when she caught sight of her she raised her hand and beckoned, then began to make her way through the press of people almost frantically. When she reached her she grabbed her by the wrist and pulled her back toward the door.

"Anna, what is it? What's wrong?"

"Come with me into the other room and take off that necklace. It's time to go."

"But it's still early!"

"Don't argue with me. Just do as I say."

Out into the cool of the hallway and into the room opposite, where Anna closed the door and took off her own necklace, laying it back on its bed of velvet in the casket.

"Anna, I can't unfasten the clasp."

"Wait a minute, I'll do it for you." As she spoke the door opened and Russell stood there. He looked from one to the other, without understanding. Then he saw that Anna's neck was bare.

"Why have you taken it off, Anna? What is it?"

"We're leaving." Her voice was cold and harsh, the voice of the young, bitter Anna he had first known. "Thank you for the loan of the necklaces." She unfastened Clara's and held it out to him.

"But it's early yet. I was going to ask your sister if she would play for us . . ."

"Another time, maybe. But we have to go." She handed Clara her cloak and threw her own around her shoulders before he could come forward to help her with it. "I have to be up early in the morning. I'm breaking in my Glenartney filly."

"But you said you wouldn't do that until the end of the racing season, when you had more time. You said you didn't believe in pushing two-year-olds."

"Backward two-year-olds, which she's not. She's big and forward in condition; she needs more exercise than cantering round in circles three times a day, on the end of a running rein. If I don't give it to her soon, she'll kick her stall down. And in any case I've decided to give her one or two races before the winter, to see how she shapes up against experienced fillies." She was already at the door. "Thank you for this evening. Clara?" As her sister passed by him on her way to the hall, she hesitated, and looked up nervously into his face.

"Yes, thank you for this evening. And for lending us the necklaces."

"You're more than welcome. And any time you want to use my piano, please come over."

Clara followed Anna to the door, where the butler was already waiting. But Anna was staring toward the bottom of the staircase, and his eyes followed hers. Lionel Tollemache's young brother stood there, a smile on his lips. He bowed toward them, his own eyes on Clara. Anna grasped her hand almost roughly and pulled her outside through the open door.

Russell watched them walk toward their post chaise. The young man from her stables who had driven them over rushed to open the door and help them inside. Then he mounted and the chaise swung away down the drive, swallowed up in the darkness. Russell turned and went back into the hallway.

Tollemache's brother had gone. Russell went back into the room, dejectedly, and picked up the necklace she had worn. It still felt warm, from contact with her skin, and for several minutes he stood holding it tightly in his hands, before replacing it in its box.

He had never understood her. He wondered if he ever would.

"Didn't expect you back this early, miss." Anna's head groom came toward them from the shadow of the coach house, buckling his belt up as he went. "Everything all right over at Lord Russell's place, is it?"

"Early start tomorrow, be up and ready by six. I'm breaking in my Glenartney filly," she said briefly, without answering his question.

"But you said you wasn't going to break 'er in till wintertime. You said you wanted to wait."

"I've changed my mind. She needs breaking now." Something about Paris irked her, something she wasn't quite sure of. But he had come with good references and there was no denying he had a way with the horses. That was good enough for her. She glanced down at his hastily fastened belt. "Did we get you out of bed?"

"No, miss, no." He looked flustered, but only for a moment. "Just an accident, really. Spilled some water from me bucket, all over me clean shirt. There was dried mud on one of the chaise wheels, and I was washing it off."

"At this time of night? I don't expect you to work in the dark," she said dryly, and went on into the house, Clara following behind her.

Jessie was still up. She was sitting in the little parlor, a bag of knitting on her lap, a half-finished supper tray on the table at her side. There was amazement in her face as she glanced up.

"Back already? It's not 'alf past ten, yet."

"Yes, back already." Clara sat down by Jessie and picked up a slice of cold meat from the plate on her tray. Anna went straight over to the decanter and poured herself a glass of brandy. She drank it all down. "I'm breaking the Glenartney filly in tomorrow. I'll need a good night's sleep. She might prove difficult."

"Not that it's any of my business," Jessie said, her needles clicking as she spoke, "but you're drinking too much of that stuff lately."

Anna put down the glass without looking at her.

"I need it. I've got a nasty taste in my mouth." She went over to the window and moved the drape with her hand. She stared out into the night. Behind her Clara and Jessie's chatter faded into blankness; only their mouths moved, she could hear no sound. She could see her own shadowy reflection in the window pane, the round, shiny disc of the full moon above it, shimmering like a pool. And then the ray of moonlight as it had fallen softly from the undraped window onto the coverlet of the canopied bed, illuminating the two white, writhing bodies, revolting and sickening her. She closed her eyes, tightly, willing the images away. When she opened them again, it was to see someone appear, suddenly, from within the darkness of the coach house, then run across the courtyard to the door.

She turned from the window and the drape fell back into place. Outside, she heard the front door open and then close softly.

"Goodnight." She looked across the room to Clara and Jessie. "Don't stay up too late."

In the hallway, the new girl Anna had hired from the village to help Bess and Ellen Troggle in the house flattened herself against the door, her face white, like a ghost's.

"Oh, it's you, miss. You fair gave me a turn!"

"Was that you outside just now?"

Color flooded into her cheeks.

"Yes, miss. I . . . I just went to ask Ben . . . I mean Paris, whether 'e'd give you that message or not. But I couldn't find 'im."

"What message?"

"About the boy what called 'ere, not long after you and Miss Clara'd left for Lord Russell's place."

"He didn't say anything about it to me. Did the boy say what he wanted?"

"I think 'e was after work, miss. With the 'orses, like. Paris sent 'im packing, but 'e said 'e'd come back tomorrow, when you was back."

"Why did Paris send him packing?"

"'E was Irish, miss. Paris reckons all Irish are no good. That's what 'e told 'im, right to 'is face."

"Paris had no right to send him away." There was anger in her voice. "I make the decisions round here. And only a fool would believe that all Irishmen are bad, the same as anyone would be a fool to believe that all gentlemen are good." She started to go upstairs. "I'll speak to him in the morning. Is Bess still up?"

"I think so, miss."

"Then ask her to help you bring some hot water up to my bedroom, would you? I need a bath, now. Then you can both go to bed."

"I'll fetch 'er right away, Miss Anna." She hurried away down the corridor toward the kitchen.

She undressed slowly. Then she hung away the white tarlatan ball gown in her cupboard. She stepped into the tub and sat down, then slid deeper beneath the warm, soothing softness of the water. Only the skin on her feet where the satin shoes had rubbed stung her, painfully; the rest of her body floated, weightlessly, and she lay back her head and closed her eyes.

She had had a bath only that afternoon; she had disliked making the maids Ruth and Bess carry pails of hot water up the stairs at the end of a long day, when they were tired and had done it once already. But ever since she had opened the door to the locked room and seen inside, she had longed to immerse herself into the cleansing water, as if what she had seen on the canopied bed had somehow made her unclean, too. But she could not tell them that.

She heard them chattering as they passed her door on their way to their bedrooms. She heard Clara call goodnight and go into her own room and close the door. For several minutes she could hear her moving about as she undressed and put away her clothes. Then there was silence once more. Clara would have hung away the white organzine ball gown, neatly, then brushed out her hair. She pictured her climbing into her bed, tired and happy, sleep coming to her almost as soon as her head touched the pillow, no ugly memories to disturb it, to keep her taut and wakeful into the early hours.

"Anna?" said Jessie's voice from the other side of her bedroom door. "Are you in bed yet?"

"No," she called, opening her eyes. She felt the draft as Jessie opened the door and came into the room. Then it disappeared as she closed it behind her. She was carrying a pile of towels in her big, work-reddened arms, and she had already plaited her hair, ready for the night.

"I'll stay and brush your 'air for you, if you like."

"It's kind of you to offer, but there's no need."

"Anything I can get you from downstairs, then? A nice 'ot nightcap would do you a power of good."

"No thanks. I don't want anything."

Jessie sat down. She shifted her weight on the chair.

"Then maybe you'll tell me what's bothering you." Anna gave her an old-fashioned glance. "And don't tell me there's nothing, 'cos I know better."

"It's nothing I want to talk about."

"Is it that Ralph Russell?"

"No, it's not Ralph Russell. Nothing to do with him."

"Then it's someone else. Someone there tonight say something to upset you?"

"My hide's too tough for that, Jessie. If it wasn't I'd never have gotten this far." She eased herself into another position in the tub. "Do you know what they call me on the course, behind my back? The bastard." She gave a small, bitter laugh. "At least they can't call me anything worse than that."

"Then shame on 'em! The good Lord'll see that they get their deserts. Jealous tongues don't need much to make 'em wag, and that's the truth of it. You turn a deaf ear to 'em, and take no notice. It's a true saying . . . sticks and stones'll break me bones, but names'll never 'urt me!"

"Whoever said that was stone deaf," Anna said, dryly. She traced patterns with her fingers upon the water. "Do you know what they're trying to do now? Get the stewards of the Jockey Club at Newmarket to make a ruling against women on the course. They'd stop at nothing to get me out. Today I merely rubbed their noses in it when Firestone ran their horses into the ground."

"And what'll you do if they get the ruling? 'Ave you thought about that?"

"Yes, I've thought about it. I'll fight them. In the courts. All the way to parliament if need be. They won't intimidate me. The more they're against me, the more determined they'll make me to get what I want." Her eyes had that hard, far-seeing look that Jessie knew so well. "All that will take time. A lot of time. Maybe years. They can't ban me from the course or ban my horses from racing on it until they have that final judgment. That's my trump card, Jessie. The time it takes. They can't act until they have a decision, from the highest court, one way or the other. While they're waiting for it I'll be free to accomplish what I set out to do. And there's nothing they can do to stop me." Her face had lost that tired, strained look. It was animated. "That's what they don't realize. That I'll fight them to the end. They think I'll crack. Back down. Slink away with my tail between my legs when the going gets rough. They'll never know just how wrong they are."

"There's nobody can say you 'aven't got your 'ead screwed on the right way round, an that's a fact!"

"Whatever happens I shall have won, one way or the other." She glanced across at Jessie. "Something else I found out tonight. Something I never knew before, never even suspected. Ralph Russell's uncle is the chief steward at Newmarket."

"Why, fancy that! Well, there's 'alf your problems solved to start with. All 'e 'as to do is to 'ave a quiet word in 'is uncle's ear!"

"But don't you see, I can't let him do that. If I asked him it would make me beholden. If he tried to influence his uncle on my behalf, it would place both of them in an impossible position . . . stewards are supposed to be strictly impartial; members of the Jockey Club risk warning off if they try in any way to exert influence on an official. I don't want either of those things to happen."

"But 'e might go ahead and do it anyway. 'E knows the others are dead set against you. Only stands to reason that 'e'll try and do what 'e can."

"Then I must make sure he doesn't." She reached for a towel, then climbed out of the tub. "Whatever I do, I have to do it alone. I don't want favors, not even from him. I don't ever want it said at the end of the day that I got where I am by climbing on the back of others. I couldn't bear that."

"What you want is a good night's rest." Jessie heaved herself to her feet and went to lay down the pile of towels on Anna's bed. She jabbed a finger in the direction of the tub. "And don't go breaking your neck over that thing, neither. I'll get the girls to empty it, first thing in the morning."

"I don't think I can sleep yet. I might go downstairs, and read awhile."
She rubbed herself vigorously. "Sam sent a book over. I haven't even had
time to open it, I've been so busy." Yes, she would try to read. In that, she
might lose herself. In that she might forget the moonlit room and the
white, writhing bodies upon the canopied bed.

While the rest of the house slept, she sat beside a lamp in her favorite
chair, the dogs asleep at her feet, restlessly turning over the pages.

She fell asleep in the chair, the book still open on her lap. When she
woke, it was just before dawn.

Quietly, she crept upstairs to dress.

Every day for weeks, Anna had been preparing the filly for the saddle.
Every day, sometimes as much as three or four times, she had tied her
quietly in her stall and stroked and gentled her, then walked around her,
stopping now and then to lean across her back. She had progressed to
fitting her with a surcingle, then exercising her on the lunge for two or
three hours a day, before turning her out into one of the big paddocks to
kick her heels as she pleased. Now, she was ready for the final lesson.

With a saddle in her hands, Anna approached her quietly, speaking in a
soft, low voice. She paused, within hand's reach, and held out the saddle
for her to smell and look upon, then jingled the girths, and the stirrups, to
make her familiar with the sound. Every day for the past three weeks she
had enacted the same unwavering ritual, until now the filly was ready to be
offered the saddle on her back for the first time. Sam's words, the words
from the book he'd given her, lilted through her mind at every movement.

*Then you shall offer him a saddle, which you shall set in the manger
before him; so that he may smell and look upon it, and you shall jingle the
girths and stirrups about his ears to make him careless of the noise . . .*

Behind her, almost silently, Paris and one of the other lads had appeared, ready to help. As Paris slowly untied her halter and held her
steadily, Anna handed the saddle to Elijah, then reached out to her, and
began, very gently and deliberately, to rub and stroke her sides.

*Then, with all gentleness, after you have his sides therewithal, you shall set
the saddle upon his back and gird it gently on . . .*

Still talking softly to the filly, Anna took back the saddle and lay it
carefully upon her back, then buckled the girth; then she adjusted the
stirrups to the length she liked them, on either side.

*Which done, you shall take a sweet snaffle bit washed and anointed with
honey and salt, and put it into his mouth . . .*

Slipping off her halter, Anna took the bridle from Elijah and gently
eased it, reins first, above her head, then slipped the bit into her mouth,
holding it open with her left hand, and finally passed the headpiece gently
over her ears.

"Now, watch me, Elijah. See how it's done? Always fasten the throatlatch so . . . so that you can always get three fingers between it and the horse's throat."

"Yes, miss."

"If a throatlatch is fastened too tight it stops the horse from flexing at the poll. But more important, it's bloody sore. All right, stand back." With the same slow, gentle movement, Anna took the reins, gathered them on the pommel of the saddle, and mounted, with a leg up from Paris. She eased herself quickly and carefully into the saddle, slipped her booted feet into the stirrups, then gripped tightly with her legs as the filly began to fidget and twist her body from left to right. "Stand away!"

The filly struggled, lashing out half a dozen times with her back legs, then bucked, from her front feet to her hind ones, moving backward and forward like a rocking horse; but Anna stayed firmly in the saddle, patting her neck, gentling her, talking softly to her all the while. When the filly finally stopped, Anna walked her slowly around the paddock, then eased her into a trot and then a hack canter, while every now and then the filly tossed her head and whinnied, champing on the unfamiliar bit.

"Open the gates!" Anna shouted to Paris. As he did she gently steered the filly's head toward it, then rode her out in the direction of the grounds.

There were acres out there. High ground. Low ground. Sloping ground. Steep ground. Every kind that she was likely to come across on any racecourse.

Now she could see what the filly was really made of.

The first thing she heard was Paris's voice, raised in anger. Then a strange voice, in protest. She dismounted, and led her filly forward into the yard, pausing to listen.

Their backs were turned to her and neither noticed her until the filly's hooves clip-clopped over the courtyard flagstones. Then they both turned. The stranger was a small, slight boy with a mop of curly hair and hands so delicate that any lady would have been proud to own them. He started to come toward her, but Paris grabbed him by the sleeve.

"I've already told you. Be on your way!"

"What's all this?" asked Anna, glancing at Paris. Before he could speak she suddenly remembered. The newcomer must be the boy that had come yesterday, when she wasn't here, inquiring after work. "Did you come yesterday?"

He pulled his cap from his mop of hair.

"Ay, Miss Brodie. And I was sent away with a flea in me ear. But I said that I'd only take no for an answer from yourself." He was Irish, Ruth had said. She could hear that for herself.

"You sent him away without waiting to ask me?" Paris was getting too big for his boots. Making him chief groom had already gone to his head.

"You never said anything about wanting to take on more help in the yard," he answered, sullenly.

"That wasn't the question I asked. I said, you sent him away without asking me first?"

"I didn't reckon you'd be wanting any Irish within a mile of the place!"

"Why, you black-hearted son of a—" The boy sprang forward, his fists clenched, but Anna grasped him roughly by the sleeve.

"That's enough. From both of you. Paris, take this filly and rub her down." She waited until he had gone before she turned back to the boy. "All right. What's your name and who did you last work for?"

"William Devine, miss. And I was with poor Mr. Randyll until lately. You already know what happened up there, at the manor." He shook his head, sadly. "One of the best, Mr. Randyll was, miss. One of the best. They done for 'im now. And all of us is out of a job."

"How long did you work for him?"

"Nigh on a year, miss. I come over on the boat from Dublin and I worked me way down to Epsom. It was Mr. Randyll who give me me first chance, and right grateful to 'im I was for it. I only wish I could have found the rogues what did what they did to 'im, that I do." He fished in his coat pocket and brought out a folded paper. "This is what 'e wrote, miss, as a testimonial, like. But you can ask 'im to 'is face about me honesty, if you care to." He handed it to her and she unfolded and read it. She glanced up, a smile playing about her lips.

"So you're hard-working and honest and you have a way with horses. How come you didn't go to one of the big yards . . . to Durdans, for instance? I've only just started out here, I don't have even half a dozen horses of my own, not yet."

"Mr. Randyll said that 'e'd put a good word in with Sir Gilbert Heathcote on me behalf, if I had a mind to go there, it's true . . ."

"Then why didn't you?"

"You're better-looking than 'e is, miss. And I always admired a lady with guts."

Anna turned away her head to hide a smile.

"Flattery won't get you a job in my yard."

"Ay, I reckoned on that, miss. But if yourself would be willing to take a chance on me for a week or two, I could show you what I could do." His words sounded very like those she'd used on Sam Loam, more than three years ago. She smiled.

"I've only Firestone and the Glenartney filly in my own stable. But I'm taking on a lot of unbroken horses for Sam Loam, to help him out. He hasn't got enough room at his yard and I've got plenty. Have you done any breaking over at Randyll's?"

"No, miss, but I done plenty on me uncle's farm since I was fourteen years old, and you can write and be asking 'im if you don't believe me."

"All right. Let's say you've a difficult colt. Never had a bridle or a saddle on him in his life. What do you do?"

"Be the only one to look after 'im. Lead 'im out, give 'im 'is feed. Make much of 'im. Then when the time come, I'd slip on a plain rope 'alter, and lead 'im out, then I'd tie 'im up secure. Then I'd touch 'im, all over, with a willow wand. Soft, like, and gentle. Get 'im relaxed, and trusting me. Then I'd lunge 'im for a bit."

"Without anything on his back?"

"To start with, for a day or two. Then I'd try a surcingle, to get 'im used to a little weight. After a few days I'd start to walk around 'im, touch 'im, smooth his back and 'is flanks. Then when he was used to me leaning on 'im, I'd put a saddle on . . . but slow, and gentle. Then I'd lunge 'im in that for a spell."

"And the next stage?"

"I'd find a little grooming stool, tall enough for me to stand on so that I was above 'im. After a while I'd mount 'im, slowly, and sit on 'im, bareback. Wouldn't attempt to ride 'im for a few days, maybe a week. Then when the time come he'd be used to the saddle and me sitting on him."

"Whoever taught you taught you a thing or two. All right. Consider yourself hired."

His pixielike face lit up.

"Bless you miss, bless you for the angel you are! You'll not be sorry, I swear it on me mother's soul!"

Anna held up a hand.

"Wait a minute . . . there's one thing more. If I take you on I don't want any trouble. No arguments. No fights. Paris might be a pain in the arse, but he knows his work inside out and I'd be hard put to replace him. You make sure you get on with him or you don't get on at all. Understand me?"

"If there's any trouble it won't be of my making."

"All right. Take a stroll over to the barn and find Elijah. He'll show you where to put your things. I'll go and have a talk with Paris."

He was wisping down the Glenartney filly with a handful of straw and looked up as he heard her approach. His face wore that dark look she knew so well, the look of a sulky schoolboy. It instantly maddened her.

"Next time anyone comes to the yard asking for work, you send him to see me, all right?"

"You weren't here, miss."

"Don't back-answer me. You get him to wait or come back the next day. Understand? That boy knows more about horses than any green-eared stable lad I'd ever come across. That's the kind of boy I want working in my yard. And because of you I might well have lost him."

Paris flung down the handful of straw.

"You're makin' a big mistake, miss. You mark my words. You take on

Irish muck and you're taking on trouble. I seen it. You can't trust 'em no further than you can throw 'em . . . and they'll lift anything in sight that's not nailed down."

"The boy's been working for Edward Randyll for over a year and Randyll doesn't hire rubbish. And he's got a good character and a recommendation from Randyll that he signed himself."

"No bit of paper would satisfy me. Randyll's crack filly gets done over, and nobody in the yard knows how the nobblers guessed she was hid in the coach horses' stall! If I 'ad ten guineas I'd wager that little Irish whelp could tell a thing or two about that!"

Anna gave him one of her coldest stares.

"Whoever gave the orders for Randyll's filly to be nobbled was someone who expected to get rich from his ruin. Not a stableboy who stood to gain nothing except the loss of his own living when Randyll went down." Paris didn't answer. "And if I hear that you've been giving that boy a hard time just to vent your own spite, you'll be out of this yard so fast it'll make your head spin." She turned on her heel and went out.

As she reached the front of the house, a small group of riders were coming up from the drive, and she stopped and shaded her eyes with her hand to see who they were. She recognized Sir Gilbert Heathcote and Lord Leopardstown, who had been one of Russell's guests from the night before. And the third, a face she was never likely to forget.

They all dismounted and removed their hats. Heathcote apologized for bothering her. "May I introduce the earl of Leopardstown, and Mr. James Tollemache?"

She made no move toward any of them.

"Is there something important that you wanted? I'm running a busy yard."

"Is there somewhere more private where we might talk, Miss Brodie?"

Anna narrowed her eyes suspiciously. Anything private Heathcote had to tell her would go straight back to Jacob Hindley if it was said in front of Tollemache's brother.

"Come into the house," she said abruptly. Inside, she called out to Clara at the top of her voice. When she appeared at the turn of the stairs Anna jutted a finger in the direction of Leopardstown and James Tollemache. "I've got some business to discuss with Sir Gilbert Heathcote. Take these . . . gentlemen into the drawing room and give them something to drink."

Clara did as she was told obediently. Anna turned her face away to hide a smile. James Tollemache looked as stunned as if somebody had hit him.

She closed the library door behind them and leaned against it. "Well, what is it? You can spare me the fanciful phrases. If you've come all this way to try to persuade me to sell up and get out of Epsom, then you've had a wasted journey."

She detected amusement in his eyes.

"By no means. You're a lady of firm resolve. I acknowledge that. I respect you for it. Though I have to admit that seeing a woman walking on the course, mixing freely with the men, and racing horses on it, is something that I never expected to see, and probably won't ever get used to, I'm personally loath to set myself up in opposition against you. Unfortunately, as you're already aware, I'm very much in a minority."

"You're telling me something I already know, Sir Gilbert."

"I feel I should tell you that every other major owner in Epsom, with the exception of Lord Russell, has insisted that I write to the stewards of the Jockey Club in Newmarket demanding that you be stopped from racing your horses on the course."

That she also knew from Lionel Tollemache, and had known for some time. But she could hardly tell Heathcote that.

"Go on."

"As chief steward here, I had no choice but to do as they asked. After all, it's my job to represent them. A petition was signed and sent with my letter to the Newmarket stewards."

Anna walked across the room and looked out of the window onto the gardens and the orchard beyond to suppress a smile. The letter and the petition were in her desk in this very room, under lock and key. "Really?"

"I feel bound to warn you that I fully expect the Jockey Club stewards to accede to the wishes of the majority here, and legislate accordingly."

She turned back to face him. Her face was composed now.

"Would you expect them to do anything else? They're all men, aren't they?" The bitterness in her voice was sharp as a knife. "They can't bear the thought of a woman in their midst, taking them on, beating them at their own game. It scares the guts out of them. It rankles. It sticks in their throats. It goes against every narrow, bigoted principle they were ever taught to believe in. Women are second-rate, one rung above children and servants. They have to be kept down, kept in their places just as a horse or a dog is. They should be obedient. Humble. Respectful. Grateful for meaningless chivalry and empty courtesies that were only devised to disguise the fact that they have no status or power at all.

"Women can't own property in their own names. They can't vote. They have no control over their own lives or even their own bodies. From the cradle to the grave they're nothing more than the property or the playthings of men, and they're treated accordingly. Even the clothes they wear belong legally to either their fathers or their husbands. They can't win, not ever. The laws are made by men and administered by men. They have all the power and all the advantages. The only reason I'm different is that I'm alone . . . my father is dead and I have no husband. And I have no intention of ever taking one."

She was surprised to see him smiling.

"You're a formidable young lady . . . and I respect you for it. Every word you say is true. I won't deny it. But I have no say in the making of the laws of the land any more than I do in the making of the laws of the Jockey Club. As chief steward here, my duty is only to do what my superiors tell me to. What I came here today to say to you is that whatever I'm obliged to do in public, in private my sympathies are wholeheartedly on your side." He saw by her expression that she was not quite sure whether to believe in his sincerity. "If the worst comes to the worst, may I ask you what you would do?"

"You really expect me to answer that question?" She gave a short, acid laugh. "That would be the equivalent of revealing my battle plans to the enemy."

"I'd hoped that you wouldn't look on me as the enemy. True, I'm a figurehead. But underneath my duties in an official capacity I should like to think you might look on me as a friend."

"The public hangman could well say the same words to someone he was about to hang. What do you take me for?"

"For your information, I voted against petitioning the Jockey Club stewards to ban you from the course. In fact, I was one of only two people present to abstain from adding their names to the list of signatures."

"If I was skeptical I could call that an empty gesture. Why else would you tell me that you're on my side if it isn't to gain my trust for the purpose of making me show my hand, simply in order to disarm me later?"

"You really don't trust anyone, do you?"

The look of mild amusement vanished from her face.

"If you'd lived through enough and suffered enough as I have you wouldn't even ask that question." She was over at the door in an instant. She had not offered him a drink, not even a chair. "Is there anything else you want to talk about?"

He looked at her. It was the closest he had ever been to her and he thought that never in his long life had he seen anyone so beautiful. But it was the sheer guts of the girl that impressed him more than anything else. She was a fighter; and he respected her for it.

He did not blame her for being abrupt. For mistrusting him. In her place he would have felt exactly the same.

"One more thing," she said, as he came forward to the door. "Don't ever bring James Tollemache inside my gates again."

It was the first thing she had said that really surprised him. "May I ask why not?"

"I don't like his face."

PART VI
September 1833

✳ 18 ✳

"The Brodie filly's in the Queen Charlotte at fifty to one!"

"Ralph Russell's lent Chifney again to take the ride!"

"If Frank Buckle was riding the nag it still wouldn't have a hope in hell. Maybe that's why she's called it Hope. I'll lay you twenty to one it'll come in last whether Chifney rides it or not."

"Don't be so sure. Anything of Glenartney's is an unknown quantity to be reckoned with. Anyone in the know'll tell you that it was only because he was pulled in the last furlong that Glenartney didn't win the Derby in '27."

"Maybe. But as a stallion he's sired nothing of any note. Remember that. And the nag's dam was never even raced in all her life!"

"But the blood's good. And whatever you say about her the Brodie girl's got an eye for the horses."

"She was right about Firestone, ay. But that was her father's horse and his mettle was already proved beyond doubt. She was just lucky."

"She's lucky to have a nag in the Queen Charlotte at all. Heathcote and the rest of them are still waiting to get the ruling against her from the Jockey Club they expected nearly two months ago."

"It won't come in time to stop her in this race."

"You told me 'Eathcote 'ad sent the petition to Newmarket demanding they warn off the bastard and stop 'er racing 'er nags . . . that was more than two months ago!"

"Heathcote did send off the petition. I was there. I saw it. It was sent on the fast mail coach the same evening together with the letter to the stewards we made him write."

"But you never saw it delivered to the mail coach. You never even saw it leave the 'ouse. You've only got 'is word for it that it was ever sent to Newmarket?"

"Heathcote's a man of honor. If he said it was delivered to the mail coach then it was delivered."

Slout spat contemptuously on the ground.

"Man of honor! I never met one in me whole life who didn't 'ave a price.

'Ow do you know the bastard 'asn't squared 'im to keep 'is mouth shut and leave the Jockey Club in the dark about what she's doing?"

"Because I know Heathcote. He wouldn't do it."

"No doubt 'Eathcote reckons 'e knows you. But then 'e'd be wrong, wouldn't 'e?" Slout opened his snuff box, took out a large pinch between his fingers, and inhaled it. "You said yourself 'im and Randyll refused to put their names on the petition. That they was both against getting that Brodie bitch warned off? Well, do you want it put plainer than that?"

"I know them both; you don't." Irritably, Hindley twisted the ring on his little finger as he always did in moments of agitation. "If it came to it, Heathcote would rather resign as chief steward than do anything he considered to be against his principles as a gentleman."

"Principles! If that bitch 'ad a nag running against one of 'is in the same race, and 'e stood to lose big brass if she beat 'im, you'd soon see 'ow much 'e reckoned on bloody principles!"

"I haven't got time to wait for that to happen. I expected her to have been forced out of Epsom nearly two months ago, when you said you'd deal with her. But she's still here, a thorn in my flesh, putting her horses into any race she pleases. You promised to scare her off before the King's Cup and fix Firestone on the day of the race . . . but you did neither!"

"That ain't my fault. When I sent three of my boys to waylay 'er in the copse, 'ow was I to know she'd be carrying a pistol . . . and know 'ow to use it? And only Chifney stood in the way of my man bringing Firestone down near the last furlong. Both times we was up against bad luck."

"Luck had nothing to do with it. Your boys bungled the jobs and Anna Brodie's still running around doing just as she pleases. When her horse beat mine in the King's Cup it cost me big brass, brass I can't afford to lose, brass I don't intend to lose, not ever again. If this Glenartney filly turns out to be any good, the bitch'll be certain to enter it for all the big races, and that won't suit me, Slout. That won't suit me at all."

Slout sighed. He took out his gold pocket watch and glanced at it. If he didn't leave soon he would be late getting onto the course and making his way through the crowds to the betting stand. "Look. Forget the filly. The nag isn't important. That lot at Newmarket won't take much longer to make an answer. Your guess is as good as mine at what they'll decide. The bastard goes. Either way, in a week or two all your worries'll be over."

"It was you that said Heathcote might not have sent the letter."

"All right, all right. I take back what I said. So you know 'Eathcote and I don't. You'll see 'im today in the grandstand, and you can take 'im up on it. Ask 'im a few pointed questions. Ask 'im why you've 'ad no answer from Newmarket. Tell 'im you're not satisfied and you want 'im to take it up again."

"That's not all I intend to do."

"Oh?" They began to walk back toward the house.

"The Brodie bitch has a sister. Not so good-looking and not so cunning.

A different kettle of fish altogether. If we play our cards right, she could be very useful."

"Don't you believe it! She might only 'ave 'alf 'er sister's brains, but she'll be nobody's fool, neither. You try and use 'er to get to the other one, an' she'll go running straight to 'er ear."

"Wait a minute. You haven't heard what I've got in mind." They had reached the house and Hindley nodded toward the window. Sitting on Slout's chair behind his desk was James Tollemache, leafing through the pages of a book and smoking one of his best cigars. "When I heard that Heathcote was riding over to the Old Brew House a while ago, I got young James to invite himself along on some pretext or other. Heathcote never suspected anything; why should he? The Tollemaches are county gentry. Respectable. Move in good circles. Now, young James with his good looks is very popular with the ladies. And he reckons that Clara Brodie took more than a fancy to him."

"What good'll that do us? Whether she fancies 'im or not, that bastard'll never let 'er out of 'er sight. And if you think Clara Brodie'll tell 'im anything about 'er sister's business, think again."

"Listen to me. One of the Brodies' maids has been seen out and about with a certain young man . . . she's our way into the house and to Clara Brodie. Now . . . James can send her a message through the maid, asking her to contrive a meeting at some given place. Not Epsom, where they'd be seen. But Egham, maybe, or Sutton. I'll tell him what to write. Clara Brodie will be swept off her feet and her sister none the wiser."

"I'm beginning to get your drift," Slout said, his mind starting to work, cog on cog. "Who's this young man the maid's bin seen around with?"

"Paris. The bastard's head groom."

"Couldn't be better!"

"And I've another idea . . . it'll work if we act quickly enough."

"I'm all ears," Slout said, grinning.

Anna's prerace tactics were entirely different this time. Knowing that nearly everyone but herself believed Hope stood no chance in the Queen Charlotte Stakes that afternoon, she let William Devine sleep in the filly's stall the night before with just the dogs let loose in the yard to give the alarm in case of trouble. But she expected none and none came. Nobody was likely to bother with an unknown filly of dubious pedigree who had plummeted from fifty to one to one hundred to one overnight.

Instead of the armed guard she had had to escort Firestone from his stable to the racecourse, she simply saddled the filly and rode her over herself, with only Paris and William Devine for company.

"Don't you reckon it'll tire 'er, miss?" Paris had said before they set out, irritating her with his predictable pessimism. "Wouldn't it be better to walk 'er over?"

"If I thought it'd tire her I would walk her over," Anna snapped back, climbing into the saddle. "You're forgetting something, Paris. I've worked this filly day in, day out, for the past two months . . . I know her inside out and back to front. She's been tested over every kind of ground there is and I know exactly what she's capable of doing, thank you very much."

"However good you reckon she is, she's bound to run green, being the first time she's ever set foot on a racecourse and all. And the carter who delivered the grain sacks this morning was saying 'e'd 'eard she'd gone to 'undred to one instead of staying steady at fifties."

Anna looked at him incredulously. "I don't *reckon* she's good . . . I know she is. And I know a damn sight more about my own horse than the carter who delivers the grain sacks does."

Paris mounted his own hack without answering, tight-lipped. During the whole ride over to the course he never spoke a word. They kept their pace deliberately slow, never more than a canter. But when they reached the course the stables were so crowded with runners for the enormous field in the first race that there was no room for Hope.

"I thought we'd be late," Paris said, speaking for the first time. "We should have left earlier, like I suggested this morning. Now she'll be so upset by all this bedlam and noise, even Chifney'll not be able to settle 'er."

"Ay, she looks a bag of nerves," mocked William Devine, holding her bridle for Anna to dismount. "For a young filly that's not had sight of a racecourse in all her life, she's as steady as a rock. Look how calm she's standing!"

"When I want your opinion I'll ask for it!" Paris snapped back.

"That's enough, from both of you!" Angrily, Anna slid from the saddle and began adjusting the stirrup leathers. "You're talking through your arse, Paris. And you ought to know better! I know this filly and I know exactly how long it takes to ride over here from the house . . . walking, trotting, cantering, you name it! And I timed it so that we'd get here with enough time in hand for her to have a breathing space before Chifney takes her to post, but not so much that she'd start to get worked up. That way she hasn't got time to be nervous."

"I still reckon she'll 'ave the edge taken off 'er," Paris said, stubbornly. "And fillies are never twice alike at the best of times."

"She'll have my week's wages riding on her tail for a hundred to one, anyhow," William Devine said, taking Anna's part. "You was right, miss. Here comes Jeremiah now."

She turned and saw him. In the distance, walking across the edge of the Warren from the weighing shed came Chifney in Anna's pale blue silks, head and shoulders above the rest of the jockeys. He waved his whip at them in greeting.

"I can tell by the color of 'is face that 'e's bin wasting like the devil to make the weight," said William Devine. "That's the penalty for being six inches taller than anyone else."

"No doubt Lord Russell pays him well," Paris's voice was bitter, and Anna turned on him.

"If you can't be civil, you can get back on your horse and ride home. And don't take it out on everyone else just because you grew too heavy to be a jockey yourself." She turned her back on him and began to walk toward Chifney, all around her the other jockeys beginning to mount and make their way to post. Something, suddenly, made her pause and glance up. Jacob Hindley and Lionel Tollemache stood there, only a few feet from her path. As she passed them, Tollemache smiled and tipped his hat.

"I see your filly's gone out to a hundred to one from fifties, Miss Brodie. What do you think about that?"

"The world is full of fools, isn't it, Mr. Tollemache? That's how the blacklegs get rich." She smiled coldly. At him, then Hindley. Then she walked on.

Clara had been lying on her bed reading when she heard the sound of horse's hooves clattering on the flagstones outside, then the sudden barking of the dogs. Curiosity got the better of her. She was expecting no one. Jessie and Ellen Troggle had gone to collect provisions in Epsom, and wouldn't be back for some while. But the dogs never barked unless it was at the arrival of a stranger. That meant that whoever it was was nobody that Anna knew. Laying aside her book she went over to the window and looked out; then her face lit with a smile. She pushed the window open and leaned out, calling to Elijah to quieten the dogs.

"I hope this call isn't inconvenient?" James Tollemache shouted up to her. "But I wanted to speak to you . . ."

Her heart began to hammer wildly. She felt color rushing to her cheeks. She ran down the stairs to meet him.

It was different from Firestone's race. He was her father's horse, tried and true, only part of her had had any doubts. The filly was different.

The nerves began to attack her as soon as Chifney had ridden out of sight to the start. The Queen Charlotte was too ambitious for an untried filly. There were too many runners. There was too vast and noisy a crowd. Maybe Paris had been right. Maybe she should never have ridden her over. Maybe she had been wrong to enter her at all. She was too immature, inexperienced, unready.

Fillies were different from geldings and colts, everyone knew that. She should have known better than to ignore that. They were different to break, to train, to handle. They didn't settle well. They were jittery. Temperamental. Unpredictable. They could be gentle and biddable one minute, wild and unmanageable the next. Surely she should have remembered that, and taken note, after three years working in Sam Loam's yard.

She could feel the men's eyes on her. Avid, curious, smirking. They wanted her to lose today. They wanted her to be humbled. Then they could smile behind their hands, then they could have the satisfaction of being proved right. About women knowing nothing about horses. About women competing against men.

They did not want her in their midst. She was an interloper. An outsider. Someone of a different breed. She was not one of them.

Despite the cold wind she felt hot. The high collar of her gray velvet gown cut into her throat and she could not breathe. William Devine, beside her, was talking to her; smiling, encouraging, but she could not hear what words he said. There was a great roaring in her ears. The din of the crowd on the public side of the course grew louder and louder, and then louder still.

It was all her own fault. Guided by her own gut feelings she had bought a filly with a dubious pedigree; on one side a line of unraced mares, on the other a sire whose only merit was coming second in a race he should have won. Sam had told her. Sam had warned her. Only her own arrogance had made her refuse to listen.

"Miss! Miss!" William Devine shrieked wildly, tugging at her arm. "Here they come!"

Her wooden limbs somehow began to move. She craned her neck forward to see the massive field thundering toward the straight, a jumble of flying turf and color. Wildly, her eyes sought Hope, but she was lost within the wall of galloping horses.

"I should have waited," she whispered, brokenly, more to herself than to William Devine. "She wasn't ready. The field's too big. I never meant to race her before she was three . . ."

"She's holding 'er own, miss! She's going to hang on for a place!"

Anna looked dazedly in the direction that he pointed. As the field split into two groups, the four fastest fillies surged forward into the final two furlongs, Hope just behind them. But they were bunched so tightly together and flashed by so quickly that Anna could not see whether the filly was going easily or was fully extended. The blood surged in her brain. Her wooden limbs at last began to move. She ran forward to the very edge of the course, shouting the filly's name.

She was not disgraced. They could not smirk and whisper now. There would be no gloating, no sneering behind hands. The filly had vindicated her judgment. She had kept pace with four of the fastest fillies in southern England and Anna could not ask more of her than that. She was inexperienced. She was completely untried. To be fifth in a race such as this was more than she could have ever hoped for.

She stood there like a dumb thing, rooted to the spot as they approached the winning post. Then to her astonishment her filly suddenly burst ahead of her rivals, beating them by a short head at the line. She was galloping on so strongly that it took Chifney more than two furlongs to pull her up.

Speechless, dumbfounded, something in Anna suddenly pulled taut, and then snapped. Burying her face in her hands, she burst into tears.

PART VII
October 1833

✳ 19 ✳

She saw him approaching from the drive as she stood at the library windows, looking out across the leaf-strewn lawns. She went outside, a cloak flung about her shoulders against the cold, and walked toward him across the courtyard, the dry, dead leaves crackling beneath her feet.

"You're up early."

"I had a visit from Gilbert Heathcote last night." He dismounted, and they walked side by side toward the stables. "About you." She said nothing. Only the noise of their booted feet across the flagstones broke the silence. "You already know that he was asked, as chief steward here, to write to the Jockey Club and submit that your horses be banned from racing on the course." Still she said nothing. "When no answer was forthcoming he was pressured into writing again, to ask for the reason for their delay in making their ruling. He received word yesterday that neither the letter nor the petition that most of the Epsom owners signed has even reached Newmarket."

She kept her face a mask.

"Are they blaming me for that, too?"

"Letters have been known to go astray, even by the mail coach. But not often. The delay merely means that the inevitable will be put off . . . but only for a while."

"That isn't news to me."

"Since there'll be no more racing on the course after next month until the end of the winter, you'll have a brief respite so that you can marshal your forces. Heathcote says that you intend to appeal any decision made against your rights, and that if necessary you'll be prepared to fight them at law."

Her eyes flashed with anger.

"Do they expect me to do anything else? Stand idle while they destroy everything that I've worked and fought for, for the past three years?" Her voice was bitter. "If necessary I'll fight them to the highest court in the land."

"I can understand exactly how you feel."

"Can you?"

"For God's sake, have you given any thought to what a lawsuit like this is going to cost you? It could drag on for months, years even, before it's resolved. It could ruin you, Anna. And at the end of it—even if you win— you'll be forced to sell the very horses you've been fighting for the right to race just so that you can pay for it."

"I'll manage if I have to mortgage every brick of this house to do it."

"And when that's gone, what then? Milk any well too often and it runs dry."

"Not if I take care to see that it's always replenished. My horses will do that for me."

"Don't be a fool." He stopped walking as they reached the stables and his horse began to drink from the water trough. He put his hand on her arm. "Firestone is nearly seven . . . you can't race him forever. The filly has promise, yes. That I'll grant you. But you can't risk pinning all your hopes on one untried horse that might never win another race in her life. And what happens if she goes lame? Sour? If she breaks down and can never race again? There's too much at risk for you to take that chance." He fell silent, suddenly, as Paris led Hope out of the stable block and into the yard.

"She's looking good, Paris."

"Ay, that she is, miss. Do you want me to work 'er the same as I did yesterday?"

"No, not now. Just get her saddled and I'll work her myself this morning. You can exercise Firestone instead."

He nodded and walked on, touching his forelock as he passed Russell.

"So you've been taking on Sam Loam's overflow as well as training your own?" He glanced toward one of the paddocks, where Elijah and William Devine were working two young horses. Her eyes followed his.

"Sam gave me a chance when I needed it. The least I can do is repay him when he himself needs help."

Russell smiled.

"If there were more men in Epsom like him the world would be a better place."

"And the Jockey Club," she said, sourly.

For several moments another, longer silence fell between them; then he spoke again. He looked at her solemnly.

"Anna, there's just a chance that I may be able to help you . . . with the Jockey Club stewards. But I can't promise anything."

"If you mean by that that you'll try to persuade your uncle to find in my favor, don't. Even if he did what you asked him he'd be overruled in the end by the majority. And you'd be accused of attempting to pervert the course of Jockey Club justice. Or worse."

He stared at her, incredulous.

"Who told you that my uncle was one of the senior stewards at New-market?"

"No one. I found out the night of the King's Cup dinner, when I over-heard you arguing with Jacob Hindley." She looked him straight in the eye. "I listened through the door. One thing I didn't understand then any more than I understand it now. Why you ever invited him into your house at all."

He looked away from her. He kept his eyes fixed on the horses in the paddock.

"I didn't do it by choice. I didn't want him there any more than I wanted any of the others. But families like ours go back a long way with certain traditions, that's all, something you'd find it hard, maybe impossible, to understand. We still observe all the rituals and courtesies that polite society demands, even if we hate each other."

"I never took you for a hypocrite."

He turned toward her for the first time, reproach in his eyes. "We don't all have your freedom to say and do exactly as we choose."

"If you haven't then the choice is yours."

He looked away again toward the horses and the paddock. He sighed. He fell silent once more. There were so many things that he needed to explain to her, but she would never understand unless he told her all. And he could never do that, for the consequences would be too great for both of them.

"He works well, your new lad."

"Yes."

"I remember him from Edward Randyll's stable. He always had a way with the horses, even the difficult ones. A boy after your own heart. And he's slight, small-boned. He'll make a fine jockey, one day."

"If you ever run one of your horses in the same race as I do, I'd put him up instead of Chifney. I'd trust any of my animals in his hands, inex-perienced though he is."

"You think he's ready for that kind of responsibility?"

"He'll never get experienced in race-riding if he doesn't do any."

"He's still only a boy."

"So was Nat Street."

There was a pause. He hung his head for a moment.

"He was nearly eighteen when I gave him the ride on my colt. Your lad is a year and half younger. At that age Nat Street was still mucking out the stables."

"I was fifteen when I started work in Sam Loam's yard. And if I'd been a boy I could have ridden any horse in any race and given a good account of myself."

He looked at her, smiling.

"Yes, but then you were different, even then."

"What exactly do you mean by that?"

"That there's only one Anna Brodie."

For a moment they looked at each other. Then before either could speak the door of the house slammed behind them and Clara began to walk toward them across the yard.

"I'd best be on my way," Russell said, remounting his horse. He doffed his hat to Clara as she came up. "Think over what I said. My uncle is at least in a position to state your case."

"No deal. I'm not afraid of a fight. If they want one they'll get it. And I'll get where I'm going without anyone being able to say that I only got there by climbing on the backs of others." Her mouth was set. Her blue eyes were hard as she looked up at him. The same look he remembered from so long ago, when she'd confronted him on his own land and made him feel that it was he who was trespassing, not she. He replaced his hat and turned his horse's head in the opposite direction.

At the bend in the drive he pulled up and glanced back over his shoulder. But she was already walking away from him.

"What is it? I'm busy." Anna strode toward the paddock, Clara running to keep up with her.

"There'll be no rain today, Jessie says. Could I take Ruth with me and ride into Ewell this afternoon? Or Sutton, maybe? It's Paris's half-day off, and he's willing to drive us in."

"If he doesn't mind, then I don't." They reached the paddock fence and Anna climbed through it. "But take a warm cloak with you and mind he brings you back before it starts to get dark."

Clara's face lit up.

"Oh, yes. I'll make certain he does." She turned and ran back into the house, shouting to Ruth. A few minutes later, Anna had forgotten her.

"She's not got enough to do, that's 'er trouble," Jessie grumbled, without glancing up from her pastry. "And she's got too much time on 'er 'ands, and all. 'Ousemaid's no fit company for 'er, neither . . . what she needs is something worthwhile to occupy 'er mind, like your ma would have wanted. Now, just 'cos you got what you want, you forget about everyone else." She picked up the pastry and lay it on top of the heaped fruit in the pie dish, then began to trim the edges with a knife. "Idling about looking in shop windows is all very well. But she'll soon get tired of that."

Anna sighed. She sank down onto the pine bench against the kitchen wall and began easing off her boots.

"I haven't heard her complaining."

"That's only 'cos you're outside all day, working with the 'orses. You don't see 'er, only at mealtimes and before you go to bed. Mooning around all day, reading books and doing embroidery. And gossipin' with the girls, stopping 'em from getting on with their work . . ."

"If you asked Clara what she wanted she'd say to spend all day buying new gowns and every evening wearing them, at some ball or dinner. And you know that as well as I do."

"There's 'er music, you're forgetting that. She's a gift for playing and singing, just like your ma 'ad, God rest 'er. You promised to get 'er a big piano like the one we 'ad at Saffron Walden as soon as the 'ouse was fit and ready . . . but you've not done it."

"I haven't had time. And in any case Ralph Russell has one that he says is never used. He invited her over to play on it as often as she cares to go."

"But she can't go unless someone goes with 'er. You know that. It just wouldn't be right."

"Oh? Why not? Nobody ever goes with me."

"Well, you're a law unto yourself, and always 'ave bin. Clara's not made that way." Jessie pushed the pie into the oven and slammed the door on it.

"She's tougher than you give her credit for. And I've never stopped her from going anywhere she chooses to. Just as long as she takes Ruth with her and one of the lads from the yard goes to look after them."

"That's all very well. But she needs more than that. She needs to mix, in proper company, with young folk of 'er own station, not maids and grooms. Just 'cos you don't reckon on getting yourself married to some nice, respectable gentleman, that don't mean to say that Clara shouldn't 'ave the chance to."

"For Christ's sake, Jessie! She's only sixteen!"

"Time soon flies. She'll be seventeen next birthday and eighteen the next. Better to be married young than end up some miserable, bad-tempered old spinster, like some I could name." She picked up the copper kettle and sat it on the hearth. "Your ma was wed before she was twenty."

"Yes, and look where that got her!" Anna's voice was bitter. "Any woman can always stoop and pick up nothing." She got up and went out, before Jessie made her lose her temper.

The library was warm and quiet. She went over to the big mullioned windows and leaned against them, looking out at the gathering dusk. Clara should have been back by now, unless something had happened on the journey back. A lame horse. A cast shoe. Maybe a spoke had worked loose on one of the post chaise wheels. Maybe she should never have agreed to let Clara go, even with Paris and Ruth, when the days were short and it grew dark long before six o'clock. Maybe she should have given Paris a pistol before he left, or a blunderbuss.

She turned, suddenly, when the library door opened.

"Oh, it's you, Ellen."

"Just come in to make up the fire, miss. It's turned right bitter since this morning. Lads reckon it could turn to frost overnight, or snow, even." She put down the basket of logs and knelt to put them one by one onto the already blazing fire. "Best place to be this weather is tucked up in bed, to my way of thinking."

"If we all did that nothing would ever get done." Anna glanced back through the window, ears and eyes strained toward the drive. There was no sounds of horses' hooves. No sounds of wheels. Across the yard, she watched as William Devine led the last of Sam Loam's horses into the stable block, followed by Elijah and the other lads, all carrying buckets and armfuls of hay. "Did Ruth say what time she expected to be back?"

"Why, no, miss." Ellen got up and smoothed down her apron. "But on 'er 'alf-day, she's never back earlier than seven."

"But it's dark by then!"

"Paris brings 'er back, miss. 'Im 'aving the same 'alf-day and all. She said 'e never minds. And no 'arm can come to 'er or Miss Clara if 'e's with 'em, can it?" Anna turned back impatiently to the window, without answering. A mist had settled together with the growing darkness, like a gray shroud draping the outbuildings and the trees. "Mrs. Tamm says shall she wait dinner?"

"Tell her she can have hers. I'm not hungry." Anna went out into the yard and ran toward the drive and then along it, all the way to the gates. She peered through them, looking and listening. But still she heard and saw nothing.

She turned and ran back toward the house.

It was so dark now that Ruth could no longer see where they were going. The bare branches of passing trees stretched out, like tortured, blackened limbs, eerie and horrible. No part of the route they were taking seemed familiar. Even Paris seemed different, now that she had done what he'd asked.

"What if they're not at the milestone when we get there? What if Mr. Tollemache's lost 'is way?"

"Shut up, will you? Of course they'll be there. Of course 'e won't lose 'is way. He's no one's fool, you can take my word for that."

"Nor is Miss Clara's sister." There was a tight, sick feeling in the pit of her stomach. "She'll be worrying already, I know it. She might even send someone to come looking, now it's got late. Miss Clara said she'd promised 'er to be back before dark."

"That's just too bad." He didn't turn to look at her. "I'll tell 'er one of the horses cast a shoe and we 'ad to walk back into Ewell to get it fixed. She'll not think to question it."

"It doesn't take that long to shoe 'orse," Ruth said, pulling her cloak further around her shoulders. She shivered. "She might get suspicious. She might even ask smithy when she goes into town. And if she ever finds out there'll be 'ell to pay . . ."

"She won't find out, not if you keep your mouth shut. And she never goes into Ewell."

"I don't like it, Ben."

Angrily, he swung round on her.

"I thought I said shut up!" He peered at her through the almost nonexistent light. "For Christ's sake, don't start blubbering. If she sees your eyes all swollen up and red, then she will start thinking. You want to get me thrown out the bloody yard?"

She bit her freezing lips, fighting back the lump in her throat. Tears stung at the backs of her eyelids and she dashed them away, frantically, with the back of her hand. Paris loathed weak, tearful women. Women who clung, women who broke down and cried at the least little thing. She cared for him so much, so desperately. She must never let him see her like this, with bloated eyelids and trembling mouth. But Miss Anna would blame her. She'd given her word that they'd be back, well before dark. And now here they were, in the middle of nowhere for all she knew, with no sign of Miss Clara or that nice young Mr. Tollemache, who'd met them in town just by chance and offered to take her for a ride in his carriage.

"It's all right," Paris said through the darkness, "I can see their barouche, up ahead."

"Are you sure it's them, Ben?"

"Don't be stupid!"

Ruth fell silent. But as she peered uncertainly through the murky gloom she could make out two pale shapes beneath the hood of the barouche, pulled off the road beneath the dripping trees half a mile in front of them. As they came closer, one of the shapes became a face, a face she knew, and she lay back against the seat and breathed a sigh of relief.

"Lord, Miss Clara, you 'ad me scared stiff!" She clung to the side of the post chaise as it drew alongside. "God only knows what time we'll be back at 'ouse!"

James Tollemache climbed out of the barouche and helped Clara up beside Ruth. He tipped his hat.

"Remember what I said to you." He smiled, whispered a few words in Paris's ear, then stepped back as the post chaise started off, and the horses got up speed. Gaily, Clara waved after him until the darkness had swallowed him up.

"Miss Clara!"

"Ruth, you're as white as candle wax!"

"And a wonder that you're not, and all, miss. Miss Anna'll 'ave our guts for garters, getting back at this hour!"

"Oh, don't be silly, Ruth. Paris can say that the horse cast a shoe, and she won't blame him for that. How can she?"

"I don't see why you can't tell 'er the truth, miss. That you come across Mr. Tollemache just by chance, and 'e took you for a ride in 'is carriage. 'E's bin to the 'ouse before . . . why, I seen 'im there meself, with Sir Gilbert 'Eathcote and the earl of Leopardstown. 'E's a nice, respectable young gentleman, after all. And Miss Anna knows 'is brother."

"How can I tell her what really happened? She'd never let me out of her sight again, unless Jessie came with me! I'm tired of being treated like a child. It's all right for you, you and Paris can come and go as you please. You can go where you like and meet whom you like on your half-day off. I'm different. I'm not allowed any freedom at all, any more than if I was a prisoner."

"Oh, Miss Clara, that's not true!"

"Yes it is. Anna hates the Tollemaches. She thinks that everyone in Epsom is against her, because a few owners don't like her racing her horses on equal terms with theirs. She'd forbid me to have anything to do with James Tollemache, just because he was a guest in one of their houses." She gripped Ruth's arm, tightly. "You're not to breathe a word, do you understand? However angry she is. Promise me now."

Ruth swallowed. Clara's fingers clutched at her arm so tightly that it hurt. "You know I'd not say anything, miss. But I don't like bein' deceitful."

"It isn't being deceitful. It's just plain common sense. Nobody can ever reason with Anna when she's angry." She leaned forward, her blue eyes bright, her face flushed with excitement beneath the brim of her wide furred bonnet. "Look. There. I can see the lights from the house coming through the trees."

It was Jessie and Ellen who ran out to them, light from the house and hallway streaming into the darkness from the porch. Two of the dogs ran after them, barking wildly.

"For the love of God, where've the three of you bin these past two hours? Your sister's bin frantic with worry!"

"I'm sorry, Mrs. Tamm." Paris dismounted and quietened the dogs. They stopped barking at once and began to sniff at his boots and lick his hands. "Two miles out of Ewell one of the horses cast a shoe. We 'ad a fair old time walking 'im back all the way to nearest smithy!" He glanced at Clara as he helped her down from the post chaise. Ruth was left to climb down by herself. "Miss Clara's bin 'alf out of 'er wits, worrying about what Miss Anna'd think . . . but there was nothing I could do."

Jessie put her arm around Clara's shoulders and bustled her inside. "All right, lad. You see to 'orses and I'll tend to these two. I'll tell 'er sister as soon as she gets back."

Paris frowned. "Gets back? Isn't Miss Anna 'ere, then?"

"She's not. When you wasn't back by seven and there was no sign of you coming, she got 'alf the lads and went out on 'orseback to look for you. Lord only knows where she is now."

Clara's smile faded. "Oh, Jessie . . . she'll be so angry!"

"Well, that's as may be. But it wasn't your fault the damn 'orse cast its shoe. She'll see that. Now, come inside the both of you, and get something good and 'ot down you. Ruth, you look like a corpse what's got up out of its coffin. You sickening for something?"

"No, Mrs. Tamm, no." Ruth gave Paris a quick, backward glance, a nervous half-smile. But he turned on his heel and began leading away the horses. "I'm just chilled to the marrow."

"We'll get some supper inside you and then you can go off straight to bed. Come on, inside the pair of you."

By the light of the coach lamp above the porch Clara's face was almost as colorless as Ruth's was.

"When will Anna be back, Jessie?"

"That I can't tell you."

There was a small light burning inside the tiny cottage at the side of the forge, and Anna pulled up her horse as they approached it. Her face was drawn and pale. This was the last smithy that she and Chifney had stopped at in a radius of almost thirty miles, stretching from Hook to the north of Epsom to as far afield as Ewell and Cheam. Dispirited, growing more anxious with every mile, they had ridden from Sutton down to Wood-mansterne by nine o'clock, and then crossed and doubled back again through Banstead to Epsom. There was only one forge left to call at, if indeed one of the post chaise team had cast a shoe and Paris had been forced to stop, and this was it.

As Anna dismounted and pounded on the cottage door, Chifney got down from his horse and came to stand beside her.

"They'll be all right," he said for the twentieth time that evening. "Paris is with them. They'll come to no harm."

"Clara said they were going in to Ewell, or Sutton. We've been along both those roads. Not a single blacksmith remembers any one of them . . . nor a black and yellow post chaise going by."

"Blacksmiths work with their heads down, mostly," Chifney said, trying to hearten her. "They wouldn't notice if the lord mayor's coach and twenty horses went by."

"Maybe you're right." She stood back as the sound of bolts being drawn echoed into the quiet night, and a woman's face peered out at them, holding a rushlight in one hand. Her mouth fell open with surprise when she saw Anna, and she called over her shoulder into the room behind.

"Jed, there's a lady out 'ere, come quick!" Then, in a loud whisper. "She's gentry, Jed!"

The man appeared in the doorway.

"Can we be 'elping you, ma'am? You got a 'orse needs to be shod?" He touched his forelock. "I can soon open up the forge. Won't take me above a minute!"

"No, our horses don't need shoeing. But you might be able to help us with some information." They were shown into the cottage. They both looked round, unused to the dull light made by the rushlights. For a moment Anna looked around her, in silence. So much in that tiny, cramped room with its cheap furniture and clothes hanging across a rope above the smoking hearth reminded her, poignantly, of her own past, the past she had fought to escape from, the past she had finally left behind. She could see that they had placed dried turf upon the fire to supplement their meager pile of sticks and logs, and the thick, acrid smell filled the tiny, low-ceilinged room, making her long to escape outside into the cold night air before it stifled her. She took a deep breath. She explained what they wanted.

"Ay, ma'am, a black and yella post chaise! I remember it well, ay I do. And two good, fine 'orses. Bays, I recall. The one I shod 'ad two white pasterns and one white 'ock at the back on 'is nearside 'oof."

"You remember the passengers?" Anna asked.

"Ay, ma'am. There was only one. A young maidservant, with a lockram cloak and 'er 'ood drawn up. Rider was a young man, dark-'aired, good-looking, about twenty-four or -five, I'd say. 'E seemed in 'urry. Kept pacing up and down, up and down."

"Are you sure there was no one else in the post chaise? Another young woman, in a dove-colored velvet cloak, edged with fox fur? Dark-haired, blue eyes?"

The man shook his head. He glanced at his wife.

"Oh, no, ma'am, nobody like that. I'd 'ave seen 'em if there 'ad bin, that's for sure."

Anna sighed noisily. She began to pace round and round the tiny room, agitatedly. She exchanged a glance with Chifney.

"What time did they have the horse shod?"

"Let me see . . . it'd 'ave bin about four o'clock, I'd say. Ay, it was about then, I reckon."

Anna stared at him.

"Four o'clock? Are you certain it was as early as that? If the horse lost a shoe and had it reshod at four, they should have been back by half past five, six o'clock at the latest!" She turned to Chifney. "And Clara wasn't with them!" She buried her face in her hands, her mind spinning. "Oh, God!"

Chifney lay his arm round her shoulder.

"Are you sure you're not mistaken about the time?"

"No, sir, no indeed. But what was so peculiar, like, was the 'orse's shoe 'e asked me to change. There weren't nothing wrong with it."

They both stared at him.

"What?"

"Not a thing, ma'am. As good and new a shoe as ever I seen. But 'e would 'ave it changed. I told 'im it didn't need doing, but 'e wouldn't listen. An' since 'e give me five shillings and didn't want no change, I never argued."

"Did you see which direction they went in?"

"Ay, ma'am. Back toward Ewell."

"Thank you for your trouble. And we're sorry to have disturbed you on such a night. One thing you can do for us . . . do you still have the shoe that you took from the bay horse? Can you find it in the dark?"

"With me eyes shut, ma'am." He took one of the rushlights and his keys and went outside to open up the forge.

"I don't understand any of this," Chifney said in a low voice.

"Nor me. Not yet. But I'll get the truth out of Paris if I have to hang him arse-side up over an open cesspit before he tells me."

She took the shoe gratefully from the smithy. Then she fished in her reticule and brought out half a sovereign. "Take this for your trouble, with my thanks."

He took it gingerly, staring at the shining coin in the middle of his work-blackened, grubby hand. Half a sovereign. Just like nothing. He shook his head and went back into the little cottage and closed the door. He could still smell the lingering scent that had hung about her in the little cluttered room, holding its own above the smell of cooking and the bitter, smoking turf that lay upon the fire.

He held out the coin and his wife stopped what she was doing, and stared at it with him.

"Oh, Jed! An 'ole ten shilling! And I never set eyes on anyone so beautiful as she!"

He went over to the hearth and reached up, then put the half-sovereign in an old, cracked pot high on the shelf.

"And she was riding astride! Just like a man does!"

She saw the lights blazing from the house through the bare trees that lined the drive. William Devine was already in the courtyard, about to lead his sweating horse into the warmth and dryness of the stable. He began to run toward them as soon as he caught sight of them.

"It's all right, miss! The post chaise is back. Your sister's safe and sound, and tucked up in bed be now, I shouldn't wonder." He paused to get his breath, and Anna could see by the state of his clothes that he himself had not long been back from searching along with the others. "One of the horses cast a shoe, and they had to walk nearly back to Ewell to get it shod." He saw the look that passed between Anna and Chifney. "Is every-thing all right, Miss Brodie?"

She got down from her horse, her face grim.

"That's what I'm going to ask Paris."

The light streamed from beneath his door in the room above the coach house; from within, she could hear the sounds of someone moving across the floor. So he was not in bed. With her quick, light step, she climbed the stairs and hammered on the door. When he opened it he stared at her in surprise, as if he had been expecting someone else.

"Why, Miss Brodie . . ."

"I hear you had some trouble with one of the horses." She kept her face expressionless. "That you had to walk back all the way into Ewell to find a blacksmith."

His eyes could not quite meet hers.

"Yes, miss. It was dark, too. And there was a bit of a mist coming up. We took the wrong turning and ended up 'alfway to Sutton."

"If you were halfway to Sutton why didn't you go on the rest of the way and get the horse shod there?"

"Sutton's right in the opposite direction to Epsom, miss. And I 'ad no way of knowing if the smithy there would be shut up or not. I reckoned turning back toward Ewell was our best bet, it being right on the route 'ome."

"But you must have passed half a dozen inns on your way back. Didn't you think of stopping at one of them and changing horses? You would have been back by seven o'clock with my sister safe and sound, and I could have sent someone to the inn the next morning to bring back the horses and return the hired ones."

He shifted his weight from one foot to the other, trying to avoid her eyes.

"I didn't 'ave enough on me to pay for 'orse 'ire, or I would 'ave done it."

"And you never thought of stopping and asking someone at one of the inns to ride back here and tell me what was happening? So that I could have sent Elijah and one of the others out with a fresh horse, and paid them for their trouble? And saved myself and all the others the work and worry of scaling half the countryside looking for my sister in case something had happened to her?"

"There was no need for you to worry, miss. She's as safe as 'ouses with me, you know that. We was never in any kind of danger. It was just an accident that could 'ave 'appened to anybody."

Anna waited for a moment. Then she reached into her leather reticule and drew out the horseshoe. She held it up to him, and his face turned pale.

"You recognize this, do you, Paris? It's the shoe that the smithy at Ewell took off one of my horses. He remembered you very well. And do you know why?" She saw him swallow. "He remembered it because you asked him to change the shoe when there was nothing wrong with it. Now, I wonder why you'd do something like that?"

"The 'orse was limping bad . . . I pulled the team up several times, thinking it was a stone got lodged in 'is 'oof, but I couldn't see nothing. I got the shoe changed because I thought the old one might not 'ave bin fitted on proper. I thought if I didn't do something 'e might go lame . . ."

"Don't lie to me. You got to that smithy at four o'clock in the afternoon, not after dark. I went there tonight with Chifney and he told me himself.

And what's more he noticed there was only one passenger in the post chaise . . . who wasn't my sister."

"She wasn't feeling well . . . she asked me to put 'er off at one of the inns along the road, so that she could rest in the taproom till we got back from the smithy. She said the jolting of the post chaise made 'er feel sick . . ."

"You left her there alone, without Ruth?"

"She said she never wanted anyone with 'er. She said she wanted to be alone. We argued with 'er, but she ordered us to go on and leave 'er be."

"Which inn was it?"

"I don't remember."

"Are you going to tell me the truth or pack your bags and get out of my yard?"

He hung his head. He turned away and walked back into the room. Then he turned and faced her, defeat in his eyes.

"I never wanted to do it, miss. It wasn't my idea. But Miss Clara ordered me and there wasn't anything I could do about it . . . I'm not 'er keeper."

"I'm listening." She made a gesture to Chifney below and he came up the stairs and stood behind her.

"We was on our way into Sutton, and then I saw a barouche coming along toward us, from the opposite direction, like it was 'eading toward Ewell. Miss Clara told me to stop the post chaise, because Mr. Tollemache was driving it, and I did."

"Tollemache!"

"Miss Clara said she was going driving with 'im and that I was to wait with the post chaise by the old milestone, ten miles out of Epsom, at about eight o'clock. I told 'er you'd said I was to 'ave her back before it was dark, miss, but Mr. Tollemache said it'd be all right."

Anna's eyes blazed with anger.

"And you let her go, just like that? With Lionel Tollemache of all people!"

"What could I do, miss? It's not my place to tell Miss Clara what she can do, or a gentleman like Mr. Tollemache. And I thought it was all right, seeing that 'e'd bin a guest in your 'ouse, with Sir Gilbert 'Eathcote . . ."

"Lionel Tollemache's never come to this house with Sir Gilbert Heathcote!"

"No, miss, it wasn't Mr. Lionel I meant. It was 'is brother, Mr. James."

Her face was as white as Paris's. A nerve twitched in her cheek. Without another word she turned and went out of the stable room and ran down the stairs.

"Anna, wait!" Chifney shouted after her. He caught her up, halfway across the courtyard.

"James Tollemache. With my sister." He could feel her arm trembling beneath his hand. "Do you understand what that means?"

"That the Tollemaches have been Jacob Hindley's house guests for the

past six months? You think they'd try to find things out about your horses
from Clara?"

"What else?"

"He could be interested in her for another reason."

"No, he couldn't."

He stared at her, for a moment dumbfounded by the enormity of what
she was suggesting.

"What do you mean, Anna?"

"I think you know what I mean, don't you?" She did not wait for his
answer. She went on into the house.

Jessie rushed after her.

"The lass is back, safe and sound. And Ruth and all. Got back more than
an hour ago." Anna made no reply and went on toward the staircase. "I
gave the pair of 'em a good 'ot supper and a warm posset, then sent 'em
straight off to bed." Anna still ignored her. "Anna?"

"Later, Jessie." She lifted the hem of her riding habit and mounted the
stairs in twos and threes.

A lamp was still burning in Clara's room. She flung open the door and
saw her sister sitting on a stool in front of the mirror, already undressed for
bed, a hair brush in one hand.

"You deceitful little bitch!"

"Anna!"

Anna strode across the floor toward her, knocking the hair brush from
her hand.

"You've been with James Tollemache this afternoon. After getting Paris
to risk his job with me to lie for you. Don't bother to deny it . . . he's
already told me everything. And I'm not leaving this room and you're not
going to get any sleep tonight until you've told me every word that Tollemache said to you!"

The fright in Clara's face gave way to sudden anger.

"You have no right!"

"I have every right! Until you marry or you reach the age of twenty-one,
you go nowhere and see no one without my approval. And my approval
doesn't extend to vermin like James Tollemache!"

"I won't listen to you! You don't know anything about him!"

"I know enough to have made up my mind that you'll never see him
again."

"You can't do that!"

"I can and I will. Even if I have to lock the gates to keep you inside
them." She grasped Clara roughly by the wrist and shook her. "You little
fool! Don't you understand that he was just trying to use you, pretending
to be interested in you so that he could prize information out of you more
easily about my horses. He's Jacob Hindley's catspaw and Hindley would
do anything in this world to see me ruined!"

"James Tollemache isn't anything to do with Jacob Hindley! He never even spoke about him. Never mentioned his name!"

"What did he ask you about my horses?" Anna pulled her from the stool and flung her onto the bed. "Tell me! What did he ask you about my horses? Because if you say he didn't ask I shall know you're lying!"

Clara began to cry. The tears welled up in her eyes and spilled over, running down her cheeks and into her mouth.

"He didn't ask about them like that. He just wanted to know which races you were putting them in, because he said he was going to bet on them, they were bound to win . . ." She crawled into a heap on the bed, sobbing into her outstretched hands. In the open doorway Jessie appeared, Ellen and Bessie behind her on the landing.

Anna turned to her.

"Don't go to her, Jessie. I haven't finished."

"Now, lassie." Jessie's voice was gentle, coaxing. "Your sister's only concerned for your safety. You must tell 'er what she wants to know."

"There's nothing to tell! There's nothing, nothing!" She raised her face to Anna's, miserably. "All you care about are your horses. Not about me. You never did. About how I feel. What I want. What I need. The first person who comes into my life that I care about you dislike and distrust, just because you dislike and distrust his brother." Anger flared in her again, and she struggled to her feet. "But what are you really concerned about, Anna? What are you really afraid of? Is it my safety, or can't you bear the thought that I might be married before you are?"

Anna's thin thread of patience pulled taut and snapped. She was worn out with miles in the saddle. She was hungry, tired, and cold. She stepped forward and slapped Clara so hard across the face that she staggered back, lost her balance, and fell full length across the bed.

"Don't you ever speak to me that way again."

"I hate you!"

"I can live with it."

"I'll never forgive you as long as I live. Not ever."

"Oh, Clara, lassie," Jessie said, shocked, "I know you don't mean that. And you oughtn't to 'ave gone meeting 'im without your sister knowing; now, you really oughtn't to 'ave done that."

"But I love him!"

"Love him!" Anna said, derisively. "You don't know the meaning of the word!"

"And you do?"

"Maybe not in the way you mean it. But I know a parasite when I see one and a cesspool rat when I smell one. You're too young and too stupid to know either."

Clara was still crying, silently. But Anna did not go to her. With one glance at Jessie, she turned and walked out of the room.

"He was a perfect gentleman!" Clara shouted after her, hysterically. "He never laid a hand on me!"

Outside the door, Anna stopped and looked back.

"That I can believe."

She went on down the stairs toward Chifney.

"Did you hear all that?"

"I heard your sister crying," he said, tactfully.

Wearily, Anna sighed. "Come in here, have a brandy to warm you before you leave. It's bitter outside, at this time of night. And Jessie always sees to it that there's a good fire in here."

"I accept, gratefully." He followed her into the library and they sat down before the fire. "I always feel the cold when I've been fasting."

"You're trying to make the weight for the Markbeech Handicap?"

"Lord Russell's planning to run White Stockings, didn't he tell you?"

She smiled, in spite of herself.

"So you told him about the name I gave it?"

"He said it suited the colt perfectly. He said he wondered why he hadn't thought of it himself."

Anna got up and poured brandy into two glasses. She handed one to Chifney and then stood beside the fire, cradling hers in both hands.

"Tell Russell I'm sorry, when you get back. For dragging him, and you, and half his men away from their firesides in this foul weather, riding around half the countryside on a wild goose chase, looking for my sister. And all the time she was with Tollemache's brother, joy-riding between Sutton and Ewell!"

Chifney sipped the brandy.

"Did you tell her? I mean the truth?"

"How could I? She wouldn't have believed me if I had, she's so besotted with him. She'd say I was making it all up, just to blacken him in her eyes." She put down the drink and held her head in her hands. "Oh, God! Why did it have to be him? Tollemache, of all people!"

"Do you have proof?"

"Yes, I have proof."

"Would it help to talk about it? Would it make you feel better?"

She turned her head away. She looked down into the leaping flames of the fire. She saw the two white, grotesque bodies together on the big bed, writhing and turning. "I'm sorry, Chifney. I can't talk about it. Not now. Not yet. Even to you."

"I understand."

She glanced up suddenly.

"But you can tell me something." He looked at her. "About Jacob Hindley. Russell invited him that night of the King's Cup dinner, even though I know he didn't want to. He said as much himself when I last spoke to him. What I don't understand is why."

"Didn't you ask him himself?"

"Yes, I asked him. And he said it was because families like his had appearances to keep up."

"What else should there be? If there is any other reason then I don't know it. After all, I'm only his stable jockey. And you've lived in Epsom far longer than I have."

Anna put down her glass on the mantelpiece. She began to slowly pace about the room. As she was standing, he got to his feet also. "On the second floor of the house, there's a room that he keeps locked. I asked one of the manservants if he knew why, but he just said it was Lord Russell's orders." She stopped pacing and looked directly at him. "Do you know anything about that?"

"I've heard some of the house servants talk about it, yes. It was Lady Russell's room. They say he's kept it locked ever since she died. That he can't bear to go into it and look upon her things. They say he can't get over her death . . ."

Anna turned away, abruptly. His words curiously hurt her, without her understanding why. Not for the first time, she wondered what she had been like, the woman Russell had loved. Had she been fair or dark, blue- or brown-eyed? Had she been beautiful, clever, dazzling, a paragon he could never replace, because after her no other woman could exist for him? Every time Anna had been inside the house she had looked for a portrait, but had never found one. Was there a painting of her behind the door of the locked room that she had not seen that night, a painting that he could neither bear to destroy nor bear to look upon?

"How long has she been dead?" she heard herself ask Chifney. There was a pause, a silence broken only by the crackling of the wood upon the fire.

"I believe nearly five years. Long before either of us ever came to Epsom."

"He must have loved her, then, never to have married again. Most men in his position would have. For land or money, or to get an heir to his estate." Without realizing it, she began to bite her nails. "They had no children, then?"

"I believe she was of frail health. Consumptive, something like that. I don't know for sure."

"Did she come from around here?"

"No, not from Epsom. I heard somewhere that she was Yorkshire born. But I couldn't be sure."

There was another silence. Then the long-case that stood in the hall struck the hour, and she was startled by it. She had not realized how long they had been talking. She had not realized the time.

"So late already. And you to be up so early in the morning. I mustn't keep you any longer, it's a long ride back."

"Think nothing of it." He smiled at her. He went toward the door.

"They'll be glad to hear that your sister arrived back safe and sound, even if it wasn't one of us who found her."

"Goodnight, Chifney."

She sat down again in her chair after he had gone, staring into the embers of the fire. There was still heat in it, the room was still warm and comforting, a haven of peace that she needed. She loved the rows of musty-smelling books that lined the walls, the enveloping softness of the huge wing chairs, and the way the dogs would wander, unobtrusively, in and out of the room, as if they too sensed that this was a special place to come, a favorite retreat.

A great weariness came over her. She could no longer think or feel. If Jessie had not suddenly come into the room she would have fallen asleep, still dressed as she was, lulled by the brandy and the warmth of the fire.

"You go on up to bed, Jessie. I'll come later. I have some thinking out to do."

"Oh, lass, I wish you'd not 'ad words like that, the two of you. It's not right, not between sisters, all this arguing and bitterness. And the poor child's still crying 'er 'eart out; I 'eard 'er as I come by 'er door." Jessie sat down in the chair opposite Anna. "You go up and talk to 'er, make things right . . . now, before you go to sleep." She smiled, coaxing. "It'll all be over and forgot by morning, you mark my words it will."

"No it won't, Jessie. Not by either of us." She lay back in the chair and stifled a yawn. She rubbed her eyes. "It's my fault, I know. I've kept her cloistered here, sheltered from the real world outside. Throwing her promises now and then, just to keep her happy. A grand piano, just the like the one Mama had . . . next week, next month, next year. New gowns. A London season. All grist for her mill. But I've been so taken up with my own ambitions, with what I want, that I've forgotten them and Clara as well. I suppose she has a right to be bitter. I made her promises and I haven't kept any of them. Even the King's Cup dinner that Ralph Russell invited us to I left early and made her come with me. Maybe I shouldn't have done that, either."

"If you 'ad your reasons for leaving you couldn't 'ave come away and left 'er there, not on 'er own. She'd 'ave understood that."

Anna sighed. "That's the trouble, Jessie. I had my reasons but I couldn't tell Clara what they were."

For several moments they were silent. They looked away from each other into the dying embers of the fire, as if seeking some answer from it.

"This James Tollemache she seems so set on . . . 'e comes from a good family, don't he? A fine catch, if you ask me, for any young girl. Now, if Clara's that taken with 'im, do it really matter that you don't like 'is brother?"

Anna got to her feet with an air of finality that Jessie did understand only too well.

"I'm sorry, Jessie. I can't talk about it. Not even with you. Just take my word for it that James Tollemache won't do, not for Clara." Slowly, she turned away. She leaned against the mantlepiece and closed her eyes. Behind her, she heard Jessie sigh and shuffle over to the door.

A piece of charred, smoking wood fell from the pile inside the grate and clattered into the hearth. A floorboard creaked as Jessie stepped on it.

Without turning round, still staring into the dying fire, Anna spoke in a soft, almost toneless voice.

"I can't let her see him again, Jessie. He's the kind who only wants to be with other men." There was a gasp, quickly smothered, from somewhere near the door. She turned round at last and looked into Jessie's shocked, white face. "It's true."

"Merciful 'eaven!"

"I found out the night of the King's Cup dinner, at Russell's place." She hesitated, swallowing, fighting down the ugly, obscene pictures that still haunted her. There was a bitter taste in her mouth, like bile. "That's why we came back so suddenly. I made an excuse to Russell and got Clara away as quickly as I could. What I saw sickened me. I had to get out of that house before I suffocated." She sat down, and covered her face with her hands. "I couldn't bring myself to tell her the real reason why, somehow. The words stuck in my throat, as if they were frozen there. But I had another reason for keeping silent, more important. The man I saw James Tollemache with has been my biggest enemy ever since I came back to Epsom and outbid him for the Old Brew House. What's more I've suspected him of a lot of things that I can't prove. Not yet. If I'd told Clara everything, I'd have had to reveal his identity to her—she'd never have believed my story about Tollemache, otherwise—and if I'd done that there was always the risk that she might, inadvertently, let his name slip to someone else. Not on purpose. I thought it all over and decided that it would have to be all or nothing. And for now, it has to be nothing. Until I have the proof that I need."

Jessie was leaning against the door, still stunned. She nodded, slowly. "I understand, lassie. I understand. But you shouldn't 'ave bottled it all up, inside. You could 'ave come to me. You could 'ave told me. Whatever you tell me'd go with me to me grave. You know that."

Anna smiled, wanly. "Yes, Jessie. I know that."

On her way to bed she hesitated, momentarily, outside her sister's door, listening to the muffled crying from within. But there was no purpose to be served by going to her, unless she could tell her the truth; and for now she could not do that. Too much was at stake.

It was better to be cruel to be kind.

Her hand fell away from the door latch. She went on to her own room.

✳ 20 ✳

A small, light traveling carriage stood in the drive at the front of the house as she rode up. She could see servants coming and going, one with rugs, another with a leather valise and luggage trunk. Russell's coachman stood by the horses' heads, a groom darted about, checking their harness and shoes.

So he was going somewhere, for several days and maybe weeks, to judge by the quantity of his baggage. And wherever it was he wanted to reach his destination quickly, otherwise he would have taken the larger, formal carriage, and not this light, sleek, giglike thing, built essentially for speed.

"Is Lord Russell going far?" She got down from her horse and gave the reins to the groom.

"Newmarket, Miss Brodie," the coachman said, tipping his hat. "'Is lordship reckons to be leaving within the hour."

She thanked him and went on into the house. The front door was already open, and so was the door of his study. She caught sight of him, sitting at his desk, and for a moment she stood there, on the threshold of the room, watching him.

"Your carriage is ready," she said. He looked up, startled. "I didn't know you were leaving Epsom."

"Anna!" He got up, and came over to her.

"Your coachman said you were going to Newmarket within the hour." The smile faded from his face.

"Yes. My uncle has been taken ill. I only got the news last night, just before Chifney came back to say that you had found your sister. I was relieved to hear that." He offered her a chair but she refused it.

"I won't keep you, if you're in a hurry."

He moved closer to her.

"Chifney said that you'd be calling here this morning, when you left Sam Loam's. I wouldn't have left before I'd seen you."

"I would have understood if you had. What I wanted to ask you can wait till you come back."

"No. Ask me now."

She could feel the warmth of his breath against the skin of her face, and instinctively she moved away. He was too close. His nearness disturbed and disquieted her as it had before. Because she had never felt wholly comfortable within herself when she was alone with him, she walked away toward his desk and half-sat on it, toying with her gloves to hide her conflict of emotions.

"You offered me your help once, if ever I was in need of it. Does the offer still stand?"

"I think you already know the answer to that, Anna."

"I'm not asking for myself. It's for my sister. If Chifney told you anything about what happened yesterday, you'll maybe begin to understand."

"Yes, he told me about James Tollemache."

"I know you haven't got to listen to what I have to say about him, or his brother. They're both tarred with the same brush. But for Clara's sake I want her as far away from him as possible." She got down from her perch on the desk and began to pace the room, clenching and unclenching her fists. "It isn't her fault. She's too young and too stupid to see men like James Tollemache for what they really are. Since our mother died I've kept her cloistered, out of contact with reality, as if she was living in a nunnery. I didn't want her to see some of things that I'd had to see. I wanted to protect her." She sighed. "I should have known better. The first personable, good-looking young man to come along can twist her around his little finger as if she was a piece of silk thread."

"You think Tollemache's after her share of your father's fortune, or after information about your yard?"

"Maybe both. As far as her half of the money is concerned, I can checkmate him . . . Clara can't marry anyone without my permission until she's twenty-one, and whether she marries or not before then she doesn't get a penny of the money until her twenty-first birthday. Even if she ran away and eloped with him he'd have to wait nearly five years before he could get his hands on it . . . and I doubt if he'd relish living on his father's charity until then.

"As for my horses . . . Clara doesn't know enough about them to tell him anything of use. She's never been interested. But if I hadn't found out that she was meeting him behind my back, he could have gotten her to find out things by feigning an interest, or asking any of my lads. And that would have been dangerous, maybe fatal, even. Look at what happened to Randyll. Someone who had no business to know, knew all about his secret plans to protect his filly. They didn't find out by themselves, did they?"

"You think Tollemache was trying to get information for his brother?"

For a moment she hesitated, held back by her natural caution.

"No. I think he was trying to get information for Jacob Hindley."

"Hindley?"

"He hates me, he always has. Ever since I came here and outbid him over the Old Brew estate, he's never forgiven me for it. He wants me out of Epsom and he doesn't care how he does it. You know that. He's told you so with his own lips."

"But you could say that about any of the other owners who want you out. They're scandalized by having a woman racing horses on the course. They're shocked. They're stunned. They just can't accept it. You've come here, all alone, and done something that they never expected to see in the whole of their lives."

"Are you making excuses for Hindley?" Her voice was bitter.

"No, I'm not making excuses for him. And if it makes you feel any better I can tell you that I detest him as much as you do. But what makes you think that he'd want to be rid of you any more than any of the others . . . or be prepared to go to greater lengths to do it than they would?"

"He has more motivation than anyone else. I made a fool of him. I snapped up the Old Brew estate right from under his nose, when he thought that it was as good as certain that Dewar would sell out at his price. I put Firestone into the King's Cup against his horse and beat him. He wanted Chifney for his horse but I got him for mine instead. His filly was one of the favorites to win the Queen Charlotte while mine was a fifty-to-one outsider, but she got her head just in front of his filly's on the line, and lost him a small fortune. Do you want any more reasons?"

Russell turned away and went over to the window. She could see him staring out at the traveling carriage outside, at the coachman, the groom, and the grounds beyond, but as if he was not really seeing them.

"Have you any proof against him?"

"Not yet. Just suspicions. But one way or the other, I intend to get it." She said nothing of her deeper suspicions, the suspicions she had confided to Chifney; nor her discovery on the night of the King's Cup. "I didn't come her to talk about Jacob Hindley. I came to talk about Clara." He turned round, at last. "You once told me you had a sister in London. If you spoke to her, do you think that she'd be willing to take Clara under her wing, for a year maybe? Then she could lead the kind of life she wants, the kind of life I can't give her here. I'd pay all expenses, of course."

"There'd be no question of that. My sister would be glad to do it."

Her face hardened momentarily.

"I don't expect charity."

"I'm offering none. On my way back from Newmarket, I shall be spending one or two nights under my sister's roof. I'll make the arrangements with her then."

"I'm grateful." Gratitude to him, thanking him, did not come easily to her. With uncharacteristic awkwardness, she looked down at her hands. "I mustn't keep you any longer." She moved toward the door. "Is your uncle very ill?"

"He had a seizure, two days ago. When I arrive I may find him better, or worse." They exchanged a glance, and she knew what he was implying. "If no decision was made about your case before he fell ill, then there's a chance it may be deferred until he recovers . . . or, if he doesn't, until a new chief steward has been elected."

"I don't want to get what I want that way."

"It wouldn't be your fault. Nobody could blame you if you did. It's fate, that's all. You know that I'll do everything I can to make them realize what their decision would mean to you."

"But I told you before. I don't want you to do that."

"Because you think it would make you beholden to me?" When she made no answer he came toward her, and she could not move away because she stood against the door. "My helping you doesn't put you in my debt, Anna. How can I make you understand that?"

"And Firestone?"

"He was a gift. He belonged to you, anyway. That's what I told you before, when you said you couldn't accept him. That's what I wrote in the note, before I went away."

"You've already done me too many favors."

"You're the one who insists on counting them, not me."

For a moment they looked at each other. Her eyes held a wary, hunted look, like an animal who fears to be trapped. To her surprise he suddenly reached out and took her hand, then raised it to his lips and kissed it.

"I must go now," she said, trying to pull it from his grasp. But he held it firmly in his own.

"Don't forget, Anna. While I'm away you can call on anyone here if there's anything you need. And your sister can use the piano any time she cares to." Slowly, he let go her hand. Then she murmured something about a safe journey, and was gone.

He watched her from the window. He stood there until she had ridden out of sight. He could still feel her presence in the room, all around him, as if part of her had not gone but still lingered.

If only he did not have to go away. If only he could have called her back, and told her everything that had happened to him in his life, until there was no more to tell.

But he could not do it.

Paris sat on the end of his bed in his room above the coach house, finishing off the polishing of a saddle, whistling a tune beneath his breath and keeping one eye on the small, slanting window, watching carefully in case Anna should come back earlier than he expected and catch him cleaning tack in the warmth and comfort of his own room instead of where he should be, in the barn or the tack shed. What did it matter, as long as the job was done? Only a woman would make a fuss about something as trivial. He rubbed in more saddle soap, and worked it vigorously into the leather, polishing as hard as he could until it shone like the shell of a horse chestnut. For a moment he forgot to glance out of the window, engrossed in the work in hand. Then his door creaked open and he almost jumped out of his skin.

"What the 'ell are you doing here?"

"Looking for you, Ben." Ruth stood there in the open doorway, shivering from the cold.

"Shut the door. And don't you knock before you come in?"

She did as she was told. "I'm sorry, Ben. But I 'ad to see you. I've bin waiting and waiting, but you've not said anything more about us going out on your 'alf-day . . ."

He turned his back on her abruptly, and went on with what he was doing. "I got other things to do besides wasting my 'alf-day driving you around."

"But, Ben, you promised . . . you said . . ."

"I never promised you nothing. I said I'd meet you when I could. When I got the time." He glanced at her coldly over his shoulder. "Now you'd best get out of 'ere, before she comes back." He jerked a thumb in the direction of the window. "I 'ad enough trouble last time, telling lies for 'er bloody sister!"

"That wasn't your fault, Ben."

"Ay, it wasn't. But to 'ear 'er ranting and raving, you'd think different. And all in front of Chifney, and all. Talking to me like I was some wet-eared stableboy that needed a kick up the arse!" His voice was bitter. "Well, what else can you expect, working for a woman? I should 'ave known better. I should 'ave gone to some other yard."

"But she pays you nearly twice what you'd get, working for someone else . . . you told me so. And in anyone else's yard you wouldn't be 'ead groom, not at your age. You'd 'ave to wait years."

"What do you know about it, ay? What do you know about anything?" He got up and put the saddle on the floor in front of him. "And I thought I told you to get out of 'ere? Do you want to lose me my job and your own as well?"

She went to him and grasped him by the arm.

"Please, Ben . . ."

He shook her off, roughly.

"I said get out of 'ere. I'm busy. I got work to do."

"You didn't say that before. Not the first time. The time you told me to come up." She started to cry. "You never wanted me to go, then." She blew her nose on her apron. "Now I've done what you wanted, you don't want me no more."

"Shut up! Shut up." He took her by the shoulders and shook her until her teeth chattered. "And stop blubbering. I can't stand women who keep blubbering, just 'cos they can't get their own way. You keep your mouth shut about coming up 'ere, and what went on between the two of us. Do you 'ear me?"

"I won't say nothing, Ben. I won't, I swear it!"

He let her go. He turned away and picked up the saddle.

"Go on back to the 'ouse, then. 'Aven't you got work to do?"

She rubbed at her reddened eyelids. She went slowly back toward the door and opened it. "When can I see you again, Ben? When will it be?"

"I don't know. On me next 'alf-day, maybe. I don't know. I'll 'ave to see. She's got a dozen more young 'orses coming over today or tomorrow, from Sam Loam's yard. All of 'em 'ave got to be broke and then wintered 'ere. It'll mean a lot of extra work. She might expect me to work on me 'alf-day to get it done."

"But she's always fair, Ben. She wouldn't expect you to work all week long, not without a break."

"Where 'er bloody 'orses are concerned, she expects everything. And if she says I 'ave to work on me 'alf-day, then I 'ave to work on it." He turned his back on her, and behind him, he heard the door click, and then close softly again. Her footsteps echoed down the narrow wooden stairs.

From the tiny window he saw her run across the courtyard and down by the side of the house, then she disappeared from sight. He turned away again and picked up the finished saddle. What a fool he had been to encourage her! She had long since begun to bore him with her slavish, doglike devotion, he was irked and irritated by her pleadings and tears. But for the moment his hands were tied, there was nothing he could do about it. And she came in useful, he had to admit, whenever he felt the need for a woman. Foolish, pointless, to throw away dirty water until he got clean.

Hoisting the saddle onto one shoulder he went out, down the stairs, through the coach house, and into the yard in the direction of the tack shed, shivering in the bitter cold.

From the window inside he caught sight of Anna, on foot, walking her horse back along the drive. He smiled. He replaced the saddle on its tree and took down another. She would never know that he had spent the morning in the warmth of his room, while the others were working in the cold outside, exercising the horses more than a mile away. Only Ruth knew where he had been. And she would never tell.

The meal had gone on for more than half an hour. No one spoke, not even Jessie. Only the clinking of cutlery and plates broke the uneasy silence. Then, as Ellen and Ruth came in to clear the table, Clara murmured something about excusing herself, and rose from the table.

"Wait a moment," Anna said, laying down her napkin. For the first time, the two sisters looked at each other. "Ralph Russell left for Newmarket this morning. He said that while he's away you could ride over any time you cared to and use the piano."

"Why, that was right kindly of 'im," Jessie said, glancing from one to the other.

"Yes," Clara said. Slowly, she sat down again.

"Well? Shall we go together this afternoon?"

"I thought you had things to do here. With those young horses from Sam Loam's."

"Paris can see to them."

"But you always like to see to them yourself."

"I can do it tomorrow. One day isn't going to make any difference, is it?"

"No, I suppose not." She got up from her place a second time, sheepishly, not quite able to meet Anna's eyes. "Yes, I should like to go. I'll go and fetch down my music."

"I'm glad you made your peace with 'er, Anna," Jessie said as soon as Clara had left the room. "What 'appened between the two of you last night upset me so, I couldn't sleep for thinking on it. What a stroke of luck 'e's gone off to Newmarket, and give you the run of the place. When you get over there, after a while, you can break the ice and tell 'er you're sorry for what 'appened."

Anna got up from her place at the table and went over to stand beside the window. "But I'm not sorry. Not for what I said to her last night. It had to be said, Jessie. She was in the wrong. What I am sorry for is that I had to hurt her. And over a piece of vile filth like James Tollemache." She repeated her conversation with Ralph Russell. "It'll do her good to be away from here for a year. She needs it. She needs the kind of life that Russell's sister can give her, the kind of life that makes her happy. That's all I want for her. To be happy. She isn't now."

"You've done everything for 'er that you could."

"But I haven't been able to give her what she really wants. Russell's sister can." She fell silent when Clara came back into the room.

"Are you ready to leave now, Anna?"

"If you are."

Quietly, she closed the door of Russell's drawing room behind her and slowly walked up the stairs. Below, the first strains of Clara's exquisite playing wafted up to her, and for a moment she paused and stood there with her hand on the banister, listening. Then she went on until she reached the second-floor landing, where she stopped outside the door of the locked room.

There were no servants to see her. She reached out and tried the handle of the door. But it was locked. Quickly she went back downstairs and slipped into the study. She closed the door behind her and turned the key. Then she went over to Russell's desk and opened each drawer in turn, going swiftly through the contents. But there were no keys. She looked around the room. There was a small, polished box on a table by the window, and she went over to it, but it contained only cigars. She shut the lid with a snap.

She unlocked the door again and went back upstairs. She stood in the middle of the landing, looking up to the floors above. Then she began to climb the stairs, first singly, then in steps of two and three until she reached the top. At the end of the landing she caught sight of a heavy oak door, different from the others, and when she went to it and opened it she saw that it revealed another flight of steps, narrow and wooden, that led not to another landing but to the attics at the top of the house. Lifting the hem of her gown above her ankles, she began to mount them slowly.

There was no light, no hand rail, even. Only a thick rope, fastened to the smooth walls by metal rings, gave her something to cling to, and she stopped, several times, as the stairs wound and twisted away before her, never ending. Then, at last, she caught sight of a low wooden door up above, and she breathed a sigh of relief. Curiosity spurred her on. The staircase seemed to grow narrower still, if that were possible, and on hands and knees she inched her way toward the door, only to find it locked.

She pummeled it with her fists, threw her weight against it with frustration, but it was so thick that it barely rattled. Then she suddenly caught sight of a key, hanging on a hook above her head. On tiptoe, standing on the highest step, she managed to reach it with the very tips of her fingers. She hit at it, then hit at it again, and it fell off, clattering down the staircase. Cursing, she had to turn around and descend the steps, not easy in her full, wide gown, until she found it.

With trembling fingers she fitted it into the keyhole and turned it, and the door creaked, and then swung open.

She stood there for a moment in the frame of the doorway, staring at the low, long room that it revealed. A ray of bright sunlight shone across the tumbled contents of the attic from the small window in the sloping roof. The floor was thick with dust, cobwebs glistened among the beams and on the stacked, old furniture and pictures frames that filled the room. Slowly, she closed the door behind her and began to walk among them, pausing to touch things at every step. A broken chair, an old picture, its paint faded and cracked with neglect. She opened boxes. She looked through piles of old, yellowed papers that meant nothing to her. She was not certain, even, what she expected to find, even why she was here. Something within that had no name compelled her, drove her on. Edging her way through the abandoned furniture stacked against the walls, she went to the far end of the attic room.

Another old picture lay against a chest; she could see its shape through the sacking that covered it, and for some reason it made her pause. It was larger than any of the others, almost life-size. It was the only one that had been wrapped and tied securely with narrow rope, as if for some reason somebody had wanted to preserve it.

She fought her way through the piles of clutter to reach it, tearing at the ropes that bound it. Wildly, she looked around her. A rusted knife lay among a dusty box of old tools in the opposite corner of the attic, and she went to fetch it. For a moment she hesitated, biting her lip. Then she hacked at the rope until it was cut through and pulled away the thick layers of cloth that had been draped about the picture to protect it.

It was too massive and heavy for her to raise. She dragged it from its place and lay it down on the dusty floorboards, where a shaft of light from the tiny window in the sloping roof picked out the faded colors on the canvas, and the chipped gold frame.

It was a portrait of a woman, and she stared at it. A woman with fair, ringleted hair, a woman with pale eyes and slightly smiling mouth. It was a comely face, but the eyes were hard and catlike; there was a cruel twist that the artist had caught, playing at the corners of the lips. And there, about her neck, was the diamond necklace Anna herself had worn in the night of the King's Cup dinner downstairs.

Woodenly, stunned, she went down on her knees on the dusty floor and wiped away the grime and cobwebs with her hands. Her heart hammered. A strange, alien, sick sensation gripped her in the pit of her stomach. In the right-hand corner of the portrait she could just make out the artist's signature, and the inscribed identity of the sitter. Her lips moved silently as she mouthed the words, half-unable to believe them.

"Mary Hindley, Lady Russell."

PART VIII
March 1834

✳ 21 ✳

Tobias Slout lay back in his chair beside the fire, the smoke from his cigar curling upward in a thin, gray column toward the ceiling. Behind him came the sound of one of his lackeys, lighting the oil lamps around the room, and Slout turned his head to look at him.

"When you've done that, send Ephraim in to me. I want words with 'im."

"Yes, Mr. Slout."

He turned back toward the fire, the light from the leaping flames casting shadows across his heavy, grotesque face.

"Take that lamp from me desk and trim the wick, when you go. It keeps smoking and smoke stinks."

"Yes, Mr. Slout. I'll take it now." He did as he was told and scurried away. No sooner had he left than there was a tapping on the outside of the door, and in answer to Slout's bellowing a small, bent man came in. He stood there in the open doorway, his beady eyes darting around the room.

"Shut that door, I can feel a draft!"

"Ay, Gov'nor. I'm sorry, Gov'nor." He shuffled over and stood beside the fire. "It's a cold night, Gov'nor."

Slout threw the stub of his cigar into the fire.

"Well, did you do as I told you to?"

"Ay, I bin watching out for that black filly of Anna Brodie's, just like you said. Wasn't easy, Mr. Slout. Mostly, she gallops it on 'er own ground. But 'alf a dozen times she's took it up on Mickleham Downs, and I was ready and waiting."

"Well?"

"She's got it entered for the Guineas and the Oaks, just like you reckoned, and the Queen's Cup, in three weeks. That'll be a big field, you can bet on it. And all quality nags. She'll be up against the best all right. I reckon if she can take the Queen's Cup there'll be nothin' to touch 'er in them classics . . . and I ain't the only one to think it, neither."

Slout swore and spat into the fire.

"That poxy Brodie bitch! She's bin in my 'air too long and I aim to 'ave 'er and 'er nags out of it! This time for good." He got up and walked over to his desk. He crashed his huge fist on it and it shook. "Do you 'ave any idea of 'ow much brass she's lost me over this last year? Do you?"

"You'll get 'er, Mr. Slout, you'll get 'er. If the stewards at the Jockey Club don't first . . ."

"The stewards at the Jockey Club! When they get up off their fat idle arses, they'll get 'er! But 'ow long is that likely to be? Next week, next month, next year? If I go on losing brass at the rate I've bin losing it over the last few months, I'll be put out of business!"

"Things isn't that bad, is they, Mr. Slout?"

"They're getting that way. They're getting close to that way." He started to pace the room.

"What you going to do, Mr. Slout?"

"I'm going to break 'er, Ephraim. That's what I'm going to do. I bin waiting too long. Much too long. And I don't aim to wait no longer. There's an old saying . . . if you want something done proper, you got to go and do it yourself. If 'er nag wins the Queen's Cup, you mark my words, it'll be the last race it'll ever win. Or run in." He smiled, and his teeth gleamed black and yellow in the firelight. "That's a promise." He sank back into his chair.

In the sudden silence there was another tap on the door. "Who is it?" He jutted a finger toward Ephraim. "Open it."

One-eyed Bill stood outside, behind him a shadowy figure that neither could see because the passage was in darkness.

"I'm busy. What do you want?"

"There's a lady to see you, Mr. Slout. Says she's got business."

"Lady?" He half got up from his chair. "I don't know no ladies. Who is it, at this hour?"

All at once the shadowy figure in the darkened passage pushed past One-eyed Bill and stood there on the threshold of the room, her lips curled in a smile. She wore a velvet gown and fur-edged mantelet of bright peacock blue, and she threw back the large hood attached to it that had hidden most of her face.

"My name is Lady Helen Gordon. I believe you and I might have a mutual interest in seeing certain someone get her just deserts."

Slout stared at her, momentarily taken aback. Then he quickly recovered himself and signaled for One-eyed Bill to come into the room and close the door.

"And who might that certain someone be?"

"Anna Brodie."

Behind her back, Ephraim and One-eyed Bill exchanged glances. Slout's thick, flabby lips curled back from his rotten teeth in a knowing smile.

"Fetch the lady a chair, Ephraim." He waited until she was seated. "Brandy?"

"I prefer gin."

Slout signaled to One-eyed Bill and he brought a glass and the gin bottle from another corner of the room.

"So you got a grudge against the bastard?"

"Let's just say I have a score to settle."

He frowned. "But you ain't nothing to do with racing or blood 'orses." Realization suddenly dawned, he smiled in understanding. "Unless it's nothin' to do with 'orses . . . something personal, then?"

"That's my business." She opened her reticule and brought out a thick wad of banknotes. Slout's lackeys' eyes gleamed. "I have five hundred pounds here. You can regard that as a deposit. If you want to earn five thousand, all you have to do is make sure that she's finished in Epsom. For good. And that none of her precious horses ever run anywhere again."

Slout whistled.

"Five thousand's a lot of brass. You must 'ate 'er pretty bad."

"I just told you. I have a score to settle. And I mean to settle it, one way or the other. I don't just want Anna Brodie ruined in racing. I want her hurt. Really hurt. And the only way to hurt her is to hurt her horses."

Slout exchanged a knowing look with One-eyed Bill above her head. "Well now, I think you and me can do a little business together." He reached out and took the money from her hands. He began to finger the notes with his big, ugly hands.

"It's all there. You can count it if you don't believe me." Her voice was sharp. "When will you do it?"

"Hold on now, lady. Just hold on. You don't realize what you're asking. For more than a year, someone else I know, besides meself, 'as bin trying to figure out ways to run that bastard out of town. Easier said than done."

Helen Gordon sprang to her feet in rage. "Just make sure you destroy her. And her horses. That's what I want. That's what I mean to get."

"Consider it done, me lady." Slout's voice took on a coaxing note. "Now, you come and finish your gin by the fire. It's a bloody cold night, that's for sure." He made a signal with his hand to his lackeys, and they both went out of the room. She sat down again. "One thing you 'aven't told me . . . one thing I'm curious about. 'Ow come you came 'ere, to me? Who told you that I 'ad an interest in seeing the Brodie bitch put down?"

She smiled over her glass of gin.

"You forget who I am, Mr. Slout. I'm in a position to hear things that other women don't. And I've been hearing whispers in certain quarters that you've lost a lot of money because of Anna Brodie's horses. Only rumors, it's true. But then I always believe that there's no smoke without fire."

"You took a big risk driving up to my 'ouse."

"At this time of night I doubt there'd be anyone to see me."

"What about your driver?"

She held up her reticule and shook it. He heard the jingle of coins. "He knows how to keep his mouth shut."

"Of course."

She put down her empty glass and got to her feet.

"I'm staying with friends of my father's at their estate near Cheam . . . until the racing starts. Then I shall be a guest of Sir John and Lady Verney for as long as it suits me to stay. You'll know where to find me."

"Supposing I need to get in touch with you? Supposing I want to get word to you about something? 'Ow do I do that? I might need to, in a 'urry."

"There's a certain gentleman you can trust with any messages. Nobody would ever suspect him because he owns no racing horses and isn't even a member of the Jockey Club. But his family have such standing that he's accepted everywhere." She smiled. "I think I can safely say that he'd be more than willing to do anything I might ask of him."

Slout was immediately intrigued.

"And 'is name?"

"Lionel Tollemache."

"I've 'eard of 'im, ay. But what makes you think 'e can be trusted indefinitely? 'E might be sweet on you now, but things can change. What 'appens if 'e cools off?"

Her eyes narrowed to slits. Her lips were taut and white.

"No man who falls in love with me ever cools off."

"You're pretty sure of yourself, ain't you, lady?"

"I have good reason to be."

He decided it would be more prudent to keep silent. He put his hand across his mouth to hide a smile.

She stopped when she got to the door, and turned to him.

"One more thing you can do for me, if you will. The earl of Leopardstown has a horse running in the Prince of Wales Stakes next Thursday. I would rather it didn't win . . . if you take my meaning?"

"'E keeping the nag overnight at the racecourse stables?"

"According to my information he is."

"Consider it done."

She smiled and went out.

Slout went to the window and pulled back the curtain enough to be able to watch her leaving, but without her knowing that he was watching. As soon as her small carriage had disappeared through his gates, he called his lackeys back into the room.

"That could prove to be a right useful lady," Slout said, pouring himself another measure of brandy. "A lady with a grudge all right."

"She stunk of scent, Gov'nor . . ."

Slout guffawed and belched. He swigged down his brandy and wiped his lips on the back of his sleeve. "That one, she's a born whore . . . I can smell 'em a mile off. 'Elen Gordon . . . she's bin in more rich men's beds

than you've 'ad tankards of ale. And she wants revenge. On the bastard.
And on Leopardstown."

"You tell 'er you knew that, Mr. Slout?"

"What you take me for?"

"But can you trust 'er, Mr. Slout?"

"I don't trust no woman, including 'er. But we can use 'er. She's got
useful connections. She gets invited into 'ouses where things are talked
about that I might want to 'ear. And she's got an advantage over even
Jacob 'Indley . . . men'll say a lot of useful things to a woman when they're
in bed with 'er!"

"Will you tell 'er that 'Indley's in with us?"

"That'd be a fool thing to do. The less she knows the better." He heaved
his bulk up from the chair. "Got a job for you, though, Ephraim. Not too
difficult. Prince of Wales Stakes, next Thursday."

"Nag need fixing, Mr. Slout?"

"Ay. A favor for Lady 'Elen. Leopardstown's horse. Make sure it gets a
bucket of cold water a few minutes afore it's saddled for the race. And put
something in it . . . not too strong . . . just enough to make the nag sick."

"Will do, Gov'nor."

"All right, you can get out."

When he was alone Slout went over and sat down behind his desk. He
lay the wad of notes down in front of him. Smiling, he began to count
them.

Lionel Tollemache lay on his back in the big curtained bed, staring up at
the ceiling, his long, tapering fingers toying idly with the loose strands of
Helen Gordon's hair. She lay on her side, naked, running her hands over
his body, rubbing her leg tauntingly against his.

"What are you thinking about?" Her thin lips gleamed in the half-light.

"About me?"

"Of course."

"Then why don't you look at me?" She rolled closer to him. "Were you
thinking that you'd never seen anyone as beautiful as I am?"

Slowly, he turned his head. Lazily, he forced himself to smile. How
boring and vain she was! It had suited him to meet her here at the Gold-
finder Inn, fifteen miles away from Epsom, where there was nobody who
knew him, but he already regretted it. If he could have decently gotten up
and dressed and left her, he would have. But he was desperately short of
money and when she had gone out of the room for a few minutes he had
opened her reticule and found it crammed with loose guineas and banknotes. He was waiting for another opportunity to help himself; after all,
she was so careless about money that she would never notice if any was
missing.

"You haven't answered my question," she said, prodding him.

"What would be the point when you've already read my mind?"

His answer pleased her. She leaned over him and began to stroke the side of his cheek.

"Are you going back to stay with the Hindleys until after the Derby meeting?"

"They invited me. And it will suit me, yes."

"Their seat is only seven miles away from Sir John Verney's," she said, slyly, with an implication in her voice that he understood only too well. His agile mind cast around swiftly for some believable excuse.

"It won't be easy for us to meet, nevertheless. You can hardly expect our hosts to let us use their homes as we might use a wayside inn."

"If I became Lady Helen Tollemache they would have no option."

Beside her he stiffened, stunned into silence by the enormity of her suggestion. He had been totally unprepared for it, even from her. And for the first time in his life he was completely speechless.

"You must have thought of it, constantly, ever since you met me at Durdans." Absently, she toyed with the lobe of his ear. "What a handsome couple we would make, you and I. A perfect match, many have been hinting at it. And it would delight my father."

Despite the cold of the night, Tollemache began to sweat. He could feel the beads of perspiration forming on his forehead, behind his neck, in the palms of his hands. He swallowed, trying to think. Married to a virago like Helen Gordon, he would be little more than a prisoner, less than a common servant—for even servants have their moments of leisure and privacy—he would be stifled, pandering constantly to her colossal vanity, forced to laugh at her cruel mimickry and spiteful jokes.

She would never let him out of her sight, not even for an hour; and she was the kind who would make a scene if he so much as raised his hat to another woman. Her father was a duke. . . .

Slowly, reluctantly, he turned toward her.

"Helen . . ."

Her catlike eyes narrowed instantly.

"What is it, what's wrong? Why are you looking at me that way?"

"I can scarcely bear to tell you this . . ." Cunningly, he took her hand in his and held it to his lips. "But I can't marry you." She took her hand from his grasp. She sat up against the carved bed head.

"Why?"

"Because a long time ago, when I was barely eighteen, my father arranged with a neighbor whose estates ran with his that I should be betrothed to his daughter. A definite promise was given, both in words and in writing, and legally it is still binding. The only reason the marriage hasn't yet taken place is that she suffers from a delicate constitution, and has lived for the past few years in Italy . . ." The lies tumbled out, one after another, with such ease that he surprised even himself. "If there had been no definite promise between my father and hers, it wouldn't matter. But there's nothing I can do."

Her eyes glittered with rage.

"But surely her father wouldn't hold you to such a promise, when she isn't fit to be married? It should be canceled. Rescinded. Tell me her name. My father can approach hers, and tell him that you want to marry me. If necessary, he'll buy him off."

"You don't understand, Helen. Her father is a fanatical churchman. He'd never consent to it. And no amount of money could ever buy him off." There, he had said it. He almost breathed a sigh of relief.

"The weakling bitch!" Furiously, she threw back the covers and snatched a robe to cover herself with as she paced the floor. "Does she think she can make herself live longer by staying in Italy and sitting all day in the sun? Why doesn't she die? Why don't you make them bring her back here, so that the cold kills her? What use is she to anyone? Was your father mad when he made such a promise?"

"When he made it there was no way of knowing her state of health. She was barely fifteen then."

"So you're not free to marry me? Not until she dies? Is that what you're saying?"

He turned his face away so that she should not see his expression.

"I'm sorry."

In the dim lamplight he watched her pour herself another glass of gin and stand at the little inn window, looking down into the deserted cobbled yard. For a while neither of them spoke again.

"I should hate to compromise you," he said at length, sliding from the bed and beginning to dress himself. "After all, a lady's reputation is her most valued asset." He suddenly realized what he had said. But she was far too angry to read anything into his thoughtless words. "I think that I should leave, and ride back to Epsom tonight. Then to all intents and purposes it will look as if you have been staying here alone."

She threw the empty gin glass across the room where it crashed against the wall and shattered into pieces. Then she covered her face with her hands and sobbed with rage. Diplomatically, he went over to her and held her to him.

"I could have any man I wanted. Any man. I have only to crook my little finger and they'd come running, all clamoring to claim the privilege of asking my father for my hand."

He kept a straight face. He knew that she was lying. With difficulty he suppressed a smile. With even more difficulty, he gently extricated himself from her suffocating embrace.

"Let me pour you some water, to bathe your eyes." He took the jug from the washstand and half-filled the bowl with warm water. "Here." He soaked his handkerchief in the water.

Reluctantly, she took it from him and held it over her closed eyes.

"I'll fetch you a cloth to dry them." Never taking his eyes from her back lest she turn round and see him, Tollemache inched his way toward the table where she had left her reticule. Keeping up a ceaseless flow of talking, still watching her, he quickly untied the drawstrings and slipped his hand inside, feeling for the wad of notes. Clutching a handful he stuffed them into his pocket and pulled the drawstring taut again. Then he fetched the cloth and took it to her.

"Sleep well," he said. Then he bent and kissed her cheek and left the room.

Downstairs in the cobbled inn yard, waiting for the ostler to bring round his horse, he breathed in the cold night air with relief. He was free again. From the stifling, half-darkened room, permeated with the odor of her stagnant perfume. From her white, clinging arms, clutching and clawing at him like tentacles. Suddenly he felt sick, disgusted. Suddenly he understood why Leopardstown had tired of her. He, too, must have felt sickness and disgust.

But Tollemache had gotten what he came for. Slipping a hand inside his coat as he waited, he felt the wad of banknotes there. And he smiled.

It still seemed strange, without Clara in the house. Even now, even after five months. As she passed her sister's empty room, lamp in hand, Anna paused for a moment; then she opened the door and looked in.

Everything was exactly as she had left it. There were books on the table beside her bed. A pile of sheet music. Her jug and water glass still stood on the linen press beneath the window. Only the cupboards, stripped bare of her clothes, betrayed that the room had not been occupied for many months.

Anna stood there, in the middle of it, looking around her, a small lump growing at the back of her throat. Only when Jessie and the rest of the house were safely asleep did she ever come here. Even to Jessie, even more to herself, she could never quite admit that she missed her. Suddenly, the click of the front door downstairs startled her, and she went out, closing the door behind her, making her way to the top of the stairs. She began to walk down them, holding the lamp aloft, peering into the gloom. On the turn of the staircase she stopped and stared at the small, white figure below her, clutching her shawl about her nightgown and gazing back at Anna with wide, frightened eyes.

"Ruth! What are you doing down here?"

"I . . . I'm sorry if I woke you, miss. But I come down for a drink of water, and I thought I 'eard a noise, outside."

"But I let the dogs loose tonight. If there was anyone out there we would have heard them barking."

"I didn't see nothing, miss."

Anna turned back and began to go upstairs again.

"Draw the bolts and come to bed."

In bed she lay back against the carved bedhead and closed her eyes. Her body was weary from working all day with the horses, but her mind would not let her rest.

She thought about Russell. Still in Newmarket, still running his sick uncle's estates. Downstairs inside her desk lay a dozen letters that he had written her, each one more anxious, each one more puzzled than the last, all of which had remained unanswered. But how could she answer them, what words could she write, after the discovery she'd made that day in the attic . . . that Hindley's sister had been Ralph Russell's wife?

Before her, in the darkness, she saw again the dust-coated frame, the gilt of its carved edges chipped and cracked with neglect and age. And then the face that had stared back at her from the faded canvas, the eyes and lips in their secretive smile mocking her, taunting her, laughing at her for not realizing the truth.

Desperately, she covered her eyes with her hands, willing away the face from her memory, but it would not go.

Before she fell into an exhausted sleep, she could still hear Tiffany's voice whispering in her ear, the words tormenting her.

They say he can't get over his wife's death . . .

❊ 22 ❊

As she rode into the deserted courtyard at Chilworth Manor her hack's hoofbeats sounded strange and eerie in the deadly quiet. She turned and looked around her.

It was a long time since she had ridden this way and the sad, neglected house looked forlorn and unloved in the bright March sunshine, like the unsightly remains of a banquet in the glare of the day.

Weeds grew in unchecked profusion through the once immaculate gravel of the drive; birds' nests protruded from the eaves. The hedges were overgrown, several windows were cracked, and some broken.

Slowly, Anna dismounted and led her back toward the front of the house. Tollemache's horse was already there, tethered to one of the stone balustrades, nibbling at the grass that had grown up between the paving stones. She tied up her own horse and walked up to the front door.

She found him, riding crop in hand, touring the enormous ballroom. Their voices echoed loudly from wall to wall.

"I didn't hear you ride up."

"Why did you send me that note, asking me to meet you here?" Her footsteps rang out as she walked slowly toward him. "I have nothing to say to you, you know that."

He smiled, his eyes on her face.

"What better place could I have chosen? Deserted. Miles from Epsom. No one rides this way anymore. No one to see us. No one to hear what we say."

"And what is it that you have to say?"

"I've come here to warn you. If you want to keep that Glenartney filly of yours in one piece until the Guineas and the Oaks, don't let her win the Queen's Cup. Better still, don't even run her in it."

"What are you saying?"

"Nothing more than that. But if you want to keep one step in front of your enemies, do as I say."

"If you know of the existence of some plot against my filly, you'd better tell me about it. Then you can come straight to the constable with me and tell him too. I want names, Tollemache. Evidence that I can do something with. And I want it now."

"Names I can't give you." He turned away and began to walk about the vast, empty space that was once a ballroom. "I only wish that I could. There are some things that a gentleman can't reveal, even if he wanted to."

"You mean that you haven't got the guts to take the consequences?" Her voice was mocking.

He was standing almost with his back toward her.

"What a sad place," he said, leaning against one of the marble pillars. "I can almost hear it weeping, can't you?" Dead leaves from last autumn, blown in through the broken windows, lay littering the dusty floor. He turned to her now and smiled, as if he had never heard her insult. "Does your sister like living in London?"

"I'm not here to talk about my sister."

"Leopardstown was toying with the idea of buying this place . . . did you know that?"

"I had already heard."

"Then some rich merchant banker from London was showing interest. Reckon he fancied himself as an owner of blood horses, looking to pick up the property cheap, because of its condition. I think Tradescant was the name."

"Never heard of him."

He came toward her and took her gloved hands in his. "Anna, why do you hate me so? Every time I try to help you turn your back on me."

Roughly, she pulled her hands from his grasp.

"I'd never turn my back on you, Tollemache. Turn your back on a viper and you can expect to be bitten." Without another word, without looking back, she turned away and walked out. Then she remounted her horse and rode away down the drive.

He ran from the house, calling after her. But she rode on without stopping.

"So your uncles think they've got another Derby winner on their 'ands, ay?" Sam Loam said, glancing across the dinner table toward Chifney. Anna stopped eating, and looked at him.

"Another Priam, my uncle Will reckons. He says if Shillelagh doesn't win by two lengths he'll eat his Sunday hat."

"Shillelagh, the duke of Cleveland's colt?" Anna lay down her knife and fork and sipped her wine. "Priam could give the likes of him a furlong start and still beat him hands down." She made a sign to Ellen Troggle to fetch the brandy to the table. "If I was betting on the race my brass would be on Batson's Plenipotentiary. He's a half-brother to Priam and won a race at the Newmarket Craven meeting the week before last; then two days later he beat Glencoe in the Craven Stakes and Glencoe's hot favorite to take the Guineas. He carries a lot of flesh, it's true. But he's got the speed and the staying power to win the Derby in a canter." She poured brandy into her empty wine glass. "Up against him I wouldn't give Shillelagh a dog's chance."

"Nor me," Sam Loam said. "Your uncles' putting much brass on 'im, then?"

"From what I hear, every guinea they can lay their hands on. If he goes down they'd have to sell every stick of furniture in Warren Hill to meet their debts."

There was a few moments' silence while they finished the meal. Ellen began to refill their glasses.

"'Eard from that sister of yours lately?" Sam said, dabbing at the corners of his mouth with his napkin.

"Not lately, no. Clara never was much of a writer. And even if she was, I doubt if she'd have much to write to me. We had an argument before she left."

"Yes, I remember you saying," said Sam Loam. Anna and Chifney exchanged a glance. "Know when that lord and master of yours is likely to be back from Newmarket?" He turned toward Chifney. "'E's bin gone a fair while."

"He left Inchcape in charge of the running of the yard. Jason keeps the house ticking over. But I know him well enough to know that he won't come back until his uncle's either better or dead. The old man never married. From what Inchcape says, he brought Russell up after his father died. Regards him as a son, more or less. Russell feels so indebted to him for what he did and what he gave him, he'd never forgive himself if something happened to the old man when he wasn't there."

Anna's curiosity was aroused at once. Here was a part of Russell's life she had never heard about. Something he had never told her.

"What do you mean, Russell feels indebted to him for what he gave him. What did he give him?"

"Why, the house and estate, here, in Epsom. I thought you knew that?" She shook her head.

"Russell was a younger son. One of four. When his father died there was nothing left to speak of, shared out between four brothers and two sisters. In his younger days the old man was the black sheep of the Russell family, the one who won and lost fortunes on horses. Russell's father and grandfather didn't approve of that. When Russell started showing more than a small interest in the turf, the old man was delighted. He made him an outright gift of the house and land here before he went back to Newmarket to his own estate, and where he became one of the chief stewards of the Jockey Club."

"I 'eard something like that, years ago," Sam Loam said. "'E's done well, that's for sure. But 'e deserves it. Ralph Russell's one of the few men I ever met what calls a spade a spade and don't make no bones about it. Me, I'm a plain man and I like plain speaking." He paused while Ellen's sister came in to take away the plates. "Great pity about that wife of 'is. Great pity. The old man was pretty taken with 'er, so I've 'eard." He did not notice Anna stiffen and sit back in her chair.

Chifney nodded.

"Yes. Inchcape says he took it very hard. Never got over it. That's why he's never remarried." He glanced suddenly at Anna. But she looked away hurriedly.

"Ellen, you shouldn't be working tonight. Isn't today your half-day off?" Ellen Troggle stopped what she was doing.

"It was, miss. But Ruth asked me if I'd mind changing with 'er, and I said I wouldn't."

"Has she gone out?"

"Bin out all afternoon, miss. But I reckon she'll be back soon. Why, it's black as pitch out there!" She picked up the remainder of the plates and took them away. Anna turned back to her guests.

At that moment, as Anna glanced toward the open door, she caught sight of Ruth, still in her outdoor cloak and bonnet, scurrying away upstairs.

"Ruth? Are you all right? Your face is the color of candle wax."

The girl turned, nervously, and gave her a small, hurried smile. Her face was white beneath her large poke bonnet.

"Yes, miss. Thank you, miss. Just a bit worn out, that's all. I'll go straight up to bed, if that's all right."

Anna turned back toward her guests.

"Well, Sam. What do you reckon's about to give my filly any trouble in the Guineas?"

Anna was sound asleep when Ellen suddenly flung open her door, frantically, tripping over in the darkness.

"Miss! Miss! Please, come quick! It's Ruth. She's bin took bad!"

Dazed with sleep, struggling up, Anna pushed back the bed covers and rubbed her eyes. "All right. I'm coming. Have you woken Jessie?"

"No, miss. I come straight for you."

Anna swung her legs over the edge of the bed and reached for her shawl, then she followed Eliza out into the passage. Just as they reached the foot of the second-floor staircase, the air was filled with piercing screams that had Jessie running out of her bedroom.

"Anna! What in mercy's name's the matter? Who's that screaming enough to wake the dead?"

"It's Ruth. She's ill. Come quickly." They hurried up the stairs to Ruth's bedroom and Anna flung open the door. She took the candlestick from Jessie and held it up.

"Oh, my God!"

For a moment they stared toward the bed, Anna and Jessie knowing at once what was wrong. The bedclothes, Ruth's nightdress, were saturated in blood. Anna rushed over to her and knelt down, grasping both her sweating hands in her own.

"Ruth! You must tell me. Who did this to you?"

Slowly, she turned her wasted face toward Anna. Beads of sweat glistened on her forehead and lips. Her glazed eyes seemed sunken into their sockets, and black-rimmed. "Oh, miss . . . the pain. I can't stand the pain. Please, miss. Please 'elp me . . ." Drawing her legs up in a spasm of agony, she clutched at Anna's hands. "Please, please 'elp me . . . miss . . ."

"God 'elp us!" Jessie said, staring at her round-eyed. "Ruth!"

"Ellen! Run and wake William Devine. Tell him to take the fastest horse in the stable and ride for the doctor. Quickly!" She pressed Ruth's limp hands tighter still. "Ruth, you must answer me. Who did this to you?"

Blood began oozing from the corner of her mouth. There were mauve patches around her lips and eyes.

"'E told me where to go . . . said I 'ad to, else 'e wouldn't see me again . . ." She closed her eyes. "Miss . . ." Anna bent her head close to Ruth's lips, and only she heard her whisper a name. Slowly she stood up. Her own face was almost as white as Ruth's.

"The doctor will need hot water. Plenty of it. And clean sheets. We must get her out of those sheets." The sickening stench of dried blood filled the room. She went quickly over to the window and opened it. "Rouse the others. We'll need all the help we can get."

After what seemed an eternity, they heard the sound of horses in the yard down below, and then banging at the front door.

Halfway downstairs, Jessie shouted to Eliza to run and open it.

"Thank the blessed Lord. 'E's got 'ere, at last."

She stood at the kitchen window, oblivious to the noise and bustle behind her, staring out into the darkness. The whole room was filled with steam from the kettles and caldrons full of boiling water on the stove.

While the doctor from Epsom was with Ruth, Anna had gone back to her room and dressed herself in her working clothes, for she knew that after what she had seen she would have no more sleep that night.

Suddenly, from outside somewhere in the hall, she heard the sound of Ellen and Bessie crying, and when she turned round, the doctor was standing there in the open doorway of the kitchen, his bag in one hand.

"I'm sorry, I couldn't save her. She'd lost too much blood."

She stared at him, as if she had not heard.

"Mrs. Tamm says you changed the sheets once, but I'm afraid there was a great deal more blood. The whole room will need a thorough cleaning in the morning. It's difficult to see now." Behind him, Anna caught sight of Jessie's ashen face. "As soon as I get back to Epsom, I'll notify the constable and the proper authorities about the body." Still she said nothing. Still she continued to stare at him. "This is most distressing for you, Miss Brodie. For everyone. I'm so sorry." He took his hat from Ellen and went out.

Bessie was bolting the front door after him when Anna suddenly walked out into the hall.

"No, don't do that yet. Go and fetch Paris."

"Paris, miss?"

"Yes, Paris." She turned away. She went and stood at the top of the stairs.

He came stumbling into the hall, rubbing his eyes, screwing them up against the sudden blaze of lights. She could see how hastily he'd dressed himself. Half his shirt buttons were unfastened. His belt was undone. He looked around him at all of them. Then upward toward Anna.

"Come up here, Paris!"

"What is it, Miss Brodie? What's all that commotion I 'eard a while ago, down in the yard? I was sound asleep when the shouting woke me."

"Just do as I tell you."

Frowning, he slowly walked up to meet her, stopping a single step below the place where she stood.

"You've been carrying on with Ruth, haven't you? For a long time. Ever since you came here. Well, answer me."

"I don't think that's anyone's business, Miss Brodie."

"I'm making it mine."

"I don't know what you mean, miss."

"I mean that Ruth's upstairs dead, lying soaked in her own blood. Blood from the knife of some butcher she went to in desperation, who hacked your child out of her because you told her that if she didn't have it done, you'd never speak to her again." He stared at her, his mouth hanging open. "And I trusted you. I let you drive my sister to Sutton, and Ewell, thinking she was in good hands, that she was safe; but all the time I thought you were looking after her, you were seducing my maid, and my sister was left alone with that viper, James Tollemache!"

"I'm not being made a scapegoat for your sister!" he shouted, angrily. "It's none of my business who she planned to meet up with, I wasn't 'er bloody keeper! And Ruth, she never needed no arm-twisting to go with me, I'll tell you that! You're not blaming me for what's 'appened, I 'ad nothing to do with it. Nothing, do you 'ear? Ay, and I'm no fool, neither, falling for the tricks of some scheming 'ussy . . . she did this, deliberate, to get me to marry 'er, and I wouldn't. When I wed, it'll be to a decent lass, what's kept 'erself pure!"

With a shout of rage Anna rushed toward him and grabbed him roughly by the shirt, hauling him behind her up the remaining stairs, along the corridor and up the second staircase that led to Ruth's room. Ignoring his wild protests and Jessie's cries, she kicked open the door and savagely thrust him through it.

"Go on, Paris!" She took hold of his head in both hands and twisted it in the direction of the blood-soaked bed. "Take a look at your handiwork. Take a good, long look. Jessie! Ellen! Bring more lights! Bring them here so that he can see better!" Desperately, he tried to break free of her grasp, but her wrists had the strength of a man's. "How does it feel, Paris, to be responsible for killing someone? Someone who loved you enough to let herself be cut up like meat on a butcher's slab? Well, answer me!" She let him go. She slapped his face, first on one side, then the other. "Have a closer look!" She tore off the top sheet that had been draped over Ruth's body. "And you stand there and talk to me about being decent and pure!" Another slap, harder than the first. Then another and another until he walked backward, cringing under the onslaught of her blows. "You bastard!"

With one mighty shove, she pushed him down the steep flight of stairs, then as he tried to struggle to his feet, she began to kick him. Like a wounded animal he tried to escape on all fours, but she would not let him go. When he reached the top of the main staircase, she let him stand up at last, bleeding, breathing heavily, falling against the banisters for support. For a moment she looked at him. Then she grasped hold of a warming pan that one of the girls had hastily left propped up against the wall and hit him so hard that he toppled backward and went crashing headfirst down the stairs. As he lay in a heap at the bottom she walked down and stood over his prostrate body.

"I wouldn't employ you to clean out my cesspit, Paris. Now collect your belongings and get out of my yard before I set the dogs on you."

Ashen-faced, he struggled to his feet. He looked at them all as they stared back at him. Last of all his eyes went to Anna. He got his breath. He dashed the blood away from his face with one grimy hand.

"You'll be sorry for this, miss. I'm telling you, you'll be sorry."

"If you ever show your sewer-rat's face round these parts again, I'll make you sorrier."

She slammed the door after him. Then she went and fetched her shotgun and stood in the yard with it until he had gone.

The public bar of the Rubbing House Inn was smoke-filled and crowded as Paris edged his way from the open door to the ale bar where he ordered a glass of gin from the landlord and leaned moodily against it while he drank, deaf to the surrounding noise and chatter. Though his body was hard and fit from working in the saddle, the long tramp from the Old Brew estate the night before had given him aching legs and painful blisters. He hadn't washed for a whole day. He hadn't eaten. After spending a few hours asleep under a hedge up on Banstead Downs he'd sat and thought awhile and decided what he was going to do. One thing was certain; after what had happened he was finished in Epsom. If he knew what was good for him he'd get the next stagecoach out and make for the North; York, or Doncaster. There were plenty of horses and plenty of racing yards looking for good grooms who knew their business; he'd have no trouble finding work in the North where nobody knew him, even without references. But he was bitter. And at that moment he hated all women, and one in particular.

Ruth was of no account. In a few weeks, a month perhaps, no doubt he'd have forgotten what she had looked like. The blood-soaked bed in her room might take a little longer to forget. But he'd never forget or forgive Anna Brodie. As he was drinking his second glass of gin he felt a hand tap him on the shoulder.

"'Ave another one on me?"

The hard, sly face was vaguely familiar to him.

"If you want to buy I will." He turned back again and stared into his half-finished glass.

"'Ear the bastard's thrown you out of 'er yard." There was a taunting note now. Paris could feel the anger rising in him. "She 'as, then?"

"It's none of your business."

"News gets about fast, round these parts. Won't find nobody else'll take you on, not when she's put the poison in. Thought about that, I s'ppose?"

"I'm going North," Paris said, roughly.

"Could be you could do yourself a favor before you go . . . if you're interested." He stopped talking while the landlord put down two drinks. "There's someone else round 'ere who'd like to teach that jumped-up bitch a bit of a lesson . . . there's some reckon that bastard's getting too big for 'er boots, with them nags of 'ers winning everything in sight . . . if you get my drift?"

Slowly, Paris turned his head. He knew the face now. Yes, it was one of Tobias Slout's men, he'd swear to it.

"What do you want?"

"You just finish up your drink and then take a little ride with me. I'll introduce you to the gentleman. Now, 'e's a man what knows a thing or two. 'E appreciates somebody like you; can't expect that from a woman, can you? Do yourself a bit of good 'fore you go off on your way, ay?"

Paris picked up his glass and swigged it down in one gulp.

"I'm not taking any risks. Not for anyone. No risks."

"Now, who said anything about risks?"

It was the unnatural silence that roused her from the heavy, work-weary slumber into which she had fallen. She lay there, seeing and hearing nothing through the thick curtains that were pulled around the bed.

She sat up. She rubbed her tired eyes. She reached out into the darkness and pushed the curtains aside. There was no wind. No sound of horses neighing. No barking from the dogs. She sat there a moment longer; then a terrified whinny rent the still air, shattering the calm and peace of the noiseless night.

She knew it instantly, as a mother knows the crying of her own child. Hope. Tearing aside the bed covers she leaped from the bed and rushed to her window, throwing the drapes aside. She could see nothing. Hear nothing in the blackness but the faint eerie rustling of the dead leaves as they blew about the courtyard below her. Frantically, with mounting fear, she called and whistled for the dogs, but none came.

Barefoot, throwing a cloak about her shoulders she fled from the room, shouting to Jessie and the girls on the floor above. She ran out into the yard, shouting to Elijah and William Devine as she went. It was then that she heard the distant barking of the dogs as they heard her voice.

As fast as her legs could carry her she ran in the direction of the tack shed. A barrel had been rolled up against the door to hold it fast. With all her strength she pushed it away, and as she opened the door the four dogs sprang out, barking wildly, jumping up, licking at her hands. She turned and raced back across the yard and they ran after her. Then she stopped dead in her tracks.

The door to Hope's stable lay wide open. In the shadow of the entrance she could see Elijah's prostrate body stretched out upon the ground, blood from the wound across his head dark and glistening. When she reached him and knelt down he rolled over, groaning, trying to speak, clutching at his head.

"Elijah! What happened? Who did this? I found the dogs, all four of them, shut up in the tack shed with a barrel against the door!"

"Hope . . ." he moaned, feebly, trying to drag himself up. "Hope . . ."

A sudden sickness gripped her. Her legs felt like jelly. Her arms and hands shook as if she had been stricken with some palsy. Woodenly, she ran to the filly's stall and then stopped, staring.

There was blood all over the straw. A pool of it oozed from beneath the prostrate filly and ran in rivulets into the gangway and one of the stalls beyond. As she rushed to her and knelt on the bloodied straw, she saw that her two forelegs had been slashed and hacked almost to the bone. The horse lay on her side, prone as young Elijah, moaning with pain.

She was too anguished, too stunned to cry. That would come later. It was rage that consumed her now; a wild, uncontrollable thirst for retaliation and revenge. She scarcely heard the sound of running feet in the yard outside, and then William Devine's voice from the stable door.

"Miss! What is it, for the love of God? We never 'eard a thing! Why didn't the dogs bark? Where were they?"

She opened her lips to answer him but no sound came out. There was a lump in her throat so huge that she could hardly breathe. She heard him and young Jonas behind her, their boots on the straw. Then she heard their horrified gasps as they looked past her and saw the injuries to the filly.

"Dear Mother of God!"

"No, miss, no! Not Hope . . ."

"Get Elijah into the house," she heard herself speak as if in a dream. Blurred, her voice obscured by a mist, not coming from her own lips. "Get Jessie to see to that wound. William, saddle up Firestone and ride for the horse doctor. Break his door down if you have to."

"I'm on me way, miss." She heard them run out. She heard the others shouting to one another in the yard outside.

A strange, unnatural calm fell over her. Gently, she reached out her hand and stroked the filly's quivering neck. She lay her head against her side. She whispered to her. She kissed her muzzle, her eyes, her flanks. Slowly, silently, she began to cry. Once she had begun the tears would not stop. They spilled down upon her cloak and dropped onto the bloodied straw. They fell onto the filly's black, gleaming coat and shattered legs.

As she turned her head she caught sight of Ellen Troggle, a blanket over her nightgown, her face thin and white. She put a hand over her lips and began to cry.

"Miss, oh, miss! What 'ave they done? What 'ave they done to your beautiful filly?"

Slowly, Anna got to her feet. She took a blanket from the side of the stall and spread it lovingly across the prostrate animal's heaving body.

"This is Tobias Slout's work." She swallowed, fighting back the lump that was swelling in her throat. "And this is the last crooked stroke that he'll ever pull." She walked up to Eliza and touched her lightly on the shoulder. "I'll be back. Don't leave her."

She went back into the house. She went upstairs and dressed. As she passed the drawing room door on her way out, she caught sight of Elijah, his head bandaged, lying in one of the big wing chairs. He opened his eyes and saw her.

"I don't understand it, miss. I don't understand why the dogs never went for 'em. Why they let themselves be shut up in the shed. They never even barked . . ."

Stony-faced, Anna was silent, for the answer was already there to see. There was only one reason why the dogs hadn't barked, only one reason why they hadn't attacked the intruders; and that was because one of them was somebody whose scent and presence they already knew. And that was Paris.

Tobias Slout had just finished a late nightcap of hot grog when he heard the sound of his dogs barking in the distance. At first he ignored them and settled back in his chair beside the fire to go over his bets for the Queen's Cup meeting, smiling to himself at a good night's work. No rich man's bastard was going to make a fool out of him; and that Brodie girl had had it coming from a long time back. Nobody ever got in his way. Nobody ever got the better of him. With her meal-ticket filly out of the way, she'd soon sell up and move out. And that was the way he wanted it.

He glanced down at his betting book, turning over the pages, pausing to write notes every now and then. Then, disturbed by the continuous barking of the dogs, he got to his feet, lit a candle, and went outside.

He whistled. He shouted at them. He waited for a moment. Then a moment more. When he whistled again and they still failed to appear, he was alarmed. Their barking seemed to be coming from the same direction, as if they were trapped somewhere. Frowning, peering through the darkness with difficulty, Slout stumbled forward through the thickly shrubbed grounds toward the stable, from where the barking seemed to come. As soon as he approached it, he noticed that the end door, an empty stall used for storing firewood and tools, was half-open, and angrily he cursed aloud. This was the thanks he got for giving them all the rest of the night off, the cretins! How many times had he told them to go round after dark, making sure everything was barred and bolted, and the dogs let loose in the grounds? With a string of foul oaths as his solitary candle spluttered and went out, he felt his way inside. As he did so someone pushed him roughly forward with such force that he was hurled across the floor and crashed into a pile of logs stacked against the side of the stall.

The hiss of a match being struck sounded; then the empty stall was flooded with light and for the first time Slout, screwing up his eyes against it, saw his assailant's face.

"You!"

"You bastard." Anna's voice was almost a whisper. "You sent your scum into my yard as soon as my back was turned, and maimed my filly." She came toward him, her long cloak sweeping across the straw-strewn stones. The look in her eyes terrified him. "She'll never race again at best. At worst, she'll have to be shot."

He grabbed up a lump of wood and shouted for his dogs, then his men. She kicked the wood out of his hand and stood over him, menacingly, as he was pinned down by his own bulk. Uneasily, he remembered the body of one of the lackeys he'd paid to waylay her, lying in his woodshed, bleeding to death from the pistol wound she'd inflicted.

"You're on your own, Slout. They won't help you now. I shut your dogs up next door. Your vermin are in Epsom, getting drunk on their blood money!"

"They'll be 'ere, any minute!"

"They won't be back in time to help you."

He tried to struggle up. "You're mad, that's what you are . . . mad. I don't know what you're talking about. I don't know nothing about no filly. Go and look elsewhere!"

"You've paid and terrorized jockeys to pull honest men's horses. You sent your hand-picked scum to put the fear of God into Russell's apprentice so that he'd ride a crooked race, but instead of doing that he went and hanged himself. You set three of your bully boys on me and got the head groom I kicked out of my yard to sell his services to you and betray me . . . how much did you pay him? You've been behind more filthy plots to line your own pockets and put more fat on your worthless carcass than I've had hot dinners. But what you had done to my filly is going to be your last one, I swear it."

He had been waiting to see if she had a pistol concealed about her, but there was nothing in her hand but her riding whip. Now he knew she was unarmed, he grew bolder, and half-rose from the floor. What was she but a slip of a girl got too big for her boots? One blow from the back of his hand would send her reeling . . . then he'd teach her a lesson she'd never forget!

"All right, miss 'igh and mighty," he said in a jeering, taunting voice, "supposing I did get the bloody nag done over, what of it? No lump of 'orsemeat's going to stop me from earning good brass! You might know it but you can't prove it, can you? You can't prove a bloody thing!" He was laughing now, his big, lopsided mouth full of loathsome yellow teeth. She could smell his foul breath from where she stood. "So what do you think you can do about it, ay?"

"Just give you a taste of your own medicine."

She moved so swiftly that he had no time to struggle to his feet, or to cry out. Raising the whip in her hand she came toward him wielding it, then brought it down across his grinning face with such force that the skin split at once, and began oozing with blood. He raised his hands to protect himself, to try to fend her off, but the blows rained down savagely one after the other, each one harder than the last. His legs crumpled beneath him. He stretched out his bleeding hands to plead for mercy, but one more lash from the whip thong cut deep into the flesh across his knuckles, and he crouched back among the old sacks and fallen legs, staring at the horrible sight of his own blood, whimpering like an animal. The last thing he remembered before he passed out was her mocking voice.

"Spread the word, Slout. Spread it far and wide. If I ever catch you or any of your scum within a mile of my yard, I'll break your neck!"

*   *   *

She got down from her horse and led it into the stable, then slowly, methodically, she began to unbuckle its saddle. The tight ball that had knotted her stomach an hour ago had gone, leaving only cold, smoldering rage. As she began to wisp the sweating animal down with a handful of straw, someone came into the stable and stood behind her near the entrance to the stall. She stopped what she was doing and turned to look at him.

"Chifney!"

His large, sad eyes looked sadder still. Something like tears made them seem brighter.

"I heard what happened. William Devine came by on his way from fetching the horse doctor in Epsom and told us what happened." He glanced down at his clasped hands, awkwardly, knowing how useless and empty any words of comfort would be. "Inchcape says is there anything he can do?"

She smiled, bitterly.

"Get my filly a pair of new front legs." She turned back to her horse and carried on wisping him down.

"Anna . . . if there was some way that I could help . . . if I could cut off my own legs and give them to her . . ." Anna turned round and looked at him. "You know that I would gladly do it."

A single tear welled up in the corner of her eye, then spilled over and ran down her cheek. She tried to answer, but the lump in her throat swelled until it almost choked her. She lay her head against the horse's neck and sobbed.

Chifney came to her and took her by the shoulders.

"They won't beat you, Anna. There'll be other horses. Other races. Other Hopes. They came here thinking that if they smashed the filly's legs they'd smash your spirit, too . . . but I know enough about you to know that you'd never let anyone do that, no matter what."

Slowly, her shoulders stopped shaking. Slowly, the sobbing stopped. She turned round to face him, her cheeks dirty and stained with her tears.

"If she lives, if she gets through tonight and the next few days, I'll nurse her back to health. I'll stay with her, day and night. I won't leave her side unless somebody else is there with a shotgun and the whole pack of dogs. I'll mate her with Firestone when he's run his last race, and I'll breed the strongest, fastest horse you'll ever see." She took his hand and squeezed it. "Thank you for being here, Chifney."

For a moment they looked at each other.

"Shall we go and find the horse doctor?" Chifney said.

He put down the brandy Jessie had poured for him, and got to his feet as she came into the room.

"I've done all I can. She's a strong filly, any lesser wouldn't make it. Not that I can give you a guarantee she will, but she has a better chance than most. That's all I can say. I'll be back first thing tomorrow, to redress the wounds . . . unless she dies in the night."

"You think that might happen?"

"I think you should be ready for the worst. I don't want to give out false hopes and promises . . . she's a sick animal. She's been tied down and battered half to death, she's lucky to be alive. If she pulls through, in a few days' time we'll have to get her up off the floor by raising her on a thick canvas sling, supported by strong ropes. Until her forelegs knit and heal they mustn't have any weight on them at all."

"They didn't break the bones?"

"A few more blows and they would have done. But I reckon the villains heard some noise or other and got panicky, then made a run for it without staying to see if they'd finished the job properly or not. Either way, she'll never be able to race again, or be ridden." He sighed, heavily. "I don't have to tell you how sorry I am." She made no answer. "I'll make sure the constable in Epsom knows what's happened, and he'll send men out searching for that groom of yours."

"They won't find him. He'll be long gone by now. But you can tell the constable that Anna Brodie's offering a reward of a thousand guineas to anyone who can give information that leads to his capture." She walked with him to the door, then out into the yard. Jonas was already there, holding his horse's head.

"Remember, she's lost a lot of blood. That's weakened her more than anything. Don't get your hopes up too high, for your own sake." He swung himself into the saddle and rode off into the night.

Anna watched him go, then she turned and walked back into the house where Jessie was waiting.

"Sit 'ere and get this down you." She pushed Anna into a chair and stuck a tankard of hot grog into her hand. "The wicked knaves, taking their 'ands to a dumb beast what can't defend itself! Curse 'em all to 'ell, that's what. And that tike, Paris, for doing what 'e did to Ruth, and then getting 'is own back on you for throwing 'im out." Anna sat there, very still, very white, saying nothing. "But don't say I didn't warn you what you'd be up against, right from the first, same as Sam Loam and all the others did. Where there's brass there's muck and villains, and plenty of both. It's no place for a lady, and never will be. And the sooner you come to your senses and realize it, the better it'll be." Anna still sat there without speaking, holding the cup in her hands without drinking.

Suddenly, Anna leaped to her feet and hurled the cup across the room where it smashed against the wall and shattered into pieces. Jessie stared at her. "If there really was a God, would he have sat there and watched those bastards club my filly half to death?" Anna's voice began to break. "Would he have stood idle while men like Hindley and Tobias Slout cheated and schemed and murdered and terrorized the innocent? While my mother coughed up her lungs on a stinking straw pallet not fit for a pig to lie on, while a pampered, idle bitch like Lilly Brodie lay in silk sheets? Where was he when he was needed, Jessie? Where was he tonight when I needed him?" Her eyes blazed like a madwoman's. She raised her arms in the air and screamed, hysterically, "Where were you, God? Tell me, where were you?"

"Anna!"

She turned and ran out.

The filly was still lying as they'd first found her, prone on the straw. But someone had taken away the straw covered in blood, and brought fresh straw for her to lie upon, and her horrific wounds had been bathed and dressed.

As Anna went down on her knees beside her and gently stroked her neck, she tried to raise her head, and whinnied, softly, in recognition.

Silently, Anna began to cry, and the tears fell from her eyes in great drops and splashed upon the filly's coat. They were not tears of thwarted ambition, for everything she had lost; the Queen's Cup, the Guineas, the Oaks, the glory and reward, the cheering crowds, all her hopes and plans, her very survival on the turf itself in dire jeopardy, for none of those things seemed to matter anymore. She was crying because this beautiful, gentle creature that she had nurtured, and schooled, and cared for as if she had been her own child had been the innocent scapegoat; Anna's enemies had cut her down because she herself had been out of reach. And if she died, it would mean that evil had triumphed and she had failed.

For the first time in her life since she had been a small child, since poverty and misery and pain had hardened and disillusioned her, Anna clasped her hands together and prayed.

"Please, God, don't let her die. Please don't let her die."

A great weariness came over her. She lay down on the straw beside the filly and slept the sleep of the exhausted.

❊ 23 ❊

Slowly, she opened her eyes. Hardly daring to look, she raised her head and glanced toward the filly. She stretched out a hand and touched her, gently, and she was warm. Her side rose and fell softly with her breathing.

Anna stumbled to her feet, brushing pieces of straw from her clothes and hair.

"Miss?" said William Devine's voice from the stable door. "Miss?"

She tried to smile, but her lips were frozen. Her eyes were sore and swollen from crying the night before.

"Miss." He came toward her, his eyes bright as he saw that the filly was still alive. "Sir Gilbert 'Eathcote rode in about fifteen minute ago . . . but Mrs. Tamm told 'im if 'e 'ad a mind to see you 'e'd 'ave to wait, you being up 'alf the night. 'E's still 'ere, in the 'ouse. 'E says 'e must speak to you."

She nodded, too weary to answer.

"You stay with Hope." She went on into the house, shading her eyes from the strong March sunshine. Heathcote was in the library, pacing up and down, and he looked up, startled, as she came into the room and closed the door behind her.

"Yes, I know what I look like," she said sourly, before he could speak. "I've been up most of the night. They told you what happened?"

"Chifney did. He's spent the night in the coach house." She could see him searching for words of sympathy. "I don't have to tell you how I feel about something like this. You'll know it."

"But that's not what you've come about." She could see disaster in his face. He was awkward, embarrassed.

"When I rode up here I had no idea what had happened, otherwise I would have waited for a few days before I broke the news to you."

Anna walked over to the brandy and poured herself some.

"What could you tell me that could be worse than what's already happened?"

"I have an answer from the chief stewards of the Jockey Club." She looked up. "Their unanimous decision was to rule that your horses be banned from racing on every course that is governed by Jockey Club rules." He looked down at his hands, unable to meet her eyes. "As to your intention to fight their ruling at law, the stewards have consulted expert legal opinion, and they wish you to know that you would have no case . . . the law of the land has no powers to intervene because the matter has nothing to do with either civil or criminal law.

"The stewards are saying that what their decision amounts to is banning your horses from racing on their recognized territories, which they are fully entitled to do because they are the elected body responsible for the governing of racing . . . you can't appeal against that any more than you could appeal to law if you wanted to come to my house for dinner, and I refused to invite you. I'm sorry."

Slowly, she set down her half-empty glass. She looked at him without speaking, dark circles beneath her eyes.

"I know how you must feel, this coming directly after what happened last night. For my own part, I wish that the task of breaking this news to you could have been delayed, or else delegated to someone else."

"Like Jacob Hindley, for instance?" she said, sourly. "How he would have loved to be the one to tell me!"

"Please . . . don't be bitter. I know you have a right to be. I would be bitter, too, in your place. You've fought long and hard against all the odds. I've always admired your courage. But in all honesty I must tell you that I don't believe racing is a fit thing for any woman to be mixed up in . . . surely last night proved that to you? Maybe it was even a blessing in disguise . . ."

Her tired, red-rimmed eyes lit with rage.

"A blessing in disguise? Tobias Slout's hired scum come trespassing in my yard and attack one of my animals, and you stand there and tell me it's a blessing in disguise? Get out of my house!"

Jessie was outside the door, alerted by Anna's raised voice.

"What is it, lassie? What's 'appened?"

One of Sam Loam's men had ridden into the yard, shouting excitedly as he leaped from his horse. In his haste to reach Anna he almost knocked Heathcote aside.

"Sam's on 'is way over! 'E sent me on ahead to give you the news! It's Tobias Slout." Chifney and Elijah, his head still bandaged, had come running from the coach house, Jonas from the barn. "Someone broke in there, last night, when 'e was alone. Went for 'im with a sledgehammer, smashed both 'is legs to pulp. They don't reckon 'e'll ever walk again." He gulped for breath. "One of 'is men's took 'im away in a cart, back to London, they reckon. That's where 'e come from. All the others 'ave bolted. Good riddance, I say!"

"Ay, I'll second that!" said Elijah, holding his head.

"'E's 'ad it coming, a long time off!"

"Must 'ave bin someone with a powerful grudge," Jonas said, "and someone with a lot of guts. To go in there, all alone, not knowin' 'ow many of 'is lackeys was still about, and them great dogs . . ."

"A man reaps as he sows," said Gilbert Heathcote. "Though nothing could ever be proved against him, I for one believe he was behind every major plot to bring racing into discredit in Epsom. How he got his information nobody will ever know."

Only Anna's face held no surprise.

"So the rats have deserted the sinking ship. That's what rats do, isn't it?" She saw Chifney looking at her, and she looked back at him, steadily, with unwavering eyes, knowing that he had guessed the truth. When everyone had dispersed he followed her back into the house.

"Anna!"

"If you want to help me, stay here until the horse doctor comes. William Devine's with the filly now."

He caught hold of her arm.

"Why did you do it? Why did you go there alone? Do you know what could have happened if they'd caught you?"

"Slout was on his own."

"But you had no way of knowing that."

"I reckoned they'd be at some ale house in Epsom until the early hours."
"But you might have been wrong." His grip tightened on her arm.
"Anna, do you know what kind of risk you took to get revenge?"

She shook his hand away and faced him with anger.

"I did what had to be done. And I'd do it again, if need be."

"You should have come for me. You should have let me go there. I would have done it, gladly. You know that."

The anger vanished from her eyes. She managed a weak, wry smile.

"Chifney, you should know me well enough by now to know that I never expect other people to do my dirty work for me. I always do it myself." She left him standing there as she raced up the staircase, her crumpled gown, with pieces of straw still clinging to it, dragging after her. She paused, halfway up. "I have to find someone, I can't stop to explain now." She turned and ran up the remainder of the stairs. He turned and walked back into the courtyard.

Lionel Tollemache knelt and closed the lid of his trunk, then glanced from the small inn window down into the yard outside. He checked the time on his gold fob watch. Another ten minutes and the ostlers would have changed the mail coach team; time to go down. Time for one last drink of gin or brandy in the taproom downstairs, while the innkeeper's lad brought down his baggage.

As he picked up his top hat and gloves he heard footsteps on the bare boards outside his door, and then a knock and the landlord's voice.

"Mr. Tollemache, sir? A lady to see you."

When he opened the door Anna Brodie stood there, the paleness of her face a stark contrast to her dark velvet hat and gown.

She looked tired, as if she had not slept. There were dark circles beneath her vivid blue eyes. But she was still the most beautiful woman he had ever seen. Recovering from his astonishment, he held open the door for her to pass through.

"How did you know that I was here?"

"I called at Hindley's house. The manservant who opened the door told me that you'd been called back to Newmarket. He told me where I could find you."

"The mail coach leaves in a few minutes." He smiled. The same slow, cunning smile she had never quite liked. "As delighted as I am to see you, whatever it is you came here to see me for will have to be brief."

"It is."

"I don't want to go back to Newmarket. Quite the contrary. But my dear father fell from his horse while he was out hunting, and while there's no love lost between us, I have to keep on his right side and pretend some concern, in case he takes it into his head to cut me out of his will. And that wouldn't suit me at all."

She lay back against the door.

"I came here to put a proposition to you."

"Oh? What kind of proposition?"

"I want you to marry me."

He was so stunned that he wondered if he heard her right. She almost smiled.

"Well?"

"I don't understand."

"It's very simple, Tollemache. The stewards of the Jockey Club have outlawed my horses from running on their racecourses. I can't appeal against their decision because it isn't a matter admissible in law. But if I marry you I can run any horse I care to in your name, and there's nothing that they can ever do about it. Well, do you agree or not?"

He leaned against the tiny window. He rocked with silent laughter. "You're a very clever lady, Anna. I always thought so. But isn't there something you appear to have overlooked?"

"What have I overlooked?"

"You do realize that once you become my wife, everything you own becomes my property. The house, the estate, the horses. If I chose to put any or all of them up for sale, there would be nothing you could do about it."

"You won't be able to put them up for sale. Before I marry you I intend to pay a visit to my lawyer, Frederick Nubbles, and transfer everything except a certain sum for working capital into my sister's name. By the terms of the trust fund that I've already set up for her, she can't touch a thing until she reaches the age of twenty-one. And I'll have got what I wanted long before then."

"But if the horses become your sister's property and are held in trust, then in effect they don't belong to me and can't be entered in races under my name."

"Only you and I will know that."

"You seem to have all the answers. Except one. What if I feel bound to refuse your more than generous offer?"

"You won't. Because if you do I'd have no hesitation whatever in making public certain facts concerning your brother and Jacob Hindley, an eyewitness account that would create a scandal your esteemed family would never manage to live down. Your brother would be arrested like a common felon. And you'd never be invited into any decent household ever again . . . and I'm sure that that wouldn't be at all to your liking. Do you know what the penalty is for sodomy?"

"You're quite a bitch, aren't you, Anna?"

"We do as we must and call it by the best names."

"Blackmail?"

"Let's just say that I'm protecting my interests." She glanced from the window. The ostlers were harnessing the last pair of horses to the mail coach below. "When you reach Newmarket make sure you put yourself up

for Jockey Club membership right away. Your father can pull a few strings
from his sickbed to get you elected quickly. Be back here a week before the
Emperor's Cup . . . I'm running Firestone in it as his last race, and he can't
be entered unless we're married first."

"You've got it all worked out, haven't you?"

"You'll have little to complain about. I'll give you a generous allowance
out of the estate for your own personal use. You can come and go as you
want to. I make only three conditions. I retain full control over the horses.
You break all private contact with Jacob Hindley. And your brother goes
out of the country on a long tour abroad. I'll pay all the expenses . . . you
can send him anywhere you like. To Paris, Holland, Italy. I don't care. But
I want him kept away from my sister. Do I make myself clear?"

"Of course. And when does this marriage take place?"

"As soon as the banns have been called."

He smiled, he came toward her and touched her cheek.

"You're so beautiful, Anna. And so clever. I always thought it. There's
something peculiarly attractive about a clever woman."

He was standing too close to her and she pushed him away.

"Don't patronize me, Tollemache. And don't ever forget that this marriage is just a business arrangement. Strictly business, do you understand?"
She opened the door behind her. "You'd best hurry. Your coach is about to
leave."

He stared at the empty space where she had been.

Strains of hymn music escaped from the doors of the little church and out
into the grassy churchyard beyond, followed by the sound of singing. The
words of the hymn were muffled and indistinct, as the chorus of voices rose
and fell in the still air, then faded into silence, replaced by the single,
droning voice of the parson as he led the congregation in prayer.

Anna got down from the carriage, followed by Jessie and Ellen, and
stood for a moment looking around her. Everything was exactly the same
as she remembered, nothing had changed. Without speaking she left them
there and made her way through the maze of gravestones until she reached
her mother's.

The headstone was darker, grayer, more aged by the elements than she
remembered. Moss and lichen had grown about the masonry, her last posy
of flowers, secured by a stone, lay dead and withered where she had left it.
She stood staring down at the wording on the headstone, the long feathers
of her elegant bonnet fluttering wildly in the strong wind. Anna Maria
would have know why she had to do this thing. Anna Maria would have
understood.

Her blue eyes downcast, Anna turned from her mother's grave and
walked slowly into the church, Jessie and Ellen following on behind her.

She saw the parson look up, the rows of heads turning to gape and stare
as she walked along the aisle and took her place in one of the pews near the

pulpit. From the corner of her eye she saw Jacob Hindley turn toward his wife and whisper behind his hand.

She ignored their staring. She was deaf to their whispers. She looked straight ahead of her, her eyes fixed on the parson's face. This was the first time since she had been a child that she had set foot inside a church, except to sit here, a year ago, and plot with William Hubbard to take the Brodie inheritance. Was it only a year, so short a time? It seemed far longer, another lifetime away, since that young, bitter girl had stood before her mother's grave, vowing revenge.

She looked away from the parson and up into the vaulted ceiling, then to the stained-glass windows in the transept, depicting the Holy Trinity, the Virgin Mary, and Saint Anne, arms outstretched, at the feet of Christ. Then she lowered her eyes. Did He see her as she sat here, and judge her for what she had done, and for all that she would have to do? Had he watched her with William Hubbard, with Lilly Brodie, with Tobias Slout? Would He look down again, when she stood side by side with Lionel Tollemache, a man she distrusted and despised, and made a mockery of the sacrament of marriage?

She closed her eyes and rested her head against the pew in front of her, and prayed for Hope. She had only done what she must, what she had to do. To avenge her mother's suffering, to stop herself and Clara being cheated out of what had been rightfully theirs, to punish Slout for his wickedness while the law stood idle . . . had she been so wrong to do all of those things?

The parson's voice came back to her, breaking into her tumult of thoughts. He had finished the service. He was looking down at her, kindly.

"The banns of marriage are announced between Lionel Tollemache, gentleman of Newmarket, in the county of Suffolk, and Anna Brodie, spinster of this parish."

She heard the gasps of dismay, people turning in their seats. She looked toward Jacob Hindley, keeping her face expressionless as a mask.

His eyes bulged from their sockets. A dark, scarlet flush was rapidly spreading from his thick, bull neck to his cheeks. Half-rising from his pew, he clutched at the cravat at his throat as if he was choking, and his wife and manservant had to help him from the church. Slowly, everyone began to rise from their places and follow, and within minutes the church was empty but for the three of them.

"Anna," Jessie said solemnly. "Are you sure this is right, what you're doing? Once it's done, you can't go back on it, you know that."

"I know it."

"You coming back with us, then?"

Anna stood up. She stepped into the aisle.

"There's something I must do first."

* * *

Frederick Nubbles looked at her across his desk with his small, clever, weasel-like eyes.

"You've thought long and well on this course of action, Anna? It's no thing to be entered into lightly . . ."

"You sound like Jessie."

He lay back in his enormous chair.

"A woman of sound common sense. You should listen to her more often."

"Don't ever tell her that. She'd never let me forget it."

He smiled.

"I shall draw up the papers you require, transferring your share of the inheritance to your sister, but leaving you with a substantial portion to be used as private expenses and working capital." He adjusted his pince-nez. "The portion transferred, however, is not to be added to the amount already set aside in her trust fund, which she has access to upon reaching the age of twenty-one."

"No. Insert a clause that states that Clara has only part-ownership in the house, the estate, and the horses. That will prevent the sale of any of them at any time without my written consent, and still give me a controlling interest, and it safeguards my share of the inheritance from Lionel Tollemache."

"Does he know of this arrangement?"

"I told him, yes."

Nubbles nodded, slowly. He got to his feet.

"I shall draw up the papers today, and call in with them tomorrow evening for you to read over and sign."

"Good. Then you can stay to dinner."

"That would be pleasant." Smiling, he showed her to the door. "I shall be no later than half past seven."

Anna shook his thin, bony hand, and looked at him with affection. "I'm sorry to make you work on a Sunday."

"I think I can forgive you for that."

It was growing dark as Frederick Nubbles steered his single-horse curricle along the deserted road. There was a strong wind, which whipped up the dead leaves and shook the hood of his curricle, and he slowed his horse down to a steady walk. He would be late for dinner at the Old Brew House, but safety was more important than punctuality. He glanced about him, peering at the passing shapes of trees and cottages with his short-sighted eyes, then as the wind began to lessen, set his horse into a trot.

He was near Tobias Slout's old property now. He looked at it, lying back among its woodland and shrubs, dark and deserted. But as his curricle passed by, a small light flickered and glowed somewhere in the grounds.

He stopped his horse at once, and stared toward it. Slowly, he stepped down from the curricle and led his horse to a thicket where he tethered it.

The house had been abandoned. No one lived in it now. Even a wandering vagrant, seeking shelter from the rain, or a poacher coming upon it by night, would hesitate before he ventured within its walls. He let himself in by the gates and walked inside, pushing away the branches and bushes with his hands. He called out, looking again for the light he had seen, wondering if one of the constable's men might have been sent here, to gather Slout's betting books and papers for the magistrate . . . but if he had, surely he would have waited until it was light?

He went on through the darkness, tripping and stumbling on the uneven ground, and then all at once the shape of a man came before him from the blackness, and he stared up, astonished, into a face he knew.

"It's gone eight o'clock!"

"He'll be here, any minute."

"That's what you said, more than 'alf an 'our ago," Jessie grumbled, casting an angry eye over the dishes spread across the kitchen table. "Look at my roast goose, and all the rest of it! Done to a turn by 'alf past seven, and 'im nowhere in sight. Menfolk's always the same. If their dinner's not ready, they'll be sat at the table 'alf 'our early. And if it is, they'll be in to it 'alf 'our late! Well, if 'e don't come soon, the 'ole lot of it'll be spoiled!"

"It's a rough night. He won't make good time in this wind."

"Then 'e should 'ave give 'imself more time to get 'ere, shouldn't 'e?" Jessie opened the stove door and shoved the roast goose back into the stove. "Well, if it's burned to a cinder when 'e gets 'ere, don't blame me. Dinner at 'alf past seven you said. Dinner at 'alf past seven you got."

Anna wandered in and out of the rooms. She went into the library and pulled aside the curtain and stared into the moonless night. The wind was stronger now. Spots of rain began to appear on the windows. She took a book from one of the shelves and sat down beside the fire. Distractedly, she turned over the pages, but she could not concentrate. She got up and began to pace about the room. When another half hour had passed by she went back to the kitchen to find Jessie.

"His horse could have gone lame. He might have broken a wheel. On a night like this there'll be nobody about to help him. And he's not a young man, either. I'm going to fetch Caleb and Jonas and go looking for him."

"You'll get soaked to the skin!"

"I can't sit here and do nothing."

She ran upstairs for a cloak.

The rain was falling heavily now. It had saturated her cloak and hood and the velvet hung limply, sodden through. She could feel the wetness of it, clinging to her skin beneath. Screwing up her eyes against the downpour, she suddenly caught sight of a dark shape in front of them, and as they came closer she could see that it was Frederick Nubbles's small, hooded curricle, the single horse between the shafts tied to a fallen, dead tree trunk a few yards from the road.

"'Orse must 'ave gone lame, miss," Caleb said, pointing to the curricle. "The wheels look all right to me!"

"I can see someone sitting in there, miss," said Jonas, "looks like 'e decided to sit and wait for someone to come by and give 'im a ride back into Epsom."

Anna frowned as they approached the curricle.

"But he shouldn't be on this stretch of road, not to reach the Old Brew House. He looks as if he was heading in the opposite direction, back toward Epsom." She dismounted and gave her reins to Jonas. She walked across the squelching ground, hoisting her hem to avoid the puddles. She called Nubbles's name, but there was no answer from the figure inside the curricle.

"'Ere, miss!" Caleb sprang down from his horse and came beside her. "I think Mr. Nubbles 'as 'ad a bad turn! Look, 'e's not moving!"

Anna glanced inside. The little old man lay slumped to one side, his hat askew over one eye, his hand hanging down limp and lifeless as she touched it. Then, as she tried to move him forward, she caught sight of the knife protruding from his coat, the blood oozing from the wound dark and glistening on her hands.

PART IX
May 1834

❋ 24 ❋

They finished the meal in silence. Anna sat back in her chair, looking at him lounging at the other end of the dining table, sipping his wine with maddening slowness. Somewhere in the house one of the clocks began to strike the half hour. Putting down her napkin Anna got up without a word and went into the library.

She poured herself a glass of brandy. She stood at the window looking out across the lawns in the gathering dusk. Then she heard the opening and closing of the door behind her, and Tollemache's hated footsteps.

"I think I'll join you with a glass of that brandy."

"You know where it is. Get it yourself," she answered, without turning round. She heard him walk across the floor, then the chink of glass and the sound of liquid being poured from one vessel to another.

He seated himself in one of the big wing chairs and crossed his legs.

"I'll be going out this evening." He lay back and sipped the brandy. "I shall need a substantial amount for expenses."

She swung round on him, anger in her face.

"Where are you going at this time of night?"

"Do you really care, Anna?"

"I don't give a damn. Stay out all night. Don't bother to come back at all!"

"There's a gaming party tonight at Charlton House. If you don't want to see me back until the early hours I shall need three or four hundred guineas to tide me through."

"Four hundred guineas? And what happened to all your winnings from the Emperor's Cup? You got more than two thousand pounds on your bets on Firestone!"

Tollemache shrugged his shoulders.

"All gone, I'm afraid."

"On what?"

"Oh . . . this and that. You know how it is. A few gaming debts, a few lost bets. We can't all be winners."

"You've been spending my money like water! How much longer do you think it can go on? Go to the well too often and it runs dry . . . haven't you got enough brains to see that?" She strode over to her desk and picked up a handful of papers. "Your bills, sent to me for paying. Tailors' bills. Hatters' bills. Shoemakers' bills. A bill for three ivory-handled walking sticks. Another for a dozen pairs of gloves. Another for twenty boxes of cigars. The cost of half your useless fripperies would pay my lads' wages and feed every horse in the stables for six months!"

"A gentleman in my position has certain appearances to keep up, wouldn't you say? Or have you conveniently forgotten your part of the bargain? If I hadn't agreed to marry you so that you could work your little trick on the venerable stewards at the Jockey Club, you'd never be able to race your precious horses at all. Don't forget that."

She gave him a withering look. She unlocked another drawer in her desk and took out some money. He sat smiling and toying with his brandy glass while she counted it.

"You can have two hundred, Lionel. Not a penny more, do you hear? If you can't make it last until next month you can go and look elsewhere for a subsidy." She bundled it into a bag and threw it at him.

"That's what I love about you, my dear wife," Tollemache answered, tauntingly. "You always give in so graciously."

"Drink up that brandy and get out of my sight."

She turned her back on him. She stood beside the window, stiffly, staring out into the gardens until she heard him get to his feet and go out. Then she went upstairs to her bedroom and slammed the door.

She deserved it. She had nobody to blame but herself. She had gone into the marriage with her eyes wide open, almost knowing how it would be, but still the reality had been worse than she had ever envisaged.

She watched him cross the courtyard and walk in the direction of the coach house. Then she saw William Devine and Caleb go into the stable and after a few moments bring out the post chaise horses.

It was already getting dark. She watched them for a few minutes longer and then pulled the curtains, shutting him from sight. If only she need never seen him again.

Even the house, the house she had rebuilt and restored from near ruins, seemed different, no longer the haven of peace and happiness it had once been. Every room but this one, where he never came, seemed permeated with his hated presence, the vile odor of his cigars, the smell of his gin. She could walk into an empty room and sense, at once, that only moments ago he, too, had been there.

"Anna?" called Jessie softly from the other side of the door. When there was no reply she let herself in. "So 'e's gone, then?"

"Would that he had gone for good!"

Quietly, Jessie closed the door behind her.

"I warned you, my girl. I told you. I said how it would be. But would you listen? Well, where's 'e gone this time? Drinking again to all hours? Or playing cards for money with 'is ne'er-do-well friends?"

"He hasn't got any friends. He doesn't even know the meaning of the word."

"No need to ask whose money 'e's bin using. I seen the things 'e's bin ordering up for 'imself, arriving in cartloads! When's it going to stop, that's what I want to know. Nobody can go on living beyond their means, not for long. If you don't watch out 'e'll drain you so dry you'll go as bankrupt as John Dewar and Edward Randyll did, and 'ave the bailiffs in, to sell the furniture for debts!"

"I told him there's no more money after tonight. He'll live on what I give him and what he can't have on that he can go without."

"You've bin a fool, Anna. And I never thought to 'ave to say that to you, of all people. I thought you was born smart!"

"Jessie, spare me the lecture!" She sat down on the edge of her bed, her face taut and white. "Do you think I like living this way? Do you think I'm happy? Don't you think that if there had been any other way out, I would have taken it?" She buried her head in her hands. "I thought I could fight the Jockey Club by using the law, but according to the law, I couldn't. What did you expect me to do? Give up everything I've fought for? Sell my horses and go back to where we came from? Just when everything that I ever wanted, dreamed about, hoped for, was finally in my reach? There was only one thing left for me to do to save it all, and I did it."

"I'm not saying getting wed was a mistake. What I'm saying is, you wed the wrong man! Ralph Russell was the one you should 'ave 'ad, my girl, and I don't mind telling you so to your face!"

Furiously, Anna turned on her.

"Ralph Russell didn't ask me!"

"Nor did this one. But marriage to any man means being tied to 'em for life, just you remember that."

"Don't you think I thought of that?"

"And what are you going to tell Clara, when she comes back? 'Ave you thought of that? It won't be easy, I can tell you. Not when she wouldn't even come down for the wedding, once you wrote and said it was Lionel Tollemache, after 'ow you'd raved and ranted against 'im. The two of you are further apart than you've ever bin, and it breaks my 'eart to see it!"

Anna clenched her fists till the knuckles were white. She closed her eyes wearily.

"If you came here to make me feel bad, you've done what you came for. Now will you please go away and leave me alone?"

"Anna, girl—"

"I said leave me alone!" She jumped up and ran out of the room, downstairs, into the yard and toward the stables. Only here could she be by herself. Only here could she find something approaching peace. She went straight to Hope's stall and flung her arms about the filly's neck, and sobbed.

*   *   *

Lionel Tollemache leaned forward in his chair and rested his chin in one hand. Gloomily, he stared at the cards. Tonight at the beginning of the game he had felt lucky, but the two hundred guineas he had started out with had long gone, and twice he had written notes for double that amount. In a minute his luck would change. If not in this game then the next, or the one after that. In the meanwhile there was plenty to drink, and, when the game was over, more than one willing lady in the outer room who had caught his eye.

He picked up his remaining cards and spread them face down on the table. A mediocre hand. One by one he turned them face upward, and there were shouts and groans from the other players gathered around him.

"Bad luck!"

"It isn't your night for winning, Tollemache!"

"Are you in for another game?"

"Double the stakes this time."

"Take my note for another four hundred."

He stretched his long legs beneath the table. He lay back in his chair, another glass of gin in one hand, a cigar in the other. It was only eleven o'clock and already he was more than seven hundred guineas in debt; no doubt before the night was over he would be in debt for far more. But it didn't matter. The money was of no account. He would go on sitting here, losing, writing out countless slips of paper for enormous sums that meant little to him, because it would be Anna who paid in the end. She would have no choice. She would have to. No gentleman ever welshed on his gaming debts and she would know that better than anyone.

He felt the gentle pressure of someone's hand on his shoulder, and he glanced up into the face of one of the women he had noticed earlier, one of many who had looked at him with an expression he recognized only too well. Afterward, he never remembered their names. Only what they had looked like. This one was green-eyed and slender, with a tumble of tawny hair that fell in ringlets about her bare shoulders, the décolletage of her ball gown so low that he could see the dark, glistening groove between her breasts as she leaned forward and whispered in his ear.

"There's a friend of yours in the other room, waiting to see you. He's come with some others, for the next game."

Tollemache put down his cards and went out, squeezing her on her thigh as he brushed past her. Boldly, she looked back into his eyes. Yes, he would find her again, later. There was plenty of time.

In the small anteroom he came face to face with Jacob Hindley.

"Shut that door behind you."

Tollemache had brought his gin with him. He leaned against the closed door, sipping it.

"I didn't see you at my wedding," he said in a teasing voice.

"You bloody fool! Can't you see how that Brodie bitch has used you for her own scheming ends? How she's done this to trick the Jockey Club?" The deep, angry, scarlet flush began to spread rapidly from his bull neck to his thick-jowled cheeks. "She knew it was only a matter of time before they stopped her racing her cursed horses, that they'd never stomach a woman competing with men. But she's clever. Oh, yes, she's clever, she thought it all out! Now she can race any nag she pleases and in any race she wants. All in your name!"

"She knows about you, Hindley. She knows about you and James." A half-smile appeared on Tollemache's lips as Hindley stared at him, too stunned to answer. "You remember the night you were at Ralph Russell's, the night of the King's Cup? You left the bedroom door unlocked, didn't you? That was very careless."

Hindley swallowed.

"But James locked the door. I gave him Mary's key!"

"You might have given it to him, but he didn't use it. My dear young brother never was very good at remembering things. After all, if he'd remembered to lock his study door after him when he went in there with another boy, he would never have been caught and sent down from Oxford. My father spent a small fortune hushing up that little affair. But if Anna should take it into her head to tell him about this one . . . you know as well as I do what it would mean. It's a capital offense. You'd have no choice but to leave the country."

"We'd both deny everything. Nobody would believe her."

Tollemache shrugged.

"Maybe. Maybe not. But there might be those whom James has known before who'd be willing to swear otherwise. And when someone throws enough dirt at you, some of it always sticks. I can hear them saying it now . . . no smoke without fire."

"That Brodie bitch!"

"That's why I agreed to marry her. Because of what she knows about James. If I hadn't done what she wanted she would have gone straight to the constable and then my father."

"She was bluffing and you fell for it!"

"I've lived with her long enough to know that she never makes idle threats."

Hindley turned away, angrily. He paced restlessly about the room, chewing on his nails.

"That was only part of the reason, wasn't it? You agreed to do what she wanted because you thought you'd get your hands on her father's brass . . . but she's cheated you out of that, hasn't she? She schemed up a foolproof way to make sure you never had access to anything worth having, as any husband has by law when he marries! Her and that little humpback weasel, Frederick Nubbles . . ."

"He won't be troubling you again, at least. Unless she finds herself another clever lawyer."

"He got what he deserved. I can still see his rat's face, his eyes laughing at me, telling me someone had outbid me over the Old Brew House. He was pleased. He was glad that bitch had made a laughingstock out of me. I vowed then I'd make both of them sorry for it!"

Tollemache sat down on the arm of a chair. He put down his empty glass.

"One more thing I omitted to tell you. James won't be coming back from Newmarket. That was another condition she made. He's to spend the next two years abroad, at her expense, to keep him away from her precious sister. I had to agree to it."

Hindley was silent for a moment. Tollemache could almost hear him thinking.

"I'll teach that bastard a lesson she'll never forget. And you'll have your chance to get even with her. That's what you want, isn't it? You tell me everything you know, everything you can find out about her plans for her horses. The filly can't run again. Firestone's a seven-year-old, she can't race him anymore, either. But her and Sam Loam are as thick as thieves, and plenty of class nags come his way . . . he'll see to it that she gets her pick before anyone else does. I want to know what she buys and when."

"She's buying a Slane colt off him, a two-year-old. That I already know. Loam worked it and he reckoned it was one of the fastest two-year-olds he'd ever seen."

"Let the bitch buy it. If it's any good you can make sure it gets a bucket of cold water before it leaves her yard for the course. With you on the inside, it couldn't be better. And another thing you can do . . . keep your eyes and ears open in case she lets anything useful drop about any other horses that might be running against mine. Ralph Russell's, for instance."

Tollemache nodded, slowly, and smiled. It was all her own fault, after all. It was really only her own doing that he had to betray her. She should never have locked him out of her room. She should never have made over her share of the inheritance to Clara Brodie.

He suddenly remembered the girl in the gaming room. He thought of her bright, tawny hair falling about her bare shoulders. The green eyes, the half-naked breasts revealed by her low-cut gown as she'd stooped toward him. The scent of her body, the pressure of her hand as it had rested on his shoulder. She was the kind who would never lock her door against a man. Never argue. Never refuse to do what he wanted. So different from Anna.

With Hindley, he turned and went back into the gaming room. She was still there. She glanced up and looked into his eyes. He recognized that look. He had seen it in the eyes of most other women that he had met. Except Anna Brodie's.

Smiling, he pushed his way through the company toward her.

It was the sound of breaking glass that woke her, suddenly. She jumped out of bed, pulling on her dressing gown, then ran out and along the passage toward the stairs. As she passed Jessie's room, Jessie came out.

"What is it? I 'eard something from downstairs."

"The dogs haven't barked. It's him, back from his gambling. Go back to bed."

The lamps in the hall had been left burning. Picking one up, Anna went into the library and caught sight of him at once, sprawling in one of the great wing chairs. He had a glass of brandy in his hand. On the floor lay the brandy decanter and several smashed glasses, his top hat and walking cane beside them.

"A little accident as I came in," he said, in a slow, slurred voice.

"You're drunk. Sodden with it!" She looked at him with disgust. "I can smell it on you from here!"

"Here's to marriage!" he said, raising the glass in his hand. "Won't you join me?"

She came further into the room.

"You make me sick. Look at you. You don't belong in a decent house. You should be in pig sty." She snatched the glass from his hand. "You've had enough of that for one night. You'd best get upstairs while you can still walk!"

He got to his feet unsteadily.

"I've never taken orders from a woman and I don't intend to start taking them now!"

"You will in my house. As long as you live under this roof you keep to my rules or get out. If you want to get drunk and come back at three o'clock in the morning, I couldn't care less. You can stay out all night if you want to. But next time you'll have to sleep in the barn, or with the little slut that left this on your shoulder"—she plucked a long, bright tawny hair from his coat—"because next time you come back after midnight you'll find the doors bolted and barred."

He lay back against the wall. He began to laugh, slowly.

"You're not jealous, are you, Anna? You can't blame me for seeking the company of other women. After all, this is a marriage in name only. It's nothing more than a farce."

"If you spent all day and all night in a whorehouse I wouldn't give a damn!"

"But perhaps you will give a damn about this." He fished in his pocket and pulled out a handful of paper. He tossed it at her. "Now have a look at those and tell me what you intend to do about them."

She stooped and picked them up from the floor. Cold-eyed, she glanced at them, then back at his jeering face.

"These are promissory notes for gambling debts. In your handwriting."

"All eleven hundred guineas' worth." He smiled. "You have fourteen days in which to settle them."

"Wrong, Lionel. *You* have fourteen days in which to settle them. What you lose around the gaming table is your affair, not mine."

His smile vanished.

"You agreed to give me a generous living allowance if I married you!"

"I've given you an allowance more than three times what you ever got from your own father and you've squandered every penny of it and more on betting and cards! I gave you two hundred guineas last night on top of a whole month's allowance that you spent before the week was out, and I've got a pile of tradesmen's bills in my desk a foot high. Those I'll pay, because the people you owe the money to are honest men, trying to make a living. But if you choose to run up debts playing for stakes you can't afford, don't come whining to me to settle them!"

"No gentleman welshes on his bets. You know that. You of all people. It's an unwritten law."

"No gentleman would ever play for more than he could afford to lose. Or expect a woman to pay for his losses."

His voice became dangerously softer.

"You're accusing me of not being a gentleman?"

"If the cap fits wear it!"

He sprang forward and grasped her roughly by the arm, and as roughly she shook him off again.

"You drunken oaf, don't you ever lay hands on me!"

"No?" He took hold of her again and pulled her toward him. "But you're my wife, remember? I can do what I like with you. The law says so. The law is on my side." He tightened his grip on her arm. "Maybe you wish I was someone else? Russell, maybe? Or Leopardstown? I've seen them looking at you . . ."

"You're out of your mind!"

"You wouldn't be so anxious to get away if one of them lay hold of you!" He thrust his face close to hers and she turned her head away to avoid the stench of stale liquor on his breath.

"How dare you! You think every man is a whoremonger like you are? Get outside and put your head in a trough of cold water; maybe that'll sober you up!"

He let go her arm.

"I may be drunk, but I know what I'm saying. Ralph Russell's been sniffing round your skirts ever since he set eyes on you!"

Anna slapped him across both sides of his face with all her strength, and he tottered backward.

"You bitch!" He made a lunge forward to grab hold of her, but she was too quick for him. She ran to the hearth and picked up the poker, and as he came toward her she held it up, threatening. He stopped in his tracks.

"I'm warning you. If you ever come near me again I won't hesitate to use this, or anything else I can lay my hands on. Understand?"

A bitter smile came to his lips. He turned away and went to the other side of the room where the spirits table stood.

"Underneath all your high-fashion hats and French gowns you're really quite a little savage, aren't you?"

She gave him one parting look of disgust. Then she went out and slammed the door. Jessie was waiting for her on the landing, night cap awry, a candle in one hand.

"Lassie, I 'eard shouting, what is it? What's wrong?"

"He's drunk."

"But I 'eard breaking glass . . ."

"That was him when he came in. He knocked over one of the brandy decanters and most of the glasses. He's still drinking now."

"Lord 'elp us!"

"It doesn't matter. I don't give a damn what he does. He'll fall asleep in a drunken stupor in one of the chairs. Go back to bed."

"But lassie . . ."

"I'm tired, Jessie. The day after tomorrow my Slane colt is running in the Diamond Stakes. I want to be up before dawn to take him out on the Downs." She managed a weak smile. "Goodnight."

Back in her own bedroom she locked the door and lay down on the bed. She fell asleep, the poker still clasped in her hand.

❋ 25 ❋

Anna stood alone on the balcony of the grandstand, her eyes searching the milling crowds that packed the course and the Warren, where horses for the first race of the Diamond meeting were already being saddled. She caught sight of Lionel Tollemache, standing among a group of other owners, smiling, laughing, jesting. Then her sharp eyes fell on Jeremiah Chifney, in Gilbert Heathcote's colors, ready to mount his gelding in the first race. She frowned as Tollemache beckoned him over, spoke a few words, then turned away again while Chifney walked back to where Heathcote's head groom was checking the saddle straps and girths.

She turned and ran through the grandstand, down the staircase, ignoring the whispers and stares. A lady did not run in public. But when she reached the lawn outside, she was too late. Mounted on the gelding, Chifney was already making his way to post. Picking up the folds of her gown she ran alongside him.

"Chifney!"

He turned and saw her, and slowed down.

"An . . . Mrs. Tollemache! What is it?"

"I must speak to you!"

"I'm sorry, I can't stop now."

"I'll meet you in the stables, after this race, before you change into my colors for the Diamond!"

He pulled the Heathcote gelding to a halt. The other horses and jockeys behind him rode past.

"I'm not riding your Slane colt in the Diamond."

She stared at him.

"Why not?"

"Your husband has engaged another jockey."

Anger flared.

"The hell he has! That colt belongs to me and I say who rides him!"

"It's too late now . . . he's already declared the name of the other rider to the stewards. There's nothing you can do about it."

"We'll see about that. I'll meet you after the race. Good luck." She turned and made her way through the crowds to the Warren. Tollemache was still there, and as he glanced up and saw her coming toward him, he excused himself and walked forward to meet her.

"Just what do you think you're doing by standing down Chifney when I'd already given him the ride on my colt?"

"My dear, please, everyone is looking at us . . ."

"Let them look. You just answer my question!"

"I told him his services were no longer required because I'd engaged another jockey . . . which I have."

"You had no right. I have sole control over my horses and who rides them. That was part of our agreement."

"Unfortunately, that kind of agreement can't be enforced in law." He smiled. "The colt has to be entered in my name, and he runs in my name . . . or he doesn't run at all. If I say I want another jockey instead of your precious Chifney, then I shall have another jockey. And I want Bill Scott."

"Bill Scott! He won't even be able to stay sober long enough to ride to post!"

"He was sober enough to win four St. Legers and a Derby, and that's good enough for me!"

"No doubt! One drunkard patronizes another!"

Tollemache's smile vanished.

"For Christ's sake, Anna, do you want everyone on the course to hear you?" Heads were turning their way. People were nudging each other and whispering behind their hands.

"I don't give a damn who hears me. As long as you hear this. Chifney rides my colt or he doesn't run at all. So you go tell Bill Scott that he can find someone else's horse to pull . . . because he won't be pulling any of mine!" She walked away from him, fighting down her anger, making her way to the edge of the course close to the judge's chair, barely acknowledging those of the men who bowed and took off their hats as she passed by.

She stood there alone, biting her fingernails, looking toward the crowds massed upon the other side.

She was too distracted and upset to enjoy the race. As the field thundered toward her she caught sight of the leaders, tightly bunched together as they galloped to the post, Chifney in Gilbert Heathcote's colors just losing the race by a short head to Colonel Anson's Penelope. She turned away. Head down, she began to make her way back in the direction from which she had come, until she was halted, suddenly, by a chorus of cries from all around her. Swiftly she looked back to see that one of the jockeys from the middle of the field had fallen from his mount and was lying motionless on the turf. One moment the prone body lay there alone. The next it was surrounded by a wall of people, rushing from all directions. She turned back and began to run toward the course again. She grabbed someone by the sleeve.

"What happened? Who is it?"

"Why, Mrs. Tollemache!"

"How badly is he hurt? Is there a doctor coming?"

"There was a collision between three or four of the middle runners, and he fell under half the field!"

"He's been trampled to death!"

"I can't see him moving!"

"It's Hardwick's jockey, I can just see the colors!"

"Move back, they're carrying him to the weighing shed!"

The vast crowds parted and Anna stood watching as the jockey was brought by, carried by two men, capless, arms dangling, his face and silks covered with blood. Then she felt someone behind her touch her lightly on the arm and she spun round and found herself face to face with Jeremiah Chifney.

"Thank God you're in one piece!" she burst out, relief in her eyes.

"I didn't think you believed in God."

"Don't joke, Chifney. It could have been you!"

"I'm all right, I wasn't anywhere near the collision. But I don't think he'll make it. Half the field trampled over him, he had no chance to roll clear."

"Poor bastard!"

"It's an occupational hazard, to any jockey. Everyone who rides knows the risks." The crowds around them began to disperse. Slowly, they walked back in the direction of the Warren and the grandstand, side by side. "If I had the choice I'd rather go like that, quickly, than end up like most of them do, worn out, penniless, forced to beg a living from racecourse crowds. I've seen it happen too often to delude myself that it couldn't happen to me, too."

"Not while I'm around, it couldn't."

He managed a grim smile.

"You don't owe me a living, Anna."

"That's better. When you called me Mrs. Tollemache back there before the race, you had me worried."

"Worried? About what?"

"I haven't seen or spoken to you since I got married. I thought that you might have misunderstood why I did it."

"It's not my place to wonder why you do anything, is it?"

"For Christ's sake, Chifney . . . you don't think I married him because I love him, do you?" Her voice was cynical. "Would any woman in her right mind tie herself to an idle, drunken lecher, who spends money like chicken feed and most of his waking hours gambling and playing cards? You must have heard what the Jockey Club stewards at Newmarket decided. The only way I could carry on running my horses was to marry him and do it under his name."

He stopped walking.

"They really mean that much to you?"

"That's one question you never need to ask." She could see Tollemache up ahead, standing in the Warren with his cronies, a frown on his face as he watched her and Chifney approaching. "Go on. Get into my colors. Bill Scott'll ride my colt over my dead body."

"I don't want to be the cause of friction between you and your husband."

"He isn't my husband. We live under the same roof and sit at either end of the table without speaking to each other, except when we're arguing about his drinking or my money. I repeated a few meaningless words in a church so that I could use his name, that's all. It's never been anything more than that, and it never will be." She glanced into the Warren from the corner of her eye, and saw Tollemache striding toward her. "Go on, Chifney. I'll deal with him and Bill Scott." He hesitated.

"Lord Russell's on his way back. He should arrive late tonight, or tomorrow. He sent word a few days ago."

Her face turned pale beneath the wide brim of her hat.

"Why tell me?"

"I thought that you might want to know."

"What Russell does or doesn't do is no concern of mine."

"I thought . . . I thought you and he were friendly."

Her face became a mask.

"I can do without his kind of friendship." For a moment they looked at one another; then Chifney vanished into the crowd. Anna stayed where she was, waiting for Tollemache. As he came up to her she stared back at him, defiantly.

"Chifney rides my Slane colt or the colt doesn't race. Will you tell Bill Scott or shall I?"

"What the hell do you think you're doing, being seen in public walking side by side with a common jockey? Do you want to make me the laughing-stock of the whole course?"

"If you're the laughingstock of the whole course it's because of your own behavior off it, not mine. And I walk and talk with whom I please."

"You might have done before you married me. But no longer." He grasped her round the wrist so tightly that she winced with pain. "You're my wife now and you'll behave like it, do you understand?"

"I understand by the way your breath stinks that you've been at the gin again!" Angrily, she pulled her wrist free.

"I'm warning you, Anna . . . don't push me too far . . . not too far . . . for your own good, you'd better listen to me!" She tried to brush past him but he blocked her path. "What a pity your friend Chifney wasn't born a few rungs higher up the ladder, eh? If he hadn't been so low-born you could have had him instead of me."

Rage flared in her, but she harnessed it and kept her temper.

"Chifney's more a gentleman than you'd ever know how to be. And if we were anywhere else but here, I'd kick you so hard down there," she nudged him in the testicles, "you'd never go whoring again!"

"You little bitch!"

". . . and don't push me too far, either, Lionel," she said as a parting shot. "Or I might have to tell a few certain people about Jacob Hindley and your sweet innocent little brother!" She walked away from him into the crowd.

Coldly furious, he turned in the other direction and went toward the grandstand. Barely nodding to acquaintances, he mounted the staircase to the private members' floor, and made his way to Anna's box. He paused to collect another bottle of gin and a glass. He needed another drink badly. He no longer cared who won or lost, who rode or who didn't. His throat and mouth were dry and parched, even though he had been drinking ever since the racing began.

He opened the door of the box and almost dropped the bottle in his hand, and the glass as well. Helen Gordon sat there, her back toward the course, her pale eyes frosty beneath the brim of her gaudy bonnet.

"What are you doing here? This is her box, don't you know that?"

Slowly she got to her feet. Then she reached out and struck him, hard, across the mouth.

"You whore!"

She hit him again.

"If I'm a whore what does that make you? I ought to scratch your eyes out, and your tongue as well for all the lies you spun me! Betrothed to someone since you were seventeen! You must have thought I was stupid!"

He put down the gin.

"You believed me."

"I believed a lot of things you told me. Because every other man who sets eyes on me would do anything in his power to get me, I believed that you would, too."

Tollemache leaned back against the closed door. He began to rock with silent laughter. "Like Leopardstown, for instance? Every servant in Heathcote's house heard what he said to you!"

"You bastard!"

"No," he said, stretching out a hand and stroking her rouged cheek, gently. "It's my wife that's a bastard, not me."

"You could have had me for the asking and you picked that base-born Brodie bitch?"

"A matter of expediency, too complicated for me to go into now." He removed the top from the bottle and poured himself a full measure of gin. "But you are right, my dear Helen, Anna is a bitch. Oh, what a bitch! But I'm sorry to say that if the two of you were stood side by side, any man in his right mind would pick her and not you."

"You stinking . . ." Her eyes became round and wild in rage and disbelief. He grasped her hand as she lunged forward to strike him again.

"Don't, Helen . . . don't. For your own sake." He squeezed her wrist so tightly that he felt her bones crack. "Whatever else she is, Anna Brodie is the most beautiful girl I've ever set eyes on. And I reckon that every other man here, if you asked him, would say exactly the same."

Slowly, he released her from his grip. She stood there for a moment, staring at him, rubbing her reddened wrist with her gloved fingers. Then she picked up the bottle of gin and poured it over him. "I never forget a slight!"

He would have given anything to have struck her, but he restrained himself. Getting his handkerchief from his coat pocket, he began slowly and methodically to mop the liquor from his clothes and skin. He knew a better way to hurt her.

"I never forget anything worth remembering, my dear Helen. Which is why I shall find you eminently forgettable." He smiled, cruelly. "After all, in a bed, one whore is very much like another."

She saw the lilies as soon as she came into the room, and stopped, staring at them, her heart beating faster. Someone had already arranged them in a vase of water, lovingly, with special care. Ellen, maybe, or Bessie. Jessie would never have done it. Jessie's big, heavy hands would have no patience with arranging flowers.

Someone could have cut them from the garden, but instinctively she knew that no one had. They were his. He had brought them. As Bessie passed by in the hall Anna called to her.

"These flowers weren't here this morning when I left the house. How did they get here?"

"Lord Russell brought 'em, Mrs. Tollemache. 'Alf hour ago, when 'e called and asked if 'e might wait for you. I showed 'm into the drawing room. I didn't know you was back from the course, ma'am."

For a moment she hesitated, fighting with herself. Part of her hated him, part of her wanted to send him away. He had lied to her and deceived her.

He had been dishonest when she had trusted him as much as she had ever allowed herself to trust any man, and part of her, that part which had been made hard and cruel by everything bad that had happened to her, wanted to punish him for it. All the conflicting feelings that she had battled with ever since she had first set eyes on him rose up and threatened to overwhelm her.

Bessie was still waiting for her to answer. Slowly, she walked over to the brandy decanter and picked up a glass. Then she replaced it on the tray and put the stopper back into the bottle. No, that was not the way. This she must do alone, without the help of the brandy to boost her courage.

"Show him in," she heard herself say.

She stood there with her back toward the door, her hands clasped in front of her, her heart racing; then she heard his footsteps and Bessie speaking his name. Slowly, she turned around to face him, wishing she had drunk the brandy after all.

The change in him shocked her, she was not prepared for it. There were dark hollows beneath his eyes. Lines that had not been there before ran from the corners of his mouth in deep-etched furrows. The words that she had steeled herself to say suddenly froze upon her lips, and she just stared at him.

"Anna, for God's sake . . . why did you do it?" He came toward her, his arms outstretched. "Do you love him?"

"Do you still love Hindley's sister?"

His mouth fell open. He gazed at her like a dumb thing.

"How did you find out? Who told you?"

"No one . . . I found out for myself. That day you left for Newmarket, the day I rode over with Clara so that she could practice on your piano. I found her picture in the attic."

"But the attic is kept locked . . ."

"I found the key."

"Anna . . ."

"Is that why you kept it locked, so that I would never find out that you'd kept her picture? So that I'd never see by the painter's inscription that you'd been married to Jacob Hindley's sister? You knew how much I hated him, and why. And all the time you've been pretending to be on my side, you've been protecting him. My God, what I fool I've been! But I ought to have known better. Blood's always thicker than water!"

"You don't understand. I couldn't tell you . . ."

"I don't need you to tell me anything, Ralph Russell. I can work it out for myself."

"Anna, please . . ."

"The Hindleys don't come from around these parts, do they? That's why nobody ever knew that your wife was Hindley's sister. I wonder why you didn't want people to find out the truth? No doubt it had something to do with all the villainy and scandal he's been steeped in, all of which you knew about! But because you were in love with his sister, you couldn't break your silence!"

"That isn't true."

"Isn't it? If you and Hindley aren't hand in glove, why does he have the key to one of the rooms in your house? The one room that you always keep locked, that nobody, even your own servants, is ever allowed to go inside? Was that her room, Mary Hindley's? I understand it all now. You've known all along what he is. And you've kept silent and protected him because he was her brother."

His face was deathly pale, like candle wax.

"How did you know that Hindley had a key?"

"That night you loaned Clara and me the Russell diamonds, the night of the King's Cup . . . I was on my way upstairs when I noticed the door of that room was open. Only a few inches. But enough for me to see Jacob Hindley and Lionel's brother. You knew what Hindley was, didn't you? You've known all the time."

"Yes, I did know. But I have my own reasons for keeping silent, reasons that I can't tell you now. I swear I never knew that he had the key to her room. She must have given it to him, before her death. And the only reason I keep the room locked is that I can't bear to go inside it." He came toward her. "But not for the reasons you think, Anna."

"I already know the reasons. Because you loved her so much that you can't forget her. Everybody says so. That you never got over her death, that you can't bear to even speak about her, that you'll never marry anyone else because no other woman could ever take her place." Tears that she didn't understand the reason for pricked at the backs of her eyes and she fought them down. "I don't want to hear any more of your lies, Russell. I've heard enough already. I want you to turn around and go out of that door and never come back, not ever again." He took her by the shoulders but she pushed him away, roughly. "You seem to forget something. That I happen to be another man's wife."

She turned her back on him. She held on to the edge of the table to stop her hands from shaking. Behind her she could sense him standing there still, hesitating. She grasped the lilies from the vase on the table and flung them at him. "Go on, God damn you! Get out!"

When he had left she turned around and looked at the flowers scattered across the floor. His flowers. Lilies, the flowers of betrayal. She paced about the room, clenching and unclenching her fists, biting her nails, cursing. She was too angry and humiliated to cry. She sat down. She stood up again. She went from room to room, distractedly, like a wild thing, covering her eyes with her hands to blot out the image of that sly, pale face that had stared out, mockingly, from its chipped, dusty gilt frame.

Outside the rain began to patter on the window panes. Still shaking, she went to the table in the corner of the room and poured herself a measure of brandy, but the shaking would not stop. He had gone. She had sent him away. She would never see or speak to him again. Only at a distance, maybe. They would pass each other by at some dinner or on the course, and he would lift his hat and incline his head, stiffly, toward her, while she nodded coldly. Like strangers.

Behind her, the door opened again.

"Ma'am?" Ellen Troggle stood there, looking first at the lilies, crushed and strewn across the floor; then back at her. "Will Mr. Tollemache be in for dinner?"

"I don't know when he'll be in. Or if." She suddenly rushed across the room to where her cloak had been left draped across a chair, and grasped it up. She flung it around her shoulders. "If he comes back late he'll either have to eat cold supper or go without. I have to leave now!"

"I'll call for the post chaise or the carriage . . ."

"No, there isn't time. I'll go on horseback."

"But, ma'am, you'll be soaked to the skin!"

"That doesn't matter!" She pushed past Ellen and ran out into the yard, then across it to the stables. Pulling a saddle from its rack she flung it over Firestone's back and fastened the girths with trembling fingers.

As she rode out of the courtyard she saw William Devine rush from the coach house, waving his hand, shouting something after her. But she did not turn back.

She hammered on the front door. As it opened and swung back she looked into the stunned face of Jason, Russell's butler, as he stared at the rainwater dripping from the brim of her hat and down her face, from the hem of her cloak and sodden gown into pools that trickled down onto the carpet.

"Is Lord Russell back?"

Quickly, he recovered from his surprise.

"Why, yes, a few moments ago, Mrs. Tollemache . . . he went straight up to his room to shed his wet gear."

"I'll go up to him."

"But, Mrs. Tollemache, he—"

"It's all right, Jason. I know the way."

She brushed past him and ran up the staircase, stumbling over the bottom of her sodden gown, her wet boots leaving muddy footprints on every step.

She did not knock on the door of his room. As she opened it and went inside she saw his wet clothes in a heap on a chair beside the fire, and Russell himself, clad only in a towel, standing beside it with his hands outstretched toward the blaze. He looked up and saw her. She stood there, blinking the rainwater from her eyes, pools of it dripping from her clothes onto the floor.

"Anna!" He came toward her, incredulously. "You're soaked to the skin!"

"I had to come after you. I wanted you to know why I married Lionel Tollemache."

Gently, he took hold of her by the shoulders and looked into her eyes. He was standing so close to her that she could feel the warmth of his breath upon her face.

"I can't bear the thought of him touching you . . ."

"He never has. Nor will he. That's what I wanted you to know."

"Is that the only reason you followed me?"

"No, it isn't."

He reached out and unfastened her cloak and gown and let them fall to the floor. Then he unpinned her hair and it fell about bare shoulders like a cape, glistening and black.

"Your chemise is wet, too," he said, almost in a whisper, and as she felt his hand slide the straps from her shoulders, the touch of his warm skin on hers sent all her pulses leaping. He ran his fingers through her mane of hair, kissing her lips, her neck, her breasts. And as she clung to him her whole body began to float; drifting, burning, carried forward on a wave of undreamed-of delight, until she surrendered herself to what she had always scorned and feared. But neither scorned nor feared any longer.

This was why Anna Maria had strayed from the path of virtue; this was the reason she had done what she did. Because of her feelings for a man that swept out all sense, all reason, all thought of the consequences. At long last, Anna could forgive her mother, because she herself finally understood.

They lay side by side before the fire, Anna's damp head cradled in the crook of Russell's arm. He held her hand in his, and as she talked he bent his head to kiss each of her fingertips, one by one.

"You were in Newmarket. You know what happened, the moment your uncle had to resign as chief steward because of his illness. Someone else took his place, and they all ruled against me. I was expecting that. I was prepared for it. What I wasn't prepared for was that I had no case in law to appeal against their decision. That was when I made the bargain with Tollemache; it was either that or go under. And I couldn't do that, not after everything I'd been through to get where I am. He married me and let me go on racing my horses, but under his name; I kept silent about his brother and Jacob Hindley."

"Your horses meant that much to you? No, don't answer, I can see that they did, and still do. I never realized it, not truly, not until now."

She turned toward him.

"Why didn't you tell me that your wife was Hindley's sister? You've known all along what he is, haven't you?"

He lay back and closed his eyes. He put his hand to his forehead. "Yes, I've known all along. I should have told you everything a long time ago, but I was afraid to. In case you didn't understand. In case it turned you

om me. I almost told you tonight, when you accused me of protecting
Hindley because I still loved his sister."

"I'm sorry, I shouldn't have said the things I did."

"I'm glad you said them. Otherwise I would never have known what
you'd been thinking." He pulled her closer into his arms. "I was young and
stupid when I first met Mary Hindley. I thought she had the face of an
angel, the kind of face you see in stained-glass windows in village churches.
I was in York with my uncle when I saw her, sitting in her father's carriage.
Because I didn't have the experience or the judgment that comes with it,
because I knew no better, I fancied myself in love with her. Only after we'd
married did I find out how cruel and vicious she really was.

"She and Hindley were inseparable. It amused her to procure young
boys and men for him, to satisfy his perverted appetites. They both sick-
ned and disgusted me. I started lying for her, lying to my uncle, lying to
everyone I knew because I couldn't bear the thought of people ever finding
out the truth . . . or of the scandal and shame it would bring not only on me
and my family, but also on my uncle. I think it would kill him if he ever
knew. She slept with any man she could get her hands on. High, low,
young, old. She didn't care. When we came to live in Epsom Hindley was
already here, and he hid the fact that he was her brother in case any
scandal came to light and got him thrown out of the Jockey Club. That was
all he cared about.

"One day, when we'd gone back to York, I came home and found her in
bed, naked. Not with one man, but with two. After I'd thrown both of
them out of the house, I told her that if she ever did it again, she would
have to take the consequences . . . and she just laughed. I can see her now,
lying back among the pillows. I can remember everything in that room. She
started to tell me what she'd been doing with her lovers before I arrived.
She wouldn't stop. To look at her nobody would ever guess that such filth
could come from someone who looked so sweet and innocent. I stalked
over to her and hit her across the mouth. She stopped laughing then. There
was a new look in her eyes. She told me that I'd be sorry.

"The next day she told me to go the top floor in the house, where she had
a surprise for me. When I got there and went into one of the disused
rooms, I found my favorite dog, hanging from a hook in the ceiling . . . she
and Hindley had done it . . ."

Anna grasped him by the arm.

"Ralph!"

". . . they both stood there, laughing, jeering. Then something in me
pulled taut, and snapped. I hit her so hard that she went flying. I kept on
hitting her, I couldn't stop. She fell backward down the stairs and lay in a
crumpled heap at the bottom. Hindley ran down to her. *You've killed her!*
he shouted at me. *You've murdered my sister!* I should have gone straight
to the constable and confessed what happened, but I didn't. That was my
mistake. Who would ever believe it was an accident, that I did it because I

was provoked beyond endurance? No one knew what she really was, ex
cept Hindley. And it was his word against mine." Slowly, he sat up an
buried his head in his hands. "I've suspected for some time that Hindle
was passing on the confidences of his racing friends to men like Tobia
Slout . . . for his own ends. I can't prove it, but I know what he's capabl
of. But even if I did have proof I could never use it against him, because h
in turn would tell the truth about what happened that day." He pulle
Anna to him and held her against his body. "If it was only me that woul
suffer, I wouldn't care. It wouldn't matter. But my family, my uncle . .
he's been like a father to me, Anna. The least I can do is let him die i
peace."

"What if I got proof against him instead?"

"You?"

"I've had my own suspicions about Hindley ever since I came to Epsom
from the time I bought the estate from John Dewar. Frederick Nubble
told me that he was after it, that Dewar had been forced to accept hi
offer—far below its real worth—because he'd been ruined by racing debt
owed to Hindley. Hindley put it about that he had first refusal, so nobod
else made a bid; he knew Dewar was desperate for money so he made hin
wait until the whole place was so run down that he'd be grateful to sell a
any price. When I came along and outbid him, that was the end of his littl
game . . . and he never forgave me for it. But I suspect him of far mor
than that."

"You mean a connection with Tobias Slout . . . before someone with
grievance smashed Slout's kneecaps? That news spread even to New
market."

"I mean besides the connection with Slout, which I'm almost certain o
but can't prove." For a moment she hesitated. "Did you ever wonder wh
smashed him within an inch of his life?"

He raised himself on one elbow, and stared into her eyes. The tone o
her voice brought him sudden understanding, and for a moment he wa
stunned by it.

"Anna! *You?*"

"You didn't see what his hired scum did to my filly . . . you didn't see he
lying whimpering in agony in her own blood, her kneecaps nearly smashe
through to the bone. She had the winning of great races in her, Ralph . . .
knew it. I felt it. She was more than special, she was everything I'd bee
waiting for. She won the only race of her life against the best there was, bu
my judgment about her won't ever be proven because of what they did t
her. I swore two things that night. I've accomplished one of them. To do t
Slout what he had done to her. That was the easiest part. And the othe
was that if she lived I'd nurse her back to health and mate her with Fire
stone . . . and produce the Derby winner my father never could."

He took her hands in his. "For Christ's sake, Anna! Do you know what
risk you took when you went to Slout's alone that night? If any of his hire

men had been there . . . vermin that would slit their own mothers' throats for a glass of cheap gin . . ."

"Don't ask me to say I'm sorry."

Gently, he reached out and touched her cheek with his fingertips. "Anna . . . this isn't easy for me to say . . . I can't bear the thought of having to leave you when I've just found you . . . but my uncle's doctors told me before I left Newmarket that another year in this climate will kill him. He has to go abroad, and I must go with him, whether I want to or not. I owe him that. I only came back here to sort out my affairs before I left, and to see you."

She nodded, slowly.

"You don't have to give any explanations."

"My steward will go on running the house, just as before, until I come back . . . and Inchcape can take care of the stables. As for Chifney . . . I shall continue to pay him his retainer, but I intend to release him so that he can be free to help you in any way he can. I know we can both trust him."

She smiled.

"Yes, I know that."

"Anna . . . there's something else you must know . . . unless you've guessed it already. If it hadn't been for what Hindley knows and holds over me, I would have asked you to marry me a long time ago . . . you must have known from the beginning how much I wanted you." He hung his head. "If I ever married again, Hindley would expose me. That night of the King's Cup dinner, when you and Clara wore the Russell diamonds . . . he came close to it then. You see, after I found out the truth about Mary, I refused to ever let her wear them. I swore she'd never have round her neck the jewelry that had been worn by my mother. He never forgave me for that, either.

"And now I'm manacled by Hindley, and you by Lionel Tollemache."

"Manacles can be broken . . . if you can find the means."

"But how?"

"I'll find a way."

A clock, somewhere in the depths of the house, struck the hour. Rain still fell, ceaselessly, outside the windows.

"It's too late for you to go back now, Anna."

"Yes, I know it."

PART X
February 1837

❋ 26 ❋

They dismounted and led their horses along behind them to the brow of the hill, then both of them stood, looking downward into the grassy hollow below. Smoke curled from the chimney of one of the little cottages, snaking upward in a thin gray column into the cold blue sky. Birds flew past them overhead.

Chifney shivered.

"What time do you expect your sister, Anna?"

She shaded her eyes against the cruel brightness of the winter sun. "The mail coach arrives from London at three o'clock . . . I'll send Elijah into Epsom to meet her with the post chaise." She walked on, along the edge of the rise, swatting at the grass with the end of her whip. "It's so long since I've seen her. She scarcely ever wrote. Maybe I was wrong in thinking that sending her away would get her over her infatuation with James Tollemache. I don't think she's ever forgiven me."

"That was a long time ago, more than three years. Surely she'd have forgotten him by now. She was only a young girl then."

"You don't know Clara like I do. She may have forgotten James Tollemache but not that I got rid of him."

"You did it for her own good."

"And then married his brother!"

"But you can tell her why, now. She'll understand why you did it."

"Because I wanted to outsmart the Jockey Club and run my horses under his name?" She laughed, a little bitterly. "Do you really expect Clara to understand that? Whatever I say, she won't believe me!"

They walked on, in silence. Behind them, the cottages grew smaller and fainter. Anna sat down on the grass, spreading her riding skirt over her booted feet. Chifney sat down beside her.

"Will you run Bloodstone as a two-year-old? Do you think he'll be ready for his first race at the end of this year?"

"Long before. I'll enter him for the Great Foal Stakes in March . . . and if he's made of what I think he's made of, he'll fly it." She gazed backward, the way they'd come. "I know what I've always said . . . that I don't believe in racing two-year-olds. I still stand by that. But Bloodstone's different. He isn't any ordinary two-year-old. If I wait to race him until he's three he's so big and forward that he'd kick down his stall."

She came slowly down the staircase, her eyes on the half-open door of the library below. When she reached the foot she could hear the crackling of the big logs they had put on the fire, and then Clara's voice.

It was different from the high, childish voice she remembered. It was lower, sweeter, more mellow. She was talking gaily, animatedly, to Jessie. Her trunks and hat boxes were stacked in the hall, and Rosina and Ellen were busy carrying them to her room. She smiled at them, absently, as she passed them on the stairs.

Jessie saw her first. Then Clara turned toward the door and for a moment the two sisters stood looking at each other.

"I'll be seeing to the dinner . . ." Jessie said, diplomatically, and went out, leaving them alone.

"It's been a long time," Anna said.

"Yes, a long time."

She had changed. She was taller, more slender. She had more self-assurance. More poise. Yes, she had reason to be grateful to Russell's sister.

"I'll go upstairs and change out of my traveling clothes, if you don't mind."

"Haven't we got anything to talk about, first?"

"I don't think so." It was still there, the bitterness in her voice. But surely she hadn't held the same grudges for the past three years, the grudges that had driven the first wedge between them. James Tollemache was long gone, forgotten. She moved toward the door. "I feel all in, too. Maybe I'll lie down. I never was a good traveler, if you remember."

"Is that all you can find to say to me after three years?"

"What else do you want me to say, Anna? That I've missed you, that I'm glad to be back? That I couldn't wait to come home again and live in the same house as James Tollemache's brother, the man you pretended to despise? Or am I supposed to have forgotten about that?"

"So you've come back still bearing all the same old grudges?" Anna sat down on the arm of a chair. "I've made another mistake about you, haven't I? I thought you'd grown up."

"I have. And I've gotten over what happened, a long time ago. But I've never been able to forget who I am or what I am. Russell's sister couldn't have been kinder, nor cared more about me if I'd been her own kith and kin . . . but there were others who were only too glad to remind me that no matter how much of Father's inheritance belongs to me, I'm still only his bastard daughter."

"Is that supposed to be my fault, too?"

"You were the talk of every drawing room, every gathering, every dinner table! Anna Brodie, the girl who used to work as a rough-rider up on the Downs, the girl who races blood horses with the men! And I was Clara Brodie, her sister. Whatever I did and wherever I went I could never get away from either you or Father! Bastard of one, sister of the other! None of those society bitches ever let me forget it!"

"Oh, now we're getting to the truth! They were jealous of you and they wanted to dig their claws in any way they could! Don't you understand that that would have happened whoever you were? It had nothing to do with Father or me, for Christ's sake! If you were a princess of the blood they'd still have found something to hurt you with, and used it. That's the price you pay for your beauty. If Mama were still alive, she could have told you that, too."

Clara stood there, not speaking.

"Did Jessie tell you I've gotten you a piano?"

There was a flash of defiance in her eyes.

"You can't buy me, Anna."

"I'm not trying to. I promised you one a long time ago, but you went to London before I could get it. I'm just keeping my word, that's all."

They went into the drawing room together. There it stood, in the far corner of the room, and slowly Clara walked over to it and sat down on the ornate stool. She opened the lid and gently touched the keys.

"It's a Domenico Perrotta . . . like Mama had at Saffron Walden . . ." She looked up, with disbelief in her eyes. "These are very rare . . . how did you manage to get it?"

"The usual way, with money." There was a wry smile on Anna's lips.

"But . . . it must have cost a small fortune . . ."

"It didn't cost me anything. No, Tollemache didn't pay for it. He hasn't a penny to his name that isn't mine," she said quickly, when she saw the look on Clara's face. "It came from the stakes I won when Hope won her first and only race before the nobblers got to her. You have her speed to thank for it." Clara looked down at the keys, not able to meet Anna's eyes. "You see, despite everything you've ever said about my horses, they do have their uses, don't they?" She moved closer to her sister and put a hand on her shoulder, suddenly remembering her, sitting on Ralph Russell's wall in her shabby, tattered clothes, the dogs tearing at the rag wound about her boots to bind the holes. Between that Clara and this one seemed a wide, unbridgeable gap that she somehow had to step across before they drifted apart forever.

"I know you've never really understood how much I care about my horses, and maybe I can never make you understand. But I know how you feel about music, how you feel when you sit down in front of this piano and play it, and sing. If I tried to stop you doing that, if everyone around you told you that you couldn't do it because you weren't allowed to, or sup- posed to, or just because you were a woman, how would you feel then? Would you accept it? Would you do what they wanted? Would you give it up without a fight because they said you had to?" Clara looked up at her, tears in her eyes. "No, I don't think you would. And how you feel about your music is the way I feel about my horses. I have to do it. It's part of me. It's in my blood and it'll be there till I die."

A tear welled up in the corner of Clara's eye and rolled down her cheek. "Why didn't you explain it that way before, Anna?"

"I don't know. I don't think I ever thought of it till now." For the first time since she could remember, she put her arms round her sister and embraced her. Behind them, the door came open.

"Well, well, what a touching sight. The little sister returns!" They both turned, slowly, and saw Lionel Tollemache lolling in the open doorway, a glass in one hand and a cigar in the other. He walked further into the room, a smirk on his lips. "What a change. Not 'little' Clara anymore." He glanced at Anna. "I can see we'll have to fight the eligible young bachelors away from the door."

"Have you been drinking?"

He raised his glass in the air.

"Just a little before-dinner tipple."

Anna's voice held scorn.

"At four o'clock in the afternoon?"

"Half-past." His eyes rested on Clara. "Well, isn't the little sister going to play us a tune?"

"Get out of here!" Anna went to the door and flung it open. "And take that filthy, stinking thing with you! I told you not to smoke cigars in the house. If you want to do it, go outside in the yard!"

"In February?"

"I said take it out of here, Lionel."

He drank down the remainder of the gin. He shrugged his shoulders. "Want to get rid of me, eh? You want me out of the way so you can whisper tales in your sister's ear. Or is it because you're afraid I might tell her something I shouldn't?"

Anna took Clara's hand. "Come on. We'll go upstairs."

"Just a minute . . . not so fast." Tollemache closed the door and leaned back against it. "Before you go, my dear little sister, there's something that I must ask you. Are you happy to be back in Epsom? Had enough of the giddy society in London, all those rich, eager young men chasing you like a pack of hounds chase the hare?" He laughed, unpleasantly. "Gotten over your little infatuation with my errant young brother?"

Clara stiffened.

"I don't want to talk about him."

Tollemache raised his eyebrows.

"Well, you've certainly changed. She's changed, hasn't she, Anna? I saw that, straightaway. Why didn't you come to your sister's wedding, Clara? Was it because you thought James might be there . . . or because you couldn't forgive her for selling herself to me? Yes, that's right. That's just what she did. But she's clever, you have to give her that. Cunning as a vixen. She only married me so that she could outflank the Jockey Club ruling that no woman should be allowed to race horses under her own name, did you know that? Once she married me, she could just go on running them under mine. And there's nothing they can do about it. That's clever, wouldn't you agree that's clever?"

"Get out of our way, Lionel."

"But I haven't finished yet, Anna. The little sister doesn't know why I agreed to this bargain. Don't you think she's old enough now to be told the truth?"

"Anna, what is he talking about?"

"I'm warning you, Lionel . . ."

"She wanted James out of your way . . . sent abroad. For your own good, of course. She had to be cruel to be kind, if you can understand that." Clara stared at him, without speaking. "He's there now, God knows where, wandering from place to place, country to country . . . your sister pays for it, of course. That was part of the bargain. If I didn't agree to marry her on her terms, she threatened to expose poor James, and bring my whole family into disgrace." He began to laugh. "And all because my little brother prefers to go to bed with other men instead of women."

"It isn't true." Wildly, Clara looked from one to the other. "Anna, it isn't true! He's lying!"

"No, I'm afraid not, little sister." He put down his empty glass. "James only pretended to care for you so that he could ask you questions about your sister's horses. But you were such a good girl, weren't you? You never told him anything worthwhile.

"But never mind. Anna can take you along to the ball the *nouveau-riche* Tradescants are giving at Chilworth Manor tomorrow night, and I'm sure you'll find plenty of young men ready to rip your gown off!"

Clara broke away from Anna and ran out of the room, sobbing.

"I ought to throw you out of this house right now!"

He leaned back against the wall and smiled at her.

"But you can't do that, can you, Anna? Not ever."

She went over and stood so close to him that he could see the pigment in her eyes. "You ever hurt my sister again with your filthy tongue, and you'll answer to me."

She found Clara in her old room, stretched out across her bed, crying, still in her dusty, travel-soiled clothes. She went over to her and took her tear-stained face in both hands.

"Don't give in to him, Clara. Don't let him do this to you. Can't you see he's only trying to hurt you to spite me? I won't pay his gambling debts, I won't hand out money like waste paper whenever he wants it to throw away on his drinking and his women, and he wants revenge on me. He hasn't got the guts to get it any other way."

Clara stopped crying. She sat up on the bed and hugged her knees. "I never really understood how much running those horses meant to you, Anna, not until now. Not until I saw what kind of sacrifice you had to make to get what you wanted." She grabbed Anna's hands. "But what are you going to do?" Her voice fell to a whisper. "You can't stay tied to him, not until one of you dies. Anna, you've got to break free somehow . . ."

Anna ran a hand through her mane of hair.

"I know, I know that. But I can't do it yet." She got off the bed and went and bolted the door. "Listen to me. You remember what I told you about him and Jacob Hindley, a long time ago? The things I suspected Hindley of?"

"Yes, I remember."

"I'm even more certain of it now, but I still have no proof. I'm convinced Hindley had more than a hand in the ruin of John Dewar, and in Edward Randyll's. You heard about that in London?"

"Yes . . ."

". . . outwardly, he's a gentleman, from good family; eminent, respectable, a member of the Jockey Club. He's in the perfect position to hear the confidences of other men, men who think that he's their friend, that they can trust him. For the last ten years or more he's been scheming and swindling, and for the last five I believe he's been passing on information about his friends' horses to Tobias Slout. There couldn't have been a better partnership. Hindley passes on stable secrets that he's heard in the Jockey Club, or in someone's drawing room . . . Slout's lackeys do the rest, and they both profit. Nobody ever suspects Hindley because of who he is, and his position in local society."

"You think he was behind the plot to nobble Hope?"

"Yes. And I suspect him of more than that . . . I think he murdered my lawyer, Frederick Nubbles."

"Anna!"

"I've thought and thought about it ever since it happened, and I'm convinced it's the truth. Think about it. Nubbles was coming here, that night, bringing the documents to sign that I'd asked him to prepare before I went ahead and married Tollemache, transferring most of my share of the inheritance to you so that Tollemache could never touch it. He never arrived. When we went out looking for him, thinking his horse had gone lame or a spoke might have broken in his curricle wheel, we found him stabbed to death, huddled on the seat, beside the road. Because his money pouch was found empty half a mile away, the local constable came to the conclusion that it was footpads, but I never believed that for a moment. I think it was taken and put there, to make it look as if he'd been attacked and robbed."

"But why do you suspect Hindley of killing him?"

"The place where he was found was in the direction opposite where he was making for . . . here. I noticed there was mud on the soles of his shoes, a peculiar color, and sticking to the mud were dead camellia leaves. There were no camellia bushes anywhere along the road he was taking . . . there wouldn't be. You'd only find them in the grounds of somebody's house. There are camellia bushes in the grounds of Slout's old house. I know, because I've seen them.

"Nubbles left his office in Epsom earlier that evening, and took the west road, because he had papers to deliver to another client. By the time he reached the crossroads it would have been getting dark, and on his way he would have passed by Slout's place . . . it lies about a hundred yards from the main road. This is only surmise, but he must have seen something there . . . a light. Somebody skulking in the grounds, maybe. But something that aroused his curiosity enough to go and look. The constable's men intended to search the place for papers that Slout might have had hidden that could shed light on his betting coups . . . Hindley could have known that very easily. He must have done. I believe he went back that night, when it was dark and there was no chance of him being seen, to look through Slout's papers in case there was anything in the house to incriminate him. Nubbles died because he recognized him at once. Hindley then bundled him back into the curricle and left it far enough away from Slout's place not to incur suspicion. He emptied his money pouch and left it where it could be found, so that it would look as if footpads had killed him for his valuables.

"But one thing Hindley couldn't have known . . . which made him make one vital mistake. He didn't know Nubbles was coming here to see me. He led the horse that was harnessed to Nubble's curricle, with his body inside it, to a spot where it would look as if Nubbles had been on his way home. I saw at once that the gig was facing in the wrong direction . . . facing the road going back to Epsom instead of here."

"You're very clever, Anna. But how can you ever prove it?"

She lay back against the carved oak headboard and sighed.

"I don't know. But I will somehow. The hardest part is going to be convincing people that Hindley isn't what he seems. I have another ally, now Chilworth Manor's been bought from Edward Randyll. Tom Tradescant. The Tradescants are a rich London banking family who want to buy their way into racing. They came here, nearly three years ago, and spent a small fortune restoring the whole place and rebuilding the stables. Tradescant's bought a fine string of running horses, some of them from as far away as Doncaster and York. He's making it pay. One thing more that he wants and that he won't get as long as Hindley's footloose and free . . . membership in the Jockey Club. Every time his name comes up for election, someone blackballs it. And you can guess who that someone is."

"Jacob Hindley? But why? What have the Tradescants ever done to him?"

"Nothing. But then neither did I. I bought an estate that he wanted. I outbid him and made him look a fool . . . so he thought. A bastard. A woman. An outsider. How dare I. That's the way he feels about the

Tradescants. Rich trade. Trying to buy their way into the gentry. That's what puts his back up."

"He's against honest men because they made their money from trading? And he is what he is!"

"Men like Hindley never play by anyone's rules but their own."

"Does Tom Tradescant know why he's being kept out of the Jockey Club?"

"He has a good idea. And I've talked at length with him. There might just be a way to trap Hindley, and destroy him for good. But even that isn't as simple as it seems." She turned to Clara in the fading light. "You see, if I expose him, he in turn could ruin someone else, someone innocent, some-one . . ." she hesitated, then went on, "who matters to me far more than myself."

"Who, Anna?"

"Ralph Russell."

✳ 27 ✳

Everybody's eyes were on them as they walked hand in hand into the crowded entrance hall at Chilworth Manor. Heads turned. Men stared. Women nudged one another and whispered behind their fans. Then a tall, dark figure disengaged itself from the crowd and came toward them, smil-ing.

"What a striking resemblance!"

"This is my sister, Clara Brodie. Clara, this is Tom Tradescant."

The new Clara, no longer tongue-tied and shy, gave him her hand and he carried it to his lips.

"Anna said that you're an ally."

He smiled. "She told me that you have a voice that would make Henriette Sontag sound like a market stall cryer . . . if that's true maybe I could persuade you to give not only my guests' sight a rare treat, but their ears as well?"

"Anna!"

"Well, it's the truth, isn't it?"

"But I couldn't . . . I've never sung in public before!"

Tradescant offered each of them an arm. He looked from one to the other, his eyes lingering on Clara's face.

"Your mother must have been a very beautiful lady to have produced two such daughters . . ."

*   *   *

He closed the door behind him.

"I'd best be brief . . . we don't have much time."

"You think that we can trap him?"

Tradescant sat down on the arm of a chair.

"I have a Catton filly running in the Empress Cup . . . the race before the Great Foal Stakes. She won three races in a row up in York before my father bought her for our stable, and our head groom reckons that if she holds her form—and there's no reason why she shouldn't hold it—she's almost bound to be made first favorite on the course. I'd like to win the race. Not because of the money, because I don't need it. My father bought this place and gave over the running of it and the racing stable to me because we enjoy the sport, not because we looked to make a profit. But if there's the slightest chance of netting Hindley, and the price of doing that is sacrificing the Empress Cup, then so be it."

"Go on."

"The filly's had five races in her life. She was third in her first, she won her last three. The only one where she came nowhere was at Doncaster six months ago. No, she wasn't nobbled. Some northern jockey had the ride and we know he rode to win because he'd backed her himself, heavily. He reckons it was a tight race, and he had difficulty in making her keep a straight course . . . so he flicked her on the neck with his whip. As soon as he did that, she pulled up so fast that he was nearly cannoned over her head."

"What are you planning to do?"

"We're engaging a suspect jockey for her, someone who my head groom reckons has taken more than a bribe or two in his life. A few weeks back, when I was invited to Heathcote's place, I deliberately told Hindley that if the filly is touched on her neck with the whip, she'll drop out. I never breathed a word of it to anyone else. We're running a second filly, a good stayer for the distance but without her finishing speed, and I'm putting one of my young apprentices up to watch what happens. If her jockey uses his whip on her neck and Hindley's filly wins, we'll know almost for certain that he's guilty. What's more, we'll have something concrete to go to Heathcote with."

"If he does use the whip on her neck to stop her, it'll still only be his word against your apprentice's . . . and Hindley will be the first to accuse you of sour grapes and a grudge against him because you lost the race."

"Have you got any better ideas?"

Agitatedly, Anna paced the floor.

"I'd like to thrash the truth out of him!" Angrily, she clenched her fists. "I've lain in bed at night, cursing myself because I didn't make Slout confess that he'd been getting information from Hindley when I had the chance to . . . but then I realized it wouldn't have done any good if I had. Who'd take Slout's word against someone like Hindley?"

Tradescant nodded.

"Just what I was thinking. But don't forget the old saying . . . give a man enough rope and he'll hang himself."

"I'd rather do it for him."

The noises from the ballroom drifted into the room, louder than before. Music, laughter. Tradescant stood up.

"We'd best get back . . . before people begin to wonder where we are." He paused, his hand on the doorknob. "And where is your husband tonight . . . or is that a question you'd rather not answer?"

"Getting drunk somewhere. Or gambling for stakes that he doesn't have." She looked at Tradescant meaningfully. "Those are just the things he's likely to be doing that I can mention." She saw by his expression that he understood. "I don't trust him, Tom. His old ties with Hindley are too strong to have been broken off altogether."

"You think he'd pass on information to Hindley about your yard?"

"He probably already has. About Bloodstone. There's no way he could live under the same roof without seeing that he's likely to be the fastest colt that's ever been bred in Epsom. I can't keep that from him. But I swore after what happened to Hope that the next man who tried to harm any of my horses would find himself looking down the barrel of my gun."

Tradescant opened the door for Anna to go through.

"One more warning . . . since I never invite people I detest into my house, you won't find Jacob Hindley out there. But I did invite the Heathcotes. What I didn't know when I invited them was that a certain Lady Helen Gordon was staying with them at Durdans as their house guest, and they've brought her along. There was nothing I could do about it."

"Helen Gordon? Wasn't she Leopardstown's mistress about three years ago?"

"Yes, she was. Until he got tired of her. And you know what they say about a woman scorned? From everything I've been hearing in certain quarters, she's no admirer of yours."

"I'll keep it in mind."

She mingled with the groups of guests, sometimes with Clara, sometimes on her own. She smiled and raised a hand at faces she already knew. From the side of the great ballroom, she stood with a glass of wine, watching Tom Tradescant make his way through the press of people toward Clara. She saw him draw her gently from the throng, smiling, bending forward to whisper in her ear; then Clara, shaking her head, her hands gesturing in protest, her eyes seeking Anna among the crowds. She put down her glass and went to them, being stopped a dozen times on the way.

"Why, Mrs. Tollemache . . ."

"Your sister is almost as beautiful as you are!"

"Is your colt still running in the Great Foal Stakes?"

She reached them, at last. Clara seized her arm.

"I can't sing, Anna . . . not in front of so many people. I might make a mistake. My voice might break down . . ."

"It's as likely to break down as Bloodstone in the Great Foal Stakes. Do it for me." Gently but firmly, she pushed her toward the flower-covered dais where the orchestra sat. "Show them what a Brodie's made of."

She stepped back into the crowd. The music stopped. Tom Tradescant stood beside Clara and began to speak. A murmur rippled through the packed ballroom, followed by such silence that Anna could hear the sound of her own breathing. Then Clara's exquisite, powerful voice rang out far above the sound of the orchestra and carried to the furthest reaches of the great room.

Tears of pride and pleasure began to sting at the back of her eyes.

"Must you go?"

"It's past eleven and I have to be up at dawn to take Bloodstone out on Banstead Downs. Then we're trying him for time over the Derby course."

"That's a tall order for an untried two-year-old."

Anna smiled. "I'd sooner find out what he's made of first than last." Beyond the open door she could see Jonas, standing ready with the post chaise. She took her cloak and Clara's from a waiting manservant. "We haven't enjoyed an evening like this one for a long while. Thank you for that."

"The pleasure was all mine," Tradescant answered, his eyes on Clara's face. As he kissed their hands someone began pushing roughly through from the back of the crowd of departing guests gathered at the door. People began to turn and stare, then whisper among themselves.

"Going home so soon, Mrs. Tollemache?" said Helen Gordon, in a slurred, tipsy voice. She swayed from side to side, a half-drunk glass of wine in one hand. She hiccuped. "When you get back, you must give my special regards to Lionel . . . dear Lionel . . . did you know that he and I were very intimate friends?" Everyone in earshot fell silent. "He isn't with you tonight, then? What a pity." She hiccuped again, then she began to laugh. "Tell me, is it true that you prefer horses to men?"

Tom Tradescant's face had gone very white. Angrily, he went toward her but Anna put her hand on his arm.

"I prefer them to titled whores who go about masquerading as ladies." She smiled, coldly. "And I didn't know that you and Lionel were intimate friends, no. I don't keep count of my husband's castoffs."

She walked on outside.

"Anna, who was she, for God's sake?"

"I would have thought that was obvious."

"But she deliberately tried to humiliate you in front of everyone!"

"She isn't the first to try and she won't be the last. But I think I gave as good as I got, don't you?" Wearily, she climbed down from the post chaise while Caleb helped Clara. Jonas was already unharnessing the team.

"'Ave a good evening, ma'am?"

"I reckon you could say that, thank you, Caleb." She looked toward the house. "Is my husband back, yet?"

"No, ma'am."

"Then why are the lights on in the library?"

"There's a gentleman called, not long after you and Miss Clara went over to Mr. Tradescant's. Mrs. Tamm told 'im you might not be back till late, but 'e insisted on staying and waiting for you."

Anna frowned.

"Did you recognize him?"

"No, ma'am, 'e rode in from Cheam, so 'e said."

"At this time of night?"

"'E said it was important business, ma'am."

She opened the door to the library. A stranger stood by one of the windows, turning one of her books over in his hands. He put it down on the desk.

"Mrs. Tollemache?"

"I'm Anna Tollemache, yes. If you're here to see my husband I'd advise you to come back tomorrow. He might be back later. He might be out all night. I couldn't say."

"I didn't come here to see your husband, Mrs. Tollemache. I came to see you." He handed her a card and she took it and read it.

"You're a doctor?"

"Yes. My practice is in Cheam."

"Does my husband owe you money?"

"No."

"Then I don't understand why you should want to see me."

He bit his lip.

"Mrs. Tollemache, this isn't an easy thing for me to ask, but I have to, for your own sake. Could you please tell me when was the last time you had marital relations with your husband?"

She stared at him, taken aback.

"How dare you!"

"Mrs. Tollemache, your husband is suffering from syphilis."

She stood there, still staring at him. The words that she wanted to say would not come.

"I know this has come as a great shock to you . . . I understand that. But I wouldn't have come all this way to warn you if there had been no necessity. Do you know how serious a disease syphilis is?"

"Yes, yes, I know, I know." She walked away from him. She paced the floor, biting her fingernails.

"Then you understand why I had to ask you that question . . . and why you must answer it. If you and your husband have had any relations within the past four weeks, there is a strong possibility that you could have caught the disease from him. Mrs. Tollemache, if syphilis is left untreated the consequences can be devastating . . ."

"I'm afraid you've had a long ride for nothing, Doctor." She went over to the brandy and poured herself a full glass. "There's no possibility that I could have caught the disease from my husband." She took a swig of the brandy. "You see, our marriage is a marriage in name only. There's never been, and never will be, any physical contact between us." She saw the look of shock in his face. "My husband never told you that?"

"No, he never told me. He came to me more than a month ago, suffering from certain symptoms, which at first I couldn't be sure of . . . but when he visited me the day before yesterday more symptoms had developed, and I was then able to confirm my earlier suspicions." He took a small bottle from his coat and handed it to her. "The only known method of treatment is with mercury. If you will give these mercury pills to your husband, the instructions for dosage are written down. When he has taken them all, he must visit me again. Would you please tell him that? Unless, of course, you'd prefer me to . . ."

"No. No, I shall give them to him myself." She turned away from him and refilled her half-empty glass. "Would you forgive me if I didn't see you out?"

"Yes, of course, I understand." She heard his voice from the door. "I'm very sorry, Mrs. Tollemache."

Slowly, she went over to one of the great chairs before the fire and sat in it. She kicked off her ball shoes. She put down her drink. She held up the bottle of mercury pills and began to turn it round and round in her hand. She felt too numb inside to think. She was too weary to feel anger, even. She lay back her head and closed her eyes.

"Anna?" said Clara's voice from the door. She was already in her nightgown, her long dark hair falling about her to her waist. "Jessie put the warming pan in your bed. Are you coming up now?"

"Not yet."

"Who was that man? Was it someone for him?"

"Yes. You could say that."

"Is anything the matter?"

"With me? No, nothing at all." She got to her feet.

"He isn't back yet. Are you going to bolt the doors, as you said you would if he didn't come home before midnight?"

"No, not tonight. When he comes in I want to see him."

"If he ever does," Clara said. She kissed Anna on the cheek and went on upstairs. She paused on the landing. "Goodnight!"

Anna stood for a moment alone in the hall. Then she called to the dogs and they followed her upstairs.

She did not undress. She sat in the chair by her window until she fell asleep.

*   *   *

She awoke, hours later, the sky still dark outside the windows, stiff and cold. At her feet, the two dogs slumbered. The clock in the hall chimed the hour. Below her, in the library, she could hear the sounds of someone moving about. So he was back. She sat there for several minutes, staring into the dim light. Then she got up and went downstairs.

He was drinking gin and smoking a cigar when she went into the room, his clothes crumpled, his shirt undone at the neck. He looked her up and down, without surprise.

"Well, well. Back from the ball. And how is our *nouveau-riche* neighbor, Tom Tradescant? Still trying to get himself elected to the Jockey Club?"

"Not while your bosom friend Jacob Hindley is doing all he can to keep him out."

"Bosom friend?" He replenished his empty glass. "I wouldn't call him that."

"Don't lie to me! I know you've been seeing him behind my back ever since I married you!"

"Which you can prove, of course?" Casually, drink in one hand and cigar in the other, he sat down in a chair and crossed his legs. Anna strode over to him and knocked the glass out of his hand. "You bitch!"

"Get up! Get up out of that chair! I'll be damned if I'll let any man sit down in my presence when I'm standing!"

The smile vanished from his face.

"Why don't you try to make me?"

For a moment they stared at each other. Then she snatched the cigar from his fingers and flung it into the grate with the ashes. "I've taken all I intend to take from you, Lionel. I've put up with your gambling, your drinking, your whoremongering. I've swallowed your insults. I've paid your dishonored debts. Well, I've finally come to the end of my tether." She took out the bottle of mercury pills and threw it in his face. "You've got one week to pack up your belongings and get out of my house. I don't care where you go. London. Newmarket. Back to your family or abroad with your no-account brother. But I want you out of Epsom and I want you out for good."

He stooped down and picked up the bottle.

"What are these?"

"You don't know?"

"I asked you what they were."

"You can read, can't you?" A jeering note came into her voice. "Or are you too drunk to see straight?"

He looked at the small, spidery writing on the label, then up again. There was a smile on his lips.

"Oh, I understand now . . . you've had a visitor. From Cheam? He brought these for me. And you decided, my pure-as-the-driven-snow wife, that this was the excuse you could use to get rid of me. Well, I'm sorry to disappoint you, Anna . . . but I have no intention of going anywhere. Now or ever."

"If you're not out of my house at the end of the week then I'll throw you out!"

Roughly, he grasped her by the shoulders and pulled her toward him.

"Oh, you'd like that, wouldn't you, Anna? Throw me out, make a clean sweep, all the old dirt cleared away out of sight under the carpet? All ready for Ralph Russell when he comes back . . ."

"Let go of me!"

"Didn't you know his uncle had died in France three weeks ago?" He shook her again. "Didn't he write and tell you that he was on his way back?"

She struggled with him, wildly. He ripped her ball gown from her shoulder. She slapped him, hard, across the face.

"I told you never to lay hands on me, you whoremongering bastard!"

"As one bastard to another, Anna, tell me how you like this!" He slapped her back, first on one side of her face, then on the other. She tried to break way from him but he grasped her by the arm. "Do you know why I caught the pox? Do you? Do you, you bitch?"

"Let go of me!" Out on the landing, she could hear Clara and Jessie calling out to her, then the dogs, barking and growling at the noise.

"I caught it going to other women . . . women I had to go to because my wife wouldn't let me in her bed! Well, if you want me to stop you know what the answer is, don't you?" He took hold of another handful of her gown and ripped it, all the way down the seam. "You'd better start behaving like a proper wife, do you hear me? A proper wife!" He hit her so hard that she went crashing to the floor, and he threw himself on top of her. He grasped her by both wrists and pinned her down with his weight. "We'll start now, Anna, shall we? Right here, on the floor. Is that how you'd like it, eh?" He let go one wrist and hit her again. "You bitch! You wouldn't struggle like this if I was Ralph Russell, would you?"

Suddenly, the dogs came bounding into the room and leaped on him, pulling him from her, tearing at his clothes. Anna struggled to her feet, gasping, half-crying, holding up the tattered bodice of her gown. As Clara and Jessie ran in to see what was happening, she pulled out the drawer of her desk and took hold of the pistol she always kept there. She called off the dogs. She leaned against one of the bookshelves, panting.

"Get up. Go on, get up!"

Slowly, he dragged himself to his feet, his eyes on her face.

"I swear, Lionel . . . I swear if you ever come near me again, I'll use this." She pushed her hair from her eyes. Jessie and Clara stood trembling in the doorway, numbed by shock. "Lionel, do you hear what I say?"

He lowered himself into a chair. His clothes were ripped and his hands bleeding from the dogs' teeth.

"All right. All right, Anna. You're holding all the cards. But we made a bargain. You can't back out of it now." He was panting. He buried his head in his hands. "I stay here. Just like before. But I won't come in drunk, not ever again. I give you my word."

"And how much do you reckon that's worth?"

He looked up at her. His eyes were red-rimmed, bloodshot, sunken. All the furious strength of a moment ago seemed to have gone out of him.

"I mean it, Anna."

The two dogs came over and sat down at her feet. She reached out her hand and patted them. Then she motioned to Clara and Jessie to go away.

"Is it true, what you said about Russell? Is his uncle really dead?"

"That's what I said."

"And where did you hear it?"

"Ah, that would be telling, wouldn't it?" He stretched out a hand and picked up the bottle of mercury pills. "You can throw these away, on your way out. I won't be needing them."

"But you have to take them. He said so. He said you must."

"Otherwise I'll die, right?" There was a cynical smile at the corners of his lips. "We all have to do that, don't we? Sooner or later?"

"If the disease is left untreated the consequences would be devastating."

"To me, yes." He tipped the pills out into the palm of his hand, then one by one he threw them into the ashes of the fire. "Why are you looking at me like that, Anna? I thought I was doing you a favor."

The last thing she had ever expected to feel for him was pity. Pity was for the poor, the weak, the downtrodden. Not for someone like him, someone born into wealth and privilege and social position. But pity flickered somewhere in her, now. She went over to the open drawer of her desk and put away the pistol. She hesitated by the door.

"On the condition that you never do anything like this again, you can stay."

He did not get up from the chair. He leaned forward and inclined his head toward her in mockery of a bow.

"One day I shall repay the debt."

PART XI
March 1837

❄ 28 ❄

Hours before the race, spectators in their thousands already lined the course on both sides and swamped the Warren and the lawns in front of the private grandstand. The ground behind it was choked with row upon row of every kind of conveyance: barouches, gigs, post chaises, carriages. In the grandstand itself every box and balcony was crammed to capacity; those that arrived too late stood on the tops of their carriages or climbed onto the wooden edifices at the back of the betting stand.

In the packed Warren where most of the runners in the Great Foal Stakes had been brought to be saddled, Anna stood to one side while Jonas and William Devine held Bloodstone's bridle and Chifney was given a leg up into the saddle. The colt backed and pulled and swished his tail, showing the whites of his eyes.

"Hold him steady, boys!"

"Watch those back legs, will you?"

" 'E's sweating up bad, ma'am. It's all the noise and the crowds . . . 'e's not used to it."

"He'll settle when he gets to post."

"It'll be worse than this in the Derby!"

"Look at Anson's colt . . . you can't see its coat for the lather!"

Anna looked up at Chifney in the saddle.

"Watch him at the off, or he'll try to run away with you. I've never ridden a horse that pulled as hard as he does. I had a job to hold him."

He smiled down at her.

"Don't worry. I'll see you after the race." William Devine let go the bridle, Anna gave Bloodstone a last pat, and they were gone, swallowed up in the density of horses and crowd. On the other side of the Warren, she caught sight of the tall figure of Tom Tradescant, Clara clinging to his arm, trying to squeeze their way toward where she stood.

She shaded her eyes against the afternoon sunlight, watching Chifney's pale blue against Bloodstone's black until they both disappeared from sight. Then she turned away.

"If it's like this for the Great Foal Stakes," Tradescant said, reaching her at last, "what will it be like for next year's Derby?"

Anna smiled.

"Go and tell Henry Dorling to build a bigger grandstand. Has your father got down from London today?"

"To his great disappointment, no. The journey was all planned and he was packed and ready to leave when he had to preside over a special meeting of the bank board."

"That's a pity. I would have liked to meet him." She turned to her sister. "You know you shouldn't be down here, Clara. You're supposed to stay in the box . . . one Brodie causing a scandal is one thing, but two of us is quite another." She and Tradescant laughed, but Clara was staring in the opposite direction. Her face had gone very pale.

"Anna . . . that groom, there, leaving the Warren with a horseblanket over his arm . . ." She grabbed her by the hand and pointed. "I know he had a beard, but when he turned this way I could have sworn that it was Paris . . ."

"Paris? Here? Back in Epsom?"

"There's four colts that were walked down from Newmarket and two from Doncaster for this race," Tradescant said. "Maybe he came with one of them . . ."

"He's gone, whoever he was," said Jonas.

"Surely 'e'd not 'ave the nerve to show 'is cheating face back 'ere, after what 'e did?" said William Devine. "I can't believe it."

"'E'd be arrested on sight . . ."

Suddenly Anna's heart began to thump wildly. "But if it is him, nobody would recognize him under those whiskers, unless they came close up . . . wait here!"

Clara caught her arm.

"Anna, wait! I might have been wrong!"

"I can go for the constable," Tradescant said.

"Which way did he go, Jonas?"

"Behind the carriages, ma'am!"

Roughly, pushing bodies aside that blocked her way, Anna began to wade through the crowds.

"But Anna," Clara called after her, "you'll miss the race!"

Her voice was lost among the noise of the crowds.

She caught sight of him, suddenly, walking back among the trees that lined one side of the Warren. Behind them lay rows of carriages and tethered horses, coachmen and grooms tending to their teams or standing up on the tops of their masters' vehicles to get a better view of the course. Then he slowed down and glanced over his shoulder, and saw her. For a moment he stood as if he had been turned to stone. Then he dropped the horseblanket he was carrying and began to run.

"Paris!" She dragged up the hem of her gown and began to run after him as fast as her legs could carry her. "Stop him!" she screamed as she ran between the carriages and horses. "Stop that man!"

People stared after her. Some followed and gave chase. In front of her Paris dodged and darted between the post chaises and gigs, knocking others out of his way; running left, then right, blindly, without direction, trying to shake off pursuit. Then he tripped and stumbled over a harness that someone had left lying on the grass, and as he tried to get to his feet again, Anna caught up with him.

She still had Bloodstone's leading rein in her hands. Throwing it round his neck she pulled it so tight that his face turned blue and he struggled for breath, his arms flailing helplessly in the air like a drowning man's.

Savagely, she swung his head round to face her.

"I've waited three years to get my hands on your traitorous carcass . . ." She shook him, roughly. "I've got a score to settle with you, Paris!"

A choking, gurgling noise came from his throat. He tried to break free from her iron grip, but he remembered, too late, the strength in those narrow wrists of hers. In front of him as the leather strap tightened around his windpipe her face swam round and round, blurred, indistinct, receding. Then she released it and the picture came back, clearly, her cold, merciless eyes a startling blue.

"Miss Anna . . ."

"Give me one good reason why I shouldn't throttle you right now!"

"Miss Anna!"

"You took Slout's blood money to sneak back into my yard like a thief and maim my filly so bad that she never ran again, just to get even with me for throwing you out!" She thrust her face close to his. "After I took you in, Paris. Took you in on trust and gave you the best job in my yard, paid you more than twice as much as you'd have gotten working for anyone else. That was how you repaid me." She tightened the leading rein round his neck. "Now you tell me what I want to know . . ." she tightened it again. "Did that bastard Hindley put you up to it? Was he working hand in glove with Slout and his hired scum, nobbling horses? You tell me, before I pull this so tight you'll never draw breath again!"

Behind her, she heard the thunderous roar of the vast crowds. Slowly, inch by inch, she released the pressure of the strap. Paris fought to get his breath.

"No . . . no. There was no one else. I only saw Slout. One of 'is men came up to me in the inn after it got round that you'd thrown me out." His eyes sought hers for some vestiges of pity. They looked back at him. Cold, remote, stony as pebbles on the shore. No hope. Trembling, tears running down his dirty cheeks, he reached up and grasped her hand, but the flesh he held seemed like stone, as if he were holding not the hand of a living woman but a statue. Slowly, he let it go. "This time I'm telling you the truth, Miss Anna. I swear it."

Behind them, people came running. The constable's men rushed upon Paris and pinioned him, arms behind his back, before they dragged him away. Then Anna heard shouting and cheering and Clara and Tradescant came running up to her, both out of breath.

"Anna, Bloodstone stormed home by three lengths! The whole crowd's gone wild! Come back, quickly!"

They each took one of her hands and led her back through the crowds to the Warren, then on to the winner's enclosure. People stepped away in front of her to let her pass, cheering, clapping, waving their arms and hats in the air. The first thing she saw was Bloodstone, tossing his head, black coat shimmering like glass in the bright afternoon sun. Chifney had just dismounted and was unbuckling the saddle.

Laughing and crying at once, she ran to him and threw her arms about his neck with joy.

Lionel Tollemache finished his glass of brandy in the packed grandstand saloon, then made his way with difficulty through the crowds toward the paddock. As he inched his way through the endless groups of people, he felt a hand on his arm.

"You're going in the wrong direction, Tollemache," Jacob Hindley said, scarcely above a whisper. "My carriage is back there, behind the trees." His fingers tightened on Tollemache's arm. "It's the only place where we can talk and not be overheard. I want you to come with me now."

"Isn't it a little unwise for you and me to be seen talking together?"

"You'd best do as I say."

Hindley's coachman and groom were standing by the carriage when they walked up. Hindley invented errands for both of them. In two minutes they were alone.

"Get in."

Tollemache lay back on the richly upholstered seats, a cynical smile on his lips.

"Did you want me to pass on a message of congratulations to my wife for winning the Great Foal Stakes?"

Hindley's face turned fiery red.

"Don't you get clever with me, Tollemache." He leaned forward and grabbed him by the coat. "I had two thousand guineas on Anson's colt, and I've lost every penny because of that Brodie bastard you married! I'm in debt. Without Slout behind me I haven't got a hope in hell of getting into her yard and fixing that black brute before it runs away with every race there is! You saw how it ran today. It was racing against the best two-year-olds there are and it trounced them. Only Anson's colt got anywhere near it, and it left that behind at the finish by three bloody lengths!" Beads of sweat had broken out on his forehead. "You're the only one that has access to that horse, Tollemache. I want it stopped before it wins again, and I want it stopped for good."

Tollemache pulled Hindley's hand from his coat and smoothed the crumpled lapel down.

"I'm sorry, Hindley. But this time I can't help you." He got up and got out of the carriage. He glanced back at him through the carriage door. "You see, the only way you can ever beat Bloodstone is to find a colt that runs faster." He smiled. He adjusted his top hat. "As you said, without Slout behind you, you're all on your own."

PART XII
October 1837

❋ 29 ❋

It was neither the lightning nor the noise of thunder that woke her, but the sound of screaming and shouting and running footsteps down below in the cobbled yard, and bright, dancing lights that lit the whole room. Her eyes sleep-laden, Anna fumbled her way out of bed and groped at the curtains, then she realized what had happened. Struck by lightning, the whole stable block had caught fire.

For a single moment she stood hypnotized by the leaping flames. Then she threw open the window and screamed down to the boys in the yard below. Caleb looked up, a half-filled bucket of water in his hands.

"For Christ's sake, get the horses out!" She turned and fled from her room and through the house, still in her nightgown, barefoot, shouting to wake everyone at the top of her voice. When she got out into the yard everyone was running backward and forward with anything that could hold water, and Jonas and William Devine were trying to break down the stable doors.

"Ma'am, it's no use, the fire's gaining on us!"

"In God's name get out of the way!"

"More water!"

"For Christ's sake get this door open with an ax!"

The night, lit by the leaping flames, was filled with the fearful neighing of the trapped horses tied inside their stalls, then a splintering, sickening sound of breaking wood as they battered down the doors. Clouds of thick, black, acrid smoke billowed out, and the boys darted inside the stable to grab the halters of the nearest horses, fighting with them in their panic, tugging at their leading reins to get them outside to safety.

Everyone inside the house had run down into the yard.

"God 'elp us!" sobbed Jessie, her arms round Clara's shivering body. "They'll never get all them 'orses out in time . . . the other end of the stable's a wall of flame!"

Her face black with soot and grime, Anna pulled her sister from Jessie's arms. "Clara, get a bucket, anything that'll hold water . . . we need every pair of hands!"

She ran back toward the blazing building, desperately trying to count the horses that had been saved. From the flames and billowing smoke, Jonas and Elijah emerged with two more.

"Bloodstone!" she shouted at them wildly. "Bloodstone's still in there!"

"We can't get to 'im, the flames beat us back!"

"I'm going in!"

"No, Miss Anna!" Someone had grabbed her by the arm. "You can't reach 'im, the fire's got too strong an 'old!"

She shook off his hand and ran into the tack shed and seized a blanket, then she dunked it into the nearest trough. She threw it round herself and ran back toward the blazing doors, fighting with anyone that tried to get in her way. Clara grabbed hold of her sleeve.

"Don't, Anna! If you go in there you'll never get out again! Do you want to be burned to death? For God's sake, come back!"

She dashed away the dirt and sweat from her eyes.

"You know as well as I do that there's nothing any horse fears more than fire! Do you think I'm going to stand here and watch while my colt's burned alive? Get out of my way!" She pushed her aside and ran into the smoke and flames, shouting the animal's name.

Inside the whole stable was a blazing inferno. All the stalls on one side had been burned away, the roof at the far end that had caught fire first was falling in, piece by piece, and as she fought her way through the fire, lumps of burning wood fell all around her.

"Bloodstone!" She pulled the sopping-wet blanket from around herself, beating back the flames as she went, trying to hold one hand over her eyes to shield them from the suffocating heat. Then she caught sight of the terrified horse, plunging and kicking, his eyes wild with fear, desperately trying to escape from the wall of flames. There was no way she could reach him without going through the fire. Tears streaming from her eyes and mingling with the soot and grime, she ran toward him and threw the soaking blanket over his head. Then she grabbed his halter and pulled him with all her strength, crying out at the excruciating pain as the flames licked at her flesh. In front of them, part of the stable roof caved in and crashed into their path, and as Bloodstone reared up in terror, Anna grasped him by his mane and swung herself onto his back. Urging him forward with one last effort, she rode him through the wall of flame and smoke out into the yard, her hair and nightgown alight. As she fell from his back she felt someone douse her with a bucket of ice-cold water, and then throw himself on top of her to beat out the flames.

She was too shocked even to feel where the fire had burned away her skin. Rolling over, panting, blinking the sweat and tears and soot out of her eyes, she looked up into Lionel Tollemache's face. The flames from the blazing stable cast shadows across it, making deep, black hollows beneath his eyes.

"By Christ," he said, barely above a whisper, "you've got real guts." She fainted in his arms.

*   *   *

The first thing she saw was her hands, swathed in white bandages. Her head swam. As she tried to move it on the pillow she felt a weight, dull and heavy, tugging at her eyes. She tried to focus them, but everything seemed foggy and blurred.

"Bloodstone," she heard herself say, "Bloodstone."

"He's safe and sound, in a makeshift stall with the others in the coach house. Thanks to you." She opened her eyes again and saw the face of Chifney swim before her. He sat down on the edge of the bed. "We saw the flames five miles away. But by the time Inchcape had roused all the men, it was too late for us to be able to help you."

"It doesn't matter," she said, faintly.

"Anna"—he lay his hand beside her bandaged one—"they got the doctor over from Epsom. He said you'll be in a lot of pain, but that your hands will heal. He said there might not even be any scars."

She smiled, weakly.

"Does he think that I really care about that?"

Chifney looked down at them.

"Not if he knows you as well as I do."

"If you want to do something for me, call Clara on your way out. I'll need someone to help me get dressed."

"Dressed? But you can't get up yet. You're still in a state of shock!"

She struggled to sit up.

"Don't try to argue with me, Chifney. You ought to know me better than to do that. I need to start building a new stable and I need to see Bloodstone at work to find out if what happened to him last night has affected him enough to warrant my pulling him out of the Cumberland Stakes. I can't do either lying here."

"You can't run him in the Cumberland! It's only four days away!"

"When you're learning to ride and you fall off, the first thing you're supposed to do is to get back on again before you lose your nerve. It's the same with a horse. If I take him out of this race and keep him stabled all winter, by next spring I won't be able to do a thing with him. And I can't do much now with my hands like this." She held them up, helplessly. "I've always taken them for granted. Now I can't even hold a knife and fork to eat with!"

Chifney put his arm round her shoulders and held her against him. "Come on. That's not the Anna I know talking. That isn't the Anna who went into a blazing stable to rescue a horse last night, when no one else dared." He looked into her pale face, then gently lifted her bandaged hands in his own. "This was the price you paid for getting that colt out of the fire. I don't even need to ask you if you think it was worth it."

A tear welled up in the corner of one eye, and she blinked it away again.

"No, you don't need to ask. Help me up, please . . . I want to go to him."

*   *   *

She stood in the yard with a blanket around her, staring at the burned-out wreckage of the stable. The blackened wood still smoldered. What had cooled and could be taken away was being shifted by the boys in wheelbarrows and dumped into one of the carts.

Without speaking, Anna walked toward the ruins and looked at them. How close she had come to being a part of them. She remembered the dull, aching feeling of anger and despair that she'd felt before, when all her cherished hopes for Bloodstone's dam had ended, but she did not feel that same anger and despair now. There was no need. Her hands would heal. Bloodstone would race again. Maybe, as Jessie believed, there was a God after all. She turned back to Chifney.

"Has anyone seen my husband?"

"I saw him walking that way, not long after I arrived."

Anna nodded. Drawing the blanket closer around her, she began to walk away.

He was leaning against a tree when she found him, gazing into the distance toward the shrubs and evergreens, hatless, his dark hair blowing in the stiff breeze.

"They tell me the storm blew some trees down last night," he said as she came up, without turning round. "Until they shift them, the Epsom road will stay blocked. The mail coach will be late today."

She watched him for a moment.

"Why did you do it, Lionel? Why did you save me?" Slowly, he turned round and looked at her. A faint smile played at the corners of his lips. He looked ill. His face was drawn and pale. There were dark circles beneath his eyes.

"The devil looks after his own, don't they say?" He held up his hands to her. "Not a single burn. Maybe I won't even burn when I go to hell."

"You still haven't answered me."

He laughed, softly.

"My dear Anna . . . I'd be the first to admit that despite being born with all my advantages, I've led a useless, idle existence. Unlike you. Perhaps what I did for you last night is the one true act of worth I shall ever do. I don't regret it."

She had never expected to feel anything for him other than disgust and pity. But at that moment she came as near as she could to liking him.

"She's crazy to run that horse! The fire was only four days ago! No high-strung animal could get over something like that in less than six months!"

"His mane and tail are still singed, I can see it from here!"

"He doesn't stand a chance."

"Walton's Otho's been walked down from Newmarket and they reckon he's the fastest thing this side of London!"

"The crowd have gone wild over her! Listen to the cheers!"

"She's got guts, you've got to give her that."

With her hands still heavily bandaged, Anna walked down into the Warren with Chifney from the carriage stand, people running to get a glimpse of her as she appeared. She could see the rows of curious, avid faces staring at her, looking at her hands, whispering behind their own. As she caught sight of Bloodstone being saddled up, his tail and mane badly singed from the fire, she felt a lump rising in her throat. Maybe she was wrong. Maybe it was a mistake to run him. Maybe he'd fail and trail in last and she would lose face. She tried to stroke his neck and muzzle with her clumsy, bandaged hands, but the pain was so great whenever she touched anything that even that small comfort was denied her. Instead, she lay her head against his singed mane, and he turned his head and nuzzled at her hair.

Chifney was given a leg up into the saddle, and she stepped back as he rode Bloodstone by.

"Don't use the whip on him. I'd rather he lost the race than you did that."

"This is the only colt I've ever ridden who doesn't need one."

She looked away and straight into the eyes of Ralph Russell.

He could only just have gotten back to Epsom. Their eyes met and held across the crowded Warren. A solid wall of people, twenty deep, prevented either from reaching the other. Then she caught sight of Jacob Hindley, inching his way toward Russell from behind.

"I'm warning you, Russell. Have anything more to do with that Brodie bitch . . . and I tell everything I know about Mary." Russell turned and looked down at him. His small, malicious eyes glinted in his face like a lizard's. "You know me well enough to know that I never make idle threats. Think about it." He disappeared again into the crowd.

Slowly, Russell tried to make his way toward her, and she to him. There was no way that she could reach the edge of the course to see the race through the vast crowds. There was no time to get back to the grandstand and watch from her box. She stood there, not hearing the noise and chatter around her, never taking her eyes from his face. When he finally got to the spot where she was she needed all her iron self-restraint not to throw herself into his arms.

"It's been a long time, Anna."

"Yes, it's been a long time." They could scarcely hear each other speak with the commotion and din all around them. "I'm sorry about your uncle."

He looked down at her hands and gently touched them.

"They told me about the fire as soon as I got back. Chifney said you were burned when you went in after Bloodstone."

"Burned hands were a small price to pay."

"No other woman would say that."

She held them up, like useless things. "I saved him, and I can't even see him run in this race."

"We'll see about that." He took her by the wrist and began leading her away toward where a solitary carriage stood, surrounded by the cheering, waving crowd. "Hold your hands high above your head so that you can't knock them. That's it." He took her by the waist and lifted her up onto the driver's seat, then climbed up beside her himself. "Carefully, now. Step backward, look where you're going. Step onto the roof. I've got you. You're quite safe." She paused, and looked into his eyes.

"Am I?"

Below them, the vast sea of heads moved to and fro, like ripples on a lake. Then the whole Downs seemed to explode in a deafening orchestra of noise.

The field sped round Tattenham Corner, tightly bunched together, and her eyes swiftly sought Chifney in her pale blue colors, but he was hemmed in within a wall of horses. Walton's Otho, his jockey a blob of brilliant red, surged into the lead with Colonel Anson's chestnut colt close to his girths, and she heard the crowd roar for Bloodstone. As the field quickly spread out, she saw Chifney urge him through the sudden opening and ride him hands and heels for all he was worth. Before she knew what she was doing, she was waving her bandaged hands in the air and screaming Bloodstone's name. For a moment she felt dizzy. Tears stung her eyes. Tears of emotion that she could not even begin to understand. Tears of happiness. Tears of pride. Then the image of smoke and fire faded and she saw him drawing level with the two leading horses, his singed tail flying out behind him in the wind.

She was crying so much that the tears blinded her and she never saw him streak past them and reach the winning post five lengths clear.

PART XIII
April 1838

❋ 30 ❋

Without speaking, the two girls entered the churchyard by the lych-gate and made their way between the headstones, picking their separate paths carefully among the nettles and cow parsley and weeds. Wildflowers had sprung up here and there, cowslips, hellebore and primroses, clumps of bluebells and celandine, and they both knelt now and then, gathering their own bouquets to add to the flowers they had brought with them. When they reached their mother's grave they lay them at the foot of the headstone and stepped back, hand in hand.

"If only she could have lived long enough to be here now," Clara said, wiping her eyes. "If only she could have, Anna. Seven years. It seems so much longer than that."

Anna was silent. She stood there staring at the words on the headstone for several more moments, then she turned and walked back the way they had come.

Tom Tradescant's barouche was waiting in the courtyard when they arrived back home again, and they caught sight of him as they rode up to the house from the drive, leaning over one of the paddock fences watching Caleb lunging one of Sam Loam's new horses. When he turned his head and saw them he smiled and waved, and began to walk across the courtyard to meet them.

"Are you coming to watch Chifney ride my filly in the Gold Cup this afternoon?" His gray eyes lingered on Clara's face. "I reckon she stands as good a chance as any if she doesn't run too green."

"We'll be there."

He smiled. "And if you can spare me a moment, there's something I have to ask you in private."

Anna glanced at Clara and saw her face turn pale.

"Yes, of course. Come on into the library." She watched her sister take the reins of their horses and walk disconsolately away, dragging her feet, eyes downcast. When Anna and Tradescant had disappeared into the house, she made her way toward the stable. She wanted to be alone, but Elijah was there, wisping down Bloodstone. When he saw her, he put down his brushes and took the reins.

"No, Elijah. I can see you're busy. Let me take off their saddles. I don't have anything else to do."

"'Tain't your job, Miss Clara."

She forced a smile onto her lips.

"There are some things I can do besides playing a piano." She began to unbuckle her own horse's girths, slowly. "How did he go this morning? Anna said you ran him with Gilbert Heathcote's colt, the one he reckons he'll run in the Derby."

"Amato? Bloodstone beat 'im by two clear lengths, and 'e wasn't pushed." He stopped what he was doing and slapped the colt on the rump. "The only thing that's going to beat this one, miss, is 'orse with wings."

Across the courtyard, Tom Tradescant emerged from the house and got into his barouche. Clara stood watching him, stiffly, her heart in her mouth. He looked around him for a moment, then picked up the reins and slapped them against the horses' backs, and disappeared in a cloud of dust down the drive. She dropped the saddle and ran into the house.

"Anna?" She hesitated in the doorway of the library, uncertainly. "Can I speak to you?"

Anna looked up from a pile of papers. "Why does everyone want to speak to me all of a sudden?" She laughed. "Get yourself a chair."

Clara stayed standing.

"I know what he wanted to talk to you about."

"Do you?"

"He asked you to marry him, didn't he?"

Anna lay down her pen and looked up. There was no expression on her face. "Actually, he asked me if he could marry you."

"Anna!" She ran over to her and seized her by the hand. "What did you tell him?"

She lay back in her chair and began to rock with laughter.

"You little fool! I told him to ask you himself."

"But he just went away! He didn't even come looking for me!"

"And I thought you were the romantic one of the two of us! Would you rather he asked you in the courtyard or in his private box in the grandstand?"

Clara went down on her knees and threw her arms around Anna's neck. "Anna . . . before I went away to London I said a lot of things to you . . . things that were hateful and mean. Can you forgive me for them?"

Anna stroked her dark, glossy, fragrant hair. It reminded her of Anna Maria's, when she had held her close as a child, in the long-distant past.

"I forgave them a long time ago."

Anna stood on the edge of the course with Sam Loam, looking toward Tattenham Corner, shading her eyes against the bright glare of the afternoon sun. The horses had been late going down to post. There had been more than an hour's delay before the start. She waited, half-oblivious to all the noise about her, every nerve and muscle tensed, her ears straining for the familiar sound of thundering hoofbeats drumming on the turf.

As the field swept around the wide bend into the straight, she caught sight of Chifney in Tom Tradescant's scarlet colors, lying close behind the leaders; but as he suddenly began to urge the filly forward, the cheer ready in Anna's throat froze there, and became, instead, a wild, strangled cry.

The horse in front slipped and pitched into his mount, and he was catalpulted over its head like a stone and tossed straight into the path of the oncoming field.

Anna screamed out his name as she ran.

She fought her way through the crowd to get to him. She went down on her knees and cradled his bleeding head in her lap. She held his hand tightly, rubbing it desperately between her own as if by doing so she could bring back warmth to its coldness.

"It's all right. Lie still. Sam's run back to the grandstand to fetch a doctor."

Chifney looked up into her face with dull, heavy-lidded eyes. There was a faint smile on his torn, bleeding lips.

"Anna . . . remember what I said." He swallowed, and blood oozed out from one corner of his mouth. "This is the best way to go . . ."

Slowly, Anna drew the curtains. She went over to the mantlepiece and leaned against it, with her eyes closed. She felt too numb to cry. The clock on the mantlepiece began to chime and she felt the vibrations beneath her hands.

"Anna?" said Lionel Tollemache from the door.

She glanced up at him, wondering why she hadn't noticed up until now how ill he looked. His eyes were sunk deeper into their dark-rimmed sockets. His skin was yellowed, and stretched so tightly over the bones in his face that he seemed older by twenty years.

"Something's wrong, isn't it? I knew the moment you came back."

"Did you?"

He came into the room and closed the door quietly behind him. "I haven't lived with you for nearly four years without learning something."

She leaned against the fireplace. She sighed and covered her eyes with her hands.

"There was an accident on the course this afternoon. One of the horses slid on the wet ground and knocked Tom Tradescant's filly." She paused. "Chifney was killed."

For a long moment there was silence.

"And you're thinking what a waste that was. It should have been me."

"I didn't say that!"

"But it's true." He poured himself a drink of brandy and began sipping it. "It isn't fair, is it, Anna? The way fate goes. Someone like Chifney, trampled to death. And me . . . I'm still here."

"It wasn't your fault."

He finished his drink and put down the glass. He smiled.

"I'm sorry, Anna. Yes, I mean that. I know how much you thought of him. Why don't you go up to your room and have a good cry?"

She turned on him, furiously.

"You bastard!"

"You've misunderstood me, Anna. What I meant was that it'll make you feel better if you do."

She went over to the window and stared out.

"I've got something for you." Behind her, she heard him walk across the floor and lay something down on her desk. "I decided on it while you were out. Here."

"Whatever it is, I don't want it."

"I think you'll want this."

She looked round at him, then her eyes fell upon her desk. In the middle of it lay a small package tied with ribbon. On top of it he had placed a single flower.

"Well, aren't you going to open it?"

Woodenly, she moved over to the desk and picked it up. She broke open the outer wrapping and pulled away the ribbon. Inside was a letter. Frowning, she unfolded and read it, then she stared up at him, open-mouthed. Her voice was a barely audible whisper. "Why have you done this?"

He smiled as he went over to the door.

"Let us just say that this makes us even."

Suddenly, the cold numbness in her limbs began to thaw and leave her. Blood pounded in her brain. Her hands shook. This was it. This was what she had wanted to bring down Jacob Hindley. As she moved to run out after him she noticed that one of the drawers in her desk was slightly open, the drawer where she kept her pistol.

And the drawer was empty.

She stood for a moment in the deserted grandstand, looking around her. How different it was without the crowds, the horses, the noise, the cheering. Her booted footsteps echoed eerily as she crossed the floor and lightly went up the wide flight of stone steps to the floor above, and stopped outside one of the doors.

She could hear talking from the other side, and for a few minutes she waited, listening. Then she opened the door and went in.

"Mrs. Tollemache!" said Henry Dorling, the clerk of the course, getting to his feet. He stared at her. Every face around the table followed suit. Her eyes fell on Russell's, and she smiled.

"Mr. Dorling. Gentlemen. Forgive me for interrupting your meeting."

Dorling pushed back his chair and came over to her.

"Mrs. Tollemache . . . I'm afraid that I must ask you to leave at once.

This is a private Jockey Club meeting . . . any outsiders are strictly forbidden entry . . ."

She looked around the company without speaking. There were many faces she knew. Mostly friends. Some indifferent. A handful of enemies. At the far end of the table she noticed that Jacob Hindley had been the last man to rise to his feet. He was watching her now, the hostility plain in his eyes.

"Did you hear what Mr. Dorling said, Mrs. Tollemache? No admittance to outsiders. You've already taken far too many liberties, pushing yourself in where no woman has any business to be, having the gall to put yourself on a par with men, taking advantage of your sex to ride roughshod over other people's rules!" His face grew redder with anger. "It was a sorry day when they let you onto the course." He ignored the shouts of protest from several of the others around him. "But don't think that because of that you can just walk in here when you please. Racing and the business of it are matters for the minds of men!"

"Then what are you doing here, you crooked little pervert?" Into the horrified silence she opened her leather reticule and brought out Tollemache's letter. "Do you recognize this handwriting?"

Knots stood out on his forehead. His eyes bulged in their sockets.

"You bitch! You've been on my back ever since you came to Epsom! I'll sue you for slander for every penny you have!"

She smiled.

"Certainly, you can sue anyone for slander. But you can't sue them for telling the truth." She held up the letter. "I always suspected it was you who was supplying information to Tobias Slout, gleaned from confidences at Jockey Club meetings and in the drawing rooms of people that thought they were your friends. You cheated John Dewar and Edward Randyll. Everything that Slout did you had a hand in; he might have done your dirty work for you but you were steeped in just the same filth! You blackballed Tom Tradescant's application to the Jockey Club out of pure spite, and you sent my husband's brother into my yard, pretending he was interested in my sister, so that he could spy on me and pass on information to you about my horses."

"That's a damned lie, Anna Brodie! I scarcely knew him!"

"That wasn't the impression I got when I saw you and him in bed together on the night of the King's Cup . . . engaged in practices of a most revolting and disgusting nature, which cannot decently be spoken of here."

He swallowed. He looked round at all the others, frantically. "It's a lie. All of it. Can't you see that? To ruin me. That's what she's always wanted. She's trying to blacken my good name, just out of spite." Slowly, they moved away from him. He stood there in the middle of the room, alone. "Surely you don't take her word against mine? I'm a gentleman. No one can doubt my word!"

"I haven't finished yet, Hindley." She handed the letter to Henry Dorling. "The biggest mistake you ever made was telling my husband . . . because before he shot himself, he wrote it all down. Including how you blackmailed Ralph Russell for years, threatening to accuse him of knocking his wife, your sister, downstairs, when you yourself admitted it was an accident." She took back the letter from Henry Dorling. "It's all here, Hindley. Every word."

Trapped, Hindley faced her like a cornered rat.

"You can't use the testimony of a dead man in a court of law!"

"That's where you're wrong. What's written down here has as much force as a man's own will."

Suddenly, he made a wild lunge toward the door, pushing her aside. He ran out, along the deserted echoing passages, down the great staircase to the public hall. Ruined. All over. There was still time. A post chaise to Dover. A boat to France. Safety from prosecution. Punishment. Death. Bitch, Brodie bitch! Never in his life had he hated as he hated her. But as he reached the bottom of the steps that led from the grandstand to the course, two of the constable's men stepped forward, barring his path with their staves, and he was trapped. He looked desperately from left to right, and back again.

But there was no escape.

Jessie was the first one she saw. She ran to her, grabbed the tray she was carrying out of her arms, and danced her round and round the hall.

"He's finished, Jessie! Hindley's finished! They arrested him outside the grandstand!"

"Oh, you mad creature, you! You've gone and upset my china! 'Urry along into that morning room right now. There's a nice young man bin waiting to see you this last hour or more . . . don't keep 'im waiting about no longer!"

Anna frowned.

"Who is it?"

"Don't ask me. Ellen opened the door to 'im and she's gone out to my 'erb garden to pick me some rosemary and thyme for the roast duck. Well, go on, then!"

Anna went along the corridor and into the little-used morning room, then received one of the greatest shocks of her life.

"Hello, Anna," William Hubbard said.

He had grown stouter from good living. The lean, clever face she remembered behind the desk at Tuke, Benet, and Tuke had coarsened and filled out. He had dressed himself in the garb of a gentleman of means, but places on the elegantly cut frock coat were worn. "You don't seem very pleased to see me."

She slammed the door shut behind her.

"What do you want?"

"Well, you do surprise me." He smiled at her. "That isn't much of a welcome, after all these years." He glanced around the room, at the silver and paintings. "You've done well, Anna, with your share of the inheritance. But then I always knew you would." He seated himself in a chair without being asked. "And to think that if it hadn't been for me you would have gotten nothing!"

So, that was his game!

"You want money?"

"I always did admire your lightning mind." He reached out and picked up a china ornament. "Very tasteful. Quite exquisite. Expensive, I shouldn't wonder. And of course, money doesn't buy everything, does it? Like your success with horses. But unfortunately it's essential for the more mundane things in life."

She stood in front of him, her hands on her hips.

"Five years ago I gave you a small fortune in exchange for your promise to take it and never bother me again. You said you were going away to live abroad. What you did for me you did out of pure self-interest, and you were more than well paid for it. If you chose to squander your share of the money that's no concern of mine. I couldn't care less. But if you've come back here looking for another handout, then I'm afraid you're going to be disappointed."

"Oh, dear, Anna. I had hoped you wouldn't say that. You have all this," he spread out his arms, "and I have so little. Not much more than the clothes I stand up in. I thought I knew you, but I see I don't. I would never have said that you were greedy . . ."

"You dare!"

"Things haven't gone well with me, Anna . . . it's expensive, living abroad, the kind of life I was living. I daresay I could have managed, if I hadn't taken a fancy to gambling for high stakes. Well, no gentleman worth the name could refuse to play when he was in his hostess's house, now could he? And habits die hard."

"Get out of here!"

"I want five thousand pounds, Anna." He stopped smiling. "You have three days to get it for me."

"Don't talk through your arse. Even if I wanted to do you think I keep that kind of brass lying around? Everything I have is invested in this house, in the stable and horses. Half the inheritance was put into a trust for my sister when she marries, or reaches the age of twenty-one. I can't touch it. If I need any large amount for an emergency, I'd have to sell something before I could raise it."

"Then sell that horse of yours. You could ask twice as much as I need for him, and they'd be falling over themselves to buy!"

"*Sell Bloodstone?*" She stared at him in disbelief. "After what I've gone through to breed a colt that can win the Derby? After I nursed his dam back from death's door to breed with her, after I risked my own life to save him from the stable when it caught fire? Are you crazy? If I was starving and didn't have the price of a crust I wouldn't sell that horse!"

"You can't run him in the Derby or in any other race unless you sell him first. You know that. When your husband died all his nominations for the rest of the year became null and void. And you can't race him anymore under your own name. Checkmate, Anna."

She walked over to the door and opened it.

"The front door's at the end of the corridor."

He got up, but made no movement to leave. "I think you're forgetting something. That you don't really have any choice. You see, if you don't sell him and get that money, I shall be forced to tell certain persons the facts about your father's will. Remember what you said to me that day in the church at Epsom, when he sent me to find you? The punishment for forgery is transportation for life." A sly note came into his voice. "You wouldn't like me to talk, would you, Anna?"

Her heart began to beat very fast.

"It's only your word against mine that the will was forged."

"It would be, but for one thing. I still have the original will."

Slowly, she closed the door.

"You're lying, Hubbard. I burned it, in the grate of that inn at Newmarket after you gave it to me."

"You burned a copy, yes. But surely you don't think I'd be so stupid as to destroy the original. One never knows when such a valuable document will come in useful . . . how does the saying go? Never throw away dirty water before you get clean."

"You bastard!"

He walked over to her, putting on his hat at an angle as he went. "No, Anna. I believe the word suits you better. My father married my mother before I was born."

She grabbed him by the collar with both hands.

"You should have been smothered at birth!"

There was no trace of rancor in his eyes as he looked at her. Gently, he disengaged himself from her grasp.

"Three days, Anna. Or take the consequences."

She wandered distractedly into the yard, then into the gardens. She walked and walked, hatless, without a cloak, her dark hair loose and streaming behind her in the wind. Even when it began to rain she went on, stumbling on the uneven ground, getting up again, pulling herself up the steep slope beyond the orchard toward the woods at the crest of the hill. Finally, out of breath, she lay against the trunk of a tree and covered her face with her hands.

This, then, was to be the end. There was no answer. There was no escape. She was caught in a trap of her own making, and there was no way out. Everything she had built, everything she had fought for would be destroyed by that one act of dishonesty, an act prompted not by spite, or wickedness, or even greed, but by her own sense of what was just. It was the final, bitter irony that because of that, she would be remembered and branded for what she herself had spent the last five years fighting against.

She looked down below, beyond the line of trees and the roof of the house and stables, and saw Ralph Russell riding into the yard. Panting, struggling for her breath, she flattened herself against the tree. Then she moved stealthily around it, hiding herself from view. This she could never tell him. Never share with him. Never expect him to forgive, or understand. For what she had made herself party to was no accident but a willful, deliberate act.

She watched him at the door. Somebody had let him inside. After several minutes he came out again, with Jessie, and she saw him beckon to Jonas and Elijah and all of them run in different directions, looking for her.

The rain began to fall, heavier, soaking her hair and clothes. But he was still there. Still looking for her. Not till he had gone could she go back.

✳ 31 ✳

She scarcely slept, for three nights. Each time exhaustion pushed her beyond the bounds of consciousness she awoke again, panting, sweating, tormented by her dreams. Dreams of leaping flames; her mother's deathbed; Chifney's blood-splattered face; Slout's screams of agony. Then they faded and she found herself instead surrounded by a jeering, hostile crowd who barred her way, and every face became the faces of Hindley and Hubbard.

Trapped by the milling bodies around her, she fought to reach Bloodstone, and Clara, and Russell, but suddenly there was quicksand all around her and she could not move. She struggled, desperately, clutching at the air while her tormentors mocked and taunted her; then slowly she felt herself engulfed in suffocating darkness, dragged down and under, deeper, and deeper than before until it enveloped her completely, blotting out all pain and fear.

She awoke with a start, her heart hammering, perspiration running from her face. Outside, the sky was growing dark. Downstairs she heard a clock chime the hour, deep and solemn like a death knell. Three days had gone by. Her time was up. As she walked down the staircase and heard the knocking at the front door, she knew it was him.

She received him in the library, her back toward the door. She heard Ellen announce him, and then his hated voice.

"All alone, Anna?"

"So you've come back."

"I said that I would." He came further into the room, forgetting in his haste to close the door. "Surely you didn't doubt my word?"

Slowly, she turned to face him. Now that the worse had come to the worst, she felt almost calm. Clara and Jessie would be safe with Tom Tradescant. He would take care of them. They did not need her now.

"Do you have the money?"

She looked at him, a smile on her lips. She felt suddenly reckless and light-headed, as if she had drunk too much wine on an empty stomach. She had gambled and she'd lost; this time it was her turn to prove that she could be a good loser, too.

"How do I know that you're not bluffing, Hubbard? You've already cheated me once. If you kept the original will that my father made, where is it?"

"I have it here." He opened his frock coat and held it out of her reach. "Shall I read it to you?"

"I already know what it says."

"There is . . . one other way out for you . . ." he smiled and came toward her. "And if you can't bear to part with that nag of yours, it's the only thing you can do to save yourself." He touched her hand. "If you were to marry me . . . after a suitable period of mourning for your husband . . . it would insure my continued silence; and I could go on living in the manner to which your money has made me very much accustomed."

She threw off his hand.

"Me? Marry you? A grubby little second-rate clerk? What bad taste you credit me with!"

All laughter died from his eyes. He walked backward, away from her. "I'm going to make you so sorry for saying that, Anna. Unless you give me that money right now."

"I haven't got the money. And even if I did have it, you'd never get your dirty little thieving hands on another penny of it!"

"All right. All right, if that's the way you want it. Now I'll have my say. Before I leave. Before I go and show this will to the constable in Epsom. This is the will your father made years ago, the will that was written out and witnessed by Old Tuke, when he was alive, leaving everything to Lilly Brodie and his two sons. Five years ago, your father changed his mind. Old Tuke was dead and his nephew left everything to do with running the business to me, while he stayed an idle figurehead. Your father knew he was dying. He sent me to find you and bring you back to Newmarket, so that he could see you for the last time." Suddenly, Hubbard started to laugh. "Don't you see, Anna? Don't you see the joke? The will that gave you most of the Brodie inheritance that was read out that day . . . that was his new will. It wasn't a forgery." He began to rock with laughter. "It was so simple. Instead of destroying the old will when the new one was written, as Old Tuke would have done, I kept it and showed it to you. I told you it was his only will, and you believed me. And the new will your father had me write out, you thought was a forgery, just because I said so. You must see the irony, Anna! You paid me for nothing. I contrived the whole scheme for my own ends, and you handed me a slice of your inheritance just on the strength of my word. It was so easy to trick you, clever as you are. You hated your father so much that you were ready to believe anything of him."

She stood watching him while he rocked with silent laughter.

"What my father left me he really meant me to have, and because of you I've gone on believing all these years that he died without leaving me a penny?"

"That's right, Anna. But unfortunately for you, who is going to believe it?" He picked up his hat and turned toward the door, and found himself face to face with Ralph Russell.

"Ralph!"

"I came looking for you three days ago, and nobody knew where you were. Since then you've been trying to avoid me, Anna." He looked from her to Hubbard. "Now I understand why."

Hubbard turned pale.

"Who in God's name are you?"

"Someone who heard every word you said and intends to kick your worthless arse right out of this house!" Hubbard tried to rush past him but Russell grabbed him roughly by the collar of his coat. "Give me that will before I break your neck!"

"Let go of me!"

Russell tightened his grip on Hubbard's collar.

"Shall we do this the easy way or the hard way? The choice is yours."

Without warning, Hubbard raised his free arm and hit Russell a stinging blow in the face, knocking him away. Then, as Russell quickly got to his feet and came toward him, Hubbard picked up a chair and hit him so hard with it that it splintered into pieces, and across the room Anna cried out in alarm. He made another lunge toward the door, but Russell caught up with him and they fought punch for punch for several minutes, crashing against the furniture, breaking everything in their way. Then Russell gave him one final, crashing blow to the jaw, and Hubbard fell backward with a shout of pain, knocking aside everything in his path. He lay there in the middle of the floor in a crumpled heap; panting, bleeding from the nose and mouth.

Before Anna could rush to Russell's side he had hauled Hubbard to his feet. He was sweating profusely. Blood trickled from the cuts about his face where Hubbard had hit him.

"All right . . . are you going to hand over that will, or do you want some more?"

Hubbard hung his head, fighting for his breath. He fumbled inside his frock coat and brought it out, then dropped it on the floor. Russell shook him roughly.

"It's your decision, Anna. Do you want me to haul him up in front of the constable . . . or shall I just throw him out?"

Slowly, Hubbard raised his head and looked at her. The flesh around his eyes was beginning to discolor and swell. There were dark, angry patches on his face and neck, and congealed rivulets of blood.

"I thought I'd seen the depths with Tobias Slout and Jacob Hindley," she said in a voice that was barely above a whisper. "But I reckoned without you." She thought of the past three fear-filled days and sleepless nights, bitterly. "Do you know what kind of hell you put me through?" There was no answer. "Take him out of my sight, Ralph!"

Angrily, crying with relief and fright, she stooped down and picked up the will, then threw it upon the fire.

She was standing with her head against the mantlepiece when Russell came back. Without turning she heard his footsteps behind her, then the soft click of the door as he closed it quietly behind him. For a long moment neither of them spoke. The only sounds in the room were the ticking of the clock and the crackling of the fire. Then Russell came across to her and lay his hands on her shoulders.

"You should have told me, Anna." His grip tightened. "You should have trusted me enough to tell me everything." He pulled her round to face him. "For Christ's sake, why didn't you?"

Slowly, she raised her eyes to his face.

"Do I really need to answer that?"

"You think I would have turned against you? You think I wouldn't have understood? In God's name, what kind of man do you take me for?"

"You heard what Hubbard said. It was all true, every single word. I did plot with him to change my father's will. I didn't need any persuading. I was an equal partner in an act of criminal forgery and I knew what I was doing every step of the way, including the consequences if anyone ever found out the truth. But just because it now turns out that Hubbard was lying and the will leaving Clara and me almost everything was genuine after all, that doesn't change what I did five years ago. In the eyes of the law I'm still guilty."

"And if I'd found myself in your place I would have done exactly the same."

"You don't have to lie to me to make me feel better."

"I've never lied to you. In the past, for reasons you already know about, I had to keep some things from you . . . yes. But that isn't the same, Anna."

"Whatever you had to do in your life, you'd never have done anything that was dishonest. I know that much about you."

He smiled. "Maybe not." His hands slid from her shoulders to her waist. "But whether something's honest or dishonest isn't always clear . . . and not everything that a man does that's wrong is punishable by the law . . . you should know that, of all people." His grip tightened about her. "I've never told you this before, Anna . . . not even on that night when you rode after me to tell me the real reasons why you'd married Lionel Tollemache . . . I don't know why. Maybe I didn't have enough courage to tell you then. Maybe I wasn't sure of myself. Maybe I still wasn't sure of you, and what you might say to me if I told you the truth." He reached out, gently, and touched a loose strand of her hair. "But every time you and I have been together, I've fought with myself not to tell you. Even when you hated me, I loved you so much that it hurt."

Her lips turned up at the corners in a ghost of a smile.

"You thought I hated you? Did I really manage to hide my feelings so well?"

PART XIV
May 1838

❄ 32 ❄

She sat on the paddock fence, watching Bloodstone at the far end of it, his black coat gleaming like glass in the hard May sunlight, cropping at the lush spring grass. There was a lump in her throat as she looked at him, the colt she had bred to win the Derby that he could now never race in. It was an irony to think that had Lionel Tollemache lived for one more month, he could have done it. But without Tollemache's name she was helpless.

Slowly, she got down and began to walk away, arms hanging at her sides, eyes downcast. Out on the Downs since before dawn there would have started massing the vast Derby crowds, teeming in their thousands like ants, every road leading to the racecourse would be clogged with riders and anything on four wheels that could hold human beings. Clara would already be with Tom Tradescant in his box inside the packed grandstand, wearing her new satin and velvet gown, gazing down across the Warren and the course; everyone she knew would be there, caught up in the excitement and the cheering and the deafening noise.

She thought of the rows upon rows of carriages, with spectators standing on the drivers' boxes and the roofs to get a better view, the crowds packed around the winning post and the judge's chair. She thought of the field thundering down past Tattenham Corner and into the long straight, hooves pounding the ground, clods of turf flying as they swept past, a blaze of shimmering coats and jockeys' colors that flashed by in a moment like a huge blurred rainbow, and tears began to sting at the back of her eyes.

She stopped walking and looked back toward the paddock. Bloodstone had stopped cropping the grass and had come over to the near side of the fence. He raised his head and neighed.

She turned away again and began to walk toward the house. Then she slowed down, and looked again over her shoulder. He was still looking at her. The farther she walked away from him, the closer he came. Suddenly, she turned and ran toward him, like a demented thing. She unlatched the paddock gate and caught him by the bridle. Then she led him into the stable and pulled a saddle from the wall.

The crowds were more vast than she had ever seen before, more jubilant, more noisy, even more difficult to make her way through. Maybe it was because for the first time in history excursion trains had come to within five miles of the course itself, bringing with them hundreds of extra spectators, most of whom had been used to walking from eight to fifteen miles for their sport.

Dismounting half a mile away from the course, Anna walked Bloodstone the rest of the way, pausing once to take a stone from her shoe and to let him drink from a nearby stream. When she arrived the horses for the Derby were already leaving the Warren, and she fought a path through the solid wall of bodies to catch up with them. But she and Bloodstone had been recognized. People were beginning to turn in their dozens, to stand and stare, whispering behind hands; gentlemen doffed their top hats, moving back as best they could to let her go past. Training grooms and stable lads, hurrying to get their owners' colts off to post, stopped what they were doing and stood gawping at her, as if somebody had turned them all to stone.

That was when she saw young William Devine, standing among the crowds outside the Warren.

For a moment he stared at her in blank dismay; then he raised his hand and waved to her, making his way toward her with difficulty through the milling crowds.

"Miss Anna! What in the world are you doing here?"

For an answer, she thrust a small bundle into his hands.

"When you first came into my yard looking for work, I asked you what you wanted to do more than anything else, and you said you wanted to ride like Jeremiah Chifney. Well, I'm giving you the chance to prove yourself." Slowly, disbelievingly, he unrolled the racing silks in his hands. "If he was here now, he'd be riding Bloodstone in the Derby. Will you take his place?"

He looked up at her, then down at her racing colors in his hands. "But Miss Anna, they'll never let you run the horse, you know that. When Mr. Tollemache died all his race nominations became null and void. And the Jockey Club already ruled against you entering horses under your own name, long before that!"

"I know his nomination for Bloodstone to run in the Derby is null and void. And what the Jockey Club ruled. But that makes no difference to me, William Devine. I bred this colt to run today no matter what, and not all the hounds of hell are going to stop me."

"But Miss Anna!"

"You haven't got time to run back to the weighing shed and change. You'll have to do it here. Hurry up! Take off your shirt and pull the silk breeches over your own."

He put out his hands in exasperation.

"But what about the weight? My cloth breeches are as heavy as a dozen pair of these flimsy things!"

"If you were wearing armor it wouldn't slow Bloodstone down."

As the crowds of spectators looked on in dismay, the boy pulled Anna's blue silks over his head and stumbled into the white silken breeches. As they began to understand what was happening, a shout went up that Bloodstone was in the race.

"It's the Brodie colt! She's put an apprentice up, in her colors!"

"The nag's not even on the race card!"

"He wasn't even mentioned down at the betting stand!"

"She can't enter him, it isn't legal!"

"Make way, make way! It's Henry Dorling!"

There was no groom to lead Bloodstone out of the Warren and down to the gate from which the others were already leaving to go to post. Anna took the colt by the bridle as soon as William Devine was in the saddle, and began to lead him there herself. As the crowds on the other side of the course caught sight of her, a great roar went up that sang almost painfully in her ears. But before she could pass through the opening at the end of the Warren, they came face to face with the clerk of the course.

"Mrs. Tollemache," Henry Dorling said, gravely, "I'm afraid you can't enter that horse. You already know why." He tried to look sorry for what he was going to say. "All your late husband's nominations became null and void from the moment of his death . . . and a long time ago the stewards at the Jockey Club in Newmarket passed an official ruling barring you from entering any horse under your own name."

"I know Tollemache's nominations are null and void. And what the Jockey Club said about me. But none of that counts anymore." She took a deep breath, then said the first thing that came into her head. "The colt isn't entered in the Derby under Tollemache's name or mine. He's entered in Ralph Russell's."

Dorling stared at her.

"This is the first I've heard of it. No Derby nomination from Lord Russell has been received for this colt or any other. And what's more, this lad is wearing your own personal colors."

"If you haven't received his nomination yet, it must have got lost, somewhere or other. That's nothing to do with me. As for the colors, I don't have any. You yourself just said that the Jockey Club stewards banned me from racing horses a long time ago . . . from that moment my colors ceased to exist, isn't that right? Lord Russell's jockey is only wearing this old shirt because his own, with the proper colors, has gotten mislaid somewhere in the weighing shed, and he hasn't got time enough to look for it."

William Devine struggled to keep his face as straight as Anna's. Dorling looked from one to the other, uncertainly.

"You're correct, of course." He gave her a stiff, frigid little bow. "I shall go myself and find Lord Russell so that he can sign a duplicate nomination for the horse."

"Are you calling me a liar?"

Dorling's white, narrow face went whiter still.

"By no means, Mrs. Tollemache. But the rules of racing as laid down by the stewards are clear. There must be a written nomination from the owner of a horse before it can be permitted to enter a race, otherwise any subsequent win would not be officially recognized. Surely you of all people know that?"

"Yes. I know that, You'd best find Lord Russell then." She gave William Devine a single knowing glance, then turned away and pushed her way back frantically through the milling crowd.

Halfway across the paddock she halted and looked back. The boy had ridden Bloodstone out of the gate, and was cantering him on toward the start. For a moment she watched him, a lump in her throat. Then she turned and elbowed her way ruthlessly toward the packed grandstand as fast as she could.

She collided with people. She stumbled, cursing beneath her breath as she nearly tripped. Her bonnet fell off and her long, heavy hair escaped from its combs and tumbled down about her back and shoulders. At the grandstand entrance she grasped a shocked top-hatted gentleman by the wrist.

"Have you seen Lord Russell? Has he come onto the course?" She was out of breath. She leaned against a marble pillar and dashed away a strand of hair from her face. "Lord Russell, for God's sake!"

When he stared at her blankly she waved her hand with impatience and brushed past him into the packed building, looking desperately around her at the sea of faces. No sign.

She ran around like a demented thing, her eyes searching every corner. Then she lifted the hem of her trailing gown and ran upstairs into the crowded salon. There were cries of dismay as she rushed by, knocking everyone from her path. Then, at last, she reached the door of his private box and flung it open without knocking.

"Anna!" For a single moment he stared at her, then came forward and grasped both her hands. "Anna, what is it, what's wrong?" He pulled over a chair and gently lowered her into it while she struggled to get her breath, but she got to her feet again and held on to him so tightly that he could feel the pressure of her fingers through his clothes.

"Ralph . . . you once said that if I ever needed your help, all I had to do was to ask for it." She swallowed, and leaned against him. "I'm asking for it now."

He smiled. He reached out and stroked her face with one hand. "Anna, you know that you've no need to ask me for anything."

In the split second before the starter shouted to the field to move off, William Devine looked down the course and saw it as he had never seen it before. It stretched away in front of him; green, daunting, infinite; rising and falling, twisting, turning, curving, every inch of it lined by the cheering, yelling crowds.

One moment he was sitting on Bloodstone's back, his eyes roving across the Downs as they rolled away into the distance. Then he was being taken along with him at such speed that he caught his breath.

Rain had begun to fall. Heavily, mercilessly; clods of turf flew up and stung his face. All around him was the deafening sound of cheers, mixed with the pounding of Bloodstone's hooves, faster and faster, cutting into the soggy turf. The air was rent with the noises of cursing and snorting and the cruel slash of whips as they rounded the curve of Tattenham Corner and galloped tightly bunched into the long, punishing, crowd-lined straight. In front of him and around him the slower, the weaker, the inferior, began to tire rapidly and fall away, leaving the cream of the field, the swifter, the stronger, the superior, to quicken their pace for the final surge toward the post, and he let the colt go off the bit at last, guiding him with deft artistry through a sudden gap in the solid moving wall of horses, fighting the rising ground with every stride and every muscle, nostrils flared with his exertion. For a fleeting second he glanced toward the crowd.

She was there, somewhere, with her heart in her mouth, he knew; trembling all over, her legs turned to jelly beneath her, fighting back tears of fear and pride and something else that he could give no name to, only feel it too.

She rushed down out of the grandstand, hatless, long hair loose and flying, pushing her way back frenziedly through the massive crowd. She shoved people out of her path, too frantic to apologize, pushing anyone who barred her way to one side as she fought to reach the edge of the course. The shouting and cheering deafened her, falling all around her like heavy rain, and shading her eyes against the steady drizzle, she stared across the course to the point where the field would any moment appear. Her mouth was as dry as old wood. Beneath her velvet gown she was sweating like a furnace.

There was not even a piece of broken fence to hold on to. Her legs shook so violently that she had difficulty in not sinking to her knees. For a single moment she held her breath as she heard the field gallop close together into the straight, then somehow she found the strength to rush forward, shouting Bloodstone's name at the top of her voice. Gilbert Heathcote's Amato was in the lead, with the black colt hard on his heels.

For the last hundred yards they battled neck and neck; one taking the lead and then the other. For a wild split second Anna had a sudden, blinding flash. All around her leaped the spiraling flames of the burning stable, in her ears she could hear Bloodstone's terrified, frenzied cries. There was a blood-curdling sound of falling wood, crashing about them, and the searing pain as it touched her bare flesh. Then the screams of the crowd all around her drowned the noise of the flames, and in front of her eyes now she saw William Devine urge the colt forward past Amato and gallop on toward the post. As he passed it, the crowd roared with approval and delight, and Anna ran onto the course toward him, laughing and crying both at once, her arms outstretched.

Shaking from head to foot, she threw her arms around his neck.

She rode Bloodstone in, William Devine leading him by the bridle, her damp face stained with tears, her tangled, windswept hair dripping rainwater down her back and into her eyes.

She looked up, without surprise, at the waving blobs that were human beings far away, lining the packed balconies of the grandstand, at the dancing mass of people that moved all around her like a brightly colored sea.

This was the thing that she had craved; fought for, suffered for; no one could ever take it away. She caught sight of Ralph Russell ahead, edging his way toward her through the crowd. Hatless, wiping the rain from his face, his eyes warm as they looked back at her.

Reaching up he placed his hands around her waist. Smiling, he lifted her down from the saddle.

❋ Author's Note ❋

Had Anna Brodie really existed outside the pages of this book she might well have seen the real Priam outside the Cock Inn in Epping high street on his way to Epsom Downs in 1830, for it was a journey that actually happened and is well documented. Priam was walked by his then owner, William Chifney, from Newmarket to Epsom—it took them ten days on foot—and that particular inn, which can still be seen today, was one of their stopping places.

The racehorse Priam, a dark bay colt by the 1823 Derby winner Emilius, was foaled in 1827; his dam, Cressida, was an unraced mare (by Whiskey out of Young Giantess by Diomed) and a full sister to the famous Eleanor, first filly in history to win the Derby and the Oaks, which she did in 1801. He was bred by Sir John Shelley and bought as an unbroken yearling by the Chifney brothers for one thousand guineas, and it was in their colors that Priam won the 1830 Derby, with Sam Day up, by two lengths. He was an unlucky second in the St. Leger of that year, narrowly losing the race—which was run in appalling conditions—to the seventeen-hand colt Birmingham, and in a long and strenuous career was in fact beaten only twice (once in mysterious circumstances), winning among other prestigious races of the time the Craven Stakes (after which he was sold to Lord Chesterfield for three thousand guineas), the Goodwood Cup (twice), the Eclipse Foot at Ascot, and a four-mile King's Plate, before being retired to stud at a fee of thirty guineas. In 1835 he was exported to America, sold to Merritt and Company, the most prolific American importers of English bloodstock, for the then huge sum of fifteen thousand dollars (he was then nine years old), and he became the first English Derby winner to head American sire lists since accurate stallion records had been kept. He stood at Virginia until 1842, when he was moved to William G. Harding's noted Belle Meade Stud in Tennessee, and there died in 1847 at the age of twenty, having led the sire list four times—in 1842, 1844, 1845, and 1846.

After his departure from England his daughters Miss Letty and Industry both won the Oaks, while his daughter Crucifix, his finest offspring, won the Oaks and the One Thousand and Two Thousand Guineas. An effort was then made to buy him back for the benefit of English breeders—but all offers were refused.

I think the last word on this great racehorse should be left to the famous nineteenth-century trainer John Kent, who wrote: *"I have seen all the best horses that have flourished and had their day for more than sixty years past, and I now repeat my well-considered opinion that Priam was the most perfect racehorse that I have ever seen. His constitution was magnificently sound; his temperament and nervous system beautifully attuned; his shape, make, and action were faultless. No weight known to the Racing Calendar could crush his spirit. All courses came alike to him."*

✳ ACKNOWLEDGMENTS ✳

Several kind and helpful people, and a number of excellent books, were of great assistance to me in my initial research into nineteenth-century horse racing, and I am more than happy to acknowledge my gratitude here.

Special thanks are due to Roger Mortimer, former racing correspondent of the *Sunday Times,* for answering my numerous questions about the racehorse Priam; to Martyn Stewart, formerly with Ryan Price at Findon; to Lady Patricia Lucas-Scudamore, descendant of the Earl of Chesterfield who bought Priam from the Chifney brothers, for the great trouble she took to find out more facts for me and for her kind interest in the book.

Books which I found invaluable: Wray Vamplew's *The Turf: A Social and Economic History of Horse Racing;* David Hunn's *Epsom Racecourse;* John Welcome's *Infamous Occasion;* and the *Biographical Encyclopaedia of British Flat Racing,* by Roger Mortimer, Richard Onslow, and Peter Willett. The long-out-of-print *Post and Paddock,* by "The Druid," for which I must thank the staff of the British Library Department of Printed Books, and, finally, the article on eighteenth- and nineteenty-century British racehorses in America, from *The British Racehorse,* all proved equally invaluable to me.

The Author
February 1985